CODE-NAME: "WHITE BUFFALO"

By James A. Martin

PublishAmerica
Baltimore

First printing

ISBN: 1-4137-6359-6
PUBLISHED BY PUBLISHAMERICA, LLLP
www.publishamerica.com
Baltimore

Printed in the United States of America

CODE-NAME:
"WHITE BUFFALO"

By James A. Martin

INTRODUCTION

The book you are about to read is fiction. Many of the incidents and operations are true in a general sense. I created the details of the many events to fit the story. Many of the characters are real people; some are fictional. I changed names, code-names and descriptions of those who are still in "harm's way." There are a few names that are the actual names of the characters. Those people will know the names that are true. I included your true name to pay tribute to your contribution to East Timor.

The historical struggle in East Timor is real. As with any conflict, there are two sides—or more. What is considered right and wrong fluctuates depending what side you are on. I wrote this book from the viewpoint of the East Timorese people. Indonesia was the enemy of East Timor for many years; therefore, this book views the actions of Indonesia as wrong. Whether the actions of Indonesia were ever wrong or not is not for me to judge, and I don't. The people of every nation have the duty to protect the interests of their country.

The many East Timor groups named in this book are real. There is an internal struggle for dominance of the newest Nation on earth. Virtually every East Timorese believe that this struggle will result in a civil war at some point. Whether this future civil war is real or imagined is not known. Time will tell.

The people who lead and make up the membership of these internal East Timor organizations believe that whatever they are doing is what's right for East Timor. Whether their actions are right or wrong does not change the fact that they are patriots too. Most of these people are doing what they believe is the best for East Timor.

I wrote this book for the purpose of entertainment. At the same time the reader can experience East Timor—the people, the culture and the land itself. Americans should be able to relate to the struggle of East Timor to our own struggle with England many years ago. I did.

TABLE OF CONTENTS

CHAPTER ONE

East Timor, September 1999

Jose heard women and children screaming in the distance as he sat with his friend, Alfonso, in the shade of a large Mango tree at the front of Alfonso's home. The East Timor sun was hot on this fourth day of September in 1999. The tropical Island of Timor is one of many Islands in the Indonesian Island chain that is located very near the Equator. It is always hot in Timor; however, September is the dry season, thus the humidity is lower, so the shade of the tree affords a degree of relief from the heat.

Jose and Alfonso jumped up and quickly moved toward the side of the home, toward the direction of the screams. Alfonso's wife came out of the house and also moved toward the sound of the screams. The 20-year-old woman was carrying a baby and followed by her and Alfonso's nearly two-year-old son. The Timorese people display very little emotion; however, anyone could see the fear in the young woman's face.

As they gazed in the direction of the screams, about two hundred yards away, they saw large clouds of black smoke gently rising into the blue and otherwise clear sky. Trees and homes of Maumela Village blocked the view of what was burning but Jose, Alfonso, and his wife knew that the smoke was coming from the burning homes of their friends who lived at the far side of the village.

Gunfire rang out in single shots and bursts of automatic fire. There were more screams and now Jose, Alfonso, and his wife could hear the crackling of the fires as the bamboo walls and grass roofs of the unseen homes were consumed.

* * * *

On the 30th of August 1999, all the people of East Timor cast their votes. The vote was to decide if East Timor would become an Independent Nation or remain as an Indonesian State. The United Nations organized the taking of the votes to assure a fair and accurate desire of the majority of the East Timorese people. To understand this Fourth day of September 1999, you should know the basic background of East Timor.

The East half of the Island of Timor was a Portuguese Colony for several hundreds of years. In the mid 1970s two political groups who were "pro-Indonesian" conducted a coup that drove the Portuguese from the main Island of East Timor.

Unfortunately for the two "pro-Indonesian" groups there was a third political group that existed in East Timor. This third group went by the name of Fretilin. The Fretilin party desired to make East Timor Independent of all outside nations. The Fretilin party was supported by the existing East Timorese military which was created by the Portuguese. Within weeks of the "pro-Indonesian" coup, Fretilin conducted a coup against the pro-Indonesian parties and quickly drove them out of East Timor. The Pro-Indonesians fled into the Indonesian State of West Timor, which is the west half of the Island of Timor.

The Indonesian Special Forces, known as Koppassus, and Indonesian intelligence united with the exiled parties and created the illusion of instability within East Timor. After several skirmishes between Fretilin forces and supposed Pro-Indonesian forces, the Indonesians launched an all out assault to take control of East Timor. This was for the purpose of establishing peace and stability in East Timor.

The Indonesians occupied East Timor ever since and made East Timor the Indonesians' 27th state. Fretilin never gave up the fight for independence. The political side of the struggle for independence remained Fretilin. The military side of this struggle for independence became known as Falintil.

The Fretilin military, Falintil, did not have the numbers or support to directly combat the Indonesian military so they became guerilla fighters who attacked the Indonesians at every opportunity. The Falintil controlled the remote mountainous areas of East Timor while the Indonesians controlled the populated areas.

Most of the East Timorese people secretly supported the independence movement, thus the Falintil forces could easily acquire what they needed to survive and operate against the Indonesians. One of the main ingredients needed to conduct a guerilla war is intelligence. To conduct lightning-fast attacks against a superior enemy, the Falintil commanders needed to know where and when the enemy would be weak.

The Falintil organized clandestine organizations that provided several services toward the struggle for freedom. The clandestine organizations, known as "Clandestinos," conducted secret operations that ranged from collecting and transporting food and supplies from the population to buying and stealing weapons and ammunition for the Falintil forces. The Clandestinos also collected information about Indonesian strengths and movements of the military and police. They even developed a propaganda campaign that was designed to confuse Indonesian commanders and at times set them up for Falintil surprise attacks.

This twenty-four-year-long struggle for freedom eventually resulted in the United Nations coming to East Timor to organize a vote of the East Timorese people to determine what the people of East Timor wanted. The Indonesians were under pressure to allow the United Nations to conduct this vote. Since East Timor was never "legally" Indonesian territory, they had little choice but to allow the United Nations into East Timor.

The Indonesians had no intentions of giving up the east half of the Timor Island. The Indonesian military had created local "Militia units" that were to supplement the Indonesian military, known as "TNI," allegedly for defense against Falintil Forces. Actually, the Militia units were used to conduct operations against the people of East Timor that the Indonesian military and police could deny any involvement.

Militia units were based in central locations throughout East Timor. The members were recruited from the villages that surrounded the central location. Each Militia unit was given a unit name. The three most notorious Militia units were; Tim Saka (Pronounced; "Team Saka") based in Baucau, Tim Alfa was based in Los Palos and Besi Merah Putih who was based in Liquisa.

The "Militia" was involved with countless capture, rape, torture, beatings, stealing, burning of homes, and murder of many East Timorese people. This Militia activity dramatically increased over the months that led up to the United Nations conducted vote for autonomy with Indonesia or independence.

The cold-blooded and ruthless activity of the Militia was closely controlled by the Koppassus (Indonesian Special Forces) Intelligence unit known as "SGI." The SGI collected information from several sources, including Militia operations, and analyzed the information. The SGI would then conduct further operations based on the previous collected and analyzed information.

* * * *

Fear surged through both Jose and Alfonso as they heard the screams and watched the smoke only a short distance from where they stood. Both Jose and Alfonso were in there mid-twenties and had served as Falintil "Clandestino" operators for several years. It was now mid-morning of the 4th of September 1999, and they had heard the announcement over the radio earlier in the morning that 78% of the East Timorese people had voted for independence. They realized that what they were seeing and hearing now was the beginning of the revenge of the Indonesians for that choice of the people for freedom.

Both men knew that they would be targeted for capture and murder by the local Militia known as Gunta Merah Putih. Both men turned to flee immediately. Alfonso hesitated briefly as he looked into the eyes of his wife. Tears streamed down her face as she clutched their baby. Alfonso's two- year-old son clung to his mother's sarong. The child had no understanding of what was going on but knew something was terribly wrong.

Alfonso's eyes were moist and his jaw quivered as he told his wife to go to the neighbors and wait. Alfonso then ran out of the back side of the village, following the same path that Jose had taken a few seconds before. Both men knew that they had to get to the nearest Falintil Stronghold that was about two and a half miles away into the deep mountains of Cailaco Sub-district. Once in the Falintil camp they would be safe. They hoped that the Gunta Militia members would be too busy burning homes and trying to catch and kill other intended victims than to bother chasing down two men who were already in the jungles and mountains of Cailaco.

Maumela Village is located in the valley of Cailaco Sub-district, Bobonaro District. This valley is one of the rare locations in East Timor that is flat. Only about 600 feet above sea level the valley is very hot. Sweat streamed down Alfonso's body as he ran down the footpath that led to the nearest mountain behind Maumela Village. Trees, brush and grass lined both sides of the narrow dirt footpath.

As Alfonso neared the river the jungle gave way to small clearings where the people of Maumela Village grew crops. For the first time since running out of the village Alfonso could see Jose's lean, muscular body as he ran through the fields about eighty yards in front of him. Jose stopped running as he reached the river bank. He closely scanned the surrounding area as he waited for Alfonso to catch up.

Nothing was said as Alfonso neared the river bank were Jose waited. Alfonso took the lead as he stepped down into the dry river bed, which was covered with gravel and many rocks. The twenty-yard-wide river bed was dry with the exception of a small stream that flowed through the center. During the rains of the wet season this river bed is full of raging waters that flow out of the mountains.

Alfonso, followed by Jose, ran up the river bed until they reached the heavier jungle at the base of the mountain. Both men stopped in the thick cover of the trees and brush. They gasped for air as they closely watched the surrounding area, especially their "back trail." Their muscular dark brown bodies glistened from their sweat that flowed stronger than the stream in the river bed. They rested for less than two minutes and then began climbing the steep hillside that led up the mountain.

The men reduced their speed to a walk as the mountainside became steeper and the terrain very rugged. There was no footpath up this mountain but the men knew very well where they were going. They had been to the nearby Falintil stronghold many times as they carried food, cigarettes, guns, ammunition, and information to the Falintil fighters in the mountains.

They stopped again at a place further up the mountain where they could look over the Cailaco valley. Tears welled in their eyes as they saw clouds of smoke rising from what once was Maumela Village. The smoke from the many burning homes filled the sky above the village. They silently watched and could only wonder what was happening to the people that fell into the clutches of the Gunta Merah Putih Militia men.

Jose was not married but he, like Alfonso, had many friends and family who lived in that village. There was nothing that could be done for those people now. Jose and Alfonso knew that they would be beaten, tortured, and killed if the Militia captured them. They had to keep going. By this time they both believed that nobody was following them but the only true safety was at the Falintil stronghold.

They turned away from the horror that was occurring at their homes and continued their trek up the mountain. They crested the top of the first highpoint and were walking along the edge of a steep grassy slope that dropped on their right side nearly one hundred feet into a ravine. As they walked the quiet of the mountain jungle was suddenly shattered by the crack of a high-powered rifle shot.

Jose was walking behind Alfonso as the rifle shot split the air and shattered Alfonso's right thigh. Jose saw Alfonso stumble and then drop to the ground. More rifle shots smacked into the trees near Jose. Jose immediately dropped to the ground to avoid being shot. He then crawled the few feet distance to Alfonso. Jose could see the extreme pain in the face of Alfonso as he tried to crawl into the thicker jungle. They heard the excited screams of the Militia men as they closed in on their prey.

Alfonso knew that he could no longer hope to escape. He thought of his wife and remembered the tears streaming down her face as he turned away from her and left the village. He thought of his young son and his baby daughter who would not understand why their father would never return home.

Alfonso stopped crawling as Jose tried to drag him into the jungle. Rifle shots were coming in short bursts of automatic fire as the Militia quickly moved closer to the two escaping Clandestino operatives. Fortunately for Jose the Militia was firing their SKS and M-16 assault rifles from the hip and while moving through the jungle rather than taking aimed shots.

Alfonso jerked away from Jose who was still trying to help him move. Alfonso had now accepted his fate but had to convince Jose to except Alfonso's fate as well. As Alfonso jerked away from Jose's grasp, he told Jose, "*Ba ona, Jose. Hau la bele halai. Ita persisa ba hetete Falintil mosu saida!*" (Translated; Go now Jose. I can't run. You have to get to the Falintil and tell them what is happening.)

Jose hesitated for a few moments, thinking about what Alfonso had said. Jose knew that Alfonso was right. Alfonso could not be saved and the Falintil guerillas needed to know what was happening. Jose nodded at Alfonso and then quickly crawled into the thick of the jungle before standing up and running for his life. He knew the Militia was very close and he had to move fast if he hoped to escape.

Jose was torn with emotion, however, the immediate danger caused him to temporarily forget the terror in his village and Alfonso's fate. He heard the triumphant Militia men only a few yards behind him as they had apparently found Alfonso. Jose knew that they would kill Alfonso. He hoped that because they still had one left to capture they would kill Alfonso fast.

Jose was moving as fast as he could through the jungle and up the steep mountainside but his strength was ebbing from emotion and physical exertion. Twenty minutes later he crested the next high point of the mountain and started to descend the reverse side of that highpoint. The muscles in Jose's legs burned from the strain of the fast and hard climb. His chest heaved as he gulped air into his lungs. His sweat soaked his cloths as if he had jumped into the sea.

The jungle thinned to a few scattered trees among the rocks and grass as he continued the descent to a small stream that spilled its waters to the valley below and lay between two high points of the mountain. Jose was nearly to the thicker jungle, near the stream, when again rifle shots cracked from his back trail. He heard the bullets as they closely passed by him, some of them hitting the ground or trees a few yards in front of him.

Jose increased his pace to reach the thick jungle, which was now just a few yards in front of him. As he entered the thicker jungle he lost his footing and violently fell to the ground, landing face first. Dirt and grass ripped across the right side of his face as his body skidded to a halt.

Jose struggled to quickly get back on his feet but his body wouldn't respond. Then he felt the burning in his lower back. Jose now realized that he had been shot. A bullet had torn into his lower back just a couple of inches to the left of his spine and flung him to the ground.

The pain from the wound increased with every second. Jose stopped trying to get up as he realized that he would soon be dead. He lay face down in the dirt and relaxed as he exhaled a long sigh of acceptance of his death. Blood quickly soaked the earth under Jose's body where the bullet had exited through his lower left lung, leaving a gaping hole in his chest large enough for a small child to put a fist inside.

As he lay helpless on the ground Jose heard men approaching. He heard the taunting of the Militia men as he saw the black combat boots of one of those men that moved near his face. Strong hands grabbed his right shoulder and violently turned him over so that he was lying on his back. Jose looked up and into the faces of five jeering men who now stood around him. All five men were dressed in tight black t-shirts, Indonesian military camouflage pants, and combat boots.

Jose knew all of these men. They were all from nearby villages. One of them was from Maumela Village. The man from Maumela, Mateus, who now stood over the dying Jose, was two years older than Jose. Jose and Mateus had played together, gone to school together, and worked the village fields of crops together. Mateus was even married to Jose's cousin, but none of this seemed to matter now. Mateus's eyes showed only hatred as he now looked down into the eyes of Jose.

The leader of this group of Mililtia men harshly commanded, "Stand him up. I want to get blood on my arrow." Two men grabbed Jose from either side and jerked him to his feet. Jose weakly dangled between the two muscular Militia men as they raised his arms above his head.

The Militia leader glared into Jose's face as he slung his M-16 rifle over his left shoulder then pulled one of seven arrows from the quiver he wore on his back. The Militia leader had made his own arrows as well as the bow that was unstrung and hung with his quiver of arrows on his back. The Militia leader clutched the wooden arrow shaft in his right fist and smiled slightly as he saw the fear in Jose's face.

The Militia leader suddenly thrust the steel point of the arrow into Jose's left armpit. The two-inch-long metal arrowhead completely disappeared into Jose's body. The very weak Jose let out a scream as the pain from the new wound surged through him. He continued to scream as the Militia leader violently moved the arrow shaft up and down and side to side causing the sharp arrowhead to tear flesh inside Jose's body.

Blood flowed from the arrow wound and ran down the left side of Jose's torso, then mixed with the blood that still gushed from the bullet wound. Jose's screams quickly subsided as he was close to being unconscious from the loss of blood.

The Militia leader could see that Jose was near death so he jerked his arrow out of Jose's body and barked out, "Kill him." The Militia leader took a step back as the Militia man who had been watching the torture session from his left side stepped forward, drawing a bayonet from the sheath he wore on his belt.

The man who was holding Jose on his feet from the right side grabbed a hand full of Jose's hair and pulled his head back, exposing Jose's throat. In one swift motion, the Militia man with the bayonet slashed Jose's throat. Blood quickly flowed from the gaping wound in Jose's throat and his body began to twitch. The two men holding Jose on his feet let go of their victim and watched his body fall to the ground.

They stood watching Jose's still twitching body as it lay on the ground at their feet. The Militia leader then calmly said, "Let's get back to the others. Stay alert. Falintil guerillas may have heard the gunfire."

The five men near Jose's body were joined by two other Militia men who had been standing a few yards into the jungle on opposite sides of the group of torturers. These two men had been watching closely for anyone who may try to approach them.

The Militia men had good reason to be concerned. They were deep in the mountains. Indonesian soldiers, police, and Militia units never went into the mountains anywhere in East Timor unless they were well armed and in large numbers. The Falintil guerillas dominated the remote areas all through East Timor. The Falintil were renowned for being able to outmaneuver and outfight Indonesian units when they tried to penetrate the jungles and mountains.

With this in mind the seven-man Militia unit quickly returned to where Alfonso had died. They linked up with the five Militia men who had remained at that location to torture and kill Alfonso. Then the combined unit returned to the burning village of Maumela.

CHAPTER TWO

Beginning a Mission

Sweat soaked my shirt and ran down my legs as I stood inside the C-130 "Hercules" United Nations aircraft that had just landed at the airport in Dili, which is the capitol city of East Timor. There were about 60 passengers aboard that plane on this late November 1999 day. All the passengers were dressed in a variety of police uniforms that represented the nations that had sent them to this little Island that lay between Australia and the continent of Asia.

There were contingents of policemen from several nations aboard the plane; however, the American contingent was by far the largest. There were thirty-four Americans who just a few weeks ago were police officers in the united States. Now these thirty-four men were standing inside the C-130 waiting for the door to be opened so they could set foot for the first time on East Timor soil.

My head hurt and my stomach churned as I waited with the others to get off the plane. The air was stale and unbelievably hot. The United States Contingent police uniforms were the military style of trousers and shirts, both with multiple pockets. The dark blue uniforms sported an American flag on the left shoulder and a United Nations patch on the right shoulder with a "Rocker" patch over the UN patch that read "police."

The uniform was designed to protect the wearer. At the moment the only value the uniform had was soaking up the huge amount of sweat that was pouring out from my body. There was a loud metallic clank followed by the whine of hydraulics as the rear tailgate of the big cargo plane began to lower. We all turned and watched as the nearby landscape was slowly revealed to us as the large tailgate slowly dropped opened.

The fresh air from the large opening did not bring any relief from the heat. The very little breeze that did enter the plane was just as hot and humid as the air already in the plane but at least it took away some of the stale scent of the aging C-130 interior. The passenger door was then opened and men began to filter through the door.

I stepped down onto the tarmac and could feel the heat penetrating through the soles of my boots from the hot asphalt. The sun on by face and body increased the temperature in my already overheated state of being. My head hurt even more than before I exited the plane. I had nobody to blame for that other than myself.

* * * *

The night before was our last night in Darwin, Australia before going to the Royal Australian Air Force Base where we stowed our gear in a big pile and got on the C-130 to take the one-hour and forty-minute flight to Dili, East Timor. As would be expected, the entire US contingent went out to dinner and had a few drinks the night before leaving civilization. We all knew that we were going into a burned out and otherwise destroyed country so a last night on the town was in order.

Unfortunately I did not have the sense to quit with a few drinks. I and one other American had met a group of people from Darwin and decided to spend a little more time with them. About four-o'clock in the morning two of our new-found friends drove us to the Northern Territory University, where we were staying, and dropped us off. The mescal I had been sipping on for the last couple of hours was hitting me pretty hard as I stumbled through the large room full of bunk beds and sleeping men.

Eventually I found my empty bunk and fell into it. The dark room spun as I lay on my back and closed my eyes. Three hours later Billy shook me until I woke up. He said over and over again, "Come on, we gotta go. We gotta go, buddy."

I opened my aching eyes slightly and said, "You guys go on. I'll be along later."

Even through my blurry eyes I could see Billy smile as he said, "It doesn't work that way, buddy. You gotta come with us. You know that."

I struggled to prop myself up on my left elbow and then struggled to bring Billy's face into focus. Billy looked fresh and was already dressed in his uniform. I fell back onto the bed as I said, "Just kill me now and put me out of my misery."

Billy pulled the sheet off from me and started to pull me out of the bunk, "You only got forty minutes before we leave."

He was still pulling on my left arm as I said, "Okay, okay, okay. I can do this."

My head throbbed and spun all at the same time. My mouth was dry as a desert and I had a sick stomach. I got to my feet and leaned forward to grab a bottle of water that was sitting on the floor near my bunk. Even at this early morning hour it was already hot and muggy. The fan in the large room did little to help cool down the room. I took a long, hard drink of the water. As I put the bottle back on the floor I could feel the effects of the alcohol even stronger than before I drank the water.

I managed to get showered, dressed, and my gear packed and outside to the gear collection point just as the bus arrived to take us to the Royal Australian Air Force Base. I had been sweating ever since getting out of the shower and now that I was outside, my sweating increased. This didn't help my drunken/hungover condition.

The bus ride wasn't too bad; however, once at the Air Force Base, we spent the next two or more hours outside in the heat of the day. Eventually the United Nations C-130 transport plane landed at the Air Force Base. We all watched as the big white plane with black UN letters painted on the sides taxied to a location about one hundred yards from where we all stood watching.

We continued to watch as people started to get off the UN plane. Everyone who got off the plane was in military uniform, carrying assault rifles, and wearing their "web gear." The arriving passengers walked from the plane toward the Flight Building that we were standing near. As the soldiers walked by us we could see and smell that they were filthy, soaked in sweat, unshaven, and most importantly, you could see the exhaustion in their faces.

Shortly after the arrival of the soldiers I heard one of our guys ask an Australian soldier, "How is it over there?" The soldier had just got his large backpack from inside the flight buildings receiving area and brought it outside where he laid it on the ground and was rummaging through it.

He looked up from where he knelt on the ground at the American police officer who had asked the question. He then looked around at all the neatly dressed men, all in their fresh, clean, dark blue uniforms and said, "Well mate, you're going to find out soon enough."

Another American standing nearby said, "I don't know how you can carry and wear all that gear. It's too hot."

The Australian soldier stood up, picked up his backpack and slung it over his left shoulder. The heavy backpack caused him to lean forward slightly to balance the weight. He was holding his Styer assault rifle in his right hand. He simply said, "It's a lot hotter in Timor." He then turned and walked away.

* * * *

I thought about that soldiers statement about being "hotter in Timor" as I walked away from the UN plane, making my way across the tarmac and through the burned-out airport terminal building. We new arrivals were following behind two men who had met us as we got off the plane. As the Australian soldier had said, the temperature and humidity was noticeably hotter in East Timor than it was in Darwin.

One of the two men who had met us was wearing an Australian police uniform. We stopped walking as we entered the parking area just in front of the airport terminal. Two large piles of our gear had been placed in the middle of the very dirty, dusty, empty parking lot. The man wearing the Australian uniform told us to collect our "kit" and stand ready. "Kit" is Australian talk for "gear."

We all rummaged through the many bags and eventually everyone had their own individual piles of bags and backpacks. We stood in the parking lot and waited for whatever was next. A couple of small white buses with black UN letters on the sides pulled into the parking lot near us and stopped. The drivers shut off the engines and got out of the buses. The two drivers moved over to a shady area that was near the buses.

I watched these men as they squatted, lit cigarettes, and smoked while they closely scrutinized us. Both men were small in stature; however, I could tell by looking at them that they were solid and very alert. Their skin was dark brown and they both had short black hair. They were both dressed in blue jeans. One man wore a short-sleeve button-down shirt and the other a t-shirt.

My attention was drawn away from the two men as the man in the Australian uniform began to give us a briefing. His Australian accent caused me to listen closely to understand what he said. He was about forty years old, five-foot-ten-inches tall, with a medium build.

He told us that we had all been selected to be assigned to several workstations throughout East Timor. Those workstations would have to be "created." There were no existing police structures or established bases of operation anywhere in East Timor other than a recently established headquarters location in Dili.

He further told us that the Indonesian-controlled Militia organizations have destroyed almost everything in East Timor. Buildings, homes, offices—everything had been burned. In addition to the mass destruction of a nation, the Militia organizations had killed many people. The man in the Australian uniform said, "How many people have been killed is not known yet. Where all the bodies are is not known yet. What happened to them is not known yet."

The Australian man paused a moment to let what he said sink into our already overwhelmed brains. He then continued, "You men have a difficult job ahead of you. We have to establish a functional police force on this east half of the Timor Island. We must establish law and order similar to what exists in any civilized country. At the same time we must start sorting out what happened here. Identify those who were murdered and build murder cases against those who killed them."

He paused again for a moment, then said, "You will have as much support as we can give you but at this time there is very little available for us to give. Do the best that you can."

The man in the Australian uniform then lifted a clipboard and began calling out one name at a time. The man whose name was called out would respond with a "here" or a "yes." The Australian man then announced the name of the workstation that man was assigned to work.

I stood next to Billy as the names were called out and waited for my name to be called. My head no longer hurt and my queasy stomach was pretty much settled now, which left me with just the lack of sleep and extreme heat to endure.

"Billy Kreiger!" the man called out.

Billy answered with a sharp, "Yo." The man with the clipboard then said, "Viqueque."

I leaned over closer to Billy and asked, "Do you know where Viqueque is?"

Billy never looked away from the man with the clipboard as he said, "I have no idea."

I watched Billy as he stood naturally in a strong and balanced stance. He had a military flair to him, as he should. He had been a police officer for the past several years in North Carolina; however, before that he spent many years in the army.

Billy began his military career in the Army Rangers running reconnaissance missions behind enemy lines during the Vietnam War. Billy was five-foot-ten-inches tall with a lean but muscular physique. His slightly graying dark hair was the only thing that gave away his almost fifty years of age. Billy's aging body may have lost some of the strengths and abilities that he possessed during his military service but his spiritual and mental strength, if changed at all, was stronger than ever. I felt privileged to have become a close friend of Billy's. I met Billy when I went to Fort Worth, Texas for the pre-mission screening, testing, and training provided by the 'company that recruited me for this East Timor mission.

On 8 July, 1999, I completed 25 years of service at the Eaton County Sheriff Department located in Michigan. I was forty-eight years old and could not draw my retirement money until I turned fifty years old; however, my retirement was "locked in," so I was free to work somewhere else if I wanted.

Shortly thereafter I heard about a company that was recruiting police officers for a United Nations mission in Kosovo. I was curious, so I called to inquire. I was re-contacted by the company a couple of weeks later and asked if I would be willing to go to East Timor and work with the United Nations. I had no idea where East Timor was. I told the recruiter that I had called about going to Kosovo.

The recruiter replied to my statement, "If you're going on a mission for our company you're going to East Timor."

There obviously was no negotiating with this company so I got as much information from them about East Timor as I could and said, "Okay, I'll go." I was actually thinking that I "might" go once I find out more about what I am getting into. I didn't say that to the man on the phone since an unsure answer would probably result in no mission at all. I wanted to keep my options open.

The next thing I knew I was on an airplane flying to Fort Worth, Texas. Twelve seasoned police officers were screening and testing for eight positions. Only seven of us made it through the first part of the program. The eighth position was filled later by bringing a man over from the Kosovo group of police officers who qualified to work for the company.

We began hearing reports about the burning and killing in East Timor, which began the day after the vote for Autonomy with Indonesia or independence. On 4 September, 1999, the result of that vote was officially announced. The people of East Timor had overwhelmingly voted for independence, which resulted in a dramatic increase of killing and burning. United Nations personnel and other foreigners in East Timor were forced to evacuate the Island.

It was during this time we were making our final arrangements before leaving the following morning on a flight that would begin our long trip to East Timor. Late that night our departure was delayed a couple of days to see how things developed in East Timor. Then it was a couple of more days. Then it was a week. Then it was another week of waiting. One month later the company sent us home until they figured out when we would be going to East Timor.

During the month that the East Timor eight-man team was waiting in Fort Worth the company put us to work recruiting for other missions around the world, distributing supplies and assisting with training new recruits going to other missions. During this time I got to know all seven of my teammates very well; however, Billy and I hit it off exceptionally well.

He couldn't believe that I did not have a Special Forces background and was really amazed when I told him I had never been in the military. Eventually he accepted the fact that I was not Special Forces but added, "You got the SF attitude and mannerism. You know the special tactics of SF operators and you got the SF team spirit," he told me, "As far as I am concerned, you're one of us."

That was a big compliment coming from someone like Billy but I doubted that I could live up to the way Billy believed in me. I didn't know at that time that the near future would provide me many opportunities to prove myself as a "Special operator."

On 14 November, 1999, I again went to the airport in Lansing, Michigan and got on a flight to Fort Worth, Texas. The company had sent me notice three days before that they were ready to send us to East Timor. Upon arriving in Fort Worth I was surprised to see that our eight-man team had grown to thirty-four.

We signed contracts the following morning. That afternoon we were on an airplane going to Los Angles. We changed planes, then endured the 14-hour flight from Los Angles to Sydney, Australia. After going through customs, and then an eight-hour long layover, we were on a five-hour flight from Sydney to Darwin, Australia.

All incoming personnel were taken to the Northern Territory University where we would sleep, eat, and go through our induction lectures and processing procedures. A few days later we were taken to the Royal Australian Air Force base to be transported by the United Nations C-130 cargo plane to East Timor.

* * * *

The man in the Australian uniform, holding the clipboard and calling out names, was continuing the process during the time that I was reflecting on the events that brought me to this destroyed country. My thoughts were interrupted as the man called out my name, "James Martin!"

I responded as Billy did with a sharp, "Yo."

The man calling out the names had, on a few occasions, asked the man whose name he had called out, "Are you a swimmer?"

Every man had responded, "Yes."

The man with the clipboard now asked me, "Are you a swimmer?"

I had no idea what he was asking me. The only thing I could think of was that it must be very wet wherever I was about to be assigned and I would need to know how to swim. I was never a good swimmer.

I answered the question with a thought out, "No."

The clipboard man looked at me hard then smiled and nodded at my ignorance. He then said, "Maliana. We will see if you swim or not."

I leaned over toward Billy again and asked, "What's a swimmer?" Billy just shrugged his shoulders. I felt a little better when I realized he didn't know what a swimmer was either.

By the time the proceedings in the airport parking lot came to an end a large truck had arrived. We were told to put our "kit" in the truck and get on one of the buses. They would take us and our kit to where we would be staying until being deployed to our assigned work locations.

The bus ride through the city of Dili was depressing. The streets were narrow and filthy. I saw the remains of many homes and businesses that lined both sides of the streets as we passed by. Most of the buildings were concrete. The walls still stood; however, they had all been burned out completely, leaving only the concrete walls.

There was very little traffic on the streets. The few cars, trucks, and motorbikes that were on the streets were obviously damaged. Windshields, side and rear windows, headlights, and taillights were smashed out of most of them.

I sat quietly in the little bus and gazed out the window during our twenty-minute or so trip across town. Nobody on the bus was talking except for one of our American police who was sitting next to the bus driver. He was trying to make conversation with the driver; however, it was soon obvious that the driver did not speak English.

I thought about the effort and coordination that it would take to so completely destroy everything of value in this city. There was absolutely nothing left—nothing which could be seen anyway. Our convoy of two buses and one large truck drove to the front of a closed gate and waited. On the other side of this gate was a parking area in front of a long single story building.

This location had been taken over by an Australian military company. The perimeter of this now military compound was enclosed by rolls of concertina wire along the top of the six-foot high concrete and steel bar wall that had existed before the violence of the Militia and the eventual invasion of INTERFET to stop the killing.

* * * *

INTERFET is the acronym for "International Force, East Timor." INTERFET was the combined militaries from several area nations that quickly formed to conduct the large-scale operation into East Timor. The Australian military maintained overall command of the combined military contributions.

In November of 1999, the mission in East Timor was still an INTERFET mission. The mission would not change to a United Nations mission until late February 2000; however, there was a desperate need for law enforcement personnel now so the United Nations sent in their United Nations civilian police prior to the united Nations-mandated mission.

* * * *

One of the two Australian soldiers who were manning the compound entrance guard post came out of the small sandbagged structure that was erected near the entrance. The soldier pulled the steel gate open and watched as our two buses and one truck drove through the opening.

Our three vehicles parked in front of the long one-story building and we all filed off the buses. We were instructed to collect our kit and find an area inside the large building and prepare to stay until we could be deployed to our assigned workstations, which could take two or three days before deployment.

I stood in the parking lot behind the truck that carried our kit and waited for the Timorese men who had been hired by the UN to unload our gear. I looked around at my surroundings while I waited. The sun was low in the sky by this time. I looked at the high mountains that rose above the backside of Dili. The mountains were covered with jungle; however, for the most part they appeared to be dead from several months of no rain. The few large trees scattered up the mountainside were the only vegetation that wasn't a depressing brown color.

The compound where we were now standing was dry and dusty. Four military APCs (armored personnel carriers) were parked in a neat line in the middle of the parking area. The building where we would be sleeping still had a roof. After seeing all the burned-out buildings as we drove through Dili I was surprised to see that this building had not been burned.

After collecting my kit from the rear of the truck I walked into the building. Although the building had not been burned I found that the interior had been badly damaged. The windows had all been broken out. The toilets and wash tanks were broken down. The walls were all damaged; however, because the walls were concrete, they still stood. The floor was covered with thick dust and debris.

I walked through one room of the large building and then into the next room and then the next. There were men in each of the rooms setting up their mosquito nets. I reached the last room and found most of the original eight East Timor teammates who were now setting up their mosquito nets, blowing up small air mattresses, and arranging their packs and bags. I picked out a small remaining area in the same room and began to organize my sleeping gear too.

By the time I finished I was completely soaked in sweat and filthy from the dust that covered every inch of the building's floor. I went outside and stood near a group of four of our American contingent who were smoking and talking. I didn't know any of these men. Out of the thirty-four Americans in our group I only knew the seven men who trained and worked with me.

I lit a cigarette and stood quietly as I smoked and listened somewhat to the four men talk. The sun was down and the only light came from military security lights mounted on the perimeter walls. The night air wasn't much cooler than the daytime. I was still sweating. I was miserable and wondered how I would be able to endure a year of this kind of living conditions. The conversations of the four men next to me told me that they were miserable too.

As I stood alone I heard a voice coming from the darkness near our parked buses and truck. The voice announced, "Get on the buses and we will take you to the UN compound and get something to eat."

I walked over to the buses. I threw my cigarette to the side before climbing onto the bus. Once everyone was aboard the buses our drivers drove out of the compound and then through the city. The streets were dark except from the headlights of our buses. We passed other cars and motorcycles driving down the street but none of those cars or motorcycles had headlights or taillights. I wondered how they could find their way down the street and how they could avoid hitting the other vehicles on the road.

Our buses pulled into another military-guarded compound. We got off the buses and were led into a lighted building. Upon entering the building I could see two dark-skinned women standing behind a long counter to the left side of the large room. This building was set up as a cafeteria-style eating establishment. There were several tables and chairs throughout the rest of the building.

I stood in line and waited for my turn to collect my dinner at the counter. The two women working behind the counter were "local staff," East Timorese women who had been hired by the United Nations. Both of these women were short with a slim build. By now I was realizing that the East Timorese as a whole were a small people. The women behind the counter both had their long, dark hair pulled neatly back into ponytails. Both women were in their twenties and attractive.

As I stepped up to the counter the first woman filled a plastic bowl with a thin broth from a large metal pot. The woman's movements were very deliberate. I watched as she seemed to completely focus on the simple action of dipping a large spoon into the metal pot and then bring the broth-filled spoon over the plastic bowl and slowly pour the broth from the spoon into the bowl.

She repeated this graceful procedure two more times. She gracefully set the large spoon to the side of the large metal pot. She then turned her attention to gently grasping the sides of the bowl with both hands. She looked up into my eyes and slowly presented the bowl of broth to me.

I hesitated as I looked into this woman's liquid, dark brown eyes. I was mystified by this woman. Though her face showed no emotion whatsoever, her eyes displayed a soft smile. Not a flirting or wanting smile, but a genuine, friendly smile. The chiseled features of her face and her soft, dark skin were very attractive; however' what held my attention were her eyes and her mannerism.

I reached out with both hands and took the bowl from the woman. I gave her a slight nod of my head and said, "Thank you."

She never said a word and her facial expression didn't change; however, her eyes seemed to brighten and smile just a little more. I didn't realize at that time that I was learning to speak a new language. The Timorese people have a way of communicating through their eyes.

I set the bowl of broth on a tray that I had taken from a stack of trays near the counter. I then moved down the counter to the second woman behind the counter. This woman's mannerism and eyes were just like the first woman's. I took the plastic plate that she offered me and sat it next to the bowl on my tray. On the plate was a handful of "chips" (Americans call chips "French fries." "Chips" is an Australian term.) and a simple sandwich of some type of deli meat topped with lettuce and tomato.

I grabbed a plastic cup that was filled with some type of fruit drink from a cluster of several filled cups at the far end of the counter. I then carried my dinner over to a table where a few of my friends were sitting. I sat with my friends and ate in silence.

It suddenly occurred to me that this night was Thanksgiving back in America. I announced to my friends at the table, "Hey, cheer up, guys. This is our Thanksgiving dinner, so be thankful."

There was a loud groan from the group of guys in response to my statement. I then added, "You should be thankful, you know. If we were eating an American Thanksgiving dinner we would all eat way too much food and then be miserable for hours afterward."

There were more groans and one, "I would gladly trade this misery for that misery any day."

After dinner, we climbed back into our buses and were driven back to our new home at the Australian company compound. We stumbled through the dark building until everyone found their own little camping area. It had been a very long and depressing day so it wasn't long thereafter that everyone was sleeping. There wasn't much that anyone could do in the near-total darkness anyway.

I was exhausted but I kept waking up from time to time because of the heat. I never stopped sweating all night long. I lay on my tiny air mattress with nothing on except my underwear. Dogs howled and roosters crowed off and on all through the night. Nobody got much sleep. At daybreak I gave up on sleeping and crawled out of my mosquito dome.

I walked outside behind the building where we were staying and lit a cigarette. I met an Australian Lieutenant while smoking my cigarette. He was very curious about this large group of policemen that he and his company were now responsible for so we talked for a long time. By the end of our conversation he offered me the use of their company shower, which was nothing more than a large canvas bag that the user filled with water.

The canvas bag was attached to a rope, which ran up a short pole and through a pulley and then extended back to the ground. The user hoisted the bag just above head high and tied off the rope to hold the bag suspended above the user. The user then opened the shower nozzle to let the water slowly run out and then showered under this dripping water.

This was not the best shower system; however, under the circumstances, it was a God send. Cleaning the filth and sweat from my body seemed to revive my inner strength. I couldn't believe how much better I felt psychologically.

The rest of this second day on Timor Island was spent just sitting around talking, smoking, thinking, and for the most part, just trying to stay cool. Late in the day, the rumor was going around about one of our contingent members who was quitting. He told the U.S. Contingent Commander that he had received a phone call from home and was offered a chief of police job and would have to return to America immediately or lose the opportunity.

There were many jokes and speculation as to how this man had a phone conversation when there were no phone connections anywhere in East Timor. That man never returned to our camp and did return to America. Although there was a lot of criticism about this man quitting, deep down nobody blamed him. Everybody still on the island wanted to go home too. But, Americans being Americans, quitting was just not the right thing to do. The thirty-three remaining Americans stuck it out.

Late in the day I was told to be prepared to go to Maliana where I would be stationed. I, one other American, and two "Kiwis" would be flown out to Maliana first thing in the Morning. ("Kiwi" is what people from New Zealand are called. "Kiwi" is the name of the New Zealand national bird.)

I was relieved to know that I was getting out of that nasty compound we were living. I realized that where I was going could be just as bad but it certainly couldn't be any worse. At least I would be someplace that I could settle into and make my home.

I spent the remainder of the day with my few friends that made up the original East Timor team. Those were the only guys that I knew and now that I was leaving I knew we would have little contact throughout the remainder of the mission. That night we returned to the UN compound for dinner.

I struggled through another night of intermittent sleep. By daybreak I was up and packing my gear for the move to Maliana. I said my goodbyes to my teammates and moved all my kit to the front of the building and waited. Eventually the other American and the two Kiwis going with me to Maliana arrived at the front of the building with all their kit. Then two other Americans came and waited with us. These two Americans were being flown to Suai on the same helicopter that was taking us to Maliana. The six of us made some small talk, but for the most part we waited in silence.

I didn't know any of the names of my fellow passengers, not even the other Americans. For some reason I didn't care if I knew their names or not. Apparently they felt the same way since none of them asked for my name either. Eventually a white mini-van with black UN letters on the sides, back and front, pulled into the compound and stopped near us. We knew the van was coming to take us to the heliport so we picked up our gear and walked it over to the van and put it all in the back.

We all had to make three trips to carry everything. In addition to mosquito domes, sleeping bags, clothes, and equipment we also had to take our supply of food. There was nothing that could be purchased on the island so all the food that we would eat had to be purchased in Darwin and brought with us.

Before leaving Darwin, UN officials told us to buy enough food to sustain us for two weeks. Someone from our assigned area would be allowed to return to Darwin after two weeks to re-supply. Most of us bought enough food to last three weeks just to be safe.

After loading all our kit in the van, the six of us got in the van and we were driven to the heliport. We then had to carry all our gear from the van to the Puma helicopter that sat quietly on its pad about 30 meters away. By the time this task was complete I was again soaked in sweat.

We were then told to have a seat on the helicopter. As we climbed into the aircraft the pilot started the engine. The turbines whined and the large rotors slowly started to turn. By the time we were seated and fastened our seatbelts, the rotors were in full motion. Within a couple of minutes the large Puma helicopter lifted off the pad and nosed forward as it climbed up and out of the city. We were on our way to another big "unknown."

CHAPTER THREE

Rescue

A warm breeze coming off the large river softly blew Caitano's long black hair away from his face. Caitano closely scanned the opposite river bank as he quietly squatted in the tall grass at the river's edge. The half moon that hung in the sky on this night was enough light for this very experienced Clandestino leader to determine if there were enemy in the jungles on the far side of the river.

The operation Caitano was leading was very dangerous but anyone looking into the face of Caitano or the other four men with him would only see a calm and natural appearance. Caitano watched and waited while the other four men with him sat very still in camouflage positions to the left, right and rear of Caitano.

All five men were dressed in civilian dark-colored clothes. As is normal for East Timorese in remote areas, they each carried a Timorese-made machete, which the Timorese called a *katana*. The slightly curved wooden handle makes the *katana* a distinct-looking machete. The *katana* is a much- needed tool used daily for everyday living. These men were carrying the *katana* as a weapon as well as a tool.

While Caitano closely looked for enemy the other four men were watching for any Australian soldier patrols that secured the East Timorese side of the border. The entire length of the border between East Timor and Indonesia's West Timor ran through jungles and mountains, making the border areas remote and porous. The Nunura River marked the border for several miles distance including where Caitano and his men now watched and waited.

The Nunura River was the normal type of river that exists in East Timor. The river bed is about thirty meters wide. There has been no rain in East Timor for several months so there was only a shallow stream of water about twenty feet wide that ran through the middle of the otherwise dry gravel and rock riverbed. On the Indonesian side of the river there was an offshoot knee-deep stream that was three feet wide near the riverbank.

The night of Caitano's mission was in the month of November, 1999. Indonesia, their East Timorese Militia, and many thousands of citizens who lived in East Timor had recently left East Timor and now were living in West Timor. The border that at one time marked the boundary between two Indonesian states now was the border between two nations.

Crossing this border during the Indonesian occupation of East Timor was no big deal. The traveler was simply going from one state to another. That situation changed when Indonesia was forced to leave East Timor. Now whoever crossed that border without proper visas or permits was guilty of illegally entering Indonesia. Anyone crossing that border for any activities of collecting information or conducting acts against the Republic of Indonesia was guilty of espionage.

Because of the nature of Caitano's mission, there would be little chance of convincing Indonesian intelligence that Caitano and his men had simply crossed into West Timor without the proper paperwork. If caught, they would be charged with espionage.

Caitano and his men grew up during the Indonesian occupation of East Timor. Since their early teens, the men had been involved with Clandestino operations. At first they were acting as couriers carrying food, supplies, and sometimes weapons and ammunition to Falintil units operating in the area.

As they got older and more experienced, their responsibilities increased. Eventually the five men conducting the mission on this November night were selected to become members of a specialized section of the Clandestino group they belonged to. The commander of this specialized group was known as "La Faik" (the Crocodile).

Caitano and his men knew very well the Indonesians' reputation for torture to extract information from their victims. These men had no intentions of getting caught; however, psychologically, they had accepted that fate should it happen. Therefore, Caitano and his men were free from the emotion of fear.

* * * *

Four days ago Caitano was summoned for a secret meeting with La Faik. Caitano arrived at the home of Augustinho, who is a commander under La Faik, in the late afternoon. Augustinho and La Faik were sitting on the front porch when Caitano arrived. Caitano respectfully approached La Faik and shook his hand. He then turned to Augustinho and shook his hand. Caitano then sat in the chair that Augustinho offered him.

Within a few minutes of Caitano's arrival, Augustinho's wife, assisted by her twelve-year-old daughter, brought cups of coffee and cookies out onto the front porch. The bowl of cookies was placed in the center of the small table that her husband and his two visitors were sitting near. The cups of coffee were then placed at the edge of the table. One cup for each man was placed at the edge of the table closest to the intended recipient.

A couple of minutes went by before Augustinho motioned toward the table and politely offered the coffee and cookies to his guests. Caitano slowly picked the cup of coffee up from the table with both hands then looked at Augustinho and said, "Colsensa."

Augustinho gave Caitano a slight nod of his head. Caitano then drank coffee from the cup. Once the customary protocols were met La Faik got down to business while the three men drank coffee and ate cookies.

Caitano listened carefully as La Faik spoke, "We have a need for a mission into Turiskai." Turiskai is a small village three kilometers on the "other side" of the border. "This mission must be conducted as soon as possible."

La Faik then explained the situation to Caitano, "Before the Indonesians were forced out of Cailaco Sub-district, I had selected men who were not known to be our 'elements.' They waited in their homes until the time came to be evacuated to West Timor by the Gunta Merah Putih Militia along with the many other people from Cailaco."

La Faik stopped talking when Augustinho's wife and daughter came out onto the porch to retrieve the now-empty cups and the bowl that contained the cookies. Once the women left, La Faik continued, "One of those men I sent to West Timor is now suspected of involvement with our *Segrada Familia*." *Segrada Familia* was the name of La Faik's Clandestino group. Translated, it means "secret Family."

La Faik continued, "The Militia have already come to the suspects new home in Turiskai to find him, but fortunately, he wasn't home. His wife was clever enough to have told the Militia that he had gone to Atambua to visit friends. We have to get our element and his family on our side of the border before he is captured by the Militia. If captured he will eventually give the names of all our elements in his team."

Throughout the remainder of the day, La Faik, Augustinho, and Caitano put together the plan to rescue their element and his family from Indonesia. La Faik had already gathered all the information possible to obtain for this mission. His network of assets, or elements, as he called them, was in position to support the rescue operation. The last ingredient for this rescue recipe was a team leader and a selected team of men who could physically carry out the task. Caitano was the team leader who La Faik believed could do this job.

Caitano spent the next few days and nights with the four teammates that he selected to participate on this mission to further plan and prepare. The five man team spent long hours every day and night on the border. They observed the activities at the illegal market that was on the Indonesian side of the river near the East Timor village of Tunubibi and the West Timor village of Turiskai.

The Indonesian soldiers and the Militia were making money from the market, which was why the market was not closed down. Many people living in East Timor were allowed to walk across the river and enter the market. The East Timorese would make their purchases and then return to East Timor.

Caitano and his team also closely watched the Australian soldiers who were stationed at this river crossing point where the people crossed over to the illegal market. At night Caitano and his team carefully scouted the riverbank north of the illegal market, which would be the area that Caitano's team would cross from East Timor into West Timor.

The purpose of these night-scouting patrols was to locate suitable crossing points and also to learn the security patrol tactics of both the Indonesian soldiers and the Australian soldiers. Through long hours of slow, deliberate movement, they found Australian patrols that were hidden in static observation positions near the river's edge.

The Australians did not use the same position two nights in a row; however, Caitano observed that the Australians did not appear to conduct moving patrols late at night. They relied on night-vision equipment and motion sensors.

Caitano picked out three different locations that he and his team could use to cross the river. From those intended river crossing positions Caitano spent hours watching the opposite side of the river. Caitano observed the Indonesian military patrols that were made along the Indonesian side of the river. He took notes on the size of the patrol, how many soldiers per patrol, and which direction they were walking and at what time. He further noted the speed of the patrol and the exact area the soldiers walked in relation to the river.

It was not an easy task for Caitano to gather so much detail. Observing detail from thirty to forty yards away on a moonlight night is not easy. Some of the information Caitano collected was more of an estimate rather than a known fact. But this was the best that he could do under the circumstances. Caitano was just thankful that the timing of this mission happened to be during the time there was a moon. What Caitano did not realize was that La Faik did not give this mission assignment to Caitano until there was moonlight.

Caitano was reasonably certain that the Indonesian military did not have any hidden static observation points along the river. Caitano knew this because during the daytime hours on the first day of these pre-mission planning operations Caitano and one of his men had gone over the border into the illegal market . While at the market Caitano met with one of Segrada Familias secret operators who had been placed in West Timor by La Faik.

During this brief meeting the West Timor based Segrada Familia member gave Caitano the information Caitano needed to conduct this mission and coordinate the mission with the West Timor Segrada Familia elements. The West Timor team already had determined that the Indonesian military were more interested in keeping an eye on the Australian military rather than trying to catch a few stray East Timorese.

The West Timor team had also determined that the Indonesians conducted foot patrols along the river through the night hours. There were static observation positions; however, the same positions were used every night. The man Caitano met in the market used natural landmarks to describe the static positions used by the Indonesians so that Caitano and his team could avoid being seen by the Indonesian soldiers while crossing the river.

* * * *

Caitano and his men spent three days and three nights observing, planning, and preparing. Segrada Familia members supported the pre-mission operations by daily meeting with the five men and bringing them food and supplies. When Segrada Familia supporters met with the five men at pre dawn on this morning Caitano sent La Faik a message through these supporters that the mission would begin tonight.

Caitano sent one of his team members over to the illegal market to make one last brief meet with the West Timor Segrada Familia teammate who was set up as a "mailbox," running a small selling stall inside the market area. "Mailbox" is a term for a person who can secretly be contacted to relay information. The purpose of this meeting was to let the West Timor team know that tonight would be the beginning of the mission and also to make sure there were no changes that had occurred on "their" side.

Late in the morning Caitanos teammate returned from the West Timor illegal market. The mission was a "go" for tonight. Caitano led the five-man team to a secluded location in the jungle about three hundred yards from where Caitano planned to cross the river. The five-man team spent the next few hours sleeping, eating, and preparing for the mission.

Two hours after the sun went down the team left their resting area and moved toward the river's edge. The team didn't arrive at the river until almost midnight. The team moved very slowly, making sure that they made no noise that anyone nearby could hear. The team came across an Australian military patrol that was set up in a hidden static position near the intended river-crossing point.

The team slipped around the Australians, then moved to an alternate crossing point. The team carefully checked the area of the alternate crossing point to make sure there was no other Australian static observation position set up. Once satisfied this alternate crossing point could not be observed by the Australians, the team deployed into hidden team security positions and waited.

The Indonesian military foot patrols were sporadic; however, Caitano knew that once a patrol went through an area there wouldn't be another patrol for at least thirty minutes. With this in mind Caitano waited for the Indonesian patrol to pass through. Once the patrol passed through, Caitano would know approximately where the Indonesian patrol was, what direction they were going, and he knew that he and his team had time to get across and away from the river.

While he waited, Caitano went through the entire mission in his mind. This was a complicated mission that required many timing considerations and probably a lot of flexibility. The team had already gotten past the first and least dangerous obstacle, which was to reach the river without being detected by the Australian military.

The next obstacle for the team was to get across the river and past the Indonesian patrols without being detected. Next the team had to find the rendezvous location to meet with the West Timor team. The West Timor team would then lead the combined teams to a secluded location in the jungle near the village of Turiskai, which was the target location of this mission.

The combined teams would spend the day at the secluded location resting, planning, and preparing for the remainder of the mission that hopefully would be conducted later during the night. The man the Militia was looking for should be with this West Timor team. After all, he was a member of the West Timor team.

Getting this one man across the border would be a simple matter if he were alone. The man actually didn't need any help to get across the border. He could sneak through the enemy patrols like any other Segrada Familia operator. The problem was getting his wife and two children back to East Timor.

Ever since the Militia came looking for the man and he wasn't home, the Militia had posted a twenty-four-hour guard on the man's home. If the wife went anywhere she was escorted by Militia members. If any of the children went anywhere, Militia members went with them.

Caitano was speculating on what plan the West Timor team had to snatch the wife and children away from the guardian Militia when his thoughts were interrupted by movement he saw in the jungle across the river. Caitano sat motionless in the tall grass and calmly watched the distant jungle.

Several minutes went by while Caintano and a second teammate whom Caitano called up to his position watched the far side of the riverbed. There was definite movement on the far side; however, the two men couldn't be sure if the movement was an Indonesian patrol or not. Whatever was moving was in the shadows of the trees the entire time.

The natural dilemma was whether to assume the movement was the Indonesian patrol or not. If it was the patrol it could be another one to two hours before another patrol came through. If it wasn't the patrol and the team crossed the river, Caitano could be leading his men into the midst of a patrol, which would probably result in capture.

To an experienced operator like Caitano, there was no dilemma in situations like this. A careless operator didn't last long in this environment. Caitano was fairly sure the movement was the Indonesian patrol; however, he was not about to lead his men into anymore uncertainties than what was necessary. He would wait until the next patrol came through. Patience and precision were normal East Timorese virtues. For Falintil soldiers and Clandestino operators these qualities were even stronger.

Approximately forty-five minutes later Caitano again saw movement on the other side of the river. This time there was no doubt what the movement was. Caitano could see the outline of several men as they walked the rivers edge where there were no shadows from the nearby trees. Caitano knew they were soldiers because they walked in the standard patrol formation and by the way the silhouettes of the men moved. There was a distinct difference between how a man who was carrying nothing or maybe farm tools walked and how a man walked when carrying a rifle. It was obvious those men were carrying rifles.

Caitano waited fifteen minutes after the patrol walked out of sight going south along the river. Caitano then made an ever-so-slight clicking sound of his tongue to signal his teammates that it was time to go. There would only be one teammate in the river bed at any one time. This tactic had several purposes. First of all, should an unexpected patrol or observation post happen to be nearby, one man moving slowly across the moonlit riverbed was less apt to be seen by the enemy. Second, one man seen crossing the border did not raise the anxiety levels of a security patrol as much as seeing five men crossing together. Third, should there be an unexpected surprise waiting on the other side, or if an unexpected surprise should develop, men on that side could signal the rest not to cross the river.

The river crossing went smoothly enough. Once the fifth man climbed up the riverbank to join his four teammates waiting for him now on Indonesian soil Caitano led the team west, away from the river. The West Timor team had told Caitano that the Indonesian military does not have any depth to their border patrols. Once away from the immediate vicinity of the river there is little danger of running into an Indonesian military patrol.

Once away from the river, Caitano gave the "point" (the lead person in formation) to a teammate, Francisco, who knew the Turiskai area fairly well. Francisco was familiar with the rendezvous site and would know better then the rest of the team how to get there.

The rendezvous site was only one mile from the river; however, when a team had to move down jungle paths in the night and also had to move slowly enough for the team to detect other people on or near the path before the team could be detected, movement became very time consuming. The early morning sun was rising by the time Caitano and his team reached the rendezvous position.

A cool breeze swept down from the mountain that Caitano's East Timor team was climbing. The rising sun behind the men cast long shadows from the many surrounding trees. Francisco knew the rendezvous site was close by. He was tired from the long walk and having to concentrate so hard to detect anyone that may have come across during their journey. The natural desire of a man in this situation is to walk a little quicker to get to where rest and security awaits. Francisco suppressed this desire and focused on continued stealth tactics. There were limited access trails up this mountain, which meant the team could run across other persons who were traveling in the area. This was not the time to get careless.

Francisco continued on until he reached the place where the team would leave the path and walk cross-country through the brush and trees to enter the even thicker jungle of the rendezvous site. Francisco stepped to the right side of the trail and squatted in the brush. Caitano, who was walking in the number two position (the second man walking in line) came up to Francisco and squatted beside him so the two men could talk.

Francisco never took his eyes off the trail in front of him. He whispered to Caitano, "The rendezvous site is forty meters to our right."

Caitano never said a word. He simply patted Francisco's shoulder twice, which told Francisco to go. Francisco slowly stood up and started moving through the thick brush that lay between the team and the rendezvous site.

Twenty minutes later the team entered the rendezvous site. Caitano was both confused and alarmed when he saw that nobody was there. He moved up close to Francisco and asked, "You sure this is the right place?"

Francisco calmly nodded yes. The East Timor team quickly searched the surrounding trees and brush for any sign that may have been left for them. There was fresh bent grass and other small signs of people having recently been loitering in the area; however, no specific Segrada Familia secret codes.

The West Timor Team's failure to be at the rendezvous site was not a good sign and could mean a lot of different things. An Indonesian military or Militia patrol could have come through the area, forcing the team away. Continued military or Militia patrols could be preventing the West Timor team from ever arriving. There was a very slight possibility that the team leader thought that Caitano's team wasn't going to make it so they left the area. This was a highly unlikely scenario. It was also possible that the West Timor team had been captured.

Caitano knew he should lead his team out of the area immediately. If the other team was captured they would soon be compelled to tell everything they knew including about meeting Caitano's team and where. It was too dangerous to go east toward the Nunura River (the border) during daylight hours. Also if the Indonesians had learned that there was a team from East Timor in the area they would expect the team to evade to the East.

Caitano told Francisco to lead the team to a secluded location toward the southwest. Turiskai Village was northwest of the rendezvous site. Going southwest put Caitanos team as far away from the Militia based in Turiskai Village as possible without going toward the Nunura River. Francisco did not hesitate. He turned and walked out of the thick jungle on the hilltop that was the rendezvous site.

Forty meters down the hill Francisco cautiously approached the same footpath they had used to climb the mountain to this point. Francisco had to use this narrow dirt path, which was lined by grass and brush, for a short distance. Toward the west on this trail, for a distance of fifty meters, a steep drop off fell from the path on the left side and thick jungle grew from the nearly straight up incline to the right side of the path.

Francisco turned right onto this path and increased his pace to a fast walk to get past this dangerous fifty-meter stretch of mountain path. This stretch of path was dangerous because if the team came across other travelers or enemy patrols, they could not move to the sides of the path and hide. Francisco continued his fast pace until he reached a smaller, hardly ever used path that veered off to Francisco's left.

Francisco quickly moved down this smaller path until he knew his four teammates following behind him were off the larger path and could conceal themselves from anyone that may come along on the larger path. Francisco then stopped and studied the path itself. He slowly moved down the path looking for any sign that someone had passed down this smaller path recently.

Grass and brush that overgrew this smaller path made it difficult to see any footprints that someone may have left behind. Francisco continued to move slowly, carefully, studying every inch of the path. Caitano moved up close to Francisco and closely watched the trail to their front. With Caitano "holding security" to the front, Francisco was free to completely focus on the path itself.

Francisco became suspicious upon seeing some bent grass when he first started his search for signs of someone passing down this path. As he continued his search, meter after meter, he saw more probable signs of someone using this path. Thirty meters later, Francisco saw a definite sign and it wasn't good.

Francisco saw more blades of grass that were bent. The long grass lay across the trail coming from the left side of the path where the grass was rooted into the hard soil. Francisco carefully moved the bent grass to the side to see what was underneath. His chest tightened as he saw a partial boot heel print in the dry dirt that was under the bent grass. The only people who wore boots like the one that made this print were Indonesian military or their Militia.

Caitano bent down next to Francisco and quickly studied the print in the dirt. There was no doubt. Militia or TNI (Indonesian military) had been down this trail recently. There were many issues to speculate about; however, Caitano didn't have time for that now. He and his men were in enemy country and the enemy was probably close to them. Caitano had to get his team off this trail as soon as possible.

Caitano looked up from the partial heel print in the dirt. He saw Francisco squatting in the grass and brush just to the right of the trail, closely watching the trail to the front. Caitano then glanced to his rear and saw that his men behind him were concealed and watching closely to the left, right, and rear of the team.

Caitano then scanned the landscape around him. To his right about forty meters away, Caitano saw what he was looking for. The terrain sharply rose about thirty feet above the surrounding terrain. Trees, brush, and rocks were so thick on that piece of high ground that it didn't look possible to enter the area. That was where Caitano decided he and his team should go until they could figure out how they were going to get back to East Timor.

Caitano made his normal slight clicking of his tongue sound to get Francisco's attention. Francisco heard his leaders summon so he turned and looked at Caitano. Caitano motioned toward the forbidding high ground. Francisco glanced over to the area and without hesitation stood up and moved in that direction. Every man on this team knew they were in trouble so as always when in enemy country the team moved slowly, carefully scanning their surroundings in all directions with each man on the team responsible for a direction to watch. The last man, following the rest of the team, carefully disguised any tracks or other signs of the team's passage.

Thirty minutes later the team had crawled under and through the thick jungle as they scaled the steep rocks and earth. That piece of high ground was only thirty feet high but it was a very tough thirty-foot climb. Caitano and his team quickly cleared the area on top of and behind the feature they were now on to make sure there was nobody in the area. Within a few minutes the team knew nobody had been near this piece of ground for a very long time, if ever. Finally Caitano and his men could take a breath and try to figure out what was happening and what they should do next.

Caitano sent Francisco and Lindo into the jungle to the rear of the feature the team now occupied to find water and food. Caitano moved to a position on the feature that concealed him while he watched the path where they had found the partial boot heel print. The remaining teammates, Mario and Jose, found concealed positions to observe the remaining area that surrounded the team's new position.

Caitano was tired, hungry and thirsty. He took a clear plastic bottle of water out of the small backpack that he carried. He took the top off the bottle and sipped at the small amount of water that was left in the bottle. He then took one of four rice balls from his pack. With his *katana* he cut the woven yellowish-green leaves that tightly packaged the rice ball. He sipped his water and ate the rice as he watched the trail below.

Caitano thought about their situation as he refreshed himself: Why wasn't the West Timor team at the rendezvous point? Who had been down this tiny and almost never used path that Caitano now was watching? What were the possibilities of someone other than TNI or Militia wearing Indonesian combat boots?

There was no doubt about aborting the rescue mission. Caitano was now concerned about just getting his team back to East Timor. For the time being Caitano believed they were somewhat safe but they couldn't stay on this rock for long. The team should move when it got dark, but where? Francisco was the only one who knew this area and his knowledge was limited.

Francisco and Lindo soon returned bringing with them coconuts and tiny pineapples that were the size of a man's fist. The coconuts furnished both food and water. In addition, they found a small stream that flowed from higher up the mountain to the north of the team. There were many things that could kill a man in Timor. Starvation or thirst were two things that a man should never die from, though. You may not be able to eat or drink what you want, but there was plenty of food and water in the jungle.

The team started rotating team security responsibilities. Two men kept watch for any activity near their position while the other three men ate and slept. Late in the afternoon Mario was on team security duty watching the trail when he saw men walking down the trail toward the larger path. Mario counted eight men who were all dressed in TNI camouflage pants and black t-shirts. Three of the men carried SKS assault rifles while the other five men carried bows and arrows.

The style of dress was the typical Militia uniform. The Militia men were walking in a single file formation; however, they did not appear to be overly alert. Militia members all received training from the TNI Koppassus; however, the Militia never did come close to the same level of discipline and woodsman skills as their Falintil enemies.

The Militia patrol walked right past where Caitano's team left that trail and made their way to this rocky and jungle covered piece of high ground. Caitano was sleeping within arm's reach behind Mario when the Militia patrol came down the trail. Mario didn't make a move until after the Militia was past the team and out of sight. Mario then slowly reached behind him and nudged Caitano. Caitano opened his eyes and slowly moved along side Mario. All Falintil soldiers and Clandestino operators have been trained to always make slow and deliberate movements. Fast movement is easier for someone to see and can produce more noise.

Mario told Caitano about the Militia patrol who had just walked by. Caitano sat next to Mario for a long time thinking over the developments of this mission. He knew the nature of the Militia very well. Militia members were primarily drawn from areas that the Indonesians had controlled, which meant that most of the members were not accustom to spending much time in rough remote areas. That is why Militia members did not have the toughness, discipline and natural woodsman skills that the Falintil possessed.

The Militia wouldn't venture into the jungles and mountains of East Timor during the Indonesian occupation for fear of being killed. They could get killed by a Falintil unit who may happen to be in the area or possibly by the villagers themselves. All villages in the remote areas of East Timore were known as "Falintil villages." Everyone who lived in Falintil villages was skilled with bow and arrows, spears, and *katanas*. They were also very knowledgeable about how to ambush and kill a handful of city boys who may wander into their homeland.

Here in West Timor, the militia's situation was different. There was no Falintil or Falintil villages in the remote areas so the Militia was free to go wherever they wanted; however, Caitano rationalized that the Militia would not leave their comfortable villages to take long walks through rough terrain unless there was a good reason for the effort.

* * * *

On the morning Caitano decided to launch his mission, Abilio sat in his comfortable concrete home on the south edge of Turiskai Village, which is two miles west of the Nunura River into West Timor. Turiskai is the location that the Koppassus SGI Intelligence Commander, Tome Diago, told Abilio to set up a base for Militia operations.

Abilio was the Operational Commander of the Halilintar Merah Putih Militia that was based in Maliana, East Timor. In late September 1999, it was time to leave East Timor before INTERFET forces arrived in Maliana. Abilio had already selected the home where he would live in Turiskai. A Halilintar Militia headquarters building had also been pre selected and was ready for use.

The Halilintar Militia was a large Militia organization that encompassed several smaller Militia groups that were scattered throughout the Bobonaro district. Every leader and member were prepared to make the move to Turiskai so when Abilio sent out the word to make the move the entire Halilintar organization easily took what few belongings remained to be moved and went to Turiskai. Along with them they took every East Timorese citizen who was still in the villages that Indonesia controlled. The people in the villages had no choice but to go.

The Halilintar Militia along with Indonesian military and several military trucks would drive into a village and tell the people to get into the back of the trucks. It was further announced that anyone who didn't want to go now to West Timor would be killed—right then. Needless to say, everyone got on the trucks.

The citizens were transported to Turiskai Village in West Timor where there was a refugee camping area already established for the new arrivals. The kidnaping of thousands of East Timorese citizens went smoothly for the Halilintar Militia until they went to Memo Village.

Memo Village was an Indonesian-controlled village; however, because of Memo's close proximity to the Nunura River, there were many Falintil secret operators and Clandestinos placed there—many more than the Indonesians realized. Falintil forces were all in their assigned cantonment areas during this time but Falintil's secret soldiers were not. This particular group of Falintil operators in Memo Village was not about to let the Halilintar Militia come and steal the citizens without a fight.

The Falintil fighters ambushed the convoy of military trucks as they entered the village. The Falintil fighters had no firearms. They used homemade bombs that could be thrown along with bow and arrows. The Halilintar Militia and the handful of TNI soldiers that supported the Militia activity were quickly routed by the fierce ambush launched by the Falintil. Three of the several trucks that had been brought to Memo were in flames from the attack and had to be abandoned. Several Halilintar members were wounded by arrows, flames and *katana* slashes.

Two hours later when the Halilintar returned with a larger support section from the TNI, they found that most of the people in Memo Village had already been evacuated by the Falintil operators. The Halilintar Militia attempted to catch the people; however, they were met by stiff resistance by the cleaver Falintil operators.

After suffering several more Militia members wounded the Halilintar Militia quit the chase. Most of the citizens of Memo Village escaped; however, their village did not. In their fury the Halilintar destroyed virtually everything in Memo Village. There was absolutely nothing left.

* * * *

Abilio sipped coffee from the cup he held in his left hand as he watched the black Kijang Surf, which was an Indonesian-made "Explorer"-type vehicle, drive through his front gate and stop near the front of his home. All four doors of the vehicle opened and four uniformed men stepped out. The four Koppassus TNI soldiers were dressed in Indonesian camouflage uniforms and wore red berets. Three of the four men carried M-16 rifles and moved to security positions surrounding the fourth man.

Abilio knew this car and the Koppassus Commander that was in the center of the now established security screen. Abilio stepped out onto the front veranda and waited. Tome Diago greeted Abilio as he stepped up onto the beautifully ceramic-tiled floor of the veranda. Abilio led Tome into the home and they sat in the front room while the other three special soldiers continued their security duties from the outside of the home.

Tome Diago is the Koppassus SGI commander that was tasked with the creation of the many East Timor Militia organizations throughout East Timor. He was perfect for the job. He was a Koppassus Special Forces soldier who worked his way up in rank quickly. His cold-blooded ruthless attitude eventually earned him a job in the Koppassus intelligence unit known as SGI. What made him even more perfect for the job was that Tome Diago was East Timorese.

A beautiful young Timorese woman quickly served the two men coffee and cake. Abilio had brought this woman into his home, choosing her from the many East Timorese who were recently brought to the Turiskai Refugee camp that Abilio now controlled. The parents could not refuse Abilio's selection of their daughter. If they caused any problem about their daughter becoming Abilio's property they would be killed.

Tome sipped his coffee and watched the young woman leave the room. He looked back at Abilio and nodded his approval of the woman. The nod was all the emotion that Tome would show. The hard features of Tome's forty-year-old dark-skinned face were like stone. His black eyes were sharp, piercing instruments rather than simply tools to see with.

Tome asked, "How are the wife and children?"

Abilio answered, "So far no new information since the first night. I don't think she knows anything more."

Tome asked, "Any possibilities of who may be working with Emio?"

45

Abilio thought about the question before answering, "The people Emio's wife told us were friends of Emio don't have any indicators of having been involved with intelligence."

Tome was sitting quietly on the padded bamboo chair, leaning forward slightly and holding his nearly empty cup of coffee. He now calmly sat the coffee cup on the small wooden table in front of him, then leaned back until he comfortably rested his back against the chair's padding. He crossed his legs as his coal-black eyes looked into Abilio's eyes.

Abilio knew Tome very well and was usually comfortable when discussing business with Tome. Abilio's failure to develop any solid information to tell Tome made Abilio a little uneasy. Abilio then said, "There have been a couple of different men who seem to be making frequent walks past Emio's home. There is nothing to indicate that they have any involvement with Emio, though."

Abilio stopped talking for a moment then added, "Maybe Emio was working alone."

Tome's expression, as always, never changed. After Abilio finished talking Tome sat motionless watching Abilio for almost a full minute before he spoke, "Start watching the two men that have been seen walking past Emio's home. Take the wife and children to the Halilintar headquarters for the next few days and keep them in the building. They are not to go anywhere."

Abilio realized that Tome had received some new and important information from one or more of his sources that were operating in East Timor. That was where the information about Emio being a spy for La Faik had come from a few weeks ago.

* * * *

A few weeks ago Tome met with Abilio and told him that reliable sources had reported a "cell" of intelligence operators who had been placed in West Timor by a Falintil commander known only by his codename "La Faik." How many members were in this cell was not known. Who the members of the cell were, other than Emio, was also not known.

Tome hoped to identify the other members of the cell by having Abilio's Halilintar Militia closely watch Emio's activities. Three days later Emio left Turiskai without the Militia members knowing that he had gone. The Halilintar closely watched for Emio's return. After a few days of waiting and watching,

46

Tome believed that Emio suspected that he was "burned," so he slipped out of Turiskai with no intentions of coming back.

Tome knew that Emio had not returned to Cailaco in East Timor. Tome's own cell of intelligence operators planted in Cailaco and Maliana would know the moment Emio came back. It was time to take control of Emio's wife and children and extract all information possible.

Halilintar Militia went to Emio's home and confronted his wife about where Emio had gone. As directed by Tome, the Militia was careful to make all appearances to outsiders that the Militia members were only interested in Emio and not conducting their normal rape and torture of anyone who fell into their clutches.

Several Militia members were constantly at Emio's home. Emio's wife and children were free to go about their business throughout the day; however, there was always a Militia escort with them. At night after the children were asleep Militia interrogators worked at extracting information from Emio's wife. She was repeatedly raped and "lightly" tortured so that no marks or injuries could be seen when she was in public.

As with any Counter-Intelligence operation the plan was to identify and capture or kill the entire enemy cell. Losing sight of Emio so early in the operation was a very unfortunate turn of events for Tome and the Halilintar Militia.

* * * *

Abilio did not reply to Tome's orders. He knew better then to ask questions. Tome would tell Abilio only what he wanted Abilio to know. Tome then continued to lay out his plan to Abilio, "I have reason to believe that someone will be coming to Turiskai from East Timor soon, probably over the next couple of days. They will be meeting with La Faik's cell that is operating here. They won't be meeting at the Turiskai restaurant in the middle of town so you have got to organize patrols to cover every footpath and village surrounding Turiskai. We must make every effort possible to capture the cell that is operating here and the men that are coming here from East Timor."

Tome and Abilio then spent the rest of the morning studying a map of the Turiskai area and planning how best to organize patrols to cover the most likely approaches and exits into the Turiskai area. They identified likely areas for clandestine meetings and also all possible escape and evasion routes from those areas.

Abilio had summoned all his team leaders to the Halilintar headquarters to be waiting for the operation briefing that would be given as soon as Tome and Abilio had completed their plans. Early in the afternoon Tome and Abilio arrived at the Halilintar headquarters. All the team leaders were waiting for them so they immediately began the briefing.

By mid-afternoon the briefing session was over. The individual team leaders immediately met with their waiting team members and briefed them on the operation and their assigned area of responsibility. By late afternoon every Militia unit either had already left or was leaving Turiskai to cover their assigned area of responsibility.

There were now almost three hundred armed Militia looking for a handful of unarmed Falintil secret operators. Tome and Abilio were fairly confident that at least some of the Falintil would soon be in their hands.

* * * *

It was now completely dark as Caitano and his team sat in the thick jungle on top of that rugged hill that they used as a hiding/observation post throughout the day. They had seen no other movement on the remote trail forty-meters in front of them since the Militia unit passed by earlier in the afternoon.

Normally this would be the time for Caitano to move his team to another location but he had an uneasy feeling about moving. Caitano was accustomed to Militia ways in East Timor during the Indonesian occupation; however, this was not East Timor. The situation here in West Timor was very different.

The moon that rose above them lit up the distant trail but the thick jungle around the East Timor team blocked the moonlight, leaving Caitano and his men in complete darkness. Caitano met with Francisco and Jose while Lindo and Mario maintained security positions. The three men discussed their situation in low tones. By the end of the meeting Caitano decided not to make a move on this night. There were just too many unknowns. The Militia was not known to be in the jungle after dark but that was East Timor where Falintil dominated the jungles and mountains. Questions kept running through Caitano's mind: Where was the West Timor team? Why was there a Militia patrol so far away from civilization? Where do we go when we do leave this rugged hilltop?

48

Caitano and his men had been in tough situations before but not like this. The West Timor team was planning to furnish the East Timor team with weapons when they met. The weapons were only bow and arrows but in the hands of Caitano's team bow and arrows was enough. The only defense this team had now was to avoid detection.

Caitano and his men were in a strange land where the enemy controlled the entire area. The enemy could operate however they liked with no fear of Falintil units finding and attacking them. Caitano realized they were completely vulnerable. They had come here to rescue a fellow Segrada Familia member and his family. Now it was Caitano and his team that needed to be rescued.

Eventually Caitano realized that he had allowed himself to fall into a negative thought pattern. This was not the Falintil way of thinking. Caitano thought, *the rescue mission that we had come to Turiskai to conduct is not going to happen now and it appears that the Militia is looking for us; however, the Militia does not have the cunning and endurance to maintain a drawn-out operation in the jungle.*

Caitano reasoned that the position they were now in may be good for another day. A Militia patrol had walked past where the team had left the small trail and made their way to where they now hid. The Militia did not notice any sign of the team's movements when they walked past so they probably won't ever see any signs that possibly exists. The team has good fields of vision and they can evade in any direction should they come under pressure. Caitano made his decision. The team would stay one more day.

At first light Caitano sent two men to collect food and water. Throughout the day the team rested and watched. At about 0700 hours two middle-aged men wearing civilian clothes came walking down the trail going toward the larger trail. At about 1100 hours another Militia patrol walked past on the trail, coming from the larger path. There were twelve men all wearing the black t-shirts and camouflage pants that identified them as Militia. Five of the Militia was carrying SKS assault rifles, two men were carrying M-16 assault rifles and the remaining five were carrying bow and arrows. At 1530 hours the same Militia patrol came back down the trail going toward the larger path.

An hour after sunset Caitano gave the signal to move out. Caitano was on point as he led his team ever so slowly down the steep rock and earth face of the feature they had dominated for so long. Once at the bottom of the feature he led the team back to the small trail. It was a slow process of taking a slow step and then scanning the surroundings while listening carefully for any and all sounds. Caitano then took the next step, slowly moving one foot forward and "feeling" the ground as he slowly put that foot down. He was feeling the ground for twigs or leaves that will make sound when weight is applied.

This was going to be a long night. Every inch of ground this team traveled tonight would be done with this same slow and methodical process. By 0300 hours the team was about halfway back to the Nunura River. This was not a time to get careless. The team could move faster and make the river before daylight but that would endanger the team. Caitano spent the last two hours of darkness finding and settling into a small patch of thick brush and weeds that was about twenty meters to the left of the line of movement that the team was on.

Once out of the mountainous foothills where Turiskai Village lay, Caitano abandon the footpaths and was leading his team through brush and jungle. The terrain in the valley favored the team. There was a lot of jungle for cover and concealment and if the team came under pressure they could evade in any direction, not being handicapped by mountainous cliffs and steep rocky faces. They were not on any footpaths so anyone who comes near the team is most likely "enemy" who is tracking the team.

By the break of dawn the team was concealed and ready to wait out the daylight hours of another day. The team again was alternating security duties and resting. They were out of food and their water supply was nearly gone. There were trees that spread over the team that provided complete shade; however, the lowlands of Timor is very hot even in the shade. This was going to be a long day.

Lindo was on security duty watching the teams "back trail." There was no breeze leaving the still air to bake under the boiling sun that hung in the middle of a cloudless blue sky. In the middle of the afternoon the feelings of heat and thirst drained from Lindo's mind when he saw movement thirty-meters away from the team. A few moments later Lindo could clearly see a man dressed in TNI camouflage clothing, wearing a red beret and carrying a rifle.

Lindo had to suppress the panic that began to surge through him as he realized that a Koppassus unit was tracking him and his team. Out maneuvering Militia was dangerous enough but this was much more dangerous. Koppassus is the best Indonesia has to throw against the team and they were close. Lindo quickly summoned Caitano.

Caitano's mind raced as he watched the Koppassus unit slowly move toward the team. Caitano could see four Koppassus soldiers but he was sure there were more. Caitanos first thought was to make a run to the river but he then realized that the TNI border patrols assuredly knew there was a team caught between the Koppassus unit and the river. There would be many TNI soldiers at the river waiting to see what the Koppassus flushed out to them.

Caitano now wished he had stayed on the trails after coming out of the mountain. They may have bumped into some military patrols or checkpoints on those trails but as long as the team saw the soldiers first the team could have worked their way around the patrol or checkpoint, thus maintaining the initiative.

There was no time to waste on thinking about what they should have done. The team was nearly trapped and would probably be captured. They had no weapons so their only hope was to move and move faster then what the Koppassus could track. The team had to move north or south. Koppassus was to their west and the Nunura River along with many TNI soldiers were to their east.

The terrain to the north favored the team better then to the south. There were no villages or any other form of civilization for several kilometers to the north. Caitano led the team out of the thick brush going north. They were moving fast, no longer concerned about running into a waiting outpost or patrol. If there was a unit north of the team there would be no escape anyway.

The only hope the team had now was in the life-long ways of the Falintil. The Falintil could move quickly through jungle terrain making very little noise and leaving very little sign of passage. Caitano hoped that the Koppassus trackers would still have to move slowly to determine the signs left by the teams movements while the team moved at a fast walk and when possible a slow run.

Caitano expected to hear gunshots ring out when the team first started to move but there was nothing. The Koppassus apparently did not see or hear the team when they started to move. The Koppassus tracking unit was so close to the team Caitano thought sure they would be seen or at least heard.

For one kilometer distance the jungle was thick and the terrain rough but then the team came across a roadway. The jungle thinned to a few scattered trees and brush surrounded by grass for a distance of fifty meters. The TNI was sure to be watching for anyone trying to cross the road.

Caitano didn't hesitate as he "button-hooked" his team to swing back to overlook their own back trail. Sure enough, shortly after the team settled into concealed positions, they saw the Koppassus trackers come walking up through the same area the team had walked through earlier. Once the Koppassus unit was out of sight Caitano slowly led the team over to their original path of travel and then moved south on the same path that they had moved north. There was a chance the Koppassus trackers may not realize the team had reused their original path of travel.

Now Caitano and his team moved slowly so that they could detect anyone in front of them. Moving slow also gave the "drag" (the last man in the formation) time to obliterate any new signs of the team's passage. Caitano hoped that this tactic would confuse the Koppassus trackers to buy the team more time.

By the time the team got back to the spot that they had rested through most of that day the sun was down and the last of the day's light shone across the darkening sky. Caitano could hardly believe that they were still free men. He kept the team moving south as the day turned into night. Eventually the moon rose above them giving the team limited visibility.

A feeling of hope began to flow through Caitano as they continued to move south. Caitano gave a lot of thought about what to do and where to go. He had to assume that Koppassus was close behind them so he knew they had to get across the Nunura River tonight. He further figured that the TNI expected the team to cross the river somewhere in the more remote area north of the illegal market. With this in mind, Caitano planned to cross the river near Memo, which is south of the illegal market.

The Australian military would be sure to see the team when they crossed, but that didn't matter to Caitano. The Australian military would capture and check the team out, but when they found out Caitano and his men were East Timorese, they would be released. All they had to do was get across that river.

Throughout the night the team moved ever-so-slowly to the south. They drank water from a large puddle they came across and ate a little grass to curb their hunger and thirst. Shortly after midnight the team made it to the river near Memo Village. They took up concealed positions in the thick jungle about thirty meters away from the river bank. Through the many trees, they could barely see the riverbed in the thin moonlight. They could hear the water as it flowed around and over rocks in the middle of the riverbed.

Every one of the team members was so tired. Safety and freedom were now in sight. They wanted to make a run for it but Caitano hesitated. He was aware that the Koppassus trackers could still be on their trail and very close to them but he also knew that TNI border patrols could be nearby too.

Caitano had not scouted out this part of the river. He had no idea what may be waiting for his team near the riverbank. He didn't have time to check the situation out now so he told his teammates in a low whisper, "We can't wait here. Koppassus could be tracking us right now and maybe very close. We got to get across that river now or we may never get across. We will make our way to the river now. Once at the river we got to go. We will walk across the river if we can but if we are challenged we got to make a run for it."

Caitano paused a few moments then added, "Don't stop for nothing—if the TNI shoot us that is okay. It is better to die in that river than get captured."

With that said the team slowly made its way to the river. When they were nearly at the river Caitano, who was on point, detected movement on his left. He figured it was a static TNI observation point. He moved to his right several meters then continued toward the river. An hour later, Caitano was squatting in the shadows of the trees along the river.

Freedom was so close now. Forty yards away, the team's homeland, East Timor, waited for their return. Caitano watched, listened, and felt for any presence of other human beings as he remained motionless in the shadows. The moonlight that he had so skillfully used in his favor for over a week was now going to work against him. The moon was not much more than a sliver but it was lighter than what he wanted right now.

There was no choice; it was now or never. Caitano gave his normal slight click of his tongue, then stood up and moved into the riverbed. His four men also stood up and followed their leader. The men stepped carefully over the uneven ground that was heavily graveled and strewn with rocks of all sizes and shapes.

Chills ran up and down the spines of the men as they waited for those Indonesian words, "Stop. Stop now or we will shoot." Or worse yet, the crack of rifle rounds as the Indonesian TNI shot the men down.

The men reached the center where water rushed down the river. The Nunura River runs deeper and faster at Memo, which is why the illegal market was established north of this point. The river was more dangerous to cross at Memo. Caintano and his men did not hesitate as they stepped into the rushing water.

The men temporarily forgot about the danger of the TNI as they had to concentrate on getting across this thigh-deep twenty-foot-wide natural barrier without getting their legs ripped out from under them by the current. The sound of the rushing water would prevent them from hearing any verbal challenges from the TNI. The only thing from the TNI they might hear now would be gunshots.

The last man stepped out of the rushing water and continued walking to the very near east bank of the river. As the men stepped up the east bank of the river they were met by a section of Australian soldiers who greeted them with their Styer assault rifles at the ready and the soldier's order of, "Come with us."

Caitano and his men couldn't be happier about being captured. They had done the impossible. Their original rescue mission was a failure; however, at this point they were satisfied that they had managed to rescue themselves.

Caitano and his men were interviewed by the Australian intelligence field officers who were assigned to the Memo area. As expected, after the men were verified to be East Timorese they were released. Caitano and his men had been taken to the Australian company compound located in the small city of Maliana to be interviewed.

When the interview of the captured team was over The Australian intelligence field officers escorted Caitano and his men to the company compound entrance and watched them walk out of the compound and into the streets. Caitano and his men were very hungry and exhausted; however, the elation of still being free men overrode their need for food and rest. They briskly walked down the Maliana street as the early morning sun shone on their faces. This mission was over. Caitano knew there would be more operations. There always was but that is in the future. For now the team could relax.

The following morning Caitano met with La Faik and Augustinho at Augustinho's home in Cailaco. La Faik gave compliments to Caitano's masterful skills of leading his team. La Faik had received information through the West Timor team "mailbox" at the illegal market that the rescue mission was in great peril. After debriefing Caitano about the East Timor team's experiences during the mission La Faik told Caitano what information had been received from the West Timor Elements.

The West Timor team never made it to the rendezvous site. The West Timor team leader realized that two of his teammates were being followed by Militia members. The surveillance of the two teammates began in the afternoon of the same day Caitano sent the message that the operation would begin that night. The team leader decided to go ahead with the mission but the two men being followed would not participate.

The West Timor team leader intended to leave Turiskai Village during the late night hours; however, by this time the team leader was aware that nearly every Militia member in the area was somewhere outside of Turiskai. The team leader decided to wait until first light to make an attempt to reach the rendezvous site. The team leader knew something was terribly wrong.

The following morning the West Timor team attempted to get to the rendezvous site. Shortly after leaving the village of Turiskai they were challenged by a static Militia checkpoint. The West Timor team was traveling in three separate groups and disguised as though they were going down to the lowlands to tend their fields of crops.

Once past the Militia checkpoint it soon became apparent that there were many individual Militia patrols throughout the area. The West Timor team leader now knew that the Koppassus and Militia somehow knew about the rescue attempt. The West Timor team had no choice but to abort the mission. There was no way possible to warn the East Timor team who was already on the way to or already at the rendezvous site. The West Timor team went to the fields in the lowlands and worked the fields throughout the day and then returned to Turiskai Village, again passing through the Militia checkpoint.

As Caitano listened to the information that La Faik relayed to him he understood why La Faik was so complimentary to him about how he led his team. With every Militia, Kopassus and TNI soldier in the area searching for his team, escape from Indonesia was nearly impossible.

Now that Caitano and his team were safely back inside of East Timor La Faik and his elements could focus on the most important question for the survival of this secret intelligence organization and future activities. That question is, "How did the Indonesians know?"

CHAPTER FOUR

Maliana

I watched the approaching mountain peak from the window where I sat on the United Nations Puma helicopter. This mountain was different then all the others that I had seen so far. The sharp rocky peaks rose above the jungle and stood over the large Maliana valley like a patient father.

We had left Dili heliport and made the twenty-minute flight to Suai, which is at the southwest corner of East Timor. I had watched as the East Timor terrain below us rose to the top of a mountain range and then dropped on the other side to what appeared from the air to be near sea level again. The next mountain range began from the base of the previous mountain range leaving no flat areas.

As we neared Suai the continuous mountain ranges gave way to a flat grassy plain with scattered trees that stretched several miles and ended at the sea. We landed at a military airstrip that was controlled and secured by the New Zealand military. We dropped off the two American policemen that were assigned to the Suai station. After a short layover in Suai we were then airborne again and heading for Maliana.

We had climbed steadily until crossing an exceptionally high mountain range that I would later learn was the Bobonaro mountain range. The next mountain was unique as its sharp peaks that shot straight up into and above the clouds that hung lazily around the peaks like a halo.

Our Puma helicopter flew to the left side of the high peaks. We started the descent into the large valley that opened up on the other side of this high rock faced mountain with the halo. The valley was huge. I estimated the width from east to west to be about fifteen miles. The valley ran north for probably thirty miles or more.

Soon we were circling over the small city of Maliana as we made our approach to land. The many homes and buildings that made up this city appeared to have all been destroyed. Our helicopter was settling into a large grassy area beside a large concrete building, which was in the center of the city. We later learned that the large building was the Maliana city gymnasium/ auditorium and the grassy area was the athletic field.

As soon as the Puma helicopter was on the ground the helicopter crew chief opened the passenger door. He then turned and motioned for us to get off the aircraft. Us two Americans and the two Kiwis (New Zealanders) grabbed our backpacks and stepped out of the helicopter and onto the ground. The helicopter pilot never shut off the engines or even slowed the rotors.

The crew chief hurriedly helped us unload our kit, which we piled a few feet from the helicopter. The crew chief yelled above the din of the whipping rotors and whining engine, "There will be someone here to pick you up. Good luck."

The crew chief turned, climbed in the aircraft, and shut the door. The pilot poured on the collective. The helicopter rose twenty feet straight up, the nose of the helicopter dropped slightly forward, and then he was gone.

The four of us stood around our sloppily piled kit in the sudden silence. The sun showed us no mercy as we looked around our surroundings. Sweat streamed down my body and dripped off my nose and chin. We had no idea who was supposed to pick us up or when. There were about twenty Timorese men, women and children standing in the shade of the trees that lined the street about thirty-feet from where we stood.

The three men with me created makeshift chairs out of some of our kit and made themselves as comfortable as they could. I walked over to the shade near the Timorese. I politely nodded at the people who responded with a variety of nods, waves and *Bon Dias* (Good Morning). The children smiled and some giggled audibly. I turned and sat down on the short concrete ledge that lined the edge of the athletic field where we had been dumped.

I watched my three fellow police officers as they sat in the sun. I wondered why they didn't move into the shade with me. By now I had learned the names of all three of them. Donny, my fellow American, was probably in his late forties, same as me. He was heavy-set and had a strong Texan accent. The two Kiwis were named Mac and Zak. I would later lovingly call them the "Mac and Zak Attack."

Mac was tall and slender with brown curly hair. Zak was about the same height but stocky build. I guessed both men were in their early thirties and in very good shape. The Mac and Zak Attack duo spoke with a heavy New Zealand accent that was very hard for me to understand.

As I was studying my three teammates a white flatbed truck with big black "UN" letters on the sides stopped in the street near where I sat. The man driving the truck was a young white man. He asked where we were going. This young man had a strong European accent that I couldn't identify.

I told him, "I don't know. Someone was supposed to be here to pick us up."

By this time Mac had walked over to the UN truck where I was now standing beside the driver's door. Mac asked the man if he could take us to wherever the United Nations police were located.

The driver looked puzzled as he said, "I don't know where the police are staying. I didn't even know there was any police here in Maliana."

The driver of the UN truck was in his mid-twenties about five-foot eight-inches tall and slender. His medium brown hair was over his ears and flared out on the sides. His short beard and mustache was a darker brown then his hair.

The young driver then suggested that he could take us up to the UNTAET (United Nations Transitional Administration East Timor) office and figure out where we were supposed to go. We readily agreed to the driver's proposal.

He drove his truck around the corner and then into the driveway that entered the athletic field where our kit was piled in the hot sun. We quickly loaded our kit into the back of the truck then the four of us climbed into the back of the truck with our kit. We sat on the flatbed, resting our backs against the short steel racks of the truck.

The young man drove us out of the athletic field, turned left then sped down the street. I looked at the many burned-out homes that we drove past. Maliana was a smaller version of what we had seen in Dili, everything destroyed. Our driver turned onto a side street that was near a large cemetery. The street we had turned onto wound steadily up a hill. The driver stopped at a white painted concrete house that was about half-a-mile away on a tall hill that overlooked the center part of Maliana town. A large Catholic Church was across the street from this white concrete house that we now learned was the newly established UNTAET Headquarters for Bobonaro District.

After making several inquiries of the UN workers at the headquarters finally we found someone who knew where the United Nations police officers who drove out to Maliana a few days ago were located. Our young UN driver knew the place where the police were staying and volunteered to drive us there, which we readily accepted the offer. We again climbed into the back of the truck and made ourselves as comfortable as possible. The young man drove us to the north end of Maliana, which is an area called Ritabou. Maliana is a small city made up of several connecting villages.

Our newfound driver pulled into the driveway of what was the Indonesian TNI army compound. The driveway was a "U" shape, entering the compound in the left driveway and exiting out of the right driveway. At the front of the complex and in between the driveways was a large concrete building. The center area of that building did not have an outside wall. There were green and brown sandbags stacked two bags deep and five-feet high in a line where the front wall of that area should have been. To the left of that open area was an office and to the right was a small living quarters.

On the left side of the entrance driveway, in line with the front building, was a concrete single-story house, which I always assumed was the TNI commanders quarters. Behind and in line with the house was a concrete building that had three small rooms. Behind and in line with this building was a long single-story concrete building that had eight doors staggered evenly along the length of the building. Each of the doors entered into a double living quarters.

The far end of this long building had two Indonesian-style toilets, which are cemented into the floor and are only a couple of inches higher then the floor. We called them "squatters" because that is how you relieve yourself: by squatting over the floor-high toilet. There were also two cement tanks that were three-feet by three-feet and four feet high that held water for bathing.

An identical long, single-story concrete building was straight across the compound from the first long single-story building and ran along the exit driveway on the right side of the driveway. A six-foot-high concrete wall enclosed the entire compound. The top of this concrete wall was lined with concertina wire. The area in between the long single-story concrete buildings was the parade ground. Large mango trees were spaced neatly along the outer edge of the parade ground. The "U" shaped driveway separated the parade ground from the buildings.

Our driver stopped the truck in front of the long building on the left. The four of us jumped out of the back of the truck and started unloading our kit. I looked up from my growing pile of gear that I was stacking to the side of the driveway when I saw a man walking toward me. The man had come out of the building behind the house. His black hair and thick black mustache accented his slightly dark complexion.

What caught my attention the most about this guy was that he was wearing a loose-fitting nightgown that dropped from his shoulders and nearly dragged on the ground. I was still trying to figure out what I was looking at as this man walked up to me and extended his hand. I reached out and shook the man's hand.

The man had a strong grip and continued to hold my hand as he moved a little closer and touched the American flag patch that was on my left shoulder with his free left hand. The man smiled broadly as he said, "We like Americans. Welcome to Maliana."

This man had an Arabic accent. I had to listen closely as the man talked to understand what he was saying. The man continued to clutch my hand and rub my shoulder as he looked into my eyes and asked, "What is your rank?"

I was so confused I didn't know what to do or say. I was looking at a man who was wearing a "nightie" in the middle of the day, caressing my shoulder, and he wouldn't give my hand back after a greeting handshake. Now he wanted to know what rank I was. I eventually answered, "I don't know. The UN hasn't given me any rank that I know about."

The nightgown man chuckled aloud as he said, "No, no, no, your rank in America?"

I lightly tried to retrieve my hand from this man as I thought about the question. I could see that I would have to be rude to get my hand back. I had many questions running through my mind by this time. I asked the most immediate question first, "Who are you?"

The man said, "I am Naif, from Jordon."

He then grasped my hand a little harder and moved beside me as he gently started to move me in the direction of the house saying, "I will show you the place that you Americans should live. It is the best place here on this compound."

I walked along with Naif, who was still holding my hand, to the house. Naif then again asked, "What rank are you?"

I thought, *what is the big deal about rank? Why is this guy holding my hand? Is this guy a fag or is this just the custom in Jordon?* Then I thought about my rank. I was a sergeant while working at the Eaton County Sheriff Department in Michigan but now I wasn't working anywhere in America.

I finally answered Naif's question, "I'm just a cop." Naif quickly stopped walking and looked at me. I could see by the look in his face that he didn't understand what I had said. I then rephrased my answer, "I am just a police officer."

Naif grinned then started walking again, dragging me along by my captured hand, as he said, "I am a captain. Gazi is a colonel."

I had no idea who this Gazi guy was that Naif was talking about. I didn't bother to ask. Naif was visibly content to learn that I was a "nobody." I took the opportunity to stumble as I walked up the two steps that entered the veranda of the house and jerk my hand away from Naif's loving grasp.

I looked through the house, which was nice. The front room was a living room. There were two bedrooms that entered from each side of the hallway that ran to the back of the house. The bathroom was at the end of the short hallway. I announced to Naif, "This is nice, but I think we've got to wait for whoever is in command here to say what he wants us to do."

Naif solemnly nodded.

I returned to where the truck had been parked in the driveway. By the time I got back, someone had unloaded the rest of my kit and the truck had left. Donny, Mac, and Zak were sitting on the edge of the cement veranda, which ran the length of the long building. I was relieved to rejoin these guys after my close encounter with Naif.

* * * *

La Faik heard the whopping rotors of the helicopter as he sat with some friends in the newly established Fretilin political party office just one hundred yards north of the athletic field. La Faik and his two friends, Domingos and Joao, walked outside the office and saw the large UN helicopter that was slowly making its way toward the athletic field. The three men walked down to the athletic field to see what the helicopter was dropping off or picking up. The Fretilin leaders and Falintil operators in the area had already figured out the UN helicopters' normal flight schedules into Maliana, every Monday, Wednesday and Friday. Today was Saturday, so La Faik was curious what the purpose was for this extra UN flight.

La Faik and his two friends stood in the shade of the trees that grew in a line between the street and the athletic field. The three men stood near other Timorese who had come to see what was going on. They closely watched five men unloading several bags and boxes from the helicopter. One of the five men then got back into the helicopter. The helicopter rotors were already rotating at full speed so the three men, along with the other Timorese men, women, and children, watched the large helicopter suddenly rise straight up then shot forward and up, quickly disappearing into the distance.

61

La Faik turned his attention to the four men who were now loitering around the large pile of boxes and bags in the middle of the athletic field. He realized that four new UN police officers had been dropped off, probably to live and work in the Maliana area.

La Faik knew that there would be a United Nations presence in East Timor for several years to come. It was important to find one or more UN police or military personnel that he could work with to support his secret operations. At the very least La Faik needed someone he could trust that could take action, at a UN level, on the information that La Faik's Segrada Familia obtained. La Faik could work his operations around the UN if need be; however, if the right connections could be established La Faik's operations could be more effective.

* * * *

The Segrada Familia "over the fence" operations were already reporting important information. ("Over the fence" is a phrase that describes the other side of the border.) La Faik's over-the-fence" cells were newly established and still struggling to settle into positions of control that could yield high-grade information. This is not an easy task for the West Timor cells.

The Indonesian SGI intelligence operators knew the game of espionage very well. As with any form of combat, both offense and defense capabilities was required to overcome the enemy. In the intelligence world, the defense half was called "counter-intelligence."

Spy stories often focus on the daring exploits of "field operators" or "special operations teams" who overcome great odds to conduct a variety of offensive operations that save the world. Nothing should be taken away from these brave operators from any country who do in fact pull off some spectacular operations; however, without a good counter-intelligence system, those operators and special teams wouldn't survive long.

A field operator's survival depends almost entirely on the agent not becoming exposed to the enemy as an operator. An agent, cell, team, or operation can be exposed from two basic points of weakness. The first point of weakness is the operator himself and the second point is anyone else who knows about the operator or the operator's locations and activities.

Operators can bring suspicion on themselves by their actions or by what they say. The operators are responsible for their defense of exposure while in the field, no matter what side of "the fence" they are operating.

The operators have no control over their defense from the second point of weakness. This is where counter-intelligence operations reign supreme and saves the day for field operators and their activities. Counter-intelligence operations seek to identify information leaks or potential information leaks, both word of mouth leaks and the flow of written documents.

The aggressive side of counter-intelligence is to discover enemy agents and their operations that are designed to collect information from the counter-intelligence organization's home country or from the counter-intelligence's organization itself.

* * * *

There were many things on La Faik's mind as he watched the four new police officers who now stood in the hot sun that bore down on the athletic field. He realized that the new arrivals were stranded, waiting for someone to pick them up. He saw the flag patches on the shoulder of the four men, which told him that two men were from New Zealand and two men were from America.

La Faik was surprised to see that the two Americans were dressed differently. One wore a light blue police uniform shirt, which was similar to the uniform shirts that the New Zealanders were wearing. The other American was dressed in a dark blue military-type uniform shirt with the sleeves neatly rolled up above the elbows. The American in the light blue shirt appeared old, heavy, and out of shape. The American in the dark blue shirt appeared to be younger, muscular, and very fit.

There were other differences that soon became apparent. The three men dressed in light blue uniform shirts made themselves comfortable in the hot sun near the pile of gear. The man in the dark blue shirt walked over to the shade, then gave respect to the Timorese people who stood in the shade before sitting down. La Faik realized immediately that the three men in the sun were concerned about protecting their gear and maybe they didn't want to get to close to the Timorese who stood in the shade. The man in the dark blue shirt behaved as though there was no difference between the Timorese people and the United Nations people.

The man in dark blue carried himself with relaxed confidence and was alert to everything around him. The alertness wasn't a product of paranoia or fear. It was a natural awareness of his surroundings. La Faik thought, *this may be a man I can use when the time is right.*

Eventually a UN truck arrived and picked the four men up and drove them away from the athletic field. La Faik, Domingos, and Joao walked back to the Fretilin office and continued their meeting. The three men had been discussing the newly arrived information from West Timor. Domingos and Joao had no idea how the information was obtained. They knew better than to ask, but they also knew that any information that La Faik presented was to be considered true. Rather than wasting time authenticating the information, they worked the problem.

Domingos shifted his position as he sat on the wood chair. He asked, "What are they planning to do?"

La Faik answered, "The training that has been observed appears to be in preparation for reconnaissance operations, but there has not been enough of the training seen to be sure of that."

La Faik knew that the Australian military was closely monitoring the activities along the border between East Timor and Indonesia. La Faik was very appreciative of the Australian presence and all the modern technology that came with them; however, he also knew it was unlikely that the Australians and all their sophisticated gadgets would detect a Militia infiltration of East Timor.

This was why La Faik came to the Fretilin office early that morning. La Faik's plan was to use the Falintil's established secret security system, the FSP. As far as the United Nations knew, or anyone else for that matter, the FSP was an organization of local men who volunteered to conduct basic security patrols throughout the area that particular FSP unit was given responsibility over.

The Maliana FSP Group was responsible for the areas along the border. Joao was the commander of the Maliana FSP. Domingos was the local Fretilin leader who had tremendous influence with the Timorese public all through the area of Maliana. Through the use of both of these men and their resources La Faik would almost assuredly know when any Militia units infiltrated East Timor.

La Faik sat calmly as he studied Domingos and Joao. Once he saw the two men had fully grasped the gravity of this growing threat in West Timor, La Faik took the next step, "The Koppassus have been training the Militia for a week at the most. There probably will not be any infiltration attempts in the immediate future; however, now is the time for us to prepare. We fought the Indonesians for many years so that we could be free. Now begins the fight to keep our freedom." With this statement La Faik "set the hook" in the hearts of the two leaders.

Domingos and Joao did not need much instruction in how to use their members or their established informants. The two leaders simply needed to know that there was a possible threat for them to monitor and what that threat was. La Faik would keep the two men updated as he received further information from his West Timor cells.

The three men spent the next couple of hours discussing strategies to tighten their current security system. Next they discussed ways to build the Fretilin and FSP information flow from remote areas in East Timor. The information flow would be very important to locate Militia units once they were in East Timor. The Militia had no organized support groups in East Timor so the Militia units would have to stay in the most remote areas to evade detection.

Late in the day La Faik changed the topic of their discussions to the other side of the intelligence coin. He told the two men that they must be very careful about their information flow, stressing the belief that the SGI have many elements in East Timor right now. La Faik did not tell the two men that his Segrada Familia had been penetrated by an SGI asset.

Since Caitano's failed rescue attempt in West Timor, La Faik had figured out who was collecting information for the SGI. La Faik told specific information to the person he believed was the SGI spy. The information itself was a double-edged sword. One edge of that sword was to identify the spy. The SGI spy suspect was the only person who knew the information La Faik told him; therefore, if the SGI in West Timor get that information then La Faik would know the suspect was truly an SGI asset.

The other edge of the information sword was the "misdirection" that the information would give the SGI if they were to receive it. There were seven families who arrived in Cailaco one week after Caitano's failed rescue mission. Those seven families had returned to East Timor from West Timors Turiskai refugee camp.

The information La Faik gave to the suspect was that the Segrada Familia members who had been placed in Turiskai to collect information has returned to Cailaco because it was believed that they would soon be exposed to the SGI. La Faik also told the suspect that Emeu, the man that Caitano was suppose to rescue had returned to East Timor but didn't come back to Cailaco. Emeu was sent to the Falintil Cantonment camp in Aileu Village, which is east of Dili.

All of this information was highly believable and near impossible to verify. Six days after telling the spy suspect this information La Faik heard from his West Timor assets, who in-fact never left Turiskai, that the Halilintar Militia believe some or all of the Segrada Familia operators who were in Turiskai had returned to Cailaco, East Timor.

The Turiskai cell was still in danger of being exposed but that danger was now reduced. It was never known if the information about Emeu being with the Falintil in Aileu was known by the SGI but it was assumed that the SGI spy in Cailaco would certainly have passed that information on to his SGI handler too.

Emeu never did return to East Timor. He went to Kupang, which is the West Timor capitol city on the west end of the Timor Island. Emeu was now on a different mission given to him from La Faik. Emeu's wife and children were still in the control of the Halilintar Militia. There was nothing that could be done for them. This was another great personal loss in this struggle for freedom.

* * * *

It was almost five o'clock in the afternoon by the time the meeting at the Fretilin office ended. La Faik stood up from the wooden chair where he had been sitting and shook hands with Domingos and Joao, who also stood up. The three men walked outside through the front door of the Fretilin building. La Faik stood near his small engine Honda motorcycle and looked across the street where there was once a large and bustling outdoor market that had many selling stalls that sold meats, vegetables, rice and products of food and cloths of all kinds. Now there were only a half-dozen or so selling stalls.

There weren't many people left in Maliana to buy the products anyway. The main street of Maliana that La Faik now looked at was once a place that was packed with people walking. Cars, trucks, and motorcycles filled the streets as people came and went from this market. Now there weren't more than forty people that could be seen here in the downtown area. There was a few families arriving back into the Maliana area from West Timor from time to time but there were many thousands of people still in West Timor. La Faik hoped that someday all the Timorese could come home and help build a good life, a free life.

La Faik grabbed the handle bars of his motorcycle then threw his leg over the bike and sat back on the saddle. He put the key in the ignition and turned the key to the "on" position. The two-cycle engine came to life when La Faik sharply depressed the kick starter. He smiled and nodded at Domingos and Joao who were standing nearby watching him. La Faik slowly drove out of the Fretilin office parking area. He turned north onto the main street heading back to Marko Village, which was about a forty-minute drive.

La Faik stopped in the street in front of the former Indonesian TNI compound in Ritabou Village, Maliana. He could see eleven men dressed in a variety of police uniforms who were sitting on the cement veranda in front of the long one-story building on the left side of the compound. The policemen appeared to be having some kind of meeting.

La Faik watched from the street for a few minutes. He took mental notes of the men he saw, the types of uniforms the men wore and also of the UN cars. There were three Land Rovers, Discovery models that were parked in the old TNI compound. All three Land Rovers were green with white "UN" letters on the hood and both sides. La Faik noted that the man conducting the meeting was wearing an Australian police uniform. La Faik started his motorcycle and slowly drove off to the north, out of town toward his home in Marko.

* * * *

It was mid-afternoon when a dark green Land Rover with white "UN" letters stenciled on the sides and the hood drove into the TNI compound that we had moved into. We were sitting on the veranda of the long one-story building on the left side of the compound, which I will refer to as the "left barracks" from here on. The green Land Rover stopped right in front of us as the driver pulled as close as he could to the left barracks side of the driveway. This allowed room for other vehicles to pass the now parked Land Rover.

The two men inside the Land Rover were wearing Australian police uniforms, which was the standard light blue shirt and dark blue military style pants. We knew that one of these two Australians was the appointed Bobonaro district commander. An hour earlier three black men from Mozambique arrived in a green Land Rover with UN stencils. These three men were policemen from Mozambique who were assigned to the Bobonaro district police workstation, which was to be based in Maliana. Two of the three Mozambique police officers introduced themselves to us when they first arrived and then went to the far end of the left barracks where they occupied three of the rooms.

The third Mozambique police officer was much friendlier. He sat down on the edge of the concrete veranda with the four of us new arrivals. The Mozambique man, Leonard, told us that he and his two fellow countrymen drove out here to Maliana yesterday. Leonard was interesting to talk with because he had been in East Timor during the time that the United Nations was organizing and conducting the vote for independence or Autonomy—before all the killing and burning.

Leonard told us that Dili and Maliana were both beautiful cities before the violence and destruction. Leonard had evacuated East Timor along with all the other United Nations workers in September. He just returned to East Timor from Darwin Australia where he and many other United Nations workers waited until it was safe for them to return.

I liked Leonard and would grow to like him even more as time went on. He was six-foot-two-inches tall, stocky build and in his late twenties. He was genuinely friendly and always had a smile. He had a strong accent but I could understand his English fairly well. We would soon learn that the young Leonard was strongly dominated by the two other Mozambique police officers assigned to the Bobonaro District.

Paul was in his mid-thirties, about six feet tall and fit. He was very intelligent. He put his education to become a lawyer on hold while he came on this mission to East Timor. A policeman can make more money in one year on a United Nations mission than that policeman could make in a life time working in Mozambique. That was enough incentive for Paul to delay his education.

Karley was just the opposite of Paul. He was five-foot eight-inches tall and overweight. Through the time that we worked together I would learn that Karley was self-serving with little regard for others. He was stubborn about everything, giving little respect to anyone, even his commander. For whatever reason, Karley liked and respected me, so we got along well for the short time that we would be together in Maliana.

Leonard had sat and talked with Mac, Zak, Donny, and I since he and the other two Mozambiques arrived in the compound that afternoon. He had told us that the District Commander was an Australian. He didn't know where the two Australians assigned to Bobonaro district had gone but he believed they would soon return. Leonard told us that he didn't know much about the two Jordanian police officers. They had driven out to Maliana a few days ago and were the first UN police to arrive here. The Australians drove out to Maliana in the third Land Rover currently assigned to Bobonaro district a couple of days after the Jordanians.

* * * *

The two Australians got out of the Land Rover and walked up to the five of us sitting on the veranda. Both men smiled broadly as they approached us. The four of us new guys respectfully stood up and shook hands with the two

Australians. After proper introductions and small talk we asked the commander where he wanted us to set up our living quarters.

The commander was known to us by his nickname "Bantam." He was about five-foot-ten-inches tall, stocky of build, with a little bit of a gut but in good shape. He was in his mid-forties. He not only had many years experience working for the Australian Federal Police Force but he had served on United Nations missions in Cyprus and in Cambodia. The Australians picked the right man to take command of Bobonaro district. Bantam's experience would prove invaluable to the men and women who worked in Bobonaro district even after he left the mission and returned to Australia.

The other Australian policeman with Bantam also was known to us by his nickname, "Snapper." Snapper was in his mid-fifties, five-foot-ten-inches tall with a slender build. His gray hair gave away his age but his actions were those of a younger man. Snapper had a way about him that naturally made people forget their difficulties and feel good. The four of us really needed Snapper's uplifting personality.

* * * *

Bantam had directed Donny and me to live in the quarters on the right side of the front building. We carried our gear to our new-found living quarters. The entrance door entered a room that we would use as our kitchen. Two interior doors that were side by side entered two separate bedrooms. Donnie and I picked one each and began setting up our mosquito domes, blowing up our air mattresses and unpacking our kit.

The "Mac and Zak Attack" was doing the same thing in the living quarters next to the Australians in the left barracks. Bantam had told us to get settled in and then we would have a meeting in front of the commander's room. By five-o'clock that afternoon Donny and I returned to the veranda in front of Bantam's room.

The three Mozambiques, two Australians, and two Kiwis were already there when we got there. Snapper stood up and walked over to where the Jordanians were living in the small building next to the left barracks. A couple of minutes later Snapper returned followed by Naif, whom I met earlier in the day, and another man.

The second man with Naif was introduced to us as Gazi. Gazi was in his mid-thirties, six-foot-three inches tall, with a slim build. He had short black hair, clean-shaven face, and a slightly darker complexion than Naif. His Arabic accent was so strong I could hardly understand what he said.

Bantam conducted the meeting right there on the veranda. He covered many issues that we would have to deal with but then focused on the immediate needs for both our day to day living and also for the work that we would be doing. None of it sounded very encouraging but when Bantam finished Snapper brought us all into a positive frame of mind when he smiled and said, "This is what a mission is all about mates. We were all selected to come to Bobonaro District because the police Commissioner believed that we are all swimmers. This is our opportunity to prove that we can swim."

I still didn't know what a swimmer was so I asked, "What's a swimmer?"

The two Kiwis and the two Australians laughed aloud at my ignorance. None of them bothered to answer my question as we broke up the meeting.

Later in the night as we sat together on the concrete veranda in front of Bantam and Snapper's rooms, Zak finally enlightened me about what a swimmer was, "So you Americans don't know what a swimmer is, huh?"

Zak was sitting next to me. It had been dark since six o'clock. It was now nine o'clock at night and the concrete we sat on was still hot from the sun shining on it during the day. The air was muggy with no breeze whatsoever. Sweat dripped from my nose and chin. I looked over at Zak. The only light we had was a candle that burned nearer to where Bantam, Snapper, Mac, and Donny sat. From that faint candle-light, I could see that Zak also had sweat dripping from his nose and chin. I answered Zak, "The only exposure we Americans have had with Australia is to Foster's beer, the Outback Steakhouse, and the movie *Crocodile Dundee*."

Zak smiled then said, "A swimmer is someone who can take anything, make it happen no matter what. You know the saying 'sink or swim?' You Americans have that saying too, right? They threw us into this water here in Bobonaro; now we either sink or swim."

I nodded my understanding and thanked Zak for the enlightenment. About that time we broke up the social gathering and headed for our beds. Donny was talking to me about our new home and assigned work station. Donny had such a strong Texan accent I could hardly understand him at times. While Donny was talking I thought, *I am the only person in Maliana who speaks understandable English. Even my fellow American slaughters the English language.*

I struggled to sleep but it was so hot that I kept waking up. The many abandoned dogs throughout Maliana howled and barked through the night. About four o'clock in the morning the roosters started their singing for our listening enjoyment. By daybreak I gave up on getting any real sleep. I looked at my watch and saw it was five o'clock.

I got up and walked out onto the back veranda of what was now being called "The American House." Donnie was already sitting on the stoop smoking a cigarette. I could tell by looking at him that he didn't sleep much either. I sat down next to him and lit a cigarette. For several minutes we sat in silence smoking as we watched the new day brighten as the sun began to peek over the mountain to the east.

I looked over at Donny and broke the silence, "This is going to be a long year."

Donny looked back at me, at first with a disgusted look, but then he broke into a smile. I smiled back and slammed him on the shoulder with the palm of my hand. Thus we transferred our relationship from fellow Americans doing a tough job together. We were now brothers.

* * * *

As briefed to us by Commander Bantam, we began to build Maliana Station. We made the office area on the left side of the front building the station headquarters. It wasn't much of a headquarters at first. There were no tables, chairs, computers, file cabinets, or anything—just an empty room, but it was now the official headquarters.

Bantam quickly established a good relationship with the Australian military commanders who were based in another compound near the center of Maliana. From them he acquired a lot of logistical support for our living and working needs. The military engineers fixed us up with a large plastic elevated tank and connected a pipe that fed water into the tank from a local line that ran into Maliana from the mountains. This tank provided us with water for showering. It wasn't much of a shower, but it was better than pouring water over ourselves with small plastic pitchers.

The Australian military also provided us materials to fix up our individual accommodations to a livable level, such as doors and grenade security screening for our windows. Within a few days we were out of bottled drinking water. The United Nations promised delivery of bottled water didn't show up for four weeks. The military gave us all the water we needed.

We were told that we would be able to re-supply our food supplies after two weeks in the field. Three weeks later we were out of food with no hope of getting out for re-supply. The Australian military gave us food. Three weeks after we arrived in Maliana the UN sent us a small generator. They didn't send us any leads, wiring or anything to make the generator functional. The Austalian military sent their engineers and the equipment needed to get our generator up and running. The Australian military took very good care of us and I thank them very much for that.

We spent our days getting our camp set up. We spent part of those days conducting general patrols throughout the very large Bobonaro district. My first patrol was in the remote, high mountains of Bobonaro sub-district. Mac and I took an interpreter with us and were exploring the areas that we could drive into. The main mountain roads were so rugged that they could be used as an advertisement for four-wheel drive vehicles.

I asked Mac, who was driving, "If we get stuck, fall off a mountain, or otherwise get stranded up here, what auto club do we call to come get us? And how do we call for whoever is going to come save us?"

Mac thought about what I said, realizing that we had no radio communications. We didn't even have a radio installed in any of the Land Rovers we drove. He eventually answered, "If we get into trouble I guess we have to walk back to Maliana." That wasn't a real encouraging answer.

Eventually we started getting information about some of the people who were murdered during the violence of September 1999. We began documenting the individual murder cases that rapidly grew in numbers. We visited grave site after grave site where men and women were buried in shallow graves where they fell. We wrote reports with paper and pen that we had carried into the mission area for our own personal use. The United Nations had not yet provided us with any equipment, not even pens and paper.

Some of the bodies were buried in shallow graves near rivers. We knew that the heavy rains of the wet season would soon be upon us so we dug up the bodies of those buried in areas we feared would be washed away. We reburied the decaying bodies in the cemetery north of Maliana. Needless to say, this was a gruesome task.

One day Bantam and Snapper went to Dili for a meeting. When they returned they brought with them about sixteen cases of beer; I don't recall the exact number of cases. They had cut a deal with some Australian businessman to purchase beer for eight dollars a case, or box, as the Australians call a case.

From that day on we helped curb the pain of the hot nights by drinking beer. At first we drank the beer hot; however, soon Bantam worked out a deal with the Australian military cooks so that we got a supply of chopped ice. Every day about five o'clock in the afternoon, one of us would make a run to the military compound and get a thirty-gallon plastic trash container half-full of ice and bring it to our compound. Now we had cold beer to drink every night.

The days went by quickly and in spite of our hard living and working environment, this was probably the best time I had in East Timor. At the time I was miserable and didn't know it, but reflecting back on this time I now realize it was good. There were no pressures, no deadlines, and no real expectations of anyone. We were just living day by day and accomplishing whatever we could with what we had to work with, which wasn't much.

By Christmas time the Mozambiques convinced Bantam that they needed to get to Darwin for a break and re-supply their food stores. We were all out of food by this time, but eventually Bantam agreed that the three Mozambiques could take the first CTO (Compensatory Time Off). As they drove out of our compound on their way to Dili to take the UN flight to Darwin they had a mattress tied to the top of the Land Rover. We went and looked at their rooms and saw that they took everything. Needless to say, they never came back. That left eight of us to run the Maliana Station.

Christmas day we were serenaded by a truckload of Australian soldiers who pulled into our compound dressed in camouflage uniforms and Santa Claus hats. Their singing was terrible but at the time it was much appreciated. So were the boxes of fresh fruits, vegetables, and a variety of meats for us to cook on the grill that the engineers made for us. That was the best Christmas present we could have received.

On New Year's Eve we sat on Bantam and Snapper's veranda getting drunk. We gave a toast to the country that each of us represented as the time in that country hit midnight. New Zealand was first, then Australia, followed by Jordan. None of us were still awake to toast America the following morning.

As we sat in the dark sweating and drinking we wondered allowed if the computers crashed as some people had predicted that they would on New Years Day 2000. It didn't matter to us where we were. There could have been a nuclear holocaust and we wouldn't have known it. There were no telephones, radios or any other forms of communications with the outside world.

The end of the first week of January, 2000, was the beginning of our CTO. Mac, Zak, Donny, and I left our compound in Maliana driving one of our three Land Rovers. We left at four o'clock in the morning to make the two-and-a-half-hour drive to Dili. The United Nations flight to Darwin Australia left Dili at 0800 hours.

The first thing anyone from the outer districts does when they get to a hotel in Darwin is to take a real shower. You can actually see your body change color as the ground-in filth is finally removed by a long "hot" shower. The first meal in Darwin by most of the deprived CTO-goers is not steak dinners. It is junk food from McDonald's or Burger King, which the Australians named Hungry Jack's.

Our six days of CTO in Darwin were spent sleeping, swimming in the hotel pools, eating at the many restaurants, drinking at bars by day and discos by night. A big part of the CTO time was spent buying food and other supplies needed to live "In the districts." This became an art to purchase food that didn't need refrigeration and still gave you a good variety of meals for at least a month.

The days went by fast and then it was time to return to East Timor. The night before going back was very depressing for me just thinking about going back to Maliana. By the time I got back to my hotel room at 0200 hours I was drunk from trying to kill my thoughts of returning. My phone rang at o-dark-thirty, which was the wake-up call I had requested from the hotel desk the night before.

I took my last shower and put the last of my stuff into the single bag that I carried for my personal clothes. Along with this single bag I had four other containers that were jam-packed with food. I was going to make sure I didn't go hungry again. I used a hotel luggage cart to take my gear to the hotel lobby and check out.

This was followed by a cab ride to the Australian Air Force base where we would take the United Nations flight back to East Timor. I was hung-over, tired, and on top of that, I had thrown my back out while carrying my heavy containers of food. I was physically, emotionally, and mentally miserable.

My condition did not change as I climbed off the United Nations plane after we landed in Dili. I stepped onto the hot tarmac and walked with Mac, Zak, and Donny toward the still-destroyed airport terminal. As we got closer I saw Snapper standing inside the terminal building. He was resting his hands on the window sill as he leaned through the broken window beside the entrance door. He was smiling from ear to ear as he said, "You guys came back. I guess you guys are swimmers."

Something about that encounter with Snapper changed the way I felt. I was suddenly genuinely glad to be back. By the time we got back to our compound in Maliana I was even happier about being back. I would go through this on every CTO I took. I never wanted to come back to East Timor until I got back. I am sure a psychologist could explain this transition in feelings. I just learned to accept it.

Our living and working routines in Maliana did not change much during the time we were on CTO; however, for me there was soon to be a change. At first that change didn't seem to be a big deal. I didn't know it and certainly didn't plan it, but I was destined to soon become a part of the secret and dangerous struggle for the freedom of East Timor.

CHAPTER FIVE

A Walk in the Jungle

Samusai crouched in the tall grass and calmly gazed at the small bamboo house that was only twenty yards in front of him. The night was very dark for lack of a moon. Samusai and the two men with him were dressed in all black clothing. In addition to their black clothes the three men wore black bandanas that covered their faces from just under their eyes down, which gave them the appearance of Ninjas. They carried Timorese-made machetes, *katanas*, and on their backs they carried bows and quivers full of arrows.

The bamboo hut in front of the three men was surrounded by hard-packed earth. The tall grass that the three men now used for concealment was the beginning of the jungle behind the house. Not more than ten yards in front of the house was the rough dirt road that ran through the middle of Aidabasalala Village.

Most of Aidabasalala Village is the typical village layout with many homes built in close proximity to each other; however, the home that Samusai and his two teammates were now looking at was on the north edge of Aidabasalala Village where there was only a few homes scattered along the roadway. There were only two other homes in sight of the "target" home now in front of Samusai. One of the nearby homes was about thirty yards south and on the west side of the roadway, same as the target home. The other nearby home was on the eastside of the roadway and slightly to the north of the target home.

Suddenly Samusai could see light flickering through the cracks of the bamboo walls of the house. He realized that someone had just lit a small oil lamp inside the home. Samusai thought, *right on time*. Samusai reached out to his left side with his left hand and touched the shadowy figure crouched next to him. With his palm resting on the arm of his teammate, Samusai began tapping his finger on the man's arm. The tapping was a Falintil code, which was developed years ago for communications at times when no noise could be made, including low whispers.

As silently directed by Samusai, the shadow began moving slowly through the grass and brush to the left. Eventually the shadow stopped where he had good concealment and could see the hut on the other side of the roadway. Samusai did not need to relocate the shadow that crouched on his right side. The home to the south of the target could be seen and monitored from where Samusai and the other shadow now waited and watched.

The men hidden on the edge of the jungle listened to the very normal sounds of a family waking up in the morning. A woman and her eight-year-old daughter came out the back door of the target home and started a cooking fire under the grass roof that extended from the rear of the home. Soon they were cooking rice and coffee over the fire. A three-year-old boy soon came out the back door. The boy's mother shooed him away from the fire, after which he occupied his time playing with some of the pieces of firewood stacked nearby.

As the sky began to lighten, a girl in her mid-teens came outside with a homemade broom and began sweeping the ground around the house, whisking away any leaves, cigarette butts, or any other debris that may have collected on the ground since the last sweeping the morning before.

By the time the morning chores, cooking, and eating were completed, it was full daylight and the sun shone brightly into this valley village as it hung in the sky over the eastern mountains. The church bells began to ring from across the village signaling to the village that the Sunday morning church service would begin in one hour.

Shortly thereafter, men, women, and children were leaving the three homes that Samusai and his men were watching from the edge of the jungle. Everyone who was going to church was dressed very nicely in Western-style clothing. The day-to-day sarongs, blue jeans, and sandals were replaced by well-made Indonesian dresses and high heel shoes, dress slacks, and button-down shirts.

Soon there was no more movement that Samusai and his men could detect. The hidden men had watched two women and three children leave the target home, all of them wearing their church clothes. No man had left the target home to worship at the local Catholic church, which was expected. Samusai had been briefed that everyone in this neighborhood goes to church on Sunday mornings except this one man who lived in the target home. Now was the time.

Samusai made a chirping sound like a Teke lizard. This signaled his two teammates that it was time to do what they had come to do. Even though it was now broad daylight the movements of the three shadow men was so smooth and subtle nobody would have noticed them as they approached the rear door of the target home. Samusai quietly opened the backdoor then stepped through the threshold entering the home.

The three shadows never stopped moving as they flowed through the few rooms of the home. As they entered a side bedroom they saw a man sleeping on his right side as he lay on a bamboo sleeping platform. Samusai never stopped or hesitated. As he approached the sleeping man he drew the six-inch, finely honed knife from the sheath he wore on his belt.

As he reached the man on the bamboo bed Samusai gently grabbed the sleeping man's left shoulder and rolled him so that he lay on his back. The man groaned complainingly at having been disturbed, but never opened his eyes. Samusai's right hand swiftly moved the knife across the man's throat. The man's eyes snapped open as blood gushed from the wound that penetrated his throat to his spine.

Samusai looked down into the now wide eyes of the dying man. The man was powerless to move. Within seconds the man's body began to twitch involuntarily as Samusai still looked into the man's now fading eyes. Blood quickly soaked the thin padding of the mattress and dripped onto the floor under the bamboo platform. Samusai turned and calmly moved through the door and checked the rest of the home, followed by the other two shadows.

There was nobody else in the home. Samusai was relieved that nobody else was there. He did not want to kill anyone other than this one man. Samusai was glad to kill this man, although he felt sympathy for the man's wife and children who would come home from worshiping God and find the husband and father dead.

The three shadows made a quick search of the contents of the home. Soon they found a notebook and other loose papers with writing on them. Samusai grabbed the documents and stuffed them in a small black bag that he carried. The three shadow men then quietly exited the home and disappeared into the jungle behind the home.

* * * *

I took off my regular glasses and put them on the dashboard of the Land Rover in front of the steering wheel. I then took my company-provided aviator sunglasses out of my shirt pocket and slid them into place on my face. Mac was a driving instructor for the New Zealand federal police. He was not very appreciative of my driving habits as he rode in the passenger seat beside me. I actually accomplished the glasses change very smoothly even though we were bouncing along the rough mountain roads of Bobonaro at the time.

Mac had already lectured me about driving using my right foot for the gas pedal and my left foot for the brake. A few minutes after that lecture the early morning sun rose above the Aimea mountain that was east of where we were driving up Bobonaro mountain. The sun flashed into my eyes time and time again as we wound our way up the mountain, which was why I made the change of eyewear.

Mac said nicely, "You know it is not proper to occupy your hands with something other than driving while you are driving down the road."

I really liked Mac but I enjoyed playfully pricking his perfectionist personality. I responded, "I was driving with my knee and had complete control of the vehicle at all times. Well, most of the time."

While I was changing my glasses I had slid my left foot back until my knee was firmly under the steering wheel. After a few moments of silence I nodded slightly and confessed, "It is a little hazardous when I drive with my knee. If I should have to brake suddenly I would have to use my right foot." Mac shook his head in surrender as I smiled mischievously.

Mac and I were going to the Kiwi military compound in Bobonaro Village, which is on top of the mountain. We had left Maliana Station just before daybreak to make the forty-five minute drive up the mountain. We didn't take an interpreter with us this morning because our business was with the military.

A few days before the Mozambiques had abandon us, Karley and I had made a patrol to Bobonaro Village. We met with the Bobonaro sub-district representative, who was appointed by Fretilin to handle government tasks temporarily. During this meeting the representative told us about four young men who were murdered in a village called Anapol this past October. Hearing about multiple murders was a common occurrence during our patrols but this case was different. What was unusual about this murder case was that the witnesses and the multiple suspects were here in East Timor. All of the other murder cases Maliana Station was handling were inactive cases because all the suspects were Militia members who now lived in West Timor along with most of the witnesses to those murders. This murder case in Anapol Village was a case that we could sink our teeth into.

Over the next few weeks the Bobonaro representative was eventually able to get two of the witnesses of the murdered four young men to make the three-hour walk from Anapol Village to Bobonaro Village to meet with Mac, Zak, and me. We took statements from the two witnesses, which started the building of this case. These two witnesses were the only witnesses who were going to come to us. To continue this investigation we had to go to Anapol Village.

We discussed this case with Bantam and asked him how he wanted us to proceed. Mac, Zak and I were experienced investigators and knew what we had to do. We just didn't know how to do it. In our home countries we could drive to wherever we had to go. We could get any additional assistance that we may need. Here we had to drive forty-five minutes through rough mountain roads to get to where we would have to leave the car and walk three hours through mountains, rivers and jungles to get to a village where their could be several murder suspects that probably wouldn't appreciate our visit to their village. On top of that we would have no radio communications to call for help, not that anyone would really know how to find us anyway.

Bantam agreed that we had to go to Anapol Village and continue this investigation. Seeking justice for the four murdered young men was important; however, Bantam pointed out that even more important was for the people of East Timor who live in these remote villages to know that there is law enforcement and security for them too.

Bantam told us that we would have to coordinate this "trip" to Anapol Village with the military. The military will have all the resources to properly assist us, including radio communications. This is why we were driving to the Kiwi military compound in Bobonaro Village. This was the military post that was responsible for the Bobonaro sub-district area, including Anapol Village.

The Kiwi military compound in Bobonaro was not the fenced in, tightly secured, and bustling of many soldiers that I was use to seeing at the several Australian military compounds around the Bobonaro district. The Kiwi compound was more like a temporary position.

There was one platoon of Kiwi soldiers who took over what was the Indonesian TNI military compound in Bobonaro Village. The TNI company installation consisted of one one-story concrete building that had multiple rooms. The eighty-foot long building had large barracks rooms on both ends. I don't know what the smaller rooms in-between the barracks rooms were used for.

This building had been destroyed, I assume by fire, when the Indonesians left East Timor, leaving just the concrete walls. The Kiwi soldiers replaced the tin roofing and some of the doors. There were no fences, gates, or any type of barriers around the building.

The first time I saw this Kiwi platoon position I was reminded of scenes of World War II movies where battle-hardened soldiers took over a partially blown-up building and slept or sat on the concrete floor, made benches and tables out of whatever they found, and so on.

These Kiwis went so far as to make a weight room out of what they could find or make. I watched a handful of soldiers dressed in combat boots, camouflage pants, and t-shirts as they lifted a variety of different sized rocks and bars with large chunks of concrete on either end. This caveman weight room was outside and to the right side of the long building that they now occupied.

We saw two Vietnam War vintage armored personnel carriers (APCs) parked in front of the occupied building. We parked near the APCs and walked into one of the central rooms where the Kiwis had established a command post. We were directed to sit on a wooden bench that was at a makeshift wooden table that the Kiwis had made.

Within a few minutes the platoon lieutenant came into the room and greeted us warmly with a handshake. After the introductions, he offered us "a brew." I thought, *It's a little early in the morning to be drinking a beer, but if that's what these guys do, I guess its okay.* A few minutes later a soldier brought Mac and me a hot cup of coffee. I didn't even bother to ask as I realized that "a brew" in Kiwi-talk is coffee, as opposed to us Americans, who use the term for beer.

We told the young Lieutenant about the murder investigation and our need to get out to Anapol Village to find the bodies of the four murdered men, identify the suspects, and hopefully find more witnesses who would be willing to give us statements. Over the next couple of hours, the lieutenant planned the mission with the section leader who the lieutenant selected to take us to Anapol Village. (What the American military calls a squad the New Zealand and Australian militaries call a "section.")

Upon completion of the operation plans the Lieutenant radioed his company commander who was based in Lolotoe Village, which is ten kilometers south of Bobonaro Village. The lieutenant gave a brief description of the operation over the radio, then asked permission to conduct the operation. There were a few minutes of silence before the platoon radio crackled back to life with the answer from the company commander in Lolotoe. The commander gave permission to launch this operation in two days time.

* * * *

I hung on tightly to the nylon strap that hung from the steel ceiling of the APC as we were driven down Bobonaro mountain on our way to Anapol Village. Had I not been hanging onto that nylon strap I would have been thrown all over the interior of that APC. It was now daybreak two days after our meeting with the Kiwi lieutenant. I couldn't see the outside terrain but could only imagine how rough the terrain would have to be to make this large steel tracked vehicle ride so rough.

I looked around at the other men that rode with me. I could see the driver of our APC at the front working his controls. The APC commander was standing in the turret. I could only see him from the waist down as his chest and head protruded through the open overhead hatch of the gun turret where he stood.

The passenger compartment where I sat was full of men. Mac sat on one side of me and Domingos, one of our interpreters, sat on the other side of me. Naif sat across me and had a look of disgust. Two of the eight-man section of Kiwi soldiers were sitting with us on the two steel benches that ran the length of both sides of the passenger compartment. The rest of the section was riding in the APC that was following us.

Eventually we reached the river that flowed in-between Bobonaro mountain and Sibuni mountain. I knew that we reached the river when the APC no longer dramatically pointed down and I could hear water rushing over and around rocks. The ride became more rough as the APCs attempted to take us down the river bed to Anapol Village.

The many large rocks strewn throughout the uneven gravel riverbed prevented these large lumbering machines passage. Our APC came to a stop and lowered the rear ramp. Daylight flooded the interior as the ramp dropped into the one-foot high rushing water of the river. We grabbed our packs and stepped out into river water and sloshed our way to the Sibuni side of the river.

I heard the APC commander as he told the section leader, "We will wait for your radio call. If we don't hear from you we will come back to this location at 1700 hours and wait for you here."

I then watched the section leader (SL), Corporal Fox, as he sloshed through the rushing water and joined us on the riverbank. The two APCs spun around and slowly made their way to the opposite riverbank. Foxy, which was the name everyone called Corporal Fox, gave a hand signal. The soldiers smoothly fell into a single file security formation and started walking up a small trail that went up the side of Sibuni mountain. Naif, Mac, Domingos, and I fell into the middle of the formation as directed by Foxy.

We hadn't walked one hundred yards up that steep trail and I was already breathing hard from the effort. Another hundred yards and I felt like I had run a mile at a fast pace. I was breathing hard and soaked in sweat. I was shocked by my lack of conditioning.

I had always been very physical throughout my life. For years I practiced karate and I was even a physical training and defensive tactics instructor at the police academy back home. I believed I was in great shape, but now as the muscles in my legs burned and my chest heaved from gulping in breaths of air, I felt as though I had never worked out a day in my life.

I watched the soldiers in front of me as they made their way up that steep mountain trail, carrying their weapon, ammunition, and other gear with no apparent difficulty. I was impressed that every soldier was very alert to their surroundings, constantly covering their areas of responsibility to protect "their team." I had all I could do just to walk on this rough path without stumbling.

Having been the founder and commander of my police department's tactical team back home I knew tactics very well and was always on the watch for teammates who was not completely focused on "team security." I was ashamed of my clumsy abilities in the face of these fine young soldiers who so expertly did their job.

I was cursing the boots the company that sent me to this mission had issued . The two-hundred- dollar-a-pair Dannon boots were great for urban wear; however, here in this environment, they were a curse. The thick soles had no flexibility and you couldn't "feel" the ground. They were heavy when they were dry. When wet, they were twice the weight. I might as well have been wearing concrete boots.

I had too much pride to simply stop and say, "I need a break," so I kept going until I couldn't physically take another step. As I stopped on the trail, leaned over, and huffed and puffed, Foxy, who was walking in the two position, announced, "Take a break."

Even in my exhausted condition I was impressed as the soldiers melted into defensive security positions, completely alert to their arcs of responsibility. Foxy came back to where I sat on the ground and sat near me. I had scrutinized Foxy closely since the planning meeting with the platoon lieutenant two day earlier. Foxy was a man in his mid-thirties. He was six feet tall with a slender build; however, he was very muscular. All of the men under his command were ten or more years younger than Foxy, health nuts, and continuously worked out. Those young men were always amazed that the heavy-smoking and never-exercised Foxy could always outdo them at everything.

Foxy lit a cigarette and simply sat on the ground. He wasn't sweating or breathing hard. He didn't say anything. I looked over at Mac and Naif who sat near us. Naif wasn't hurting, either. I could tell that Mac was tired but he wasn't in as bad a shape as I was. I guzzled water from my canteen, then said to Foxy, "I'm sorry about holding you guys up. I thought I was in better shape than this."

Foxy looked at me and gave a little smile as he said, "You're doing all right." That was all he said. Foxy wasn't much into conversations.

Foxy finished his cigarette, then announced it was time to go as he stood and walked back to the second position. I struggled to my feet, slipped my backpack on, and instinctively looked behind me. Mac, Naif, and Domingos were up and ready to go. The first soldier in line behind them was so focused into covering his "arc of responsibility" as he lay in a covered position on the ground that he had not noticed that we were getting ready to go. I looked at Mac who was walking in front of that soldier and motioned toward that soldier. Mac turned and gave a subtle click of his tongue to the soldier to get the soldier's attention. The soldier then got up and prepared to move out.

Eventually we got to the top of the mountain. We talked with the village chief and found out that we didn't even need to climb this mountain. The village chief took us to a place where we could look down on Anapol Village, which is about four "klicks" (Kilometers) away and sits on the edge of two rivers that join together at Anapol Village.

Using a different trail we walked back down the mountain to the riverbed. We walked through the river bed for about two klicks. We then climbed up the side of a short mountain. The path up the side of this mountain was so steep that in some places I had to grab onto rocks or brush to help pull myself up. We crested the top of this mountain and walked down the reverse slope. The bottom of the mountain stopped at a large river. Across the river was Anapol Village.

I had never been so exhausted in my life. I couldn't think straight and I couldn't get enough water into my body. By the time we got to Anapol I had drank every drop of the three liters of water that I carried. I wasn't much good to Naif and Mac, who were trying to conduct this investigation, but I did the best I could. It didn't really matter anyway. The people of Anapol were not going to cooperate. I couldn't blame them. We would take their statements and leave. They had to live there.

After our investigation inquiries were completed, Foxy moved us to the outskirts of Anapol Village where we took a lunch break. Lunch was outdated "ration packs" that consisted of canned spaghetti, or something similar, followed by canned fruits, crackers, etc. There was even a chocolate bar in the bag of food we were each provided. The chocolate was so old it was white but it tasted somewhat like chocolate at least.

One of the many things I did wrong for this mission was carry to much kit in my backpack; however, one of the many things I did wrong turned out to be right: I had packed my tennis shoes. During our lunch break I took off those dreaded Dannon boots and put on those tennis shoes.

What a difference that made. Even in my already exhausted state, making the trip back to the rendezvous point with the APCs was fairly easy after getting those cement blocks that Dannon calls boots off my feet. We left Anapol and crossed the low mountain range that separated the two rivers. Once we were in the next riverbed it began to rain. At first the rain was a steady drizzle. Soon it changed to a steady pour.

Our interpreter, Domingos, told us, "This is very dangerous. You must watch for the big water. If you see the big water coming, you must run to the sides of the river."

I didn't know Domingos very well at that time. I eventually would call Domingos my son, but in the river on that day I knew little about Domingos; however, Domingos was Timorese and if he was concerned about dangerous waters coming down the river that was enough for me.

Domingos was a young man in his early twenties. He was well-groomed, very polite, and educated. His English was pretty good. He had worked for the United Nations as an interpreter since the UN's arrival in East Timor in early 1999. I would later learn that Domingos was from a remote Village in Cailaco sub-district. Domingos and his family had a strong Falintil background, which nearly cost Domingos his life in September of 1999.

We were walking upriver as the rain continued to pour down on us. I didn't mind being wet from the rain. I was already completely drenched in sweat anyway and the rainwater cooled my overheated body.

For a distance of at least one kilometer, we couldn't get out of the riverbed because of the impenetrable jungles and cliffs on both sides of the river. We sloshed our way across the fast-moving knee- and sometime thigh-deep water several times as we struggled to find passable points up the river. The rushing water constantly ripped against your legs as the current almost purposely tried to drag you down into its control.

Eventually we came to a point where we could climb out of the river and go cross-country to avoid walking the long curve of the river. We soon reached the river again and started to cross to the opposite bank. We all felt relief because that opposite bank was where the APCs were planning to return and pick us up at 1700 hours.

I was just entering the river when I looked up river and saw a wall of rushing water about one hundred yards away. Mac was right behind me and saw the water coming too. He yelled to the men behind him, "The water is coming, guys."

We all knew that to get across the river meant we'd get a ride up Bobonaro mountain, hot food, and a comfortable, dry place to sleep. If we didn't get across, it was going to be a long, wet, and cold night.

Everybody rushed as fast as they could to get across the river. The "big water" almost took the Kiwi "drag man" (the last man in the formation); however, a couple of his teammates were able to help him get out of the now-raging water. We all breathed a sigh of relief and started walking in the direction of Bobonaro, thinking we would meet the APCs since it was almost 1700 hours.

Twenty-meters later the point man stopped. There was a raging torrent of water in front of him that was at least thirty feet wide. A quick survey of our surroundings revealed that we were on a very small island that was surrounded by chest-deep rapids that promised to kill anyone stupid enough to try and cross the river. We were trapped.

The Kiwi soldiers quickly set up a tarp to shield us from the rain and planned to stay the night on this little island. By this time the rain was stronger than any downpour I had ever seen in Michigan. We were all out of drinking water by this time so we filled our canteens from the rain water that collected on the erected tarp. It was raining so hard that it didn't take long to fill the canteens.

Then we heard the deep-throated diesel engines of the APCs over the roar of the water rushing down the mountain. The APCs stopped on the opposite riverbank. A thirty-foot distance made the difference between a cold wet night and a ride home. The next thing I knew, the APCs actually attempted to cross that thirty-foot span of water to get us. The lead APC was about halfway across when we could see the heavy steel vehicle being pushed sideways slightly by the strong current. The APC driver had no choice but to go back to the opposite bank.

We had completely given up on getting off that little island when we saw several Timorese approach the APCs on the opposite bank. Soon the Timorese were walking along the opposite bank followed by the APCs. When the APCs were about fifty feet to the left of our island the Timorese they were following pointed across the river. The APCs turned into the river, drove halfway across the river, then made a ninety degree left turn and drove to our island with very little difficulty.

The Timorese saved us from a miserable night by knowing that riverbed well enough to get those APCs to us. As the APCs climbed out of the river and onto our little island we gleefully grabbed out packs and jumped on top of the APCs. The APC commander told us we couldn't ride inside because we would get wet. I guess he hadn't noticed that we and our kit were already completely drenched.

The low valleys and coast areas of Timor are always hot. There will never be a time that a person will be cold in those areas. The mountains are different. During a sunny day low areas like this river can be hot; however, when it rains and at night it becomes cold. We were all tired, soaked, and now cold. Domingos' teeth chattered as we made the drive through the raging water to get to the riverbank. I was cold too but not near as cold as Domingos. I stripped off my shirt and handed it to Domingos. The shirt was soaked but it helped him some.

The APCs stopped after climbing up the riverbank so that we could get off the top and climb inside. The twenty-minute ride up Bobonaro mountain was very rough and seemed to take forever but none of us complained. We were just happy to get back to civilization and not have to walk up another mountain to get there.

We ate with the soldiers who took care of us all day at their mess hall upon arriving at the Kiwi compound in Bobonaro Village. We gave a detailed description of our results of the investigation to the Lieutenant. When finished I stepped outside with Foxy and smoked a cigarette with him. I thanked him for his services and patience with me.

Foxy smiled and said, "You did fine once you got those boots off your feet." He hesitated for a moment then added, "If you want to get rid of those boots I'll trade you something for them."

I looked at Foxy in surprise as I said, "I thought you said those boots were bad?"

Foxy answered, "They are a curse in the jungle but around the base, inspections, and parades they are perfect."

I shook hands with Foxy and told him to figure out what he wanted to trade and let me know. I then walked to our Land Rover where Mac, Naif, and Domingos were now waiting for me.

We got back to Maliana about ten o'clock that night. Bantam, Snapper, Donny, and Zak were sitting on the veranda drinking beer. We pulled up and parked near them. They laughed when they saw our condition as we walked into the light near the veranda. Our clothes were fairly dry by that time; however, we were filthy from head to toe. Bantam asked, "You men have a rough day at the office today?"

Mac answered as he popped the top of the can of beer he just took out of our trash container cooler, "Yeah, it was a tough day."

We first gave an account of the adventurous side of the day, which started going bad when the APCs couldn't get down the river and had to dump us out to walk. The investigation side went well even though we couldn't get any more statements. The Anapol Village chief had enlightened us about the details of the incident; however, he refused to give a statement.

The village chief told us that in Early October 1999, four young men wondered into Anapol Village late in the afternoon and asked if they could spend the night. Someone in the village recognized one of the four men as a low-ranking Militia member of the Halilintar Militia that was based in Maliana. The person who recognized the Militia member in Anapol went to Molop Village, which is about two kilometers west of Anapol Village. The man informed a group of Falintil Clandestino operators who lived in Molop Village about the Militia member sleeping the night in Anapol Village. The Falintil never wasted an opportunity to kill their hated enemy, so the Molop- based unit came to Anapol and killed the four men.

By the time we finished telling our war stories to Bantam and the others I had drank three beers. The alcohol, along with the activities of this long and exhausting day, hit me all at once. I was planning to clean up before going to sleep, but after stripping off my mud-covered clothes I lay down on my air mattress. The next thing I knew Donny was banging on my door and asking if I planned to work at all today.

I looked at my watch and saw that it was almost noon. This was my first night in East Timor that I didn't wake up from the heat, howling dogs, roosters crowing, or even to take a piss. Other than sore muscles, I felt pretty good.

CHAPTER SIX

Strategic Information Division

Shortly after the Anapol operation Bantam was summoned to a meeting in Dili. That night during our normal gathering on the veranda to drink cold beer Bantam told me that I would be the "Field Information Officer" (FIO) for all of Bobonaro district.

I asked, "What's that?"

Bantam said, "You have been requested to be the FIO. Someone from the newly formed Strategic Information Division (SID) will be meeting with you and giving you details."

About one week later I was summoned to Dili for a meeting with the SID commander, whom I choose not to name or describe. The SID commander went through the details of my current position as FIO, which came down to collecting "intelligence." I had been selected because of my intelligence training and work while I was a police officer in Michigan. The SID commander was an ex-narcotics officer himself so we related with each other very well.

The basic rundown was this: The United Nations does not become involved with any form of aggressive intelligence collection and certainly has nothing to do with espionage; however, there is a need for the United Nations commanders to know what is happening within the mission area. Therefore the UN establishes an information division within mission areas to collect "readily available information" that may forewarn UN commanders of potential threats to UN personnel or property.

I sat at the small table within the SID office at police Headquarters in Dili. I leaned back in my chair and lightly tapped the table top with my left index finger as I thought about what my new commander had told me so far. The commander sat in a chair across the table from me and watched me closely. He asked, "What's on your mind?"

I looked up from my tapping finger and into the eyes of my commander, "You have told me all of the politically correct bullshit. Is that all you want me to do or is there more?"

My commander smiled, apparently liking my question. He responded, "I have told you what the UN information collection program is and what the parameters are for that program. If you are caught going outside of those parameters, the United Nations will have no choice but to charge you and repatriate you."

My commander then leaned slightly over the table toward me and said slowly and quietly, "If you are caught."

* * * *

I had a lot to think about during my three-hour drive back to Maliana that night. The safe thing to do was simply collect the readily available information that the UN outlined in the job description; however, I knew that information taken from the "surface" has little value. If you want to know what is going on behind the scenes you have to go behind those scenes. That was what I did as a narc back home. I penetrated into targets and took drug kingpins and their organizations down from the inside out.

Indirectly that was what I was being asked to do now, or so I thought anyway. The difference was that working for a Narc unit my actions was supported by my commanders. Here in East Timor I was being told up front that I would be charged if caught conducting any type of aggressive operation.

By the time I got back to Maliana I had decided that I would take this one step at a time. I would start out with simply collecting that readily available information and scope out the possibilities of penetrating targets if and when the time or need came, although I did decide to begin one passive penetration as soon as I could figure out whom the target was.

It made sense to me that for the Falintil guerillas to have fought the Indonesians so effectively for twenty-four years they must have had some type of organized intelligence organization in place. It also made sense that if there was an organized intelligence outfit that organization would still be active. All I had to do is find the link to penetrate that organization and use what they have already established. It sounds easy enough but how do you find someone like that who doesn't want to be found?

The answer to that question was simple. I just didn't realize yet that tactics in the international intelligence theater is pretty much the same tactics that I used as a narcotics officer in Michigan. I also did not know at that time that the target I was looking for was actually looking me. We would soon find each other.

* * * *

Bili Tai held the butt of the M-16 assault rifle tight against his shoulder as he lay on the ground and prepared to fire. The light of this early morning sunrise allowed Bili Tai to easily put is rifle sights on the enemy soldiers that struggled to walk up the narrow mountain path.

Bili Tai and the five men with him had been stealthily walking since ten-o'clock the night before. It took the team two hours just to get across the Nunura River, which divides East Timor and West Timor. Once on the enemy side of the river Bili Tai's team had to move very slow. They knew that the Australian military conducted several patrols and observation positions along the river and also for several kilometers inside East Timor.

SGI Assets who live in East Timor had studied the patrol habits of the Australian military for several months; however, because of the Austalian's tactics it was difficult to determine habits of the Australians that the Militia guerillas could exploit during an infiltration operation into East Timor. The Australians maintained very tight security of their established positions. Their patrols and static observation positions never did the same thing two nights in a row.

Bili Tai and his team were well trained by the Indonesian Special Forces organization Koppassus. The team knew how to work their way through enemy forces without being detected. Bili Tai and his team were the best of all the Militia teams being trained by the Koppassus, which is why they were selected as the first Militia team to infiltrate East Timor.

Bili Tai and the other five Halilintar Militia members with him all wore full Indonesian TNI camouflage uniforms and black combat boots. They wore small black backpacks and web harnesses that were loaded down with hand grenades and several magazines of ammunition for the M-16 and SKS assault rifles they carried.

Augustinho Bili Tai was known as a harsh and cruel Militia leader from the Cailaco Village of Atudara. Atudara Village is a remote village located near the northern tip of Lailaco mountain, which is the highest mountain near Maliana that has high rocky peaks. The SGI commander of the Militia cleverly chose Bili Tai for this "First" mission into East Timor.

Tome Diago had several secret meetings with Bili Tai to plan the operations that Diago wanted Bili Tai to conduct while the Bili Tai team was in East Timor. Most of those meetings between Bili Tai and Tome Diago took place at the Koppassus secret training facility in the jungle near the Indonesian city of Atambua, which is in West Timor.

The objectives of the Bili Tai team penetration of East Timor in February 2000 were to identify hidden locations throughout Lailaco mountain that could be used by Militia teams now and in the future.

A second objective was to begin taking control of the remote villages scattered throughout the mountain area, starting with Bili Tai's home village of Atudara.

The third objective was to collect as much information possible on the activities of the Australian military in and around Lailaco mountain. Diago was careful to make it clear to Bili Tai, "Do not engage the Australian military unless you have no other choice but if you engage them kill as many Australians as you can."

* * * *

Bili Tai thought about what Tome Diago had told him now as he held his rifle sights steady on a young Australian soldier who appeared to be struggling just to get up the steep and very rough dirt path. Bili Tai had spent hours slowly and methodically working his team through two kilometers distance of jungle to avoid any contact with the Australian military who patrolled those areas.

By daybreak Bili Tai and his team reached the base of Lailaco mountain and started up the mountain. A short way up the mountain the Bili Tai team detected an Australian Patrol who had spent the night at the side of the trail. The same trail that Bili Tai and his team were now using. Bili Tai led his team around the Australian overnight position then continued their climb up the mountain.

Bili Tai's "drag man" (the last man in the line) soon realized that the Australians whom they by past was now following the Bili Tai team up the mountain. Bili Tai feared that the Australian patrol detected his team while they skirted around the Australian position. The Australians were probably tracking his team.

Bili Tai was not too concerned about eight to twelve Australian soldiers. This mountain is where Bili Tai grew up. Once he knew the Australians were following his team Bili Tai simply increased the pace. Intelligence from SGI Assets in East Timor was that the Australian military always carried full packs while on multiple day patrols. This caused them to move slowly and have to take frequent breaks.

Eventually Bili Tai found a good ambush location along the trail that his team now walked. Bili Tai moved up into the "point" position and led his team about one-hundred-meters past the ambush site that Bili Tai planned to use. He then led his team off the trail and "button-hooked" his team through the jungle as they walked back to the ambush site that they had passed one hundred meters before.

The six Militia soldiers formed a linear ambush formation about twenty meters to the left of the trail and waited. It was almost an hour later before the first Australian soldier on point came into view as he walked up the steep trail. Then another soldier came into sight and then another.

As the column of Australians entered the "kill zone" of Bili Tai's ambush the thoughts of Tome Diago's instructions ran through his mind. Bili Tai wanted to kill these Australians but he realized as he watched the twelve soldiers now in the rifle sights of his team that the Australians were not tracking them.

If he initiated the ambush Bili Tai would have to immediately take his team back to West Timor. His team's mission would be over and they would not have achieved their objectives. Bili Tai relaxed his grip on his assault rifle and watched as the Australian drag man went out of sight walking up the mountain.

* * * *

The first few weeks following my meeting with the SID commander were busy. I established a good working relationship with the Australian military Field Intelligence team that was assigned to the Bobonaro District. This was a good team. There hardly was a day that they didn't capture at least one ex-Militia member who returned from West Timor to live in East Timor.

Most of the ex-Militia who returned to East Timor during this time period was low-level members who were more like victims than Militia. These were men who were recruited into the Militia ranks in the last few months of Indonesia's occupation of East Timor.

Most of these members willingly joined the Militia organizations because of the "clout" being a Militia member gave them. Some had no choice but to join. The Indonesian strategy was to swell the ranks of the Militia organizations during the election period so that they could better control the East Timorese population; however, the SGI did not trust the new recruits so most of them were never given any important positions or conducted any secret activities.

The intelligence value from these recruits was little to none but the Australian Field Intelligence team knew that there were a few hardcore Militia members who were now living in East Timor that did have good intelligence hidden away in their brains. The difficulty was, "How do you know which Militia members have the secrets and which ones do not?" The only way to know the answer to this was to detain all the members identified and interview them.

This Australian Field Intelligence team was relentless at finding, capturing and then extracting information from Militia who returned to East Timor. One piece of information that kept coming out of the many interviews was that there was some type of military training of Militia members going on just over the border near Atambua Village.

This is naturally a big concern for the security of East Timor. The only purpose for military training is to prepare an organized force for some kind of hostile action. Since there were no conflicts of any type in West Timor it could be assumed that if there was military training in West Timor the probable target of those being trained was East Timor.

This military intelligence team was a good contact for me; however, they were not the connection that I was really looking for. The "high grade" intelligence I was looking for could only come from the Timorese or Indonesians. With this in mind I studied the young Timorese men and women who served as our interpreters. These were the only Timorese that I could communicate with so I had to find a beginning link among our interpreters.

Through daily, seemingly normal, conversations I learned that two of our interpreters had strong Falintil backgrounds. These were the two men I focused on. I developed closer and closer relationships with the two men. They were aware that I was the new United Nations information officer. What I didn't know was that both of these men had a strong relationship with La Faik. I didn't even know yet that La Faik existed.

One of the Falintil connected interpreters that I targeted was Domingos, whom had gone with us on the Anapol operation. Domingos was in his early twenties, intelligent, educated and starved for all the education that he could get. He was five-foot ten-inches tall, lean build but strong. He was so honest about everything that he spoke about. If he couldn't or shouldn't talk about something I prodded him for he would simply say, "I can't tell you that. I am sorry for that."

Alfonso was completely different from Domingos. He was a married man in his mid-thirties and had several children. He was five-foot-six-inches tall and muscular. He too had a hunger to learn. Alfonso was a medic by Indonesian standards but he desired to further his medical education and one day become a doctor.

I had continuously pushed both Alfonso and Domingos to introduce me to East Timorese people that had an inside track in the intelligence world. I met and talked with political leaders from several Sub-Districts and FSP leaders from those same areas. I took their information and wrote out SID reports on that information and sent the reports to my commander in Dili. My SID commander was happy with the information that I was turning in but I wasn't happy. I knew there was a pot of intelligence gold to be found.

* * * *

A few days before the "Augustinho Bili Tai" infiltration of East Timor Alfonso approached me early in the morning. He told me, "Mr. Jim, if you have time we should go to Cailaco. There is a friend of mine that may be able to give you some important information."

I naturally tried to find out who this man was and what the important information was about. Alfonso simply said, "I don't know what the information is but you should go with me."

I did drive Alfonso to a village north of Marko Village. A very small village named Maumela. We arrived at a school facility that consisted of three buildings, which was all painted a dark green color. There were no children at the school when we got there at mid-morning. There were several people sitting on the ground outside of the longest building that was at the rear of the school grounds. The people sitting calmly outside the building were mostly middle-aged men, about twenty of them.

I looked into the eyes of several of those men as I approached and then walked past them as Alfonso led me into the school building. These men looked back at me in a friendly manner but I could see in their eyes that they were different from the many Timorese men that I had met. All Timorese people are alert, intelligent and amazingly strong of body and will. These men captivated my heart and soul with their demeanor that was above and beyond what I had ever encountered to this point of my mission in East Timor.

The other thing that grabbed my attention about these men was that each man had a long piece of wood that was carved to resemble a Portuguese G-3 assault rifle. Actually these carved pieces of wood didn't just resemble the Portuguese weapon, they were nearly identical. To see these pieces of wood at a distance a person would believe that they were looking at a G-3 assault rifle.

These men looked like soldiers even though they wore a variety of street clothes such as blue jeans, slacks, t-shirts and button down shirts. Their footwear was flip flops, sandals, or tennis shoes. There was not one piece of uniform clothing on any of these men.

There were twelve men sitting inside the school building that Alfonso led me into. Three men sat on wood chairs near the right wall of the large room that we entered. The remainder of the men sat on wood chairs facing the three men. There were two empty chairs to the left side of the three men sitting near the wall.

Alfonso brought me to the three men sitting and introduced me to the men. The man sitting in the middle was the obvious leader of this group. He warmly and respectfully greeted me but I could tell by the glint in his eyes that he was closely studying my every move. He was introduced to me by his proper name but I will stick with the "code name" that I have selected for this book.

I could feel the strength of La Faik's grip as we shook hands. His dark brown eyes showed the strength of his inner-being as he looked into my eyes. This fifty-year-old man was five-foot-ten-inches of lean muscle. His long black hair hung loose, falling over his shoulders and down to the middle of his back.

La Faik politely directed Alfonso and I to the two empty chairs. Alfonso and La Faik talked for a few moments. I could not understand the East Timor language of Tetum yet. These men were speaking in the Kamak language. East Timor is made up of several ancient tribes. Each tribe had its own language. Eventually there was a common language that all East Timorese understood which is the Tetum language. La Faik and Alfonso were using the Kamak tribal language.

Soon two women and two teenage girls entered the building carrying trays of cups and pitchers of coffee. The women served each of the men in the room coffee and crackers. We sipped at the coffee and ate crackers as La Faik got down to business. He asked me through Alfonso if I would be willing to go with him and some of his men to locate two of his men who were killed by Militia in September of 1999.

La Faik explained the circumstances of the two dead men to me through Alfonso. The bodies of the two men were buried in shallow graves where the bodies were found by a Falintil patrol. The Falintil patrol had heard gunshots coming from the area where the two men were killed. When they went to see who was doing the shooting they found the body of Jose Soares. The Falintil saw the many TNI boot prints in the area near Jose's body.

The Falintil patrol followed the tracks of Jose's murderers in an attempt to catch up with and kill the murderers. Eventually the Falintil patrol came across a second body. This body, Alfonso Moniz, was found at the bottom of a steep grassy ravine. The East Timorese guerillas were filled with sorrow for their two fallen Clandestino operators who had recently been tortured and killed.

The guerillas continued their pursuit but soon realized that it was too late to track and catch the TNI or Militia who had killed their friends. The Falintil patrol quickly returned and buried Alfonso at the bottom of the ravine and then returned to Jose's body and buried him too.

* * * *

I felt true sympathy for these people who suffered the loss of two East Timorese patriots but I was very confused. I thought that Alfonso was taking me to meet someone who had some intelligence value. Now I was being asked to go find a couple of bodies somewhere in the jungle. Over the first two months that I was working out of Maliana Station I had gone on many short walks to locate shallow graves where murdered people had been buried where they fell. I was a little upset with Alfonso for bringing me here for this purpose but I figured that as long as we were there I would go and identify two more grave sites. I would give the information to the Maliana Station Investigators who would conduct the inquiries when they had time.

I told La Faik that I would go with them. There was no hesitation as La Faik stood up and walked outside of the building. Everyone who was sitting outside respectfully stood up as La Faik stepped out of the school building and into the bright sunlight. I walked to my Land Rover and grabbed the small backpack that I always took with me everywhere I go. I carried my expected everyday needs in that backpack. I carried everything from paper and pen to a medical kit with multiple medicines and bandages. The backpack also contained basic camping needs such as matches, small flashlight, compass and one canteen of water, which was an additional canteen to the one I always wore on my gunbelt.

By the time I walked back to where La Faik waited in front of the school building I could see that the men who were waiting in front of the building with their replica G-3 assault rifles were going with us and taking their wooden weapons with them. I was very concerned about this. I knew that the Australian military conducted patrols in the area. If these men were to be seen in the jungles carrying what looked like assault weapons we could end up on the receiving end of the Australian military firepower, which is impressive.

My Australian intelligence buddies had told me that there was a lot of concern about a large group of men who were conducting military drill training in the Cailaco area. Australian military personnel had often seen these men training in both Marko Village and Maumela Village using wooden rifles. I reflected about that information now as I observed these men with their wooden weapons, *I guess I now know who the military have been observing with the wooden weapons.*

I respectfully told La Faik through Alfonso about my fears of the Timorese men carrying the replica rifles into the jungle. La Faik simply smiled as he said, "There is no danger. The Australians will never see us."

I countered La Faik's comment, "You don't understand. The Australians have many patrols and hidden observation posts (OPs) throughout this area. We will probably never see the soldiers who form these OPs but they will see us."

La Faik softly looked at me and smiled. He then glanced at Alfonso for a moment. He then turned and gave a nod of his head to a man named Augustinho. Augustinho barked out an order and the twenty plus men carrying the wooden rifles formed into a single file formation and started walking toward the jungle behind the school.

As Alfonso and I joined into the middle of the formation of men Alfonso told me, "La Faik wants me to explain to you that you don't need to worry. La Faik and Augustinho know where the Australians are. These Falintil soldiers with us now often train in the nearby mountains and the Australians have not seen them. They will not see us today, either."

I realized that if these men have been training in the nearby mountains then it is true that the Australian military have not seen them. The military intelligence reports were only about military drill training at the school. I was sure that the military intelligence guys would have told me about men in the jungles with replica weapons. Then I wondered how Alfonso knew that La Faik wanted him to tell me anything. La Faik never said a word to Alfonso before we started our march.

We walked out the backside of Maumela Village and followed a dirt path through the flat valley jungle. Soon we broke out of the jungle into a series of open areas that were used by the people of Maumela to raise crops. Next we stepped down into a gravel bottom riverbed. A small stream ran through the center of the otherwise dry riverbed. We walked up the shaded side of the riverbed that gradually became steeper.

After one-kilometer or more we abandon the somewhat easy walking up the riverbed. The line of men we followed made a sharp left turn, climbed up the riverbank and started to ascend the steep side of a mountain. The further up we climbed the steeper the mountainside became. Since the Anapol operation I had been on two short operations with military units walking through jungles and mountains. I felt confident that I could keep up with the military.

These men I was now with were completely different. They carried nothing but a knife on their belts, a *katana* (machete) in a leather sheath slung over their shoulders and the wooden rifles. They didn't carry any food or water.

There was no path up this mountain we climbed. These men were not hampered by the rough terrain or the occasional heavy foliage. They kept a fast pace, smoothly walking through anything that we encountered. They flowed over the difficult terrain like apparitions.

As for me I was struggling to keep up. I had not worn those dreaded boots since the Anapol operation. The cheap tennis shoes that I brought with me from America were all that I had. They were better then the boots; however, the soles of the shoes had no value for traction while walking in the mountains.

When we started up the mountain La Faik moved back in the line of marching men so that he was walking in front of me. As I frequently stumbled or slipped La Faik began pointing at the ground, showing me where to step and sometimes where not to step. Alfonso told me to watch how La Faik walks and to try to walk the same way.

By the time we finally crested the top of this mountain I was exhausted. We descended the reverse slope a short distance before La Faik stopped the moving column of men. I watched as the column of men instantly melted into the jungle to form a security screen for our position.

I was impressed how these men conducted their security tactics while moving through difficult terrain at a fast walk. Upon stopping these men flowed into static security positions effectively and naturally. This was a very good team. I knew that if they could fight together using real weapons like they move together this was a force that I would never want to go up against. These guys were good.

Two men who were not handling security positions climbed two different coconut trees that were inside our security perimeter. The two men cut several coconuts from each tree. The coconuts hit the ground with a loud thud as they fell from the high trees. Other men not on security detail gathered the coconuts. They used their *katanas* to cut one end of the coconut so that there was a silver dollar size opening into the center of the coconut.

Each man in the patrol was given a coconut. I took the coconut that was handed to me and drank the water from the hole cut on the top. Water dripped down the sides of my face and onto my chest as I drank the sweet water from the small opening in the shell of my coconut. My shirt was already soaked from my sweat so I wasn't concerned about water from the coconut making me any more uncomfortable.

Once I drank all the water one of the Falintil who stood near me politely took the coconut from me. He sat the coconut on a rock and chopped the coconut into two halves with one hit of his *katana*. The man then cut a slice of the shell of the coconut that I could use as a spoon. He handed me the two coconut halves and the coconut shell spoon that he had cut.

I scraped the thin and very moist coconut meat from the inside of the shell and ate. I had never eaten the meat of a young coconut before. The taste was different from the thick, hard coconut meat that I had eaten on occasion back in the States. The young coconut meat was very sweet and the texture so soft it nearly melted in my mouth.

The most amazing thing was that after drinking the water and eating the meat of the coconut I felt completely refreshed, almost energized. My instant refreshed condition was a good thing because once everyone had drank and eaten their coconut we were walking again.

Eventually we came to the body of Alfonso Moniz who was buried at the bottom of the ravine. A short ceremony of some type was conducted and a stone and wood cross was made and placed at the grave site. We then walked back up the grassy wall of the ravine and continued on to the grave of Jose.

Once the ceremony and the marking of Jose's grave were complete we began our return trip to Maumela Village. We returned using a different route, which I believe was even more difficult terrain then the route we had used to get up this mountain. La Faik and Alfonso continued their attempt to teach me how to walk in these mountains. I was actually learning rapidly. God knows I was getting plenty of practice.

We got back to Maumela Village shortly after sunset. I was surprised to see that many people waited for us at a group of homes across the road from the school. There were two long tables that were loaded down with platters of food, big bowls of rice, a variety of meats, vegetables, and salads. I didn't know what most of the food was. I was so tired and hungry I would have eaten anything.

I took a sample of everything on the table, which filled my large plate to the point of overflowing. I had never eaten most of the vegetables and some of the meats before this night but everything tasted very good. The feeling that I had while eating this feast with the men that I had walked the mountains with all day long was a very bonding experience.

My farm boy memories flooded my mind as I felt the exhaustion of a hard day at work followed by moms and families of us workers having a large farm style meal waiting for us when we got home from the fields. The feeling this night in Maumela Village was much stronger because of the large number of families involved and the patriotic purpose of our efforts today.

I was hooked. The camaraderie of the Falintil and their supporting families was like nothing I could have ever imagined. I thought of my American ancestors who fought the English for our freedom so many years ago. There probably was not much difference other than the American fight for freedom was a couple hundred years ago. The East Timor fight for freedom had just ended, or so I thought.

Before I left Maumela Village to drive back to Maliana that night La Faik talked to me briefly. He first thanked me for accompanying this important operation today. He then said, "The Koppassus is training the Militia near Atambua to begin operations here in East Timor. Their first infiltration operations will begin next week. Augustinho Bili Tai will be leading a team into the Cailaco area."

La Faik paused for a moment to let what he told me sink in. He then continued, "We will meet again when you have time." He turned and walked away.

This had been a long and unusual day. I came to Maumela Village for the purpose of collecting some intelligence. I didn't get the intelligence I came for but unexpectedly ended up going on a patriotic operation with Falintil guerillas who seemed bent on teaching me the ways of the Falintil. Then at the end of a very long day I got a potential intelligence bombshell dropped on me.

I had no idea who Augustinho Bili Tai was or how valid La Faik's information was but if his intelligence is as good as the Falintil I spent the day with today then this information source was the gold mine that I was looking for. My instincts told me I had found the man I was looking for. My next thought was, *I didn't find him; he found me. This whole day and night was a feeling out process as well as a training exercise.*

During the drive back to Maliana that night Alfonso talked openly with me, which confirmed my thoughts. Alfonso happily told me, "La Faik likes you so far. I have never seen him take a *malai* [*malai* is the Tetum word for "foreigner"] into the jungle with his elements before. He has a plan to work with you, Mr. Jim."

I simply nodded in response as I thought, *I will have to wait and see what La Faik's credibility is before I get too involved with him.*

CHAPTER SEVEN

Guerilla War

La Faik and I quickly formed a good working relationship. A few days after my long walk with La Faik and his elements, La Faik told me that Augustinho Bili Tai was in East Timor with a small team. The purpose of Bili Tai's mission was not known. La Faik further said that there was one or more Militia units that had infiltrated into the Suai area, which was the Kova Lima District that bordered Indonesia to the south of Bobonaro District.

I did reports on La Faik's information; however, I still didn't know how credible the information was. I indicated my doubts on the reports that I turned into my SID commander. Almost everyone in the intelligence field didn't believe my reports were true. I responded to the criticism with one sentence, "I don't start the rumors I just pass them on."

The response to my statement from most intelligence operators was a smile, a nod and a, "That's true. That's the job of an intelligence collector."

The Australian military Field Intelligence (AMFI) team was skeptical of a Militia infiltration; however, they were open-minded enough to aggressively seek out further information. They began to receive countless reports from villagers in remote areas of crops being stolen, cows stolen and slaughtered by unknown people from the jungle, and some reports from villagers who actually saw the Militia.

The AMFI interviewed the people who said they saw the Militia; however, every sighting was at night or at long distances. None of the reported sightings could be considered credible. Anyone could have stolen crops or slaughtered cows. There just wasn't any piece of intelligence that could be verified.

I had several long talks with the AMFI team leader about this sudden flood of information about Militia units allegedly operating in the Maliana and Cailaco

Sub-Districts. Eventually the team leader confessed that he believes that it is very possible Militia is here in East Timor. The AMFI has seen TNI military boot prints in some of the areas where people were reporting having seen Militia. The team leader then sighed as he said, "That's not enough proof for the Sector West commander. They will not believe until there is bloodshed."

* * * *

La Faik was growing frustrated with the lack of military response to Bili Tai and his Militia team who have had the run of Lailaco mountain for over two weeks now. La Faik displayed almost no outward signs but by now I was learning how to "read" the Timorese people, especially La Faik. As I sat on La Faik's front porch and sipped the coffee his wife had served me I could see the frustration in his eyes.

I was still skeptical about the Militia infiltration myself but I didn't let on to any of the Timorese that I had doubts, especially La Faik. I had decided not to waste time trying to develop proof of the many reports from local citizens. I relayed my thoughts to La Faik, "We cannot control what the United Nation militaries do or do not do. We should continue to monitor Bili Tai's positions and actions but we need to know what else is being planned." La Faik nodded his agreement.

Our focus was on the Militia in West Timor. Armed Militia units operating in East Timor is an immediate threat to be sure. Our purpose was to collect "information" that could be used by the military to "neutralize" current operating guerilla units. More importantly was to collect information about the Militia guerillas power base. Intelligence personnel always seek out answers to questions like, "Who organized the units? Who trained them? What are they trained to do? What are their short and long term objectives? What equipment and weapons are available to them?" and so forth. This is all important information that the enemy goes to great lengths to conceal.

La Faik was a soldier before he was an intelligence operator. He knows that the weakness within military units is human nature. Human beings are all different in many ways; however, all human beings have needs to exist on this planet. Physical, psychological and emotional needs can be exploited against your enemy if you know your enemy.

With this in mind La Faik sought to identify each person who was a member of these Militia guerillas, especially the leaders. He would find out everything he could about the identified members background such as religion, family, where he was born and raised and so on.

Armed with this type of personal information gave La Faik three different angles to use against the enemy. The first angle: Knowing the team leader gave you clues as to how he would conduct his team on operations.

The second angle: Knowing the team members opened the door to getting indirect information from the family of a team member. There was always an outside chance of "turning" a team member into a "double agent."

The third angle: By knowing the individual members, a propaganda campaign to weaken or destroy the members resolve can be designed more effectively.

By now I was aware of at least some of La Faik's operations in West Timor. La Faik had a six-man cell operating in the Halilintar Militia base in Turiskai. In addition to monitoring Halilintar Militia activites the Turiskai cell maintained a "mailbox" system of communications with East Timor. The "mailbox" was a selling stall at the Tunubibi illegal market, which was located just over the river into Indonesia.

There was another eight-man cell that was operating in Atambua, West Timor. This cell was collecting information about the military training. The training site was a secluded area near Atambua. The area around the training site was secured by Koppassus, which made information collection in that area very dangerous. The Atambua cell was also closely monitoring the Besi Merah Putih and Aitarak Militia groups who were based in Atambua.

Then there was a single Segrada Familia operator who was on a mission into the West Timor Capital of Kupang. I knew about this man but I did not know yet what his mission was. I had learned patience during my undercover operations as a narcotics officer back in Lansing, Michigan. Asking questions makes drug dealers suspicious. When they were ready they would tell me what I wanted to know. I used the same tactic here in East Timor. The information would come when the time was right.

La Faik presented me with an idea that he had been thinking about. He told me that his Turiskai cell had befriended two TNI soldiers who patrol the Tunubibi illegal market. Both of these TNI soldiers are disgusted with the behavior of the Halilintar Militia. They have made remarks to the Turiskai cell that the East Timorese who come over the river to shop at the market should capture the Militia members and take them across the river and give them to the Australians. La Faik commented, "I think we can capture a Militia member and bring him here to be questioned."

I thought that what La Faik had said was a good idea. I also thought that a kidnaping operation was out of the question. This would be very dangerous for anyone involved. Besides that, it would be next to impossible to pull off. The TNI soldiers who patrol the market would almost assuredly see what was happening and capture La Faik's elements.

I talked with La Faik about these concerns that I had about any kidnaping operations. La Faik told me that he and his elements have already made the plans to begin the kidnaping operations. They haven't conducted any of the operations yet because there is one obstacle that they have not been able to work out so far. That obstacle was the Australian military.

La Faik said, "The two TNI soldiers have already agreed to help with the kidnaping by making sure there is no soldiers close by when the time comes to make the grab. We can make the snatch and get the captured Militia member across the river but the Australian military who have established a permanent base on the East Timorese side of the river will detain my elements and take our prisoner away from us."

I thought about the possibilities of kidnaping an active Halilintar Militia member from West Timor. The potential for high-grade information was very good, especially if the kidnaped Militia turned out to be a commander. If the captured Militia member had been through the Koppassus training in Atambua we would know the details of the training, who was conducting the training, the name of the instructors, what weapons the Militia would be using against us and what types of military operations the Militia units were prepared to do.

The key to collecting the information locked inside the head of the kidnaped victim is the interrogators of the captured Militia. La Faik's elements would no doubt get every piece of information from any captured Militia. The problem was to get the captured Militia member to a location in East Timor to be interrogated. Getting past the Australians at Tunubibi was just not going to be an easy task. Then it hit me as if someone had turned on a light. We could use the Australians at Tunubibi.

I told La Faik, "If your elements can grab a Militia member and get him over to East Timor—let the Australians take control of the prisoner. The soldiers at Tunubibi will call the AMFI who will come and conduct an investigation. Once they find out he is a Militia member they will interrogate him. The AMFI will tell me most of the information that they get from the interrogation, which I will pass on to you."

La Faik would rather have his elements interrogate the prisoner but the plan I outlined was the second best option. There were some sideline benefits too.

The Australians would be getting information firsthand without reports from me, which takes me further away from any involvement with espionage. The firsthand information is always more credible to the Sector West commanders so they would be more apt to take action on any information extracted from the prisoner.

The negative side of any kidnaping operations is the havoc that the Indonesian military would create once they find out about the kidnaping, which they certainly would find out. The political side of this particular boat would be rocked by Indonesian accusations made against the United Nations and the Australian military who wouldn't know anything about any kidnaping plots.

The last issue of any kidnaping operation was how to protect the Segrada Familia structure from exposure. La Faik decided on a little sleight of hand tactic. The kidnaping team would snatch the target Militia man and get the target over the river to a location where several local villagers would be waiting. The captured Militia would be handed over to the waiting local villagers who would maintain control over the prisoner while the kidnaping team simply walked off. By the time any Australian soldiers arrived the kidnaping team would have no apparent connection to the prisoner. The local villagers would tell the Australians that they had grabbed this Militia man who had walked across the river onto the East Timor side.

Protecting the Turiskai cell was a simple matter. The Turiskai cell simply passed on the information about who the two soldiers were. One of the East Timor elements developed the situation with the two soldiers to the point of the soldier's participation. Actually the soldiers believed that they had come up with the plan not realizing that they had actually been manipulated. The only elements in danger of capture were the East Timor elements.

By the time La Faik and I finished talking about this kidnaping plot it was well after dark and my interpreter and I had a long drive to get back to Maliana. I told La Faik that the kidnaping operation probably wasn't worth the risk that his elements would be taking. I was also concerned about the political fallout that would definitely happen as a result of the operation.

I wasn't concerned that I may get caught being involved with this very aggressive espionage operation. Other than La Faik and the interpreter, nobody knew that I had discussed this operation or even had knowledge about it. Any elements that may be captured in Indonesia or in East Timor could not give my name to interrogators because those who would conduct the operation didn't know who I was. I didn't know who they were either.

* * * *

A few days later the AMFI team leader (TL) told me about a strange incident that he and his team encountered. The TL told me that the Australian platoon whom secures the Tunubibi area called for the AMFI to come and take control of a Militia member that the platoon had detained.

AMFI members who responded to Tunubibi found out that this Militia member had walked across the river to the East Timor side of the river. He was recognized as a Militia member by some local citizens who immediately attacked the man and held him until Australian soldiers arrived and took custody of the suspected Militia member.

The AMFI TL and I were sitting alone inside the Australian company compound in Maliana, which is where the AMFI were based. We sat in the drab green tent that was both the AMFI sleeping quarters and also their office. The floor of the tent was a wooden platform built a couple inches above the ground.

I looked into the TL's face and could see that he was studying me for my reactions. I responded to his story, "So what's so strange about local people beating up a Militia member that they found. I'm surprised they didn't kill him."

What I told the TL was well known by everyone. Anytime a Militia member is found in East Timor by citizens who suffered at the hands of that particular Militia member or that members Militia group it was a certainty that the found Militia member would be attacked, beaten, and in some cases, killed.

The AMFI TL shook his head saying, "That's not the point. During our debriefing of this Militia he said that three East Timorese men clubbed him over the head several times and then dragged him to the local villagers who turned him over to the Australian platoon at Tunubibi. The problem is that he claims to have been standing in the illegal market , which is in Indonesia, when he was attacked."

I steadily looked into the TL's eyes as he told me this story. I was studying him to see how he was reacting to this situation. The TL then asked, "Do you think any Timorese may be involved with kidnaping someone from West Timor?"

I hesitated to answer for a few moments as I thought about what a good job La Faik and his elements did. They actually pulled off a difficult operation smooth as silk. I told the TL, "Hundreds of East Timorese go over to that market everyday. It was just a matter of time before something like this happened—if he is telling the truth." The TL nodded his agreement of my analysis.

I asked, "So what did this kidnaped Militia from West Timor have to say?"

The TL told me that the man confirmed the military training of Militia. So far the training was for reconnaissance type operations, ambush and escape and evasion tactics. I looked long and hard at the team leader after he finished speaking. I knew he was holding back.

I decided to play an ace that I wasn't sure was in my hand of cards. If the TL believed that I was a valuable source of information this move would probably draw out what he was holding back. I said, "Come on, Randy. [Nobody in Australia is named Randy] Our bosses tell us we can't share information but on our level we have to share. You work with me and I'll work with you."

The TL hesitated for a moment longer then finally gave me a little more, "The Militia member gave us the names of six men who infiltrated East Timor three weeks ago. Augustinho Bili Tai is one of those names. He also said that a Militia commander named Martinho will be leading a team into East Timor soon."

Now I knew that La Faik was the "pot of gold" that I believed he was. In addition to that my credibility as a field intelligence agent just shot to the top of the charts with the confirmation of the information I had reported weeks ago. The kidnaping operation was a better success then what I could have hoped for. The operation was pulled off so successfully that I didn't think there would even be too much political upheaval.

* * * *

Two day later we received more confirmation that there were intentions to commit military actions against the United Nations military Forces in East Timor. The Australian detachment that was standing guard at the Nunura River bridge was attacked by men who snuck up on the Australian position and threw a hand grenade into the sandbagged guardhouse. Fortunately for the Australians, the grenade went into one large window of the guardhouse and then out the back window. The grenade exploded harmlessly a few meters away.

The Australian soldiers actually saw the four-man team as they approached from the nearby Indonesian border. The soldiers did not fire on the four-men because the United Nations rules of engagement state that UN soldiers cannot fire on anyone that does not pose an immediate threat. The soldiers saw weapons in the hands of these men but they never saw the men raise the weapons to shoot so the soldiers couldn't fire.

After the grenade exploded the Australian soldiers had the four men in their sights and could have killed them. They still saw rifles in the hands of the running men as they were quickly returning to Indonesia a hundred meters away. The soldiers did not fire because the United Nations rules of engagement forbid the shooting of anyone who was not posing an immediate threat at the time of the shooting. These four men tried to kill those Australian soldiers moments ago but because they were now no longer a threat the soldiers couldn't shoot.

Needless to say, the following day the United Nations rules of engagement were the same but the UN rules were now superseded by the Australian military rules of engagement, which meant the next time Australians was attacked there would be some hell for the attackers to pay.

Like turning on a faucet, suddenly there was a constant flow of documented incidents involving uniformed and well armed Militia guerillas all through the two East Timor Districts that border Indonesia. Bobonaro district was getting the brunt of this Militia activity but Kova Lima district to the south of Bobonaro district would realize the greatest loss.

Australian tracking teams were following the tracks of Militia units on several occasions. One tracking team followed the tracks of what they believed was twenty men. They lost the trail of tracks when they reached the outskirts of Maliana and the men they were tracking walked on the paved streets of Maliana. That was a little close to home.

From time to time we started hearing the deeply accented voice of a man who spoke over the police frequencies of our newly acquired police radios. The voice over the radio would always say something along the line of, "We know where you police are. We will kill you police. We will kill you all if you don't leave."

There were a few "by-chance" encounters between UN military forces and marauding Militia units that resulted in a quick exchange of gunfire and an occasional hand grenade explosion. Most of these encounters resulted in no casualties on either side.

One such encounter happened about halfway up the big mountain just east of Maliana. The "contact" was short but fieriest. Everyone in Maliana could hear the many gunshots and hand grenade explosions. The muzzle flashes and bright light from the exploding grenades was easily seen from Maliana in the near dark sky of this early evening.

Within an hour of the violent firefight we had witnessed, Donny and I were paid a visit by the United Nations Bobonaro District Administrator. We had been warning the UN civilian workers in Maliana about the growing threat of

Militia units operating in the area. This district administrator acted as though he was just now finding out about the threat.

Johnny, the district administrator, stopped his UN Land Rover in front of the American house veranda where Donny and I sat drinking a beer. He quickly got out of the car and approached us. I could see the panic in Johnny's eyes. I could hear the panic in his voice as he excitedly asked us if we had seen what had happened up the mountain. Before we could answer, Johnny continued, "The Militia are here! They are right here right now! You got to do something to protect us!"

Johnny was an experienced United Nations worker. He was in his forties, of slender build and about five-foot-ten-inches tall. His thinning black hair was always well-groomed. His Italian accent gave away his native homeland. He had served in other countries around the world that were more violent than this little firefight in the mountain. I was surprised that Johnny was so panicked.

As I stood up and walked into the American house kitchen area, I heard Donny tell Johnny, "We had known the Militia was here for several weeks. You have known it too. You and I have discussed the security of the Civilian UN staff who live in Maliana."

By the end of Donny's statement to Johnny, I walked back onto the veranda carrying a folding chair and a cold beer. I handed both of the items to Johnny who looked like he really needed a beer. Johnny opened the can of beer and sat on the chair. He sighed, "Yes, I have known the Militia was here, but I just didn't realize they were a threat until tonight."

I walked over to Mac and Zak's veranda to let Donny handle calming Johnny down. I liked Johnny, but I didn't have the patience to deal with someone who was out of touch with this type of reality. I sat and talked with the guys who were hanging out in front of the Kiwi house, Mac and Zak's veranda, until I was tired enough to go to sleep.

The next morning I met with the AMFI who told me what happened in the mountain the night before. An Australian platoon had bumped headlong into a Militia unit who was going the opposite direction. The Australian platoon opened fire on the Militia unit who also opened fire as they flashed through an "immediate action drill" (IA).

The AMFI TL shook his head then said, "The encounter was less than ten feet apart in heavy jungle. The platoon fired over two hundred rounds of small arms fire and threw five grenades. There were no bodies found or even a blood trail. They didn't kill anything other than trees and bushes." The good thing was that the Militia had fired many rounds and thrown at least one grenade and they didn't hit any of the Australians, either.

* * * *

Segrada Familia elements in East Timor were in the field day and night as they tried to establish the movements and locations of the Militia units. The strategy was to identify the militia's positions and then give that information to the United Nations miltary forces so they could close in and capture or kill the Militia members. It would have been easier if the Segrada Familia could have neutralized the Militia units when they found them but even these special operators couldn't go up against assault rifles and hand grenades with bow and arrows.

La Faik collected a tremendous amount of information from West Timor through the Turiskai cell "mailbox" at the Tunubibi illegal market. One piece of information that was exceptionally valuable came through the illegal market mailbox from Emeu, who was on the secret mission into Kupang, West Timor. The information from Emeu was six two-way radio frequencies that the Militia units were using.

La Faik had a scanning two-way radio that was capable of programming radio frequencies. La Faik immediately began to monitor the six frequencies. He soon established that the frequencies were in fact being used by Militia. Eventually, he was able to figure out the timing patterns and frequency changes of the Militia infiltrators.

Signal intelligence (SigInt) organizations such as Americas NSA would laugh at this very crude SigInt operation; however, it was the best we had to work with. Most of the enemy communications over the radio was in code; however, some of it was not. The information that we were able to get from the radio communications became important pieces of a puzzle when those communications was blended with information from other sources.

* * * *

It was about this time period when I was given a mysterious message from someone further up the "food chain." Bantam and Snapper had ended their missions in East Timor and returned to Australia. My American brother,

Donny, was appointed as the Bobonaro district commander. One night after Donny returned from a meeting in Dili, he wanted to talk to me alone. I had been sitting on the veranda where Mac and Zak lived. Mac, Zak, one new Gambian police officer, two new Argentinean police officers, and I were drinking beer together.

I walked with Donny to the veranda of the American house where we could talk alone. Donny told me that he was told to give me a message. The message Donny gave me was, "With the increased activities of the believed Militia guerillas, there is a much more desperate need for real and hard intelligence. Do whatever is possible to provide hard intelligence. There would be no questions asked as to how you collect the information."

Of course I wanted to know who this message was from and of course Donny was "sworn to secrecy." Donny added, "You are to give your reports to me in a sealed envelope. Do not give any reports to the SID office. Also, I am to give you any support that you need. So what do you need?"

I recognized what was happening right away. Whoever sent this message was using the same tactic I used when I wanted to distance myself from an operator who was in danger of being captured during an operation. I told Donny, "I don't need anything."

I sat on the American house veranda for a long time thinking about what I had gotten myself into. I was already directly involved with an organization that was running several espionage operations inside the borders of Indonesia, including kidnaping. There was equal intensity with the Segrada Familia operations on the East Timor side of the border as well. As the West Timor cells rooted up names of suspected SGI operators who were living in East Timor, Segrada Familia conducted surveillance of the suspects to establish their contacts. In some cases, the SGI suspected assets were openly questioned.

Sometimes the asset could be used as a conduit to deliver misdirecting information to the SGI. Others were considered to be of little threat and were monitored only. La Faik had told me that there was one SGI asset who had managed to penetrate into the outer edge of the Segrada Familia. This man gave information to the SGI that nearly caused the destruction of the Turiskai cell. One man lost his wife and children to the control of the Halilintar Militia based in Turiskai. This SGI asset was eventually murdered in his home.

La Faik never said who the man was or even what village he lived in but I was fairly certain it was a man who was murdered in his home one Sunday in Aidabasalala Village. The Maliana investigators who handled that case told me the details of this murder. I knew this wasn't the normal killing of a Militia member. That murder in Aidabasalala was a planned-out organized "hit."

So far my only infractions of the United Nations rules of conduct was "guilty knowledge," some planning of operations, and occasionally giving a ride to a group of guys going someplace that it was better that I didn't know where they were going. I was already deeper involved than whoever sent that message to me through Donny probably realized. Now I was considering becoming actively involved. I would have to think about that for a while.

* * * *

La Faik's combined teams of the Turiskai cell and the East Timor Segrada Familia operators who kidnaped the Militia member from the Tunubibi illegal market didn't stop with the one kidnaping. They snatched two more Militia members on two different days following the first kidnaping. Both "snatches" were smoothly executed and the AMFI wound up interrogating both kidnaped men.

The two additional kidnaping led to the political upheaval that I had feared would happen. The Indonesian military was infuriated that "Indonesian citizens," as they called the East Timorese Militia thugs, were being stolen by the Australian military. I thought, *I don't know what the Indonesians are so upset about. The Australians gave the kidnaped men back to the Indonesians after a few days.*

The AMFI TL and two of his team members sat with me on the American house veranda one night. They were telling me about the kidnaping and all the trouble that this aggressive action was causing for both the United Nations and the UN military commanders. The TL then gave a little chuckle as he said, "We don't mind. We have been getting some good information from the kidnaped victims."

The TL looked at me solemnly for a moment before he continued, "Sector West High Command is sending some investigators up here to get to the bottom of these kidnaping accusations. I would strongly suggest the kidnaping stop, for a while anyway."

It was apparent that the AMFI suspected that I had something to do with the kidnaping operations. I knew about the first one but I had no idea about the next two kidnaping until the AMFI told me about them. I responded, "I don't have any control over what the East Timorese do any more than you guys. The crime is occurring in Indonesia. What is up with the TNI that they can't catch whoever is snatching these Militia?"

The TL thought for a minute then said, "Good point. Why haven't they caught any of the kidnapers?"

I warned La Faik about the Australian military Investigators who would be closely looking into these kidnaping cases. La Faik's response was, "I don't care who they send or who they talk to. Nobody involved is going to tell them anything."

La Faik was right. United Nations rules of conduct didn't apply to East Timorese citizens. Any criminal investigations would come up empty handed. No Segrada Familia operator is going to give up information during a normal interview.

La Faik's elements had pulled off two more successful kidnaping; however, the two TNI soldiers were coming under a lot of suspicion from their commanders. It was time to stop the kidnaping. To this day, I am still amazed that nobody involved with these kidnaping operations ever got caught, especially the two TNI soldiers. I suspect there were TNI commanders who equally didn't like the Halilintar Militia members. Those commanders must have been turning a blind eye to what their soldiers were doing.

As for me, I was still wrestling with just how much more active I was going to get in this intelligence game. I really wasn't scared of getting caught. According to the mysterious message I received through Donny, nobody was going to be asking me any questions, which I never believed. I wasn't scared of getting caught because I would only work with Segrada Familia elements. I would never directly involve international outsiders.

I didn't know it yet, but there would be two incidents that would push me over the line that separated the sidelines from the playing field. That violent "nudge" over that line was coming very soon.

CHAPTER EIGHT

Attack on Aidabasalala

Todd looked hard through his night-vision goggles that hung in front of his eyes from the nylon straps that secured the goggles to his head under his helmet. Aidabasalala Village has no electricity so the interior of the village is dark throughout the night hours. Early in the evenings, people who lived in the many huts and few scattered concrete homes burned oil lamps or candles, which gave a small amount of light to the otherwise darkness of the night. By eleven o'clock at night, the last of the crude home lighting devices was extinguished as the citizens of Aidabasalala Village slept.

Todd was a young private in the Australian Army. A couple of months back, the Australian military established a platoon position in this very remote valley village. There had been many reports of Militia infiltration activity in the area. Most of those reports were not credible; however, the Australians decided to create a presence in the Aidabasalala area so that they could directly monitor activities throughout the area.

The platoon set up their base position in a small school complex that was not being used. They moved into the two concrete buildings of the school grounds. Barbed wire and concertina wire marked the platoon position perimeter. They built two small sandbagged positions on either side of the small compound to protect whoever was on sentry duty.

The Aidabasalala platoon situation was different on this night. There was a report of four uniformed and armed Militia sighted by villagers in the area of Moliana Village, which is about five-kilometers north of Maliana city. The AMFI investigated the report and found TNI boot prints in the area. The TNI boot prints led north into the Atabae Forest. The north edge of the Atabae Forest is a short distance south of Aidabasalala Village.

By now the various United Nations Militaries were taking any reports of Militia activities very seriously. The Australians launched a Force from the Maliana based company of soldiers to sweep the Atabae Forest for the Militia unit that entered the Atabae Forest from Moliana Village. Two of the three Sections of the platoon that was based in Aidabasalala were sent about half-kilometer to the south of Aidabasalala to establish a hidden static position on the north side of the Atabae Forest. The plan was to drive the Militia unit out of the Atabae Forest and into the waiting rifle sights of the Aidabasalala Platoon.

There was one section of soldiers along with two armored personnel carriers (APCs) and crews to secure the platoon established position in Aidabasalala Village. One section of Australian soldiers supported by the two machine guns on each APC is much more firepower then what would be needed against any of the six to twelve man individual Militia units now scattered throughout the two East Timor districts that border Indonesia.

* * * *

Todd began his sentry-duty watch at 0200 hours. Todd and his section leader were in the sandbagged guard post that overlooked the west side of their platoon perimeter. By now both soldiers were straining hard to see through their night vision goggles. Todd had seen a movement near a hut that was twenty meters straight west of them. A moment later he saw movement near the hut just south of the first movement seen. The village animals didn't move around at this time of night. It was possible that someone could have come out of one of the huts to take a piss but it was highly unlikely that two people would have come outside to take a piss from two different homes that were side by side and at the same time.

The section leader decided to put the whole section on alert status. The section leader walked the short distance from the guard post to the concrete building that acted as a barracks for the platoon. He announced the "alert" to the few sleeping men that was curled up on their thin foam sleeping pads inside the building. These young soldiers quickly got up, grabbed their weapons and started going to their defensive positions along the perimeter. As the section leader stepped outside of the barracks he heard a thud, followed by another thud a moment later.

At first the section leader thought the sound was a coconut falling out of a tree and hitting the ground. The section leader quickly remembered that there are no coconut trees near the platoon position. The section leader was knocked off his feet by the blast of the grenade that ripped the air a few meters away at the front of the barracks.

Before the team leader could get up off the ground, a second explosion rocked the barracks. Automatic rifle fire tore at the ground, buildings and sandbags all through the tiny military compound. More explosions erupted next to one APC that was parked in a defensive position on the perimeter. Dozens of bullets hit the sides and front of the APC.

Then there were explosions beside the other APC which was parked at another perimeter position. Bullets were hitting the iron hull of that APC too. Todd's M-60 machine gun chattered continuously. At first Todd's weapon was the only weapon returning fire. He was feeling pretty lonely as he put up a one man defense from his sandbagged guard house.

Todd felt better as he heard an Australian Styer assault rifle open up on the enemy from his right side. Soon two more Australian's were firing from Todd's left side. Todd felt the concussion of a grenade that exploded behind him but he never quit firing that M-60.

Todd watched the bright red tracer rounds that flashed from his machine gun's muzzle. The tracers moved straight and quick for twenty to thirty meters but then the red glowing bullets appeared to begin a dance as they bounced off the ground, rocks and the sides of some of the concrete homes that were nearby.

Todd was putting the full firepower of his weapon into the muzzle flashes that he saw flickering in the darkness. There were so many flashes all along the front of the western side of the perimeter that Todd couldn't keep up. He fired into one area of muzzle flashes then another and then another. Then there were more flashes from where Todd had just fired.

The attack ended as quickly as it had begun. Suddenly all the muzzle flashes stopped. The Australians fired on for a few seconds in hopes of hitting the apparently withdrawing enemy. A few seconds later the section leader yelled above the din of firing weapons. The Australian weapons fell silent.

* * * *

Augustinho Bili Tai walked through the dark jungle that grew between the river and the road. The road ran north and south through the center of Aidabasalala Village. The road continued south of Aidabasalala Village, ending at the Atabae Forest. The same road ran to the north of Aidabasalala for five kilometers, ending at Ouipua mountain. The river flowed to the north and was about thirty-meters east of the road. The river was the dividing line between Cailaco and Atabae sub-districts of Bobonaro district.

Bili Tai was feeling the rush of adrenaline from the attack on the Australian platoon position in Aidabasalala Village just a few minutes ago. Bili Tai was moving his combined Militia units through the jungle at a normal pace. He knew that the Australians in Aidabasalala would not be able to pursue him. Bili Tai also knew that the Australian Reaction Force in Marko Village would be coming into Aidabasalala from the East. They moved to the north, which was going away from the large concentration of Australian Forces now in the Atabae Forest.

* * * *

The plans for this vicious attack on the Australian military in Aidabasalala began the moment the Australian platoon began to establish their permanent compound. There were several Militia informants who lived in Aidabasalala Village. Once the information about the platoon's presence in Aidabasalala reached West Timor there was great concern among the Halilintar Militia. The platoon's presence in Aidabasalala was intolerable.

Aidabasalala was an important strategic location for the current and future Militia operations. Aidabasalala and the handful of smaller villages to the north had always been "Militia villages," which meant that most of the people who lived there were either Militia members or families of Militia members. On top of this one of the Halilintar top leaders, Paulo Gonsalves, was from a village just north of Aidabasalala. What all this amounted to was "The Australians had to go."

SGI Assets were sent to Aidabasalala to begin the preparations for the attack. The Assets studied the Australians activities day and night. They recorded every detail of everything that they saw. Eventually the SGI Assets created situations that would cause immediate reactions of the Aidabasalala platoon and the platoon's parent company located in Marko Village just a few kilometers to the east.

The SGI assets were eventually reinforced and began putting pressure on the current Fretilin party established "Nurep," Paulo Jose ("Nurep" is a government leader). Paulo was easy for the SGI to control. Paulo was a sincere political leader; however, he had become involved with some other men from Atabeleten Village who exploited the greedy side of Paulo.

Paulo traded his good values for money little by little as he began to extort money, food, and other possessions from the very people that he was given responsibility to take care of. This was a massive opportunity for the SGI assets who were sent to manipulate Paulo Jose.

Eventually more SGI assets were sent as the time drew near for the inevitable attack on the lone platoon in Aidabasalala. These assets would locate approach and escape routes for the attacking forces. They would also assist with the coordination of the combined Militia units that would conduct the attack.

Augustinho Bili Tai was given the responsibility to command the attack. Bili Tai had returned to Turiskai with his team to rest and re-supply. His return to East Timor was delayed as he studied all the collected information. He was meeting day and night with Abilio De Araujo, the Halilintar Militia operations commander and Paulo Gonsalves, who is a Halilintar Militia commander from the Aidabasalala area.

Finally the plans for the attack were complete. Bili Tai led his now-reinforced team of nine men back into East Timor. Two days later Bili Tai's team linked up with Rodino who was commanding an eight-man team operating in Lailaco mountain east of Maliana. Bili Tai took command of both teams.

Bili Tai led both teams to Ouipua mountain, which is north of Aidabasalala. Ouipua mountain was not as large of a mountain as Lailaco but the mountain was so rugged that nobody lived there. Martinho and his twelve-man Militia team who were operating in Atabae Sub-District were waiting for Bili Tai in Ouipua mountain when Bili Tai's combined Cailaco teams arrived. The SGI Assets who were responsible to identify the approach and escape routes for the attack soon arrived in Ouipua. Augustinho Bili Tai took command of all the elements present.

The next few days were filled with planning sessions and training to fuse the combined elements into one Force. Finally Bili Tai was satisfied that the combined teams were ready. He announced that they would launch the attack in two days. The SGI Assets with Bili Tai in Ouipua mountain radioed the SGI Assets monitoring the Australians in Aidabasalala to tell them the attack was "a go" in two days' time. The SGI Monitoring team prepared for their part of the attack.

The SGI Monitoring team slipped out of the village the following day. The four-man monitoring team walked deep into the Atabae Forest to where they had hidden four sets of TNI camouflage uniforms and combat boots. The men changed into the uniforms. They picked up four carved wooden rifles that was hidden with the uniforms then walked to the south side of the forest. The four men had to move through the forest very carefully for fear of bumping into an Australian patrol.

During the last hour of daylight the four men moved close to Moliana Village and made sure that they were seen by some local villagers. The four men walked in a single file formation through the flat open area three hundred yards northeast of Moliana Village before disappearing back into the forest.

The four man monitoring team then returned to Aidabasalala Village after changing back into their civilian cloths. The following day in the early morning several of the soldiers at the Aidabasalala compound were seen climbing into the two APCs. The soldiers were carrying full packs so the SGI Assets knew that the soldiers would not be back in Aidabasalala tonight. The APCs drove the soldiers south toward the Atabae Forest. The APCs returned to the Aidabasalala platoon position early in the afternoon.

The SGI Monitoring team radioed the SGI attack support team who was still with Bili Tai and his forces in Ouipua mountain. The information from the monitoring team told Bili Tai that the Australians in Aidabasalala were ripe for the picking. Two hours later the SGI attack support team led the three combined Halilintar Militia units under the Command of Augustinho Bili Tai toward Aidabasalala for the purpose of killing the few Australian soldiers still at the tiny compound.

* * * *

Everything seemed to be pointing to something "big" that was in the making. The Turiskai cell had reported the many meetings between Abilio, Paulo, and Bili Tai. The Segrada Familia elements monitoring Militia activities in Lailaco mountain became aware that Bili Tai had met with Rodino's team upon Bili Tai's return to East Timor. The Lailaco mountain Elements then tracked Rodino's and Bili Tai's teams as they moved together toward Atabae sub-district.

One month ago, La Faik had heard that there were several SGI Operatives in Aidabasalala Village. La Faik could no longer trust Paulo Jose, the Aidabasalala Nurep, so he could only insert a couple of his elements into Aidabasalala Village to try and figure out who the SGI operatives were and what they were doing.

The enemy radio communications that La Faik snatched out of the air was heavily coded; however, by this time La Faik had received some of the Militia code from Emeu, La Faik's element in Kupang, through the Turiskai cell's "mailbox."

A combination of the information coming in from the Turiskai cell, the East Timor operators in Lailaco mountain, the two elements in Aidabasalala and the snatched radio messages convinced La Faik that the Militia was going to conduct some type of aggressive action somewhere near Marko Village or possibly Aidabasalala Village. La Faik didn't think the hostile action would be in Aidabasalala because there was nothing there to attack other than the Australian platoon. Forty well armed men is a dangerous bite to try and chew for the Militia so La Faik believed that the Marko area was the target.

I was turning in reports of the information that I was getting from La Faik but by the time I doctored up the information to disguise where the information was coming from the information was rated as F-6, which meant that the credibility of the information could not be judged.

The AMFI TL that I had worked so well with had recently rotated back to Australia. His replacement was a good intelligence commander, but unfortunately he was not as "user-friendly" for me. Had the first team leader still been in Maliana, I could have talked to him more openly about the information we were collecting.

The afternoon before the attack La Faik was fairly certain that there was going to be a strong hostile action committed either that night or the following day. La Faik was guessing the hostile action would be in the form of an ambush of either military or United Nations personnel along some lonely roadway.

I returned to the Maliana Station in the early evening with all these pieces of information swarming through my head. I told Donny as much as I could about the information and suggested that he advice the United Nations security unit so that they could issue travel restrictions on all UN movement throughout Bobonaro district.

I had tried to contact the AMFI team leader at the Maliana company compound but the entire AMFI team was supporting the operations in the Atabae Forest. I started to suggest to Donny that he contact the Australian company commander at the Maliana compound and tell the commander that I believed that a Militia attack was eminent. The problem with that was we would be violating all the chain of command and chain of information flow rules in the book.

The other problem was that the company commander did not know me. All he would hear is, "This guy who you don't know has information that cannot be verified that makes him believe there is going to be a Militia attack sometime over the next twenty-four hours somewhere in the Marko or Aidabasalala area."

Donny and I discussed whether to break the chain of command or not. Eventually Donny decided he was obligated to go talk to the company commander, which he did later that night.

The next morning the new AMFI team leader and three of his teammates were on the veranda of Donny's and my American house wanting to talk to me right away. Donny woke up every morning before daylight for the entire year that I lived with him in Maliana. I never got out of my mosquito dome bed before seven o'clock in the morning unless there was a good reason.

The sky was just beginning to brighten as the new day approached Maliana. Donny sat on the back veranda of the American house smoking a cigarette and drinking the instant coffee he made. Two military Land Rovers pulled around the back of the American house and stopped in the driveway in front of Donny. Four men wearing Australian military uniforms climbed out of the two four-wheel drive vehicles and approached Donny.

Donny knew three of the AMFI soldiers who approached him from the past several weeks of the men coming to visit me here at the American house. Donny had not met the new team leader before this morning. As the men stepped up onto the concrete floor of the veranda Donny sat quietly studying the four men.

The soldiers looked haggard. Their uniforms were dirty, which told Donny that these men had been in the jungle. Donny commented to the men as they approached, "You boys are up early this morning."

The new team leader responded, "We haven't been to bed yet."

He then extended his hand to Donny and introduced himself. Donny shook the man's hand and told the new TL his name. The team leader asked, "Could we speak with Jim?"

Donny realized that these men were here on important business. Normally he would have joked with the men about having to wake me up early. Donny stood up from the chair where he was sitting. He walked into the kitchen area then pounded on my bedroom door saying, "You got some friends here who need to talk to you. I think it's important."

I struggled to wake up at first. I unzipped my mosquito dome opening and rolled off my air mattress onto the cement floor beside my mosquito dome. I slipped on my pants then wandered out onto the back veranda. Donny had furnished a bench and two chairs, which the four soldiers now sat on comfortably. The four men greeted me with a couple of, "Good mornings," one nod of the head and one "Must be nice to sleep till noon every day."

I responded to the men by raising my hand with my index finger extended as a visual sign that told them, "Wait a minute."

I stepped off the veranda and around the corner of the American house and took a piss. By the time I got back on the veranda, Donny was bringing cups of coffee to the four soldiers. He even brought me a cup of steaming instant coffee that demanded me to say something cute, "It's about time you started waiting on me."

Donny responded to my comment as he walked away, "Fuck you, buffalo man."

The AMFI team leader looked at me and asked, "buffalo man?"

I explained, "A couple of weeks ago I went on a day-long operation with a section of Kiwis up in the Bobonaro mountains. Our interpreter Domingos went with us. It was the typical mountain adventure of walking up and down rough mountain trails, crossing wild rivers and getting rained on."

I took a sip of my coffee and lit a cigarette before continuing my story, "When we got back to Bobonaro I looked at Domingos and then at myself. Domingos' clothes and shoes hardly had any mud on them. I was covered in mud from the waist down. So I asked Domingos how he could be so clean after walking the same path that I walked. Domingos told me, 'Yes, I noticed that you walk through the mountain like a water buffalo.'"

I paused for a moment, then added, "The name stuck."

I looked at the team leader and asked, "So what's on your mind?"

The team leader said, "The platoon in Aidabasalala was attacked last night. They hit them real hard."

I asked, "Anyone dead?"

The team leader answered, "No, but it's a miracle. The barracks was badly damaged by hand grenade blasts. Two APCs were damaged by grenade blasts too. There were some minor wounds but nothing serious."

I thought for a moment then asked, "How about the bad guys, any bodies?"

The team leader shook his head then said, "The company commander told me that you knew the attack was going to happen last night. We need to talk to your source or sources of information."

I clarified the team leader's information, "I knew the Militia was getting ready to attack something. I had no idea that they would attack that platoon in Aidabasalala."

The team leader was becoming demanding as he said, "We need to talk to your sources, now."

I looked back into the team leader's eyes as I said, "I can't do that. You know that."

The team leader calmly said, "Those Militia are trying to kill us. They have attacked our position at the Nunura Bridge twice and now they have conducted a very serious attack at one of our platoon positions."

I nodded my head in understanding as I said, "Go talk to Senior Alfredo."

There were several sources of information that the AMFI and I both talked to. Senior Alfredo was one of those sources. Senior Alfredo and I had become close friends as time went on. Senior Alfredo was a Fretilin leader from the Cailaco area but was living in Maliana. He was not involved with the espionage operations; however, La Faik trusted him enough to tell him a lot of information. Of course this was for the purpose of using Senior Alfredo's Fretilin resources from time to time.

La Faik was wise enough to know that the day may come when I was pressured to "give up" the name of my source of information. La Faik, Senior Alfredo, and I worked out this plan several weeks ago. If I ever had to give the name of my source I would give Senior Alfredo's name. Senior Alfredo would take care of the rest.

Armed with the name of my source of information the team leader and his AMFI members left the American House in route to speak with Senior Alfredo. I quickly got cleaned up, dressed, and then went to meet La Faik. We had a lot of work to do. The news of the strong Militia attack on the Australians in Aidabasalala was what pushed me over the edge.

A couple of weeks before this attack we had received word that a Kiwi soldier had been killed in Kova Lima district. A section of Kiwis was on a patrol in the remote areas of Kova Lima district when villagers told the section leader that they had just seen Militia men a short distance away. The section leader radioed in the information then led his section to where the Militia had been seen.

Up to this point and time the Militia had always runaway from any approaching UN military patrols. This time the Militia unit set up an ambush. As the Kiwis walked into the "kill zone" of the ambush, the Militia opened up with everything they had. The Kiwis flashed through an IA (immediate action response to the ambush), which meant the Kiwis unleashed all their fire-power at the ambushers while they quickly and systematically withdrew from the ambush site.

Young Private Manning didn't make it out. His body was recovered when the Kiwi rapid reaction unit along with Private Manning's section swept back into the ambush site. The 5.56 machine gun that Private Manning carried was gone.

PTE Leonard William Manning of the New Zealand Armed Forces was killed in action on 24 July, 2000, at 1730 hours. Nobody in East Timor felt the pain of his death more than his section; however, all military and police personnel grieved for this young soldier who was first to die in combat in East Timor. First came the grief, next came the desire to pay the Militia back.

I had two urgent matters on my mind as I drove up to Cailaco to see La Faik that day. One was that I had made up my mind to do whatever I could to get some payback against these marauding Militia units. The other thing on my mind was that I was driving into the same area where the Militia who attacked the Australians the night before most likely was now. I drove cautiously scanning the area I was driving through for any sign of an ambush.

CHAPTER NINE

Ghost Soldiers

Cpl. Lance slowly climbed up the large rocks that protruded from the steep side of Lailaco mountain. This was in the area of Lailaco mountain known as The Manapa Jungle. Cpl. Lance was the point-man of the Australians Charlie Company Sixth Regiment Platoon that was on a patrol in Lailaco mountain. The sun was high in the sky but its rays were powerless to penetrate the heavy foliage of the tall trees that grew on the side of this mountain.

The platoon had been driven to the west base of Lailaco mountain early this morning in APCs. The platoon rushed out of the APCs as the rear ramps dropped open. The soldiers quickly moved a few meters to the front, rear and both sides of the APC convoy then dropped on the ground into firing positions as they formed a perimeter security screen that encompassed the five APCs that brought the soldiers to this mountain.

Within moments of the platoon's arrival the platoon commander gave the order to move out. The soldiers got to their feet and began their cautious ascent up the mountain as the APCs drove away. The platoon's objective was to seek out a Militia unit that was believed to be operating in that area of the mountain. Everyone in the platoon knew that the enemy was close.

The platoon snaked its way up the mountain through heavy jungle all day long. Since the Militia attack on the platoon in Aidabasalala soldiers and their commanders knew that the strength of a full platoon was not a deterrent of a Militia attack. A platoon was more like a target for a Militia attack.

As Cpl. Lance reached the top of a two-hundred-foot-high rocky face on the side of this mountain it was about 1400 hours. From the rocky face that Cpl. Lance just climbed the terrain changed to a slight incline for about one-hundred-meters before again becoming a steep climb. The soldiers of this Charlie

Company platoon was carrying full packs, which made their days work of climbing a mountain while looking for a very real and dangerous enemy an exhausting ordeal.

Cpl. Lance continued his slow walk along the side of a mountain stream that flowed from the height's above them. This was the only way that Cpl. Lance could take the platoon who followed him without using a machete to cut a path through the dense jungle that grew on both sides of the rocky stream.

Cpl. Lance was about to step into the rocky streambed when his section leader signaled him. The platoon commander had called for a lunch break. The platoon melted into the floor of the jungle as they formed a security perimeter. The whole platoon seemed to disappear into the terrain as half the platoon quietly removed ration packs to eat while the other half maintained platoon security.

Cpl. Lance calmly lay on the ground in the jungle at the edge of the stream. His "arc of responsibility" was to the front looking up the mountain stream. As the first half of the platoon ate Cpl. Lance kept a diligent watch for danger. Fifteen minutes later Cpl. Lance saw movement in the streambed. A few moments later Cpl. Lance could see that the movement he saw was men slowly walking down the steep streambed.

At first it was difficult to distinguish who these people were because of the dark shadows from the high trees that blocked the sun. Soon the walking men came close enough that Cpl. Lance could see the rifles that they carried. He signaled the soldier who was a few feet behind him but it was too late to pass on information. The time to act was now and Cpl Lance knew it.

By now Cpl. Lance could clearly see the approaching men who were only twenty-five-meters away walking in the streambed toward him. There were six men wearing TNI camouflage uniforms. Five of the enemy soldiers were carrying their assault rifles in the "ready" position. The enemy point-man carried his rifle raised in the firing position. The point-man held the butt of his rifle against his shoulder as he pointed the muzzle to wherever he was looking as he scanned the streambed in front of him and the jungle to both sides of the streambed.

Cpl. Lance had this very alert Militia point-man in his sights as he exhaled slowly to relax his tightening chest. Cpl. Lance ever so slowly began to squeeze the trigger of his Styer assault rifle. He didn't feel fear. His chest tightened because of the adrenaline that surged through his entire being. The same type of adrenaline that a deer-hunter feels when he is about to kill that trophy buck.

Cpl. Lance knew he was about to kill the enemy and it felt good. This is what he was trained to do but more importantly Cpl. Lance was about to get some payback against the Militia that have terrorized every human being in East Timor for months now.

As Cpl. Lance completed his calming exhale he also completed the gentle squeeze of his rifles trigger. Three metal 5.56 bullets screamed from his rifles muzzle. The enemy point-man walking in the streambed never knew what hit him as all three bullets from Cpl Lances rifle struck him in the chest, knocking him backward off his feet. The man was dead as he fell onto the rocks of the streambed, his heart destroyed by one of those bullets that tore through his body.

The reaction of the Militia unit was instantaneous. Without thought the five remaining Militia raised their weapons and opened fire to the front and sides of where they now stood. Cpl. Lance didn't flinch. As he saw the point-man drop he raised the muzzle of his weapon until his sights were on the next Militia that was a little higher in the streambed. The next burst of automatic fire from the muzzle of Cpl. Lance's rifle hit and dropped the second Militia too.

Suddenly the ground near the Australians was rocked by exploding grenades. The three remaining Militia had thrown grenades and continued to fire their rifles on full automatic, spraying the entire jungle around them with deadly lead while they quickly retreated back up that streambed. The Australian soldiers who had a "line of sight" on the Militia in the streambed opened fire on the now fleeing Militia. The whole firefight was over in less than two minutes.

Twenty-minutes later the platoon began a sweep operation up the streambed. One section swept the left side of the streambed while the second section swept the other side. The remaining section swept up the streambed itself. The section sweeping the streambed found the dead body of the Militia point-man; however, the second Militia who Cpl. Lance shot was not where he fell. The soldiers in the streambed knew the second Militia was badly hurt. They saw a lot of blood and small pieces of body tissue on the rocks.

The platoon slowly swept up the mountain. They didn't know if the Militia would keep running or if they would set up a counter-ambush. Two-hundred-meters up the streambed they found the body of a Militia soldier. His body was draped over his assault rifle in a hidden position on the left side of the streambed. He obviously could not continue to run so he planned to ambush the Australians who would certainly be coming up this mountain streambed in pursuit of their fleeing enemy. The wounded Militia soldier didn't live long enough to execute his "last stand" ambush.

As the section in the streambed continued up the stream from the second Militia body they saw blood splattered on the rocks. This told the soldiers that at least one more of the fleeing Militia soldiers were wounded. By this time there was less than one-hour of daylight left. The platoon pulled back to a defensible position and prepared for the night.

* * * *

I was with the AMFI team when we got the news about the firefight in Lailaco mountain. News of a firefight between Militia units and United Nations military Contingents was nothing out of the ordinary. This time the news of a firefight had a happy ending. The firefight results were two Militia confirmed dead and at least one more wounded, no friendly-forces casualties.

Three of the AMFI soldiers and I were in the Atabae Forest following the footprints of a Militia unit that was seen near Moliana about mid-morning today. The TL was carrying the team radio when the squelch broke. The voice on the other end was calling, "Dingo one Dingo one this Charlie base, over." Dingo is the call sign for the AMFI. Dingo One is the AMFI TL. We were walking in a single-file formation through the steamy hot jungle. The TL was walking in the second position about twenty-feet behind the point-man. I was in the third position about thirty-feet behind the TL.

The TL stepped to the right side of the trail and squatted into the foliage as he answered the radio call. I squatted to the left of the trail and covered our left flank. The drag-man covered our rear and of course the point-man covered our front. The TL covered our ride side while he communicated over the radio.

* * * *

The three AMFI soldiers were at the Maliana Station talking with me when they got the radio call from their base about the Militia sighting. We had been studying the Indonesian military map that hung on the front wall of the Maliana Station office. We had sat down at the small table that was now a part of the few items of office equipment that we had acquired. Brad's long legs reached to the opposite side of the table as he stretched out on the wooden chair where he sat. We all grumbled in complaint of Brad taking up all the leg room under the table.

Brad was in his late twenties. He stood over six feet tall and was built like a football player. His short blond hair looked a little darker in the dim light of the Maliana office. His boyish face broke into a smile at our grumbling.

I looked down at Brad's combat boots that protruded to the opposite side of the table and asked, "What size are those boots? They have got to be at least size twelve."

Tim laughed as he added, "All the length went to his feet. His dick got left out of the deal." Brad smiled as the rest of us laughed.

Tim was a young Corporal who had recently joined this team of AMFI. His boyish face was a product of truly being very young, unlike Brad. He was five-foot nine-inches tall with a slim build. His light brown hair was just long enough to give away that his hair was curly.

The playful bantering and laughter abruptly stopped as Charlie Base called Dingo One. The TL answered the radio call. The Charlie Base radio operator relayed the information of the Militia sighting in Moliana. The three AMFI soldiers were anxious to go check out the report but they hesitated. The Atabae Forest was still a hotbed of Militia activity, which meant the sighting would almost assuredly turn out to be true. A quick response to the report was important but that was dangerous ground.

The AMFI team leader said, "There are only three of us. The Charlie Company commander has most of his company out in the field so we can't get any help from Charlie Company."

The team leader looked at the two soldiers with him and then looked at me, "We need another gun."

I looked back at the team leader. We looked at each other in silence for a few moments before I asked, "Sooo—what? You want me to go with you?"

The team leader jumped up from the chair where he was sitting as he said, "Thanks for volunteering. Let's go." Brad, Tim, and I looked at each other questioningly as we too stood up.

The team leader walked to the waiting military Land Rover parked in the driveway followed by his two soldiers and me. I told the team leader as I was climbing into the back of the truck, "You have noticed that the only weapon I have is a nine-millimeter Berretta pistol, right?"

The team leader replied, "That's no problem. You can walk point. The point man usually is the first man hit in an ambush anyway so your weapon isn't important."

I smiled and nodded my head in understanding as I said, "Oooh, okay, I'm the target to draw fire away from you guys."

My three knew teammates laughed as the engine of the Land Rover fired to life. Brad drove out the exit driveway and turned north on the roadway heading to Moliana Village. As we bounced along the rough roadway I asked, "You guys happen to have one of those orange reflective vests for directing traffic? I could put that on so the Militia don't make a mistake and shoot one of you guys instead of me."

The three men responded with laughter and one, "That's a good idea, but no, we don't, sorry."

Upon arriving in Moliana we talked with the several villagers who saw eight men dressed in TNI uniforms and carrying rifles on the edge of the Atabae Forest. After collecting all the information that we could from the witnesses we went to the edge of the Forest to look for boot prints or any other sign of a Militia presence. As expected we did find TNI combat boot prints in the mud near a small stream.

The problem of following tracks that someone has made is that there "is" someone at the other end of those tracks. When that someone is well armed and intend to kill whoever may be stupid enough to follow those tracks it becomes dangerous. Normally a supported platoon would handle a tracking operation. Today it would be four men armed with one 5.56 machine gun, two Styer assault rifles and one Beretta pistol.

The team leader wanted to follow the tracks just far enough to get an idea of where the Militia are going. That was reasonable. The team leader showed mercy on me and put me in the third-position instead of the point-position (the third position" is the third person in the order of March). Brad would walk the point-position.

I had got to know all the men who served on this AMFI team very well. The team members rotated out of the team as they completed six months of service in East Timor. Their rotation dates were staggered so there was always someone rotating home while a new guy rotated in. All of the soldiers I had worked with were fine young men and outstanding soldiers. Every one of them made Australia proud.

I knew Brad best of all the soldiers who currently served on the AMFI team. Brad always got the "Bush" operations when intelligence duties demanded that intelligence personnel accompany a "straight up" military operation. It was Just a few weeks before today that I had been with Brad on a military operation into Letoresi mountain. The Letoresi mountain ops turned out like all the others before it, which was one difficult day.

* * * *

A Militia unit prowling through East Timor had come across five men from a remote village. The Militia knew that anyone who lived in this remote area were either ex-Falintil soldiers or supporters of the ex-Falintil. The Militia never wasted an opportunity to kill their long time enemies. The Militia unit fired on the five men as they approached.

The ex-Falintil soldiers had no weapons so all they could do is escape and evade. One of the five men was killed before he could get out of the "kill zone" of the Militia ambush. A second man was badly wounded but he managed to keep going. The dead ex-Falintil soldier had to be left behind as the four remaining ex-Falintil split into three different directions. One man took the badly wounded ex-soldier with him as they evaded the Militia who may be searching for them.

Late that night we received information about the attack on the five ex-Falintil soldiers. The three uninjured men left their wounded friend in a village where the local medic could treat the man's wounds. The three uninjured men walked six-kilometers to Maliana to report the incident.

The following morning a section of soldiers was flown out to the ambush site accompanied by Brad, Zak, and I. The operation objectives were to process the crime scene of the murder, which included bringing the dead body out with us. Zak was the Chief of Investigations for the Bobonaro district so that was Zak's responsibility. The second objective was to "run a track" on the Militia unit to determine where they were going. We would also locate any other witnesses that may be able to give us information about the Militia unit operating in Letoresi mountain.

This was supposed to be an easy operation that should only take a couple of hours on the ground. The Ambush site was on the edge of a little grassy valley between Letoresi mountain and Lailaco mountain. The two Iroquois helicopters could drop us off right into that valley (Iroquois helicopters are known as "Hueys" to Americans).

I was reminded of Vietnam War news footage as I sat on the floor of the Iroquois helicopter with my feet dangling out the side. The helicopters swirling rotor blades increased the whopping sound as the aircraft flared just above the tall grass of Letoresi valley. The door gunners sat behind their M-60 machine guns ready to fire at anything that threatened this insertion.

Soon the skids touched the ground. We slid out of the aircraft and onto the ground. I could see the men piling out of the Iroquois helicopter that had landed in front of us as I dropped into a prone security position in the dry grass.

Within a matter of seconds I could feel the strong wind tearing at my back as the helicopter that brought us to this hot valley poured on the collective. The tall grass slapped my face and dust engulfed me as the Iroquois raised off the ground, nosed forward and then shot out of the valley. Then it was quiet.

The dust raised by the helicopter's exit quickly settled. The section leader barked out an order. The men of the section, along with us "tag-alongs" got on our feet and started a cautious movement across the valley floor. The sun's burning rays were unabated from the cloudless sky above.

By the time we reached the trees at the base of Letoresi mountain a hand full of local villagers approached us as they walked down from the mountain. Brad and I interviewed the villagers as Zak looked over the ambush site. By the time we finished we had a good idea what we were up against.

The Militia unit was only five men strong. They had left the valley, walking up Letoresi mountain. The body was no longer at the ambush site. Family members had come and took the body to their village, which was on top of Letoresi mountain. This easy operation just turned into a mountain climbing ordeal.

Letoresi mountain is a high rugged climb even for the Timorese who have lived in that mountain all their lives. By the time we were a quarter of the way up the mountain the section medic was in trouble. He was carrying his medic kit and armed with a 5.56 machine gun. The steep climb up this rough terrain was exhausting him. By the time we were half way up the mountain the young medic traded the machine gun for a much lighter Styer assault rifle.

Three-quarters of the way up the mountain we called for a helicopter to come and medevac our medic. He could no longer walk and the terrain was becoming much more difficult. The helicopters came but there was absolutely no place where they could land. We had to take the medic to the top of the mountain with us. We divided the medic's gear among us, including his weapon, grenades and ammunition.

Eventually we made it to the little village at the top of the mountain. We found the body that the family had laid on a table in the front room of their home. The stench of the decaying corpse filled the home. Zak did his investigator thing of examining the body while Brad and I interviewed more witnesses.

There was not much daylight left when we called for the extraction. Soon there were two Australian Iroquois hovering over us. The pilots of the hovering aircraft gave us the bad news that there was no place to land. The closest location that they could land was three-quarters of the way down the mountain. We watched as the two helicopters flew off into the distance.

We were in a bad way. The medic was in very bad shape by this time. We would have to carry him down the mountain. The rest of us were exhausted from the hard day of climbing too. Then on top of that, the night was fast approaching and there could be enemy nearby.

We were pondering our situation in the fading daylight when suddenly there was a voice over the section radio. The voice over the radio had a strong Kiwi accent. We herd the whopping rotors of two Iroquois helicopters as the voice announced, "Get your kit ready to go; we are coming to get you out."

We didn't know who these guys were or where they were coming from. We didn't bother to question them. We just picked up our kit and waited for our rescuers to come and save us.

The Kiwi pilots of the two Suai-based helicopters had heard the radio communications about our plight. They got permission from their commander and immediately launched from the Kiwi airfield in Suai to come get us. I had learned from the several mountain operations on which I had accompanied Kiwi soldiers that the average Kiwi military man is a gutsy individual who has never heard of the English word "quit." I loved working with the Kiwis except for one attitude that they all possessed: If there was an easy way or a hard way to do something, they would do it the hard way every time, just because it was hard.

Now as I saw the two Kiwi Iroquois helicopters orbiting above us I thought *If anyone can get us out of here, it's these guys.*

The voice on the radio directed us about one-hundred meters to the right side of the village. The voice further told us that he would not be able to take the dead body. We would soon understand why.

We reached the location where the pilot directed us. There was a small opening in the trees on the steep slope of the mountain. I looked at that opening in the jungle and thought, *There is no way a helicopter can land here.* What I didn't know was that the pilots had no intentions of landing.

I watched as the first helicopter slowly dropped into this tiny clearing until the front of one skid lightly touched the hillside. The pilot held the aircraft steady against that mountain side while half the section climbed aboard, starting with the medic who was in very bad shape.

The first Iroquois slowly lifted straight up, the tips of his rotors only inches from the mountainside to his front and the trees behind him. Once the helicopter was above the trees he turned the nose away from the mountain and he was gone. The second helicopter slowly squeezed into this little opening like the first helicopter did. As the front of his skid touched the mountainside the rest of us climbed in. The pilot slowly rose straight up until he could clear the trees. The helicopter then hovered as the nose of the aircraft turned away from the mountain. The pilot nosed forward and we were gone.

The cool air that swept my feet to the side as they dangled out the side cargo door felt good. I watched the terrain below me as the helicopter sped along about three hundred feet above the treetops. Ten minutes later our two guardian angle helicopter pilots landed in the athletic field in the center of Maliana. They never slowed the rotors as we jumped out onto the ground. Once everyone was out of the Kiwi aircraft both helicopters rose up into the air and sped off into the darkening sky.

Two military trucks and one APC were waiting at the athletic field for us. Company medics took control of our section medic whom was now so sick he couldn't walk. The following day I would hear that the section medic almost died. The cold air of our ten minute flight home that refreshed us caused the section medic to go into hypothermia.

I never knew the names of those two Kiwi pilots, co-pilots, or their door gunners. If any of you should ever read this book, I give you a long overdue and very sincere thank you for getting us off that mountain that night.

* * * *

The Atabae Forest was thick enough that any ambush would have to be from close range, which meant that the firepower that I possessed in my Beretta pistol would have some effect. Knowing that I had a chance of hurting the bad guys made me feel a little better about being on this operation.

I really was nervous about Brad being on point. He had two weeks before he rotated home. I understood why the team leader put Brad on point. Brad was very good at soldiering. He was the best point man of the four of us on this tracking operation. We were on dangerous ground. It was better to focus on doing the operation rather than clouding our minds about the future.

By mid-afternoon we had a good fix on where the Militia unit was going. We turned around and headed back to Moliana. We were walking back over the same ground that we tracked the Militia. I didn't like the idea of walking the same ground a second time. But then again I understood the team leader's theory, too.

If we moved to the left or right of the trail that we tracked the Militia during our returned to Moliana we could bump into a Militia force that was trying to evade us. I didn't know why an eight man Militia unit would evade a four man tracking team but it was always possible. I didn't have any say over our tactics so I just stayed alert and covered my "arc of responsibility" as we moved through the jungle.

We were at the south edge of the Atabae Forest when word came over the AMFI radio about the firefight in Lailaco mountain. Upon hearing the news the team leader looked at me and said, "Looks like your information paid off."

I replied, "I told you before. I don't start the rumors; I just pass them on. It's not my information." It wasn't my information but I had a lot to do with getting the information to the right place in a timely manner.

* * * *

After the Aidabasalala attack I jumped into the "intelligence game" with both feet. I met with La Faik the day after the attack on Aidabasalala and announced that I was ready to go to work. I would do whatever it took to help neutralize this rapidly growing Militia threat in East Timor. I knew that one of the keys to destroy the Militia power base was in the West Timor operations, which is espionage. The other key was to use the resources available in East Timor to take away the ability of the Militia to operate in East Timor.

I spent several hours over the next few days strategizing with La Faik through the only interpreter that he trusted completely. Our police interpreters, Domingos and Alfonso, had a Falintil background; however, for the secret operations that we were conducting La Faik only trusted one person as his interpreter. The problem was that this interpreter was not from the Bobonaro district.

Now that I was going to become more involved La Faik arranged for the interpreter to live in Maliana. We had a lot of work to do. We could not afford time delays caused by having to wait for an interpreter to meet us somewhere. It was an easy matter of making it appear that the interpreter moved to Maliana to work for the United Nations Administrative personnel, which the interpreter did begin work for the administrators. Daytime meetings with La Faik were still restrictive because of the interpreter's day job, so most of our meetings were in the evenings.

First we analyzed the current activities of the three operating entities in West Timor. The single Kupang element, Emeu, had not made contact with the Turiskai cell "mailbox" for three weeks. The last information received from this Kupang spy was a portion of the Militia radio code. We suspected that the Kupang spy had been exposed. The Kupang spy never did send another message. The fate of Emeu would never be known.

The Atambua cell was operating well; however, they were coming under pressure. On two separate occasions Koppassus soldiers who were securing the immediate vicinity of their jungle training area discovered the presence of Atambua cell operators. The first cell members caught was a husband and wife team posing as refugees searching that area of the jungle for herbs used to make home remedy medicine. The couple was detained for several hours for questioning. Their appearance, sixty-plus years of age and the fresh picked herbs they carried in a canvas bag convinced their captors that the couple was harmless. They were released.

The second team caught couldn't use the same story. The two Timorese men in their late-thirties told their Special Forces captors that they were exploring jungle areas outside of Atambua. They wanted to find a place where they could move their families away from the Atambua refugee camp.

The Koppassus knew that life in the refugee camps was not easy but it was unlikely that any of the East Timorese would want to move away from the other East Timorese living in the camps. The two men were detained for two days. SGI informants monitored the two men and their families every movement upon their release.

The Turiskai cell has been under pressure ever since Emeu was named as a spy. The pressure was reduced when La Faik had given the false information to the SGI spy in Cailaco about the Turiskai cell members returning to Cailaco. The Turiskai cell was now functioning smoothly. The "mailbox" system at the Tunubibi illegal market was very effective. Surprisingly the kidnaping of the Militia members from the illegal market never brought any suspicion onto any of the cell members.

La Faik and I discussed several ways to improve the current operations. During our "head shedding" meetings we came up with a new long term operation for the West Timor cells. There were many East Timorese living in the West Timor refugee camps who wanted to return to East Timor; however, the Militia groups who ruled the individual camps would not let them return. We decided to establish a system for smuggling people back into East Timor where they were free from the clutches of the Militia.

We had to be careful how we conducted these operations. If the Militia suspected a secret mass exodus was underway they would crush the operation along with the two West Timor cells. We would select those to be smuggled home carefully. East Timorese who had potential intelligence value were the first priority. The second priority was East Timorese who were in danger in West Timor. La Faik wasn't accustomed to giving operations a code-name. Since I was accustomed to this practice I referred to this ongoing endeavor as Project Homecoming.

Project Homecoming had three obstacles that we had to overcome. The first obstacle was coordinating with the people whom we intended to smuggle "over the fence" into East Timor. This would have to be done under the noses of the many watching Militia.

The second obstacle was the Indonesian side of the border. TNI troops patrolled the length of the border. It would be impossible to smuggle someone through a populated location such as the Tunubibi illegal market . There were always many soldiers in and around the market. Militia members were always at the market too. The soldiers could care less if East Timorese returned to East Timor; however, if the Militia recognized someone they didn't want to return to East Timor they would stop them. The soldiers would backup the Militia. The operations would have to sneak through the Indonesian patrols in more remote locations.

The third obstacle was the United Nations controlled East Timor side of the border. The many soldiers who patrolled the eastside of the border were no threat to returning East Timorese or any of our elements who would be helping them. The danger on the East Timor side of the border was villagers who may recognize Militia members or their family members that we may be bringing home.

The other threat was that a smuggling team may be being pursued by angry Militia who want to stop the returning East Timorese. Project Homecoming could use some military support. La Faik could handle the plans for the first two obstacles. It was up to me to handle the plans for the third Obstacle.

The next project we devised I named Project Freedom. The Militia units operating in East Timor had been attacking East Timorese and United Nations military forces for months and getting away with it. This had to change. La Faik and his elements were collecting good information on the Militia intentions and movements through informants, tracking elements and radio communications.

The problem was that our information was taking too much time to get to where the information needed to be by using the "proper channels" of

139

information flow. The other problem was that the military commanders at Sector West did not put much importance on information that was not confirmed by their military intelligence operators. The fast moving Militia was easily outrunning our information. By the time our information reached the company commanders the Militia was long gone.

I decided on a risky endeavor to get the information to where it needed to be in a timely manner. I would have to break both the "chain of command" and the "chain of information flow." This operation was certain to ruffle the feathers of a few important people but something had to be done if we were ever going to get our information working against these invading Militia units. The problem was how to get the information to the right people without my being charged with violating United Nations rules. I had a plan for that.

I told La Faik to get me all the information he could from both sides of the border about the Militia activity in East Timor and their future plans. I would get that information to the United Nations military commanders "directly" who could act on the information.

* * * *

My American house-mate and Bobonaro district commander had a close relationship with the military company commanders throughout Bobonaro district. I planned to use his established relationships with the company commanders to "penetrate" my targets. To support Project Homecoming I needed to penetrate the company commander of the company responsible for the security of the Tunubibi area. To support Project Freedom I needed to penetrate the Maliana based company commander.

The penetrations of both commanders had to be handled very carefully if I was going to professionally survive. The penetrations would have to be based on friendship. The information that I passed to them directly would have to be from friendly conversation about current events. This tactic not only protected me but it protected the commanders too. My defense against accusations of violating the chain of command would be my big mouth while talking to friends.

I began to join Donny as he made his regular visits to the Tunubibi and Maliana company compounds. I encouraged Donny to make more frequent trips to those compounds by dreaming up reasons for him to go. Both commanders knew that I worked intelligence for the United Nations so there was a natural curiosity for me to exploit.

The Maliana company commander, Carl, was a man in his mid-thirties. He was energetic along with being very physically fit. He handled his job at the company Command Post; however, he never missed an opportunity to go out into the field with his men. He was a man of action.

Carl and I hit it off right away. I had never been in the military but I had been a student of strategy for many years as I studied Martial Arts. I also had extensive training in police Special Operations including training with the U.S. Army Rangers RAID team. All of this plus my experience of accompanying many military operations here in East Timor gave me the tools to quickly penetrate Carl.

There were many nights that Carl and I talked tactics and strategies as Donny nagged at me to leave. It didn't take too many meetings like this before Carl and I had developed a true friendship built on common interest and respect. When the time was right during our conversations I would mention a "hot" piece of information about Militia activities. This naturally resulted in Carl prodding me for more information, which I let him drag out of me. Soon we would be standing in his Command Post (CP) studying the large map that covered one entire wall.

The AMFI team leader was becoming upset with me because I was telling Carl information that was supposed to be reported through the Chain of Command or the Chain of Information.

I always responded with, "I am sorry for that. Carl and I were just talking about different things and it just came out of my big mouth." My apologies to the AMFI team leader only worked the first couple of times. After that the team leader became very suspicious. I am sure he knew what I was doing, which was dangerous to me.

The Tunubibi company commander, Greg, was very different from Carl. Greg was enthusiastic about doing what he could about the Militia incursions. Greg was responsible for everything along the border. Every time Militia units crossed into East Timor from West Timor the Militia was slipping past Greg's defenses against these infiltrations. Greg's defenses were good. They intercepted many attempts of Militia infiltrations, forcing the Militia to retreat back across the river into Indonesia but Militia still were making it "over that fence."

Greg was a very experienced company commander. He was well trained and educated. At first he played the game that I was playing, which was allowing himself to be penetrated by me. Greg knew exactly what I was doing. He didn't mind because it served both of our purposes. I fed him information about

Militia units that would be infiltrating across the border. Sometimes that information was complete with names of the Militia members and where they intended to cross "the fence."

As our friendship grew our trust in each other grew too. One night I had gone to the Tunubibi compound alone. Greg and I talked in his office. During our conversation Greg enlightened me that he knew what I was doing and he appreciated the results of my efforts. Then he said, "You have other support needs from my company. What do you need?"

I was suspicious that I was getting set up. I came halfway to hanging myself by saying, "I just want to get information to the right people in a timely manner."

Greg smiled as he said, "When you're ready let me know what you need."

Passing information to Carl was all that was necessary to support Project Freedom. Project Homecoming was different. I had to divulge at least some of my involvement with my across the border activities. This was a dangerous thing if Greg was actually being controlled by Sector West Command for the purpose of exposing me.

* * * *

Segrada Familia Elements had successfully smuggled a family of East Timorese from the Turiskai Refugee camp into East Timor. The family had little importance to the Halilintar Militia. The family members had no involvement with the Militia in East Timor prior to September of 1999, so there was little risk of encountering problems upon entering East Timor. The first smuggling operation was done without support. We chose this family for the purpose of developing the tactics to conduct future Project Homecoming operations when we would need support.

The first Project Homecoming operation had a couple of "kinks" to work out so we decided to conduct a second operation smuggling a family into East Timor that posed little risk. We made some minor adjustments in the way cell members made contact with the Target family. We also made adjustments as to how the family would get to the "rally point," which is the secluded location where cell operators from East Timor would meet the family and begin the journey home to East Timor.

The second Project Homecoming operation was better. The adjustments in tactics smoothed out the operation. Now it was time to run an operation to get a "hot" target across the fence. By this time there were several possibilities developed by both of the Segrada Familia cells operating in West Timor. La Faik didn't hesitate to choose the most important target.

We were sitting in the front room of Augustinho's home. Augustinho was La Faik's 2IC (second in command). The three of us smoked cigarettes in the dim light of an oil lantern that sat on the low table in front of us. The yellow light from the flickering flame seemed to dance on La Faik's dark face. La Faik's coal-black eyes displayed his sincerity as he calmly said, "We must get Emeu's wife and children home."

I nodded my head in response knowing that La Faik was right. The "team" and their families always come first.

Every Segrada Familia member was encouraged by La Faik's choice to bring home the family of one of their members. The Turiskai cell didn't hesitate to begin the dangerous task of contacting the target to work out the details of this operation. The Halilintar Militia was still monitoring Emeu's wife and children; however, the intensity of their surveillance was greatly reduced.

The details took almost two weeks to complete. The Turiskai cell realized that the only opportunity to get Emeu's wife and children out of Turiskai without the Militia knowing it was to move them during the night hours. Militia members have not been spending the night at the families home during the last two months or longer.

Finally the Turiskai cell was ready to get Emeu's family home. La Faik was given the operation launch date and details through the "mailbox" at the illegal market . La Faik contacted the team leader of the four-man team from East Timor who has been handling these Project Homecoming operations. La Faik told me the operation was a "go" when I met with him that night.

La Faik, his interpreter, and I sat in the living room of his home. Two small oil lamps burned in the living room to furnish us light. One of the oil lamps sat on the edge of the small table that was in front of where the three of us sat. The other oil lamp was on the four-foot high chest of drawers that was against the wall behind the interpreter. We sipped the coffee that La Faik's wife and daughter had served us as we talked about the upcoming operation.

La Faik told me the details of this Project Homecoming operation step by step. The first step was to make sure that the target family was not being monitored by Halilintar Militia or their informants before the family is moved. This would be done by cell members systematically checking every feasible location from where someone could be watching the family's home.

Other cell members would check the planned route of movement from the home to the Rally Point. At 0200 hours two cell members would approach the family's home from the rear and make contact with Emeu's wife. She and the children should be prepared to leave when contacted. The two cell members would then take the family to the Rally Point, which is almost two kilometers away. The cell members and the family will have to walk on some rough trails without using any flashlights.

The cell team and the family will meet the Project Homecoming operators from East Timor at the Rally Point. The East Timor team will infiltrate Indonesia during the evening hours of that same night and should be waiting at the Rally Point when the family gets there. The Turiskai cell operator's part of this operation is now over so they will return to Turiskai. The East Timor team will bring the family the rest of the way home.

The East Timor team would have to avoid any Indonesian TNI patrols that are in the area. They will try and get the family across the river and into East Timor before daylight. The Halilintar Militia is almost certain to discover that Emeu's family is gone once it turns daylight. When the Militia discovers that the family is gone they will alert the TNI to attempt to intercept the family at the border. While the TNI secure the border the Militia will try to figure out where the family went and then pursue them.

La Faik sat calmly on the wooden chair as he told me the plans for this operation. He then leaned forward and took a cigarette out of the pack of Indonesian-made Marlboros that I had placed on the small table in front of us. La Faik put the cigarette in his mouth then leaned forward a little more as he put the end of the cigarette into the flame of the oil lamp burning on the same table. He held his long hair back away from the open flame as he lit the cigarette. He then sat back into his chair and crossed his legs as he exhaled smoke from his lungs.

La Faik continued, "The East Timor team cannot abort this mission once they have control of the family. It is imperative that they are not captured. They will wait at the river for the opportunity to get across safely. If they are detected by TNI patrols or pursuing Militia they will have to try and run across the river. The chances of them making it across that wide open river are very doubtful. The TNI or Militia will shoot them down before they are halfway across."

La Faik then paused as he took a drag on his cigarette and slowly exhaled the smoke. He continued, "The United Nations rules of engagement allows military or police to fire their weapons into Indonesia against anyone in Indonesia that is an immediate threat to a known East Timorese citizen, isn't that right?

La Faik was looking at me with his normal calm demeanor. I knew what he had on his mind as I answered, "Yes, that is right. UN military and police can even fire on Indonesian TNI or police if we see that they are about to kill or seriously injure an East Timorese citizen."

La Faik gave me a little smile. I smiled back as I realized what I had to do. Before I could do my part of this operation I had to know the "window of time" that the East Timor team bringing the target family would be coming across the river. I also needed to know the crossing points. The last piece of information I needed was the description of the East Timor team.

The Project Homecoming operation was laid on to begin in three days. The following morning La Faik and the East Timor team TL took me to the two selected river crossing points. I identified both locations on the Indonesian military map that I carried. I got the physical and clothing descriptions of the four men who would infiltrate Indonesia and bring home Emeu's family.

That afternoon I went to Tunubibi and met with Greg. It was time to use his resources that he had offered me. I just hoped that I wasn't stepping into a trap. I believed that Greg was sincere. If he wasn't sincere than I would be caught being involved with espionage, charged with violating United Nations rules and repatriated, which is sent back to the United States. That was a chance I had to take.

Greg was receptive of my afternoon visit. I had never stopped in to visit in the afternoon before. I knew that everyone was very busy during the day. Greg knew that something was up but his disciplined patience outweighed his curiosity. As soon as he could break away from his work he stepped out of the command post room into the larger receiving room where I waited. I was drinking the coffee that one of Greg's soldiers had made for me.

Greg walked over to the little side room and poured himself a cup of coffee. He offered me a refill on my coffee, which I accepted. Greg led the way outside where there was a temporary wood floor built on top of the ground. Camouflage netting was the roof strung over the wood floor. A table and several folding chairs were on the floor of this outdoor break room. Greg offered me a seat as he sat down on one of the chairs. I sat on the chair across the table from Greg. Even under the shade of the camouflage netting it was very hot.

Greg looked at me calmly as he studied me. There was no point in beating around the bush. If I was about to hang myself I might as well do it like a man, with confidence and strength. Beside that Greg was the kind of commander that appreciated the truth presented directly. If he was sincere we needed to work closely together. I just came out with it, "There is an operation that will begin tomorrow night. The people conducting this operation may need a little help coming back across the river."

Greg asked, "What kind of help?"

I took a pack of cigarettes and a lighter out of my shirt pocket. I knew that Greg didn't smoke so I didn't bother offering him one. I took a cigarette out of the pack and thumped the butt end against the table as I said, "There are four East Timorese men who will be bringing an East Timorese woman and two children across the river. The Halilintar Militia has held this family captive for several months now. It's time they come home. The problem is the Militia will do everything they can to stop them." I put the cigarette in my mouth and lit it.

Greg understood immediately what assistance the operation may need. I didn't have to tell him that the river crossing may be "hot." Greg didn't ask me for any details about the operation prior to the East Timor team and the family entering East Timor. He didn't ask why the Halilintar Militia didn't want the family to return to East Timor. This was a good sign that Greg was being sincere.

Greg simply said, "I have to know where your team will across the river. I will also need to know how my soldiers will identify your team when they see them coming across the river."

I produced the Indonesian military map that I carried and went through the team re-entry plan with Greg. Greg wrote down the grid references of the planned re-entry point and the alternate re-entry point.

By the end of our meeting Greg told me, "I will have a section of soldiers conducting hidden static OPs (observation posts) at the two re-entry points and throughout the window of time you gave me. You must understand the sections can give your team supporting fire as your people cross the river; however, the section cannot enter the river or cross to the Indonesian side under any circumstances. Your team has to get themselves across the river."

I replied, "That's good enough. Thanks for that."

Greg then added, "One more thing. Nobody else is to know about this, including your AMFI friends. My soldiers will not know that this river crossing is an operation. They will think they just happened to be at the right place at the right time."

This concluded our meeting so Greg went back into the CP while I walked around the building to my Land Rover and left. I met with La Faik and gave him the details about the military support that would be in place at the two river crossings. La Faik was pleased about getting secret support from the Australians.

The following night the third Project Homecoming operation was conducted. The operation went smooth other than the team was late getting back to the river. As the team started across the river with the family in broad daylight a TNI patrol nearby challenged the East Timorese party but the soldiers were too far away to make an attempt to capture the East Timorese in the river. When a section of Australian soldiers suddenly appeared on the East Timor side of the river the TNI simply ignored the crossing East Timorese and continued their patrol.

Emeu's wife and children were reunited with their family in Cailaco. There were many hugs. Tears flowed down the cheeks of many of the family members as they excitedly talked and hugged and hugged again. Seeing this reunion made all those who helped to bring this woman and her children home feel a deep emotional contentment of a job well done. The only black spot on this moment was knowing that the missing husband and father, Emeu, was still missing and probably would not be coming home—ever.

* * * *

Project Freedom and Project Homecoming was up and running full on. A combination of our intelligence and the military intelligence system gave the military the ability to be at the right places at the right time. Citizens, Militia units, and at times the TNI would be surprised time and time again when United Nations soldiers appeared out of the jungle at just the right moment to crush what the Militia was trying to do.

Project Freedom helped to tip the scales against the Marauding Militia units operating in East Timor. The Militia was still there but they were now on the defensive. They spent most of their time in East Timor evading aggressive UN military operations and sweeps.

Project Homecoming helped to prevent several Militia attempts to infiltrate units into East Timor. Project Homecoming operations continued to bring people home as well as smuggle some stolen documents into our hands from West Timor. Every time there was a need for military help the soldiers just seem to be where they were needed.

The reputation of the soldiers that were based in Maliana and Tunubibi grew rapidly among the Timorese on both sides of the border. Soon the people referred to these aggressive Australian soldiers as "ghost soldiers." That was a well deserved title for the soldier's skills of moving through the jungle and not being seen until the time was right.

As Militia morale plummeted there were cases of Militia members abandoning their infiltrated team and going home to their East Timorese

Village. There were two incidents of an entire Militia team, complete with TL, who defected as soon as they entered East Timor to conduct guerilla operations.

One night Greg's static OP position three-kilometers north of Tunubibi heard the sounds of a vicious firefight just out of sight to the north of the OP and in the jungle on Indonesia's side of the river. Multiple rifles fired on full automatic. The volume of fire increased, decreased then increased again. After several minutes the gunfire stopped as suddenly as it had begun. The Australian soldiers could only speculate as to who was doing all the shooting.

* * * *

The following day we knew what happened when we got a report from the Turiskai cell. A six-man Militia team had decided to defect as soon as they entered East Timor on an Infiltration operation. The Halilintar Militia had already lost two teams in this manner so the SGI began monitoring Militia teams to detect intentions of defection.

The SGI discovered that Martinho and his team intended to defect. A ruthless Halilintar Militia leader, Joao Baptista, was sent to disarm and arrest Martinho and his team. Martinho became aware that Joao Baptista was coming for them so Martinho and his men made a dash for the border. They intended to cross over to East Timor and surrender to the Australians before Baptista could arrest them.

Martinho led his men three kilometers through the jungle. They were almost to the Nunura River when Baptista and his twenty-plus men caught up with them. The resulting firefight was what the Autralian OP heard. Several Militia members from both groups were wounded but Baptista succeeded in capturing the escaping team.

There was no doubt that for the time being we were winning the war. The Ghost soldiers were continually outmaneuvering the Militia. They were also outfighting the Militia during contacts. Our intelligence operations were running full on. Segrada Familia elements had outmaneuvered the Militia and SGI intelligence at every turn. We had stolen there documents and even some of their members. We ferreted out their secrets and brought them home to be used against them. We snuck people out from under their noses and brought them home. We helped to demoralize their troops through targeted propaganda. We were kicking their ass in an intelligence sense.

CHAPTER TEN

Under Pressure

By September of 2000, Segrada Familia was in trouble. The Australian companies in Maliana and Cailaco were still besting the Militia at every turn. The Kiwi and Nepalese militaries were experiencing the same success all through Kova Lima District and the Bobonaro Sub-District where the one single Kiwi platoon kept the Militia at bay. The Australian company at Tunubibi made it all but impossible for the Militia units to move back and forth across the border.

As firefights between UN military Forces and Militia continued the Militia was getting the worse end of the combat encounters. We always knew who the UN military killed by reports we received through the Tunubibi "mailbox." The first time I heard the names of Militia killed in action inside of East Timor was a report about that first firefight in the Manapa Jungle.

I felt good about the Australians killing those two men but when I heard the report from West Timor I felt a pang of guilt. It was the way the Timorese tell things. The report was, "The wife and children of Rui Bere Mau and Fransisco Lopes are crying."

I asked La Faik, "So what does that mean?"

La Faik smiled at my ignorance as he said, "That means those two men are dead."

I hadn't thought about the families of these Militia boogie men before that day. Of course the enemy has families who loved and needed their husbands and fathers.

On two different occasions at two different locations the Australian military tracked and chased a small Militia unit throughout most of the day. By nightfall on both occasions the Australians had the Militia unit trapped against a solid rock mountain face. The Australians set up a containing cordon around the trapped Militia to wait for first light when they would move in and capture or kill the Militia. Both times the Militia slipped out of the trap.

The Kiwis in Bobonaro did the same thing on one occasion. Two Kiwi platoons had a Militia unit trapped near the top of Aimea mountain. The next morning they would move in and kill the Militia. The next morning the Militia was gone. They some how slipped out of the trap during the night.

I often discussed the military tactics being used with my friend Billy. We worked in different districts but I ran into him from time to time while I was on CTO (compensatory time off) or sometimes when I went to Dili on business. Billy had spent several years serving in the U.S. Special Forces. He had even trained with Indonesia's Special Forces Koppassus a couple of times.

I told Billy about the Militia guerillas uncanny ability to slip through enemy containment cordons during the night. Billy just smiled and said, "Sure they do. That's what they are trained to do. If they don't slip out they will be captured or killed. Special Forces are not in the habit of getting captured or killed, no matter what country they are from."

I certainly understood what Billy was telling me. I asked him, "So what can be done to capture an evading unit?"

Billy thought for a moment then said, "The UN militaries are doing the right thing. If they tried to finish the enemy team off during the night there would be many friendly casualties." Billy suggested to me to let the military do their thing. Just give them the information and let them do the rest. That was good advice.

While the United Nations various military contingents were knocking the snot out of the Militia in East Timor the Segrada Familia was starting to get the snot knocked out of them in West Timor. The Atambua cell only had three operators left. The older man and his wife who was caught near the Koppassus secret training site had returned to East Timor. The SGI didn't necessarily think that the couple was spies but even the light suspicion made it dangerous for them to continue to operate.

The next two men who had been caught near the training site were being closely monitored. La Faik believed that the men would be arrested once the SGI identified all the people they associated with. La Faik brought them home through the Project Homecoming system along with one other man that La Faik thought the SGI may have identified through their surveillance of the two suspected operators.

The Turiskai cell was under pressure again too. Suspicions were raised one night during a Project Homecoming operation. Two cell members were caught coming back into Turiskai after escorting a family to the rally point. The two cell members were eventually released. Both men and their families were brought home through the same system that they had helped to develop and operate.

So far La Faik was doing well to get all his people back home with the exception of Emeu who was still missing. There wasn't much hope that Emeu would ever come home. La Faik's SigInt operation was stalled because the Militia units had changed all the radio frequencies that they had been using. That's a good indication that they know that we know what frequencies they are using. Emeu was most likely captured and compelled to tell his captors everything.

The end was in sight for the "over the fence" Segrada Familia cells. The hard part about commanding operations on foreign soil is knowing when to pull your elements out. So far La Faik has done well but it only takes once to wait too long, which results in a great personal loss not to mention the intelligence the enemy would extract from the captured cell member.

As La Faik considered pulling the rest of the cell members back to East Timor the remaining Turiskai cell sent information through the "mailbox" that delayed any immediate extraction of the Cells. The wife of one of the Militia soldiers killed in East Timor wants to defect. The wife of Rui Bere Mau, Paulina, has become very bitter about the death of her husband.

Rui had been a mid-level Halilintar Militia leader for several years before the September 1999 violence. He was a team leader for the Koppassus trained Militia teams infiltrating East Timor. Because of his position he had many meetings with his commander's reference upcoming infiltration operations. These meetings included intelligence reports from assets operating in East Timor. Several of those meeting were held at Rui's home. Paulina over heard some of the discussions as she served the visiting commanders coffee and otherwise listened in from the next room.

Rui had also kept several documents of operation plans and even intelligence reports at his house in Turiskai. Halilintar Militia leader, Abilio De Araujo came to talk to Paulina shortly after the death of Rui. He gave Paulina his deepest condolences. He told her that the Halilintar Militia would take care of her and her three children so she didn't need to worry. Before Abilio left the house Abilio asked Paulina for all of Rui's Militia issued equipment and any documents that he had in the house.

Paulina surrendered all of the Militia gear. She gave Abilio all the documents except one. The document she had cleverly separated from the pile was a letter to her husband from a political leader in East Timor. Abilio looked through all the gear. He then looked through all the documents that Paulina had handed over to him. Abilio was satisfied that he had everything of importance and left the home of the fallen Militia soldier.

Paulina and her three children were well taken care of by the Halilintar Militia; however, under the pretense of taking care of her she was being monitored very closely twenty-four hours a day. Militia "body guards" escorted her everywhere she went. They even spent the night at Paulina's home.

Paulina may have only been the wife of a Halilintar Militia leader but she had learned how the intelligence game is played. She kept back the most important document. The kind of document that makes intelligence analysts excited, a written document that gives proof of the espionage involvement of a political figure.

The other extraordinary thing she did was figure out how to get a message to the secret intelligence cell that the SGI and all their training and gadgets couldn't expose. At first we suspected that this defection desire of Paulinas was a trap to expose and capture the Segrada Familia operators; however, the more we looked into the facts of what Paulina presented to us the more we thought she truly wanted to defect.

She dangled the document she held like someone using a carrot to coax an unbroken horse closer and closer so that the person holding the carrot could catch the horse. Like the horse that didn't want to be ridden but wanted the carrot, we went one little step closer and then another little step.

All of our instincts were telling us to walk away from this one. But then La Faik re-considered. He told us, "Rui and his entire family have always had Militia ties but Paulina is different. Her family has always had Falintil ties. Paulina herself had assisted covert Falintil Clandestino operations before she married Rui. The evidence of her sincerity is the Militia watching her every day and night. Why would they do that?" It was finally decided that we would try to bring her and the three kids into East Timor.

This turned into "Mission Impossible" as the planning for the Project Homecoming operation and coordinating with Paulina began. Paulina told the Turiskai cell contact person that she would not come to East Timor unless her mother and father were also brought with her and the children. Her father had been a Falintil soldier many years ago. Because of his old age and poor health, along with his daughter being married to a Militia leader, nobody bothered him; however, Paulina feared that if she defected and her parents were still in West Timor the Militia would seek revenge on her father and mother. She was probably right.

Paulina tantalized us with information from the letter that she possessed. She gave us the name of the man who wrote and sent the letter. She gave us the intended targets the letter asked Rui to hit, which were the operations her husband intended to conduct but he was killed before the operation objectives were achieved. The letter described the support the author's political group would provide to realize the success of Rui's mission.

The political leader who allegedly wrote this letter was known to us. He was the leader of the newly established CPD-RDTL group. Up front the CPD-RDTL was anti-Indonesia and their Militia. The CPD-RDTL took the stance of wanting independence from all outside nations. The CPD-RDTL believed that the rightful constitution and president existed for the time period of one month prior to the invasion of Indonesia in 1975.

We knew that the doctrine of the CPD-RDTL was a lie. Our "over the fence" cells had collected information about the true intentions of the CPD-RDTL. The CPD-RDTL was very much involved with both Indonesia and the Militia. From the collected information it appeared that the CPD-RDTL top leaders who were not even living in East Timor planned to rule East Timor when they had run the United Nations out of the country.

The brother of the exiled intended president of East Timor, Paulino Gama, was a highly respected ex-Falintil commander known as Eli Seti, which is Portuguese for L-7. Eli Seti is from the Baucau District of East Timor. Eli Seti was the CPD-RDTL leader in Baucau. Our first evidence of the truth of this information came one night when an impromptu Australian military roadway checkpoint captured two men who were smuggling one SKS assault rifle, one M-16 assault rifle and four hand grenades into East Timor from Atambua, West Timor.

The investigation into this weapons smuggling case resulted in the discovery that the two men caught smuggling the weapons were clandestine members of Eli Seti. The ex-Falintil commander had sent the two young secret operators to Atambua to meet with the Militia leader of the infamous Baucau Militia organization known as "Tim Saka" and bring the weapons back to Eli Seti in Baucau (the "Tim" is pronounced "team").

An actual captured document written by a CPD-RDTL leader reference his involvement with the Militia guerilla activity in East Timor would be invaluable. We realized that it was possible that the document was a lie. Paulina may be telling us the letter exists so that Segrada Familia would put forth the effort to get her along with her family home. That was a chance we decided to take.

153

Coordinating with Paulina was difficult because of the constant Militia presence with her. Most of the contacts happened during church functions. Paulina's body guard service waited outside the church while Paulina worshiped. That was their mistake and our good fortune.

The cell coordinators worked out all the details with Paulina except for one very big hurdle. There was not enough time that the Militia body guards were not with Paulina. The maximum time to get a head start on the Militia who would pursue the family was two hours. The two hours head start would only exist if the cell operators could sneak Paulina, her kids, and her parents away at the same time. This simply was not possible.

The next option was to get the Parents across the border before we brought Paulina and the kid's home to East Timor. Paulina believed that if her parents disappeared from Turiskai the Halilintar Militia would suspect what she was doing. She was probably right.

We then considered snatching Paulina, the three children, and her parents when they went to the illegal market. The problem was the two TNI soldiers who had assisted with the kidnaping operations were no longer patrolling the illegal market . A snatch attempt would almost certainly fail. The Militia body guards could be eliminated at the time of the snatch but with so many TNI soldiers close by the snatch team and the family would be captured before they entered the river. We had no choice but to wait for an opportunity to present itself. That could take a long time.

To make matters worse I started coming under pressure from the United Nations. One day two serious crimes investigators came to Maliana from the UN police headquarters in Dili to talk to me. They offered to buy me lunch at the new Portuguese restaurant that had opened in Maliana, which was Maliana's first restaurant. I knew both of these investigators. I had assisted them with a couple of their investigations of the September 1999 murders in Bobonaro district.

There was nobody else in the restaurant by the time we finished eating our lunch. The Canadian serious crimes investigator surprised me with a question, "What would it take to get someone from West Timor into East Timor?"

I suspected a trap immediately. I responded with a question, "What makes you think I would know?"

The Canadian investigator said, "It's well known what your doing out here. We just figured if anyone could get a job like this done you would be able to do it."

I studied the mid-fifty-year-old Canadian as I thought about what he was doing. The Canadian, John, had short gray hair, a slender physic and a personable manner about him. He had been an Investigator for many years as a member of the Royal Canadian Mounted Police. I then thought about the current United Nations police commissioner whom was a high ranking commander in the Royal Canadian Mounted Police.

I asked John, "So, does the person you want to get across the border want to come across the border or is this someone your Investigation Division want to arrest?"

John looked over at his partner and smiled. He was still smiling when he looked back at me, "This is someone we want to talk to."

I knew then that I was being set up. John masked his response well, but his partner did not. John's smile was a smile of me guessing his intentions. His early-thirties Nepalese partner smiled like Sylvester the cat who was about to eat Tweety Bird.

I told John that I didn't know anything about that sort of thing. He would have to talk to the military to see if they cold lend him a hand. John thanked me for my advice as I saw the excited Nepalese investigator's face drop from a smile to a disappointed frown. The man didn't have a poker face. John and the Nepalese man drove me back to the Maliana Station and dropped me off.

I knew there was big trouble coming at me and probably very soon. I had been on the receiving end of inner-department witch hunts back in Michigan. I figured there wasn't much difference between a police department in the United States and the United Nations civilian police. I knew they could get me if they wanted me bad enough but I could stall the outcome. There was a chance that I would be going back to America with a shroud of shame hanging over me, but I couldn't change that now. I had no regrets for getting involved in all this "cloak and dagger" stuff. I just hoped that I could survive long enough to help accomplish getting Paulina and that letter into East Timor.

On the same day that John tried to trap me, La Faik gave me more stressing news. The Turiskai cell reported that a top Halilintar Militia leader named Armindo Soares was going to a secluded location on the Nunura River three kilometers north of the Tunubibi illegal market . Armindo was overseeing the black market deliveries of gasoline, kerosene and diesel fuel. The fuel was purchased by businessmen from East Timor. The fuel would be heavily taxed if it was brought across the established border checkpoints. The Halilintar Militia was making money by smuggling the fuel across the border to avoid the taxes.

La Faik told me, "We have a chance to try and grab Armindo and bring him across the river into East Timor."

I realized the importance of capturing Armindo immediately. Armindo Soares was from the Hauba area of Bobonaro sub-district. He was second-in-command under Abilio De Araujo, who is the operations commander. Armindo Soares would be a great catch if an operation could be pulled off.

The United Nations Serious Crimes Division had several warrants for Armindo's arrest for his involvement of many murders. How ironic. John, who works for the Serious Crimes Division, came to see me about snatching someone from West Timor and now we are presented with a possible opportunity to snatch a top Militia leader who is wanted by the Serious Crimes unit. I doubted that there was any connection.

As we examined the information from West Timor the idea of executing a "snatch" operation began to look promising. Armindo went to this Nunura River location every time there was a delivery of fuel. Their system for making the delivery was simple. Trucks from Kupang, West Timor loaded with five-gallon plastic containers full of fuel would drive to the fuel drop off point located on the West Timor road that paralleled the Nunura River.

The fuel would be off loaded and hand carried to the Nunura River by East Timorese who worked for the businessmen that purchased the fuel. The East Timorese workers would then carry the fuel across the river entering into East Timor and loaded the fuel into trucks to be transported to Dili.

This was a good system for us to work with. We knew there would be no TNI patrols near the smuggling operation at the river. The Indonesians don't want to be seen as having any knowledge of a black market smuggling enterprise much less being seen as taking an active part. We would not have to contend with TNI troops.

The smuggling location on the Nunura River was secluded on both sides of the river, which meant there would be little chance of local citizens getting in the way or being witnesses. The smuggling was taking place during daylight hours, which would give our team full visibility.

The multiple combat incidents in East Timor gave the United Nations and concerned neighboring nations the ammunition they needed to put pressure on the Indonesian government to disarm the Militia. Because of this pressure the Militia members no longer were allowed to carry their weapons in West Timor. Armindo and his two body guards were not armed with assault rifles when they came to oversee the smuggling operation.

The Project Homecoming operation to bring Paulina and her family back to East Timor was now just waiting for the opportunity to get her away from the Militia body guards. That could be a long wait. Our ability to operate in West Timor was now reduced and probably soon would be eliminated all together. My days of operating in East Timor could be numbered as well. We decided to make an attempt to grab Armindo.

I met with the Austalian company commander at Tunubibi, my friend Greg. We started making the plans for the military support that this kidnaping operation would need. The Segrada Familia team making the snatch would need some help once they got on the East Timor side of the river.

Greg had supported several operation Homecoming operations that we conducted. I had always been completely honest with Greg. Eventually I started giving Greg some of the background information so that he understood the need for the operations that we conducted.

The kidnaping of a high ranking Halilintar Militia leader was a potential powder keg in a political sense. I could have told Greg that we were simply conducting another Project Homecoming operation but I couldn't do that. I decided to tell Greg the whole truth about this operation. I expected him to say, "You're crazy. I'm not getting involved in that."

I was partly right about Greg's response. When I finished telling him what we planned to do and how we planned to do it Greg said, "You're crazy—but it just might work."

Greg told me that he had been monitoring the smuggling operation at that point along the river for the past two weeks. They had not closed it down because Sector West Command wanted Greg's company to collect information of the smuggling operation. Greg has had his recon teams in hidden locations observing the activities, taking photos, recording descriptions and license plate numbers.

Greg and I were sitting at the wood table under the camouflage netting roof that was behind his CP in Tunubibi. There was no breeze, so the night air was hot. The build-up to the wet season had begun so comfortable, nights of sitting outside were rare. I sipped semi-cold Coke from the can of Coca Cola that Greg had offered me.

Greg and I sat in silence while he thought deeply about what I had presented to him. He then said, "Let me know when your boys will make their move. I will have a section of recon there to give them some help."

Greg knew the importance of Armindo Soares. There were many Militia leaders that would be worth capturing but they were all in West Timor where they were safe from being forced to pay for the horrible atrocities that they committed. Here was a chance to get some good intelligence and then turn this monster over to the justice system.

Greg told me in confidence, "You have got to be careful. There is an investigation going on about some UN worker in Bobonaro who is involved with espionage activities. I was questioned a few days ago by my commanding officer about who this UN spy is."

I said, "Yeah, I figured." I asked, "You have any idea who is behind the investigation?"

Greg said, "The investigators are United Nations police so it must be coming from the police commissioner."

Two nights later Donny returned from a meeting in Dili. He parked his United Nations Nissan pick-up truck behind the American House. I was sitting on the back veranda drinking a beer as Donny walked up onto the veranda. He looked like someone had kicked him in the gut. I stood up and went to get him a cold beer as he sat on a folding chair on the veranda.

I returned and handed him the can of beer as I asked, "What's up? You look like someone stole your favorite hunting dog."

Donny shook his head despairingly as he said, "We're in trouble, big trouble."

I could see that Donny was greatly stressed as I asked, "What's up buddy? What happened?"

Donny lit a cigarette then took a long drink from the can of beer that I had handed him, "The police commissioner knows about your spying activities. He is conducting an investigation to catch whoever is responsible for the espionage that has been going on out here. He said that he will show no mercy on those involved."

As Donny ventilated, I was picking up on a lot of positive points. I also realized that Donny was a true friend. I knew this by the very first thing he said, "*We* are in big trouble."

I was a hostage negotiator and instructor for many years. Negotiators learn psychology for the purpose of manipulating the desired response of the hostage-taker, which is usually their eventual surrender. A negotiator learns to pick up on what a person under stress says to determine his true intentions.

When Donny said, "*We* are in big trouble" I knew that he didn't sell me out. I listened to Donny's step by step description of everything that was said during his meeting with the commissioner.

By the time he finished I knew the commissioner didn't have any facts. The commissioner was reacting to rumors that he had heard. The situation was still dangerous to me but I had room to maneuver. I told Donny, "Hey, don't worry about it. The commissioner don't know shit. You don't either for that matter. You know that I have been collecting information but that is the job the UN gave me to do. You don't know where I get that information or how."

I paused for a moment for effect, "When this investigation comes down to actual interviews by investigators you just tell them what you know. Don't tell them what you think you know and we will be fine."

I could see the extreme stress flow out of Donny's face as he realized that he really didn't know anything. I stood up from my folding chair and held my hand toward Donny. Donny looked at me questioningly as he grabbed my hand. I shook his hand and said, "Thanks for being a true friend. If this investigation should turn out bad I will be the only one taking the fall. I take care of my friends too."

Donny laughed as he said, "You are so full of shit, Martin."

I went to our garbage can cooler in the kitchen and retrieved two more beers. I came back out onto the veranda and handed Donny a beer as I sat back down. We sat in silence for a couple of minutes before I broke the silence, "So you wanna hear what I am working on now?"

Donny yelled, "No!"

I continued, "I'm thinking about kidnaping a Militia leader from West Timor. You want to hear how?

Donny screamed again, "No!"

I sat for a moment, then said, "Okay, then, I'll just keep it to myself."

I was making light of this situation but I actually had a solid purpose in mind. I was joking about something that any normal human being would think was impossible. If or when the kidnaping operation was conducted I wouldn't be anywhere near the Nunura River. My joking about something that was unthinkable and then have that unthinkable thing occur at a time that I couldn't have had any involvement was one small "fail safe" for my survival.

When investigators take statements from their witnesses who may possibly have overheard something I said, I can fall back on, "I was just joking around."

Besides that, I wanted to see the look on Donny's face if this kidnaping operation actually happened. I could picture him scratching his head in deep thought as he remembered my joking around on this night about kidnaping a Militia leader from West Timor and then a week or two later it happens.

During this same time period more stressing news came to La Faik from the Atambua cell through the Mailbox. The news was the Militia who control the Atambua Refugee Camps is planning some kind of action against the United Nations UNHCR people who work and live in West Timor. We were not surprised to hear that.

There had been isolated incidents of intimidation against the refugee assistance group known as UNHCR. One week before hearing this news from our cell in Atambua a UNHCR convoy was attacked as they drove through Turiskai. A mob of rock throwing East Timorese who live in the Turiskai refugee camp broke out windows and dented the UN vehicles with the rocks they threw. For a few minutes the convoy was trapped by the mobs of people who blocked the vehicles passage. Then suddenly the road in front of the vehicles cleared and the convoy sped through.

Our Turiskai cell reported that Abilio De Araujo stood on the sidelines observing the riotous attack. As the crowd closed in on the trapped UN workers who huddled in the damaged vehicles Abilio barked out an order to the crowds, "*Para. Hotu ona.*" (Translated, "Stop. It is finished.") The crowd stopped immediately. The many people in the streets watched as the panicked UN workers saw their opportunity to escape and sped away.

The SGI had been tightening their counter-intelligence noose in an attempt to stop the flow of information that had been flowing to our side of the border. It appeared that the SGI believed that the UNHCR workers were a probable source of obtaining secrets from West Timor and delivering that information to East Timor. The SGI decided that the UNHCR had to go.

I didn't know what action the Aitarak and Besi Merah Putih Militia in Atambua intended to do but I knew whatever it was would be violent. I completed a report sealed it in an envelope and wrote "Urgent" on the front. As I had done since Donny gave me the mysterious message months ago I handed Donny the envelope. As Donny held the envelope I tapped the word I had wrote on the front. I said softly, "Don't waste no time getting this to whoever you give these reports to."

A couple of days after I delivered that report to Donny, The UNHCR workers in Atambua were attacked in their compound in the early evening. Many men dressed in black, wearing bandanas to cover their faces and blackening the exposed areas of their face with charcoal, entered the United Nations compound. The machete-wielding men in black hacked, stabbed, and terrorized the international workers.

The end result was three United Nations workers dead, several injured, and all of them completely horrified. The Indonesians gave the Australian military permission to enter Indonesia for the purpose of evacuating the United Nations workers. The Australian military drove their evacuation Force the three kilometers to Atambua and removed the traumatized workers and the three bodies. The United Nations presence in West Timor was over.

Three days later Donny was summoned to Dili for a meeting. We naturally figured, "Here we go. The official investigation is beginning."

Donny returned to Maliana in the early evening. He stepped up onto our back veranda and said, "Well, it's over."

I asked, "What's over?"

Donny didn't hesitate a moment before answering, "The investigation, everything." I thought *That was quick. I never saw any investigation go that fast before.*

Donny continued, "The police commissioner called me into his office. All he said was that the espionage investigation is completed and they could find nothing to substantiate the allegations. My meeting with the police commissioner was over in less than two minutes."

I was stunned. I sat and just looked at Donny for what seemed like ten minutes. I think my mouth was even hanging open. Donny laughed at my silent reaction. He then said, "The person who gave me the message to give to you a few months ago was waiting at my truck in the parking lot of the Headquarters when I came out. He gave me another message for you."

I sat and waited for Donny to tell me the message but Donny just sat there looking at me. I finally grew impatient and asked, "Well—you going to tell me or what?"

Donny chuckled some more. He was obviously enjoying toying with me. Donny finally said, "He said for you to take a CTO and relax. Your work is finished. Ride out your last few weeks in this mission and go home."

I responded quickly, "I can't just quit. We got shit going on that you don't just turn off like a light switch. I got to fini—"

Donny cut me off as he said, "The man also told me to tell you good job."

I thought about what Donny had told me. Obviously this mystery man had some clout to stop the police commissioner's investigation dead in its tracks. Apparently I was too "hot" to continue my secret work since I was being told nicely but firmly to quit. The "heat" could be coming from the United Nations, the military, Indonesia, or any combination of these.

It went against my grain to quit when there was still work to do. Actually it was more than just the work. I had developed strong relationships with La Faik and several other Segrada Familia operators. In addition to that I had come to know the Timorese people as a whole. I related to their struggle for freedom during the Indonesian occupation of East Timor. I believed in the struggle that was occurring now to keep the freedom they had fought so hard to get.

* * * *

I told La Faik what had happened. I told him that I would still pass on information to support Project Feedom but that I had to back off on the Project Homecoming operations. I did finish coordinating the support for the kidnaping operation though. This operation had hit a couple of snags but eventually we got them worked out. The kidnaping attempt happened on the day that Donny and I were going to Dili to start our CTO one week after I was told to quit.

Donny and I were driving out of Maliana at mid-morning when we heard the radio traffic about some East Timorese men who tried to drag some man across the river from West Timor. They got the man halfway across the river but then the man suddenly recovered from some head injuries and fought the East Timorese like a man possessed. The man eventually broke free of his captors and ran to the West Timorese side of the river. The report of this incident came from an Australian military Patrol that just happened to be at that location at the time.

As we heard the report over the radio Donny looked over at me as I drove down the road. I could tell that he was remembering the night I jokingly told him that I was thinking about kidnaping a Militia leader from West Timor. The look on his face was exactly what I had pictured other than he wasn't scratching his head. As Donny silently kept looking at me I said, "I'm going on CTO. I didn't have anything to do with it."

Donny just kept looking at me as I approached the Nunura Bridge. I finally asked, "What?"

Donny finally said, "You are spooky. Thank God our year is almost up."

I smiled as I replied, "I have three weeks left in Maliana after we get back from CTO. That is plenty of time for me to get us both fired." Donny just shook his head as I drove on down the road.

* * * *

The CTO was a much needed break. Donny and I both had not been on a CTO for over sixty days straight. Every UN worker takes a CTO after every thirty days of straight work; we more than doubled that. When we returned to Maliana we were on what was known as "short-timer" mode, which meant the end of our mission was near so you try not to get involved with anything more than necessary. The problem with both Donny and me was we just couldn't sit back and not do work that was there to be done. We both put in an honest day's work right up to the last day we were in Maliana.

One day I needed to get out to Aidabasalala Village and get some information from the Nurep, Paulo Jose. The military no longer kept a platoon in Aidabasalala Village so there was no support in this remote area. The Militia activity in East Timor was greatly reduced by this mid-October day but it was still possible to run into a Militia unit. Maliana Station was short of available cars, which delayed my going to Aidabasalala.

When I finally got my hands on a car it was late afternoon. I took three Segrada Familia members with me and went to Aidabasalala. By the time we got there it was almost dark. I always felt very much at home when I was with the Timorese. This night in Aidabasalala Village was a pleasant evening. A soft breeze drifted into the village from the nearby river making the hot night air almost comfortable.

First we took care of business as we sat on Paulo Jose's veranda. Once the business was over several villagers joined us on the veranda. We all were joking at times and then other times telling war stories. I always enjoyed listening to the stories of the struggle for freedom. I still couldn't speak Tetum but the people were patient while my interpreter translated for me.

It was well after dark by the time we left Aidabasalala. I had been so absorbed into the conversations that I lost track of time. I drove my Segrada Familia friends home then drove to the American house. Donny was used to my wanderings at all hours of the day and night so he didn't think much of my getting home at mid-night.

Two days later a Portuguese Jesuit priest came to the Maliana Station praising my courage to Donny. He had heard from some of his followers about my night time visit to Aidabasalala. Donny called me into his office to meet the priest. I was surprised to hear this priest talk about what an important person I was for the Timorese people. I thanked the man for his comments several times but he just kept on praising me. At first all this praise made me feel pretty good but it soon got old.

The priest was a short man, slender build with short gray hair. The sixty-year-old priest wore all black clothing with a little splotch of white at the front of his collar. Donny announced to the priest that we would be leaving Maliana in about two weeks.

The priest looked at me with a combination of surprise and disappointment as he said, "Oh, no, you can't leave now. The Timorese need you." The priest paused for a brief moment then softly smiled saying, "I will pray that God sends you back again."

I smiled back at the priest as I tried to break the bad news of my leaving East Timor, "I am sorry to say that I will not be coming back. I am very tired and I miss living in America. I won't be coming back here or going on any other missions to any other country."

The priest kept smiling as he stepped closer to me and patted my left shoulder with his right hand. He firmly said, "I will pray that God sends you back. I already know that God will send you back here."

I kept smiling and nodding but I had made up my mind. I was going back to America and I was never going to leave again.

La Faik organized a farewell dinner and fiesta for me Timorese style. There were many speeches, handshakes, hugs, and even some tears during the event. I felt proud to be a part of these people. We reminisced about the many operations we had run together. We laughed together at some misfortunes that fell upon us during operation that at the time was serious but now that it was over some of those misfortunes were funny.

The Timorese always think of things in a positive light. Even though most of the "over the fence" operators were forced out of West Timor, Paulina and her family still had not been brought home and we failed at kidnaping Armindo Soares, these people did not think of it as failure. These were all just temporary setbacks that would be overcome in time. I couldn't shake the Western way of thinking, which was, "We did a good job for a while but in the end we got our butts kicked."

The one thought that did sadden everyone was the loss of Emeu. Emeu was solemnly remembered during La Faik's speech to the many attending Segrada Familia members and families. After the dinner, speeches, and other formalities, a Timorese band played Timorese and Portuguese music as many people danced. This was still going on when I left at almost two o'clock in the morning. I was told that this dance would not end until daylight. I couldn't hold out that long.

Donny's and my last night in Maliana was on Halloween night, 31st of October 2000. We had a nice going away party at our compound that night. UN workers and Local Staff all attended the party, which didn't end until three-o'clock in the morning. The following morning Donny and I deflated the air mattresses we had slept on for the past year, took down our mosquito domes, and threw our kit in the car. We drove to Dili, for the last time.

Once again the remaining members of the first American contingent were together again. We spent six days in Dili going through the United Nations checkout of mission procedure. The leaving American contingent then took our last ride on the United Nations C-130 cargo plane that flew us to Darwin, Australia. We spent a few days in Darwin before being flown back to the United States.

I had a lot of time to reflect on the past year that I had spent in East Timor during the few days in Darwin. I thought about when we had first arrived "in country." At the time, one year seemed like an eternity. Now I wondered how one year could have gone by so fast. I thought about all the Timorese people that I had come to know so well. I already missed them. I thought about my narrow escape from the clutches of the police commissioner who so desperately wanted to catch a spy.

I never really thought I was a spy or even committing espionage. That was all stuff that trained secret agents did. I was just a cop who was doing whatever I could for the cause. As I thought about my exploits in Timor, I realized that I was guilty of espionage, but I wasn't an agent of the CIA, NSA, FBI, or any other acronym, therefore I wasn't the spy that some people accused me of being.

All I knew as I cooled my heels in Darwin was that I was going home and I wasn't coming back. My little secret war was over.

CHAPTER ELEVEN

Coming Home

It was eleven-thirty at night as I watched the lights of Lansing, Michigan, from the window of the American Eagle airplane that carried me here from Chicago. We were only a few miles away from the small capitol city of Michigan. Even at night I could pick out the road near Charlotte, Michigan where I lived. Our plane began to circle the north side of Lansing as the pilot moved into his landing approach. As we dropped altitude, I could begin to recognize specific buildings and neighborhoods.

I had flown out of this same Lansing airport one year ago on this date, 15 November. I hadn't returned since that day. I had thought that I would be very excited about this moment, but I wasn't. I chalked my lack of excitement up to just being tired. This was the end of spending twenty-five hours in the air. That was actual flying time, not counting the layovers in different airports on my way home.

The American Eagle touched down on the runway and soon we taxied to the small city passenger terminal. I stepped down onto the tarmac as I pulled the collar of my uniform shirt up around my neck to shield me from the very brisk air. I had worn one of the same uniforms that I wore for one year in East Timor. The dark blue military-style uniform shirt once again was helping to protect me from nature's elements.

As I entered the terminal I saw my wife who was standing and waiting anxiously for my entry. A short distance behind her were my three sisters. Nancy and her husband Walt had driven all the way from Detroit. Lucille and her husband Don had brought Joan and made the thirty-mile drive from Ionia.

I was surprised that they all made the trip to Lansing to greet me so late at night, but really appreciated the unexpected reunion. My mother had passed away back in 1984. My father had died in June of 2000, while I was in East Timor. My two brothers died in recent years. I was looking at the last of a generation. This was a very nice surprise.

I greeted my wife with a long hug and kiss. I hadn't seen her since June 2000 when I met her in Darwin, Australia during one of my CTOs. I then greeted my sisters with a hug and then a handshake from Walt and Don. I collected my bags from the baggage carousel then walked with my family to the parking area at the front of the terminal. We drove to the Denny's restaurant where we drank coffee, ate, and talked. I felt like I had only been gone a short time as we all sat together and talked.

It was two o'clock in the morning by the time my wife drove into the driveway of my home. It had been a year since I had driven on the left side of the car and the right side of the road. I was a little intimidated, so I told her to drive. As I walked into my house, I remembered the moment that I had walked out of that house one year ago. It had been so hard to leave, knowing that I wouldn't be coming back for a very long time. Now that I was again inside my home, it was just normal. This was nothing like I had expected.

Over the next two weeks I met with friends I hadn't seen, went to restaurants that I used to like, and so on. I suffered because of the extreme cold of Michigan in late November. I was now used to temperatures over one hundred degrees and high humidity. Now I was being subjected to below-freezing temperatures and snow.

I was also subjected to a bank account with less money than what was supposed to be there. I got a couple other surprise bills that my wife had run up during my absence. This wasn't the first time that my wife had spent money behind my back. I had been paid well during my time in East Timor. I had prepared a budget that paid all the bills and also gave my wife more than twice the spending money she could possibly ever use. Obviously, that wasn't enough for her.

After two weeks of being home I was ready to leave. I was cold, I had no income, and the money I planned to live on was gone. Living in America was actually feeling strange to me as the days went by. Everything was so different from the life I had lived for the past year. I missed Timor. I missed my friends. I missed the action.

Three weeks after returning home, I called the company and told them that I was ready to go back to work. I was called back a couple of days later. The voice on the phone told me to be prepared to return to East Timor by the middle of January 2001. A few days later, I received a second call. This time the voice on the other end of the line told me that my redeployment would be March or April. I told this unknown company worker that I could take an assignment in any country; it didn't have to be East Timor. The voice answered me, "You're going back to East Timor when the time is right. Be ready to go, but it will probably be March or April."

The days went by one by one. I watched the snow pile higher and higher and the temperature drop lower and lower. I was bored and freezing to death. One day I talked with a friend of mine who was a policeman. He was currently assigned at the Tri-County Metro Narcotics unit, the same unit where I had done two tours of duty. He was an old-timer narc who knew my reputation as an undercover officer. He told me how the work has completely changed now. They could no longer do the undercover operations the way we use to do them.

After our conversation I thought about what a waste of good undercover tactics we had developed. I realized that soon there would be nobody left who really knew how to work undercover. This inspired me to write a book in an attempt to capture the tactics and pitfalls of true undercover work. I occupied the next few months of freezing and waiting by writing the book I entitled *Shades of Gray*.

The first part of March, I got a call from the company. The voice told me that I would be flown to Washington, D.C. on 9 April, 2001. I would then be taken to a pre-deployment training location near Washington D.C.. I was given my flight itinerary over the phone. By the time I hung up the phone I had mixed emotions. Part of me couldn't wait to get back to Timor. Another part of me didn't want to go.

I felt a lot of love for my wife even though she had lied to me on many occasions. After every incident of her deceit, she always promised not to do it again. I always hoped that the promises would be the truth. I tried to keep a positive frame of mind about her, but by now I believed that she could never change. I knew if I left home again she would pull some outrageous act of destroying our finances.

I wouldn't have minded it so much if she was using the money for herself, but I knew that she was being manipulated by her three grown-up kids. I warned her the next time she pulled off one of her "sneaking money for her kids" acts that I would divorce her. She swore that day would never come. By this time I no longer believed her. I would wait and see.

On 9 April, 2001, my wife drove me to the Lansing Airport. Once again I was packed and leaving America for one year. I didn't bother going to the airport to get my flight tickets before today. I figured I would just pick them up when I flew out. That proved to be a mistake.

I went to the airline counter to pick up my ticket. The lady behind the counter asked, "You don't watch the news much, do you?" I looked at the middle-aged lady and asked, "Why?" The lady told me, "This airline is on strike." I thought, *This is a great start.* The lady told me that there was no problem. There was another flight leaving thirty minutes later for Pittsburg where I was to catch a connecting flight into D.C.. About the time we were to board the flight to Pittsburg it was announced to us waiting passengers that the plane was broken. They were bringing another plane from Dayton, Ohio to take us to Pittsburg.

By the time I got to Pittsburg, my connecting flight had already left. I caught the next flight to D.C. an hour later. By the time I got to D.C. I was three hours late. I went to Pier Five where someone from the company was supposed to meet me. I was carrying all of my kit that I packed for a one-year trip, which was a lot of kit.

I got to Pier Five and looked around, but nobody from the company was there. I asked a security guard assigned to Pier Five if he knew where the _____ people were, giving him the name of the company. The security guard looked at me questioningly and asked, "Who?"

I responded to the security guard with a frown, "That's what I thought."

I dragged all my kit over to the nearest payphones and called the contact number I had been given. I got a voice message. I then called the alternate contact number and got another voice message. I hung up the phone. I stood there for a moment with my hand on the phone thinking about what to do next. I though about how typical this was when working for the company. I smiled a genuine smiled as I said to myself out loud, "Well, I'm back."

* * * *

The top Militia leaders and those who control them had changed their strategy by October, 2000. They could see that they couldn't win a guerilla war against East Timor and the supporting United Nations. They decided on the long-term approach of insurgency.

Many things happened while I was freezing to death in Michigan. The CPD-RDTL recruited more and more members into their ranks. When willing participants started to become fewer and fewer the CPD-RDTL began pressuring villagers who lived in CPD-RDTL dominated areas to join the group.

The pressure they used ranged from outrageous propaganda to turn the villagers against the United Nations and the government that they were creating to out and out intimidation.

Several villages became split between the CPD-RDTL supporters and those who were loyal to building a true democracy for Timor Leste (East Timor). A few villages in remote areas became totally engulfed by the CPD-RDTL. The people who live in remote villages have received little education. There interests are in the day to day living of raising rice and corn, tending their chickens, pigs and maybe a cow or two. These people stood little chance against organized "bullies."

The fact that the CPD-RDTL could so quickly take control of so many people and areas was a testament to whoever was behind the CPD-RDTL group. This feat took a lot of organizational skill and planning. From the onset of this CPD-RDTL movement there was a plan to build a fighting force. An ex-Falintil leader, Daniel Mota, from Holmesel Village located in the Bobonaro sub-district was named the CPD-RDTL Defense Force Commander / Trainer. Mota was organizing the young men of the CPD-RDTL membership into an alleged military force. Actually, they were an organization to force the will of the CPD-RDTL onto East Timorese citizens.

While Mota developed a training program another Bobonaro sub-district figure focused on strategies to gain control of Timor Leste for the CPD-RDTL. Rosalino Cardoso was a respected school teacher in Bobonaro for many years. He now was the CPD-RDTL coordinator for all of Bobonaro district. Rosalino was perfect for the job. He was educated, influential, respected by the community, he had a Falintil background, and as it turned out, he was ruthless.

While he promoted his CPD-RDTL group he managed to always dig away at his newfound enemies, which were the Fretilin supporters for democracy. Rosalino conducted his CPD-RDTL activities in the face of the Fretilin supporters in a manner to provoke his enemy to make a hostile action against the CPD-RDTL activity. The idea was to make the Fretilin break the new laws.

An example of Rosalino's strategy would be conducting a flag raising ceremony in a Fretilin Village. Under the new laws of a free land this group could raise any flag they wanted on private property. Rosalino would plan a flag raising ceremony at a CPD-RDTL member's home that happened to be inside the Fretilin Village. Many CPD-RDTL members would come from several villages to participate in the ceremony. They would march through the village to the flag raising location and through a great display of loyalty to their CPD-RDTL flag and cause they raised that flag to fly in that village for a long time to come.

The Fretilin side of this coin was, "Why do we have to tolerate a flag flying in our village that represents what we fought against for so many years?" Timorese custom from centuries past would not tolerate that kind of disrespect of the majority of the villagers, which would result in using whatever force necessary to prevent outsiders from coming into the village and raising a foreign flag.

Rosalino planned for this possible violent reply from the villagers he was antagonizing. A large percentage of the CPD-RDTL members who attended the flag-raising ceremony were Daniel Mota's defense force prepared to deal with any violence against the CPD-RDTL ceremony.

The Militia, still organized in West Timor, was supporting the CPD-RDTL organization. The Militia was no longer infiltrating guerilla teams into East Timor; however, they were sending small groups of two to four men who would go to a CPD-RDTL controlled village and assist with military training. One of the villages where they were assisting with this training was the village of Lugululi.

Lugululi Village was a remote village a quarter of the way up Lailaco mountain on the edge of the Manapa Jungle. Through lies and intimidation the CPD-RDTL had taken control of Lugululi. The Koppassus trained Militia teams entered East Timor as Timorese citizens. They carried no weapons and dressed in civilian clothes. They would stay in Lugululi Village for a couple of weeks to assist with the training of the young men then return to West Timor.

By April of 2001, La Faik had no elements left in West Timor. The "mailbox" system was still in place but now the only information coming across the border was low grade rumors. La Faik's Segrada Familia still dominated many areas in East Timor. He was closely monitoring the growing threat of the CPD-RDTL. He was also aware of the Militia training teams coming and going from Lugululi.

La Faik attempted to feed information to the United Nations police and the United Nations military about this activity in the hopes that they would take action to stop this military training activity on the edge of the Manapa Jungle. By the end of April it was apparent that the United Nations was not going to do anything about this situation. The Segrada Familia would have to "clean their own back yard."

* * * *

Darwin hadn't changed a bit since I had flown out of that Australian city five months ago. It was still very hot. The small group of new company policemen and I had made the long flight from Washington, D.C. to Darwin pretty much non-stop. Our layovers in Los Angeles and Sydney were just long enough to make the plane change and go through customs before climbing onto the next flight.

We had two days and two nights in Darwin before taking the United Nations C-130 flight over to East Timor. Since I knew Darwin, a few of the new guys wanted me to be their nighttime tour guide of the local discos. I took them into many of the several nightlife clubs as I reacquainted myself with Darwin. We nearly got into a fight while drinking a couple of beers at the Blue Heeler Bar on our last night.

The next morning as we prepared to go to the airport for our flight to East Timor one of the guys that were with me at the Blue Heeler told the story about our near-combat experience. The company coordinator responsible for our welfare on this mission heard the man tell the story. I knew this coordinator from my last tour of duty to East Timor.

He was a good man, fair to everyone, but strict. As he listened to the recounting of the Blue Heeler experience, the coordinator looked at me hard as he listened to the story. His dark brown eyes bore into my eyes harder and harder as the story went on. When the man finished the story the coordinator asked me in a harsh tone of voice, "You took these guys to the Blue Heeler?"

I knew the coordinator was a little pissed at me. I should have been helping to keep these guys out of trouble, not leading them to it. What cold I say? I was guilty. I responded to the coordinator's question, "I was showing these guys where not to go while in Darwin. I was very stern with them while drinking inside the premises. I told them don't ever, ever come into this place." The middle-aged ex-Special Forces coordinator just glared at me. He didn't seem to appreciate my humor. I looked into those brown eyes that displayed his disgust. I shrugged my shoulders and hung my head slightly as a show of shame as I said softly, "Sorry."

The coordinator continued to look at me disgustedly for a few moments then smiled a slight smile, "I got to put up with you for another year? I am going to have to inquire about the company's re-hire program." I knew now that the coordinator had forgiven me. I raised my head from my shameful pose smiled and excitedly said to the coordinator, "Yeah, I'm back. Isn't it great? We will have sooo much fun together, just like the last time." The coordinator shook his head at my comments as he turned and led us to the front of the hotel where vehicles were waiting to drive us to the airport.

As I walked away from the C-130 after landing in Dili, East Timor, I was greeted by the American Contingent Commander with a warm smile and friendly handshake. Mike was near sixty years old. He was slender of build and in good shape. His gray hair was the only thing that revealed his age. He welcomed me back to Timor and in the same breath said, "You will be going back to Bobonaro."

I had decided while I was going through the pre-mission training that I was going to take this mission easy. I intended to work like any other United Nations worker, which was do my job and take my CTOs every thirty days. I reflected those thoughts as I told Mike, "I'm here to do my job like everyone else. I'm not looking for trouble."

Mike smiled and patted me on the shoulder as we continued to walk toward the terminal, "You have been requested. Do what you want when you get there, but you're going."

I stopped walking at the surprise of hearing that I had been requested, "Who requested me?"

Mike laughed at me as he said, "You'll find out when you get there." I could see that Mike was enjoying raising my curiosity level. I didn't push for any further information as I again started walking with Mike.

A few days later I drove out to Maliana with two other American police officers that had been assigned to the Bobonaro district with me. We drove across the Loes River that entered Bobonaro district along the north coast near a village named Atabaleten. It felt good to be in Bobonaro district again. An hour and a half later we pulled into the Maliana Station Headquarters, which had been moved to a prepared location near the center of town.

I looked around at the many strange faces of the United Nations police officers who worked there. I was surprised to see many East Timorese who were wearing police uniforms. These were East Timor's police academy graduated police officers who were being trained in the field by us UN police contingents. I recognized one of those East Timor police officers as I stepped out of the UN Nissan truck we had driven to Maliana.

Fatima saw me as I walked toward the main office. She was five-foot-three-inches tall. Her body was slim but visibly strong. Her short black hair was just long enough to touch the collar of her light blue uniform shirt. As she saw me both of her hands snapped up to cover her mouth with the tips of her fingers. Her dark brown eyes widened with excitement as she stood motionless and watched me approach her. Fatima's dark brown complexion accented the beautiful features of her face.

I walked up to Fatima who still stood where she had first seen me and froze into this excited statue. I lightly hugged Fatima as we exchanged a kiss on the cheek, which is the Timorese custom for greeting a close friend of the opposite sex. Fatima surprised me by speaking English to me. When I left five months ago, Fatima couldn't speak any English.

Some people had suspected that Fatima and I had been lovers; however, anyone who knew us realized that my relationship with Fatima was like a father and daughter. Fatima had been one of our cleaning girls during my first mission. I had got to know her well as she taught me some Tetum words. She was selected to go to the very first police academy that began the building of an East Timorese police force.

Donny and I were so proud of our little Fatima who worked so hard at our compound to keep us neat. Both of us were sad when she cut her long hair short two days before she left to begin her new career. I took pictures of her beautiful hair that hung lower than her butt the day before she cut her hair.

As I looked into Fatima's tear-filled brown eyes, Domingos and Alfonso walked up to me and greeted me with a handshake and a hug. The moment was as joyful as any reunion I had ever had with friends or family. We stood in the hot sun, oblivious of its burning rays. I knew now that I was home. I had come home.

CHAPTER TWELVE

Another Secret Mission

The sun had dropped below the western mountain on the far side of Maliana valley. The mountain on the eastern side of the valley, Lailaco mountain, already seemed cooler with the absents of the sun. Augustinho walked through the Manapa Jungle with ease in spite of his fifty-plus years of age. His body was lean but his muscles from a life time of living a harsh life along with many years of fighting the Indonesians were hard like iron. Augustinho was dressed in blue-jeans and wore a white t-shirt that had "LAPD" written in big black letters across the front.

The twenty-seven Segrada Familia ex-Falintil members following Augustinho up this rugged mountain path were dressed similar to their commander. Augustinho carried a bamboo bow and several arrows. His *katana* (machete) inside its leather sheath bounced against his rib cage as it hung from his shoulder. The other twenty-seven men with Augustinho also carried bow and arrows along with their assortment of *katanas* and knives.

The Segrada Familia Assault Force quickly walked past the few villagers from Lugululi Village that they met on the trail. Everyone that seen this civilian force knew why they were coming. La Faik had sent word to the Lugululi Village chief that this attack would happen. La Faik's message, simply put in English, was, "Militia special teams from Atambua coming into East Timor to train the young men of East Timor to wage war on fellow East Timorese people will not be tolerated."

One week ago a team of four men arrived at Lugululi Village. This four man team was highly trained Halilintar Militia members from Turiskai West Timor. As had been the practice by other Militia training teams this four man group arrived wearing civilian clothes. They carried no weapons other than a sheathed knife on their belt and a *katana*. The knife and *katana* are normal tools carried by almost every Timorese man that lives in remote areas.

La Faik heard about the arrival of the four men on the same day they walked into Lugululi Village. He immediately notified his team Leaders to begin preparations to rid East Timor of this outside influence. As Segrada Familia prepared for the assault La Faik waited a few days to collect any information that may be obtained from this new training team. One of La Faik's informant was a mid-level commander of the now organized men who live in Lugululi Village. Once La Faik was satisfied that his informant had collected all the information available from these outsiders he put his plan in motion.

* * * *

Before Augustinho and his Assault Force could enter Lululugi Village the alarm warning the people of the eminent assault could be heard. The members of the Assault Force heard a man's voice yelling, "Their coming Segrada Familia is coming!" The words were echoed again from deeper in the village.

As Augustinho entered the lower edge of the village he slowed his pace to a slow walk. His twenty-seven members quickly moved into a defensive security screen as they slowly made their way through the village. This was a dangerous moment for the Segrada Familia who was now nearing the center of the village. It was possible that the now organized and trained men of Lugululi would attack the invaders.

Augustinho walked up to the home of the Lugululi Village chief. The village leader walked out onto his veranda and respectfully greeted his visitors. Even in the near darkness of the coming evening Augustinho could see the fear in the chief's eyes. Augustinho was respectful to this man but firm as he demanded to see the four men from Atambua. The Lugululi chieftain said, "They are not here. They ran away when the alarm was given that you were coming."

Augustinho then calmly said, "Show me where they slept." The village chief did not hesitate as he stepped off his veranda and led the way to a bamboo home. There was nobody in the home when Augustinho and his men got there. Segrada Familia members searched the home. The search results were better then expected.

The Segrada Familia informant who lived in Lugululi Village had told La Faik that the Militia teams from West Timor live in this bamboo home during their stay. The home was erected for this purpose. Therefore there was never a time that anyone else entered the home except for a cleaning lady. La Faik realized that there was a good possibility of finding documents inside that home that may have intelligence value.

The Segrada Familia searchers came out of the bamboo house carrying a file folder that was full of loose documents. They also had found two thick hardcover ledgers. The Segrada Familia member who carried the documents out of the home walked up to Augustinho who was standing beside the village chief at the left side of the target home's veranda. Augustinho took the documents and scanned through the contents. By now it was completely dark. Augustinho read the documents from the light of an oil lantern.

After a few minutes Augustinho looked up from the captured papers into the face of the waiting village chief. Augustinho scolded the village chief for becoming involved with men who want to take control of East Timor for their own personal gain. He then lectured the chief about the responsibilities of being a leader stressing that the welfare of the people is the most important of those responsibilities.

The Lugululi Village chief listened to Augustinho quietly but Augustinho could see that the man really didn't care what Augustinho thought. Augustinho didn't care what this village chief thought either. The village chief was a devout puppet of his CPD-RDTL higher leaders and that was not going to change. As Augustinho ended his lecture he was content to know that he had accomplished all of his objectives.

Augustinho's first objective was to march his force into Lugululi Village using the main path that the villagers use to go and come from Maliana. He was to move his force quickly up the path and actually enter Lugululi Village just before dark. The strategy for this first objective was two-fold.

Augustinho and his Falintil could have moved into Lugululi Village in broad daylight without being detected by anyone. The Segrada Familia Force moving up the heavily traveled path would easily be seen by many people. The force quickly moving up that path showed aggression. The people would believe that they were about to be attacked. This gave the Lugululi "defense force" and their trainers the option of defending the village, which is what they had been training to do, or they could turn tail and run for their lives. They would know that the invading force was Segrada Familia Falintil, which nobody in their right mind wants to go up against. It was expected that the Militia trainers and the Defense Force would run.

The next objective was to recover any documents that may be at the Militia bamboo house. The Segrada Familia Force could have simply walked to the house without contacting the village chief. The Lugululi informant had already identified the home for La Faik; however, by Augustinho leading his force to the home of the village chief and receiving the chief's assistance Augustinho set the stage for the third objective.

The third objective was to put the Lugululi Village chief in his place. Augustinho showed the village chief the proper respect by contacting him for his assistance. When the village chief cooperated with Augustinho everyone in the village could see that the strength of this CPD-RDTL leader was subordinate to this renowned Falintil commander. Many Lugululi villagers would have heard Augustinho's scolding and then lecture of the village chief as they stood in the shadows watching what was taking place.

The purpose of the third objective was not so much to weaken the resolve of the true CPD-RDTL followers. The main purpose of forcing this village chief into his place, even if just for a few moments, was to give encouragement to the many Lugululi villagers who have been pressured to become CPD-RDTL members.

Augustinho led his men out of the village on the same path that goes to Maliana. Once away from the village Augustinho made a sharp right turn off this path. He led his men through the Manapa Jungle. It would take this Segrada Familia Force most of the night to get home but it was better to spend a few extra hours in the jungle then to walk into an ambush.

Augustinho suspected that the young men of Lugululi may have recovered from their initial panic. It was unlikely but it was possible that the young men could be waiting in ambush for the returning Segrada Familia Force. Augustinho and his Segrada Familia members were not scared of being injured by any attack from the young men. These novices of jungle warfare could easily be defeated. What these battle hardened warriors feared was possibly having to hurt or even kill some of these kids. It was better to simply take a long night walk through the jungle.

* * * *

The four Halilintar Militia men in Lugululi Village heard the men shouting that Segrada Familia was coming. These four men were well trained by the Koppassus; however, without their rifles and hand grenades they couldn't defend themselves. There wasn't enough time to organize their two platoons of trainee's into a defensive position. Besides they knew that the Lugululi trainee's couldn't hope to win against the Falintil even if the trainee's were armed with rifles, which they were not. The Militia Special Forces operators had no choice but to escape and evade the Segrada Familia.

The four men grabbed their light-weight black backpacks and fled out the back of the village. All four of these Militia soldiers had operated in the Manapa Jungle in the year 2000 during the guerilla campaigns against the United Nations. These men had outmaneuvered UN Forces many times in this same mountainous jungle. They were confident that they would easily escape.

The four men moved quickly up the mountain. They moved along a seldom used path that went straight up the mountainside. The last light of this day could be seen in the gray sky over the mountain. The jungle where these men walked was almost completely dark now. The four evading men had walked about three hundred meters away from Lugululi Village.

The team leader decided to wait for the moon to rise high enough in the sky to give them some light to walk through this jungle. He moved his men off the trail about ten-meters. The four men settled down into the jungle floor. They closely watched and listened for any movement around their temporary position.

Two hours later a three-quarter moon showed its bluish light through the high trees. The Militia team leader gave the signal to move out. The four men slowly made their way back to the little path and started working their way up the mountain again. The team leader hadn't taken a dozen steps up that mountain trail when he heard a sound that sent a chill up his spine. It was a sound he had heard many times from the time he was a young boy.

The team leader was walking in the two-position behind his point-man. As he heard the sound he saw the shadowy point-man's shoulders jerk back. The point-man let out an involuntary series of agonizing grunts as he brought both hands up to clutch the left side of his chest. The team leader yelled out, "*Menyerang! Menyerang!*" (Ambush! Ambush!)

The Militia drag-man began to scream a painful scream as the team leader (TL) heard two more high-velocity swooshing sounds from his front. The point-man was hit again as he crumpled to the ground. By now the team leader could see two arrow shafts that protruded from the chest of the man in front of him. The team leaders point-man and life long friend was down on his hands and knees trying to move to the right side of the trail.

The TL melted into the grass and brush at the right side of the trail. He quickly crawled to the front until he was along side of his dying friend who was now halfway into the brush. He was laying on his side, his legs still out on the trail. The TL put his hand on his trembling friends shoulder and rolled him onto his back. The dying man grabbed for his friend and tried to talk but the only sounds he could make were pain-filled grunts.

The TL knew his friend would soon be dead. He patted him twice on the shoulder, then quickly crawled away into the jungle. Soon he was up on his feet and moving as fast as he could without making noise. Many thoughts raced through the TL's mind as he ran for his life. The screams of his drag-man had ended quickly, which meant he was dead. The TL never seen or heard anything from the man who was walking behind him. There was a good possibility that he was evading right now too.

The team leader cursed himself for waiting for the moonlight. He figured the Falintil had tracked his team from Lugululi Village. Had he not waited for the moonlight the Falintil never would have caught up them. The team leader was getting so tired as he struggled to move through the thick jungle. He was having trouble moving quietly. The poor visibility combined with the thick tangled undergrowth made it impossible to move completely quiet. The team leader feared that these renowned Falintil warriors would easily track him down and kill him.

Thoughts of the ambush came back into the team Leaders head. He realized that the ambush was launched from both ends of the trail. Had the Falintil been using rifles they couldn't have attacked from both ends without shooting each other too. Using short range bow and arrows gave the Falintil the ability to shoot from both ends. The team leader thought as he remembered feeling his friends trembling body *Why did I wait? Why didn't we just keep moving?* Tears welled in his eyes as he continued his struggle against the jungle to escape.

* * * *

La Faik squatted comfortably in the thick brush that grew in the Manapa Jungle one hundred meters up the mountain from the rear of Lugululi Village. A soft mountain breeze tossed his hair that was pulled back into a ponytail and hung to the middle of his back. The rugged features of his face were calm as he waited patiently. His bow and arrows lay on the ground beside him as he looked across the Maliana Valley and watched the sun slowly drop behind the western mountains.

La Faik had led a Force of twenty Segrada Familia soldiers into the Manapa Jungle the night before. They spent the day resting in a secluded part of the jungle near the top of the mountain. At mid-afternoon La Faik's force made the two-hour march to Lugululi Village. The men deployed in pre-planned hidden locations one hundred meters behind the village. There was nothing left to do but wait.

There were several paths that ran out of Lugululi Village. La Faik would not have known which paths were the most likely routes of escape the Militia men in Lugululi would use to escape if it hadn't have been for his Lugululi Informant. The Informant was a mid-level commander of the "Lugululi Defense Force." Because of his position in the Defense Force the Informant was aware of the planned escape routes should the need ever arise to escape.

Defense Force members had designated trails to use to make their escape. The Militia trainers had their own escape trail that they alone would take. The strategy of escape was to disperse the fighters quickly in several directions. This would make it difficult for an enemy to effectively entrap the Lugululi Force.

The CPD-RDTL commanders had expected that there would be a day coming when United Nation's forces may come to effect arrests of certain individuals. This was why the Militia Training team had a direction of escape that they alone would take. On the outside chance that the Militia team was captured by authorities there would be no proof that they had any direct involvement with anyone from Lugululi Village. They didn't think that a force like Segrada Familia may come for them.

The Segrada Familia members hidden in the forest could hear the distant yells as the alarm was given in the village. None of the Segrada Familia members moved or even so much as changed facial expressions. These were well experienced warriors. They calmly waited in their jungle positions like statues. They effectively had become part of the jungle.

There were two paths that climbed Lailaco mountain from Lugululi Village. One of the paths was a well used route through the Manapa Jungle. The other path was seldom used. The jungle had all but reclaimed this path. Grass grew on the hard packed earth and brush hung across the path sporadically. La Faik guessed that the seldom used path would be the one that the Militia team would use to make their escape.

It didn't matter which path the escaping men used. The paths were close enough together so that La Faik and his Force could take action on either path. The main body of the Segrada Familia Force was hidden in-between the two trails. Segrada Familia OPs (observation post) was set up on both trails.

The two men who manned the OP hidden near the seldom used trail saw four men moving quickly up the mountain. The Jungle was almost dark as the trees above blocked most of the remaining light from the sky overhead. La Faik showed no change of expression as he received the signal from the OP.

After the four men passed the OP the Falintil warriors stood up from there hidden positions. They cautiously followed the four men up the mountain. Their caution was not out of fear. They knew their prey carried no weapons. They were cautious so that the four men would not become aware that they were being followed.

La Faik knew his Militia enemy very well. The Militia was well trained by the Koppassus. During the daylight hours the Militia could be difficult to deal with. Their night time skills were good but not anywhere near the skill level of Falintil's night time abilities. Falintil trained in the darkness, maneuvered in the darkness and many times attacked in the darkness. The night belonged to the Falintil.

La Faik knew that the Militia would only operate at night if they had to. He planned to follow the Militia until they found a place up the mountain where they would spend the night. La Faik's Falintil would then slowly and very quietly creep into the militia's overnight position and kill three of the four men. The Segrada Familia could have easily killed the Militia near Lugululi Village; however, La Faik didn't want the people in Lugululi to know that their trainers were dead.

As the jungle turned to complete darkness the Militia moved off the trail. La Faik guessed that the team leader had decided to wait for the moon. Two-teams consisting of two-men each of the Segrada Familia members ever so slowly made their way in the direction from the trail that the Militia had gone. These teams would locate the Militia men who they believed was hiding nearby. La Faik arranged an ambush position on the trail.

If the Militia team was waiting for the moon they would come back to the path and start up the mountain again. If they were bedded down for the night the Segrada Familia would wait until the early morning hours before launching their slow and silent attack. It didn't matter to La Faik what the Militia did. They were going to be killed either way.

The light from the rising moon began to brighten the jungle floor as the moon beams filtered through the foliage above. Thirty minutes later Caitano saw the black silhouette of a man enter the path from the jungle. The silhouette tuned and started walking up the mountain on this path where Caitano waited in ambush position. Soon a second silhouette appeared on the path from the jungle and followed the first silhouette.

Caitano knew the time to kill was near. He held his bamboo bow in front of him with his left hand. His right hand gently held the butt of the arrow against the bow string. Caitano felt no fear, no excitement and no remorse for what he was about to do. Killing these unarmed men was no threat or challenge. Like killing a water buffalo to feed the people, this was a necessary chore for the survival of friends and family.

Two of Caitano's teammates squatted in the jungle on either side of Caitano. They held their bows at the ready just like Caitano. They would shoot their arrows into the point-man when they heard Caitano shoot. Caitano began to slowly pull back the bowstring as the Militia point-man walked closer. Caitano and his men could easily have shot the point-man by now but they had to wait until all four of the Militia was in the kill zone of this ambush.

The point-man was only five meters away when Caitano loosed his arrow. The bow string twanged as the arrow sped to its mark. The point-man was so close that Caitano could hear the thud as the arrowhead struck the point-man high in his chest. The victim threw his shoulders back as he reached up with both hands and clutched his chest near the arrow that had buried itself deep into his chest.

The two men on either side of Caitano waited for this common response of the victim. The two men could see the exposed areas of the victim's torso. They loosed their arrows into the point-man. One arrow buried deep into the man's solar plexus while the third arrow found its mark in the man's lower right chest cavity as he crumpled to the ground. A voice from the group of four men yelled out in the Indonesian language, "Ambush, Ambush!"

Caitano and his two teammates prepared to shoot another round but didn't. They could have easily killed the man walking behind the point-man but La Faik had instructed them not to. They were only to kill the first man. Caitano calmly watched their victim as he painfully struggled to get off the trail and into the jungle. By now the second man in line was out of their sight. The agonized screams coming from the darkness behind the first two men told Caitano that the other half of this Segrada Familia ambush was experiencing the same success.

* * * *

I boldly walked into the Bobonaro District Commanders office at the Maliana Station followed by the two Americans who rode out to Maliana with me. There was a tall, stocky black man standing near the coffee pot at the right side of the office. He turned to see who was coming as we walked through the door. He looked at us three unannounced visitors questioningly as he asked, "Can I help you?" I didn't recognize the flag that he wore on the left shoulder of his uniform but from his accent I knew he was from an African country.

Before I could answer, a man sitting at the large desk on the left side and to the rear of this office stood up with a big smile as he said, "Jim, you're here." We both stepped toward each other and firmly grabbed each other's hand for a reuniting handshake. The five-foot-eleven-inch stocky man had a strong grip. His reseeding hairline and close cropped black hair exposed the dark complexion of his face.

I had bumped into a woman at Dili Headquarters the day before driving out to Maliana to begin working at my assigned station. The woman was a police officer from Namibia whom I had worked with in Maliana before the end of my first mission. She had come to Maliana with her Namibia police contingent commander who was assigned as Donny's 2IC (Second in Command). I was surprised to see this woman because the Namibians were scheduled to end their mission in East Timor two months after Donny and I left.

I found out who was requesting my presence back in Bobonaro from this woman. She told me that she and Jasper, Donny's 2 IC, had received an extension of mission time. Jasper was now the Bobonaro District Commander. She also knew that Jasper had been trying to get me back into the mission area and assigned to Bobonaro district since January.

Jasper Meyer was a high ranking commander in the Namibian police force. He was very intelligent and well-educated. He was an aggressive leader who was not afraid to take calculated risks when necessary. He took his responsibilities seriously. He rarely went on CTOs because there was too much work to do.

Jasper and I got to know each other during the last two months of my first mission. Jasper was impressed by my aggressiveness to get the job done. He realized that the real work in East Timor is in the remote areas where a vehicle cannot be driven. I was the only UN Civilian policeman that could and would go anywhere to do my job. He was also impressed with the quality of my intelligence reports that he saw.

I was impressed with Jaspers devoted leadership abilities. He knew everything about everyone under his command and in the upper ranks at National Headquarters. He used this knowledge along with his training and skills to do the best job possible for the people of East Timor and his United Nations employers. I am proud to say that I served under Jasper's command.

* * * *

I introduced Jasper to the two Americans with me. Jasper warmly greeted the two men then asked the three of us to sit down. Jasper gave my two fellow countrymen the usual welcome to Maliana speech complete with the do's and the don'ts. It was strange to me because I felt like I had never left Maliana. Jasper must have felt the same way because he treated me like an old-timer instead of a new arrival.

Jasper then turned to me and asked, "Would you be willing to be the sub-district commander of Bobonaro? There are a lot of problems in those mountains that need to be handled. I know it is rough living conditions up there, but I need you there." I was surprised that Jasper wanted me to take command of the largest and most populated sub-district in all of Bobonaro district. But then again Bobonaro sub-district was like the Wild West. There was no electricity, only a few villages could be reached by vehicle, limited communications with anyone in East Timor and no communications with the outside world. Most UN workers couldn't stand the harsh living conditions of Maliana. Bobonaro made Maliana seem like a thriving modern city.

I answered Jasper, "Yeah, sure, whatever you need. I love those mountains." What I said was true. The entire year that I lived in Maliana I often longed to move to Bobonaro Village at the top of the mountain. I never did get use to the heat in Maliana. Bobonaro mountains was like Michigan in the summer time. The days were tolerably hot and the nights cool. The country atmosphere reminded me of the farm where I grew up.

Jasper turned toward the black man that we had seen when we first walked into the office. The man had sat down at his desk at the front of the office. Jasper asked the man, "Could you take our two new men here and show them around? Jim and I have some catching up to do. I don't want to bore them to death before they have a chance to look around." The three men stood up and walked out the front door. I knew Jasper well enough to know that something was up. I would have thought that I was in some kind of trouble but I hadn't been in Maliana long enough to do anything wrong.

Jasper and I were alone now. Jasper told me, "I need you in Bobonaro to legitimately take command of the Bobonaro police station. There are six East Timorese police officers (ETPS) stationed there along with three Nepalese police officers. We need to build a functional police Department in Bobonaro and give those new East Timorese police officers in-the-field training." I looked at Jasper and frowned slightly as I waited for what was next. There were several United Nations Civilian police that could do a better job of building and running a police department than what I could do.

Jasper continued, "I expect you to build the police department in Bobonaro but I have a more important mission for you." I didn't know what Jasper was about to ask me to do but I knew whatever it was would be tough and probably dangerous. Jasper's brown eyes telegraphed his heart felt concerns as he again continued, "I have reason to believe that there is some type of insurgency activities occurring up there. What I would like you to do is to find out what is going on in those mountains. Train a team of police officers who can operate in the mountains and then, if possible, conduct the operations to act upon the information that you have collected."

I sat quietly and thought about what Jasper was asking me to do. Training a team to operate in the mountains wouldn't be a problem if I had the right people to train. I had tried to build a team during my first mission but my attempt failed miserably. There were high quality UN police officers who could do the job but they lacked the will power. Most of them were more interested in going on CTO and getting themselves transferred to Dili where there were restaurants, discos and women.

Getting the information about insurgent activities was not a big deal. That was something that I knew I could do. I needed some clarification from Jasper on the "operations to act on the information" part so I asked, "What kind of operations against these possible insurgents do you want?"

Jasper was quick to answer my question, "We will go after the insurgents with the Law. You identify those involved and what their activities are. When you are ready we will take statements from victims and witnesses to build criminal cases. Then we will conduct the operations to arrest the insurgents and bring them to trial."

That all sounded pretty straight up to me so far. Even the operations to actually grab these bad guys wouldn't be difficult. I had coordinated with the different United Nations militaries several times in the past to conduct operations of this nature. The military has the radio communication, the firepower and the manpower. Once in a while the military provided airlifts into and back out of "Targets" in remote areas.

As I thought about the combined operations with the military Jasper took the wind out of my sails when he said, "Things have changed since you were here last. The military can no longer be directly involved with police operations. We have to conduct our operations without military support. That is why you have to build a team that can do the job." Jasper paused for a moment then added, "Oh, one more thing. Nobody believes that there is anything wrong in East Timor. There isn't anyone that wants any kind of aggressive information collection conducted. What you do up in those mountains must not be known by anyone. Not even the Civilian police who are working with you. You report directly to me. I will support your activities the best that I can."

I thought, *There it is. There is the potential monkey wrench to get thrown into the works.* Everything was sounding so normal. There was no talk of invading Militia units, kidnapings, smuggling of documents or people, no espionage. Just collect information, build a criminal case and go arrest the bad guys.

But then I am told that I cannot use the resources needed to go out into those mountains that are dangerous enough just walking through them. Now there may be armed insurgents who aren't going to like it when investigators take statements from villagers for the purpose of criminally charging the insurgents. The suspects definitely are not going to like it when we come to arrest them.

Then to make matters worse there will be no support from National Headquarters. They don't even want to hear any information about possible insurgency in East Timor. I didn't understand why the complete secrecy. I figured Jasper wasn't telling me everything, which was all right. Jasper's job was to handle the political side of things in Dili. My job was to build a police station and go collect a little mountain gossip.

I had a lot of respect for Jasper. I trusted him as a commander and a friend. I didn't hesitate for a moment. I told Jasper, "Whatever you need Jasper. I'll build you the best team that I can but that is going to depend on what I have to work with when I get there. I'll find your Insurgents too. We'll work out the operations against them once we know what we are dealing with."

Jasper smiled and said, "Thank you, Jim" As he stood and shook my hand. He then added, "I hope we can neutralize this growing threat in East Timor by legal means."

I was still shaking Jasper's hand as I raised an eyebrow, frowned a little and said, "Yeah, me too. I get the feeling this little mission your giving me has deeper waters then what your telling me."

Jasper just smiled and replied, "I'll take care of you." I nodded my head slightly still wearing the frown as I thought *Yeah, well, who's taking care of you?* I knew that I would never know the answer to that question.

CHAPTER THIRTEEN

Insurgency or Criminals?

The early morning sun flashed into my eyes time and time again as I drove up the winding mountain road. There was only one vehicle assigned to the Bobonaro police station in Bobonaro sub-district. Jasper had given me the second best vehicle in the Bobonaro district fleet, Jasper drove the best one. Jasper knew that I would need a strong dependable four-wheel-drive to get me to the places that I would be going.

The United Nations provided their civilian police force with three types of vehicles, which were Land Rover Discoveries, Indian-made Tatas, and Nissan club-cab pick-up trucks. I was a now the proud owner of a white Nissan pick-up that had big black UN letters stenciled on both sides and the hood.

I pointed out different sights to my only passenger as we made our way to Bobonaro Village, which was about a forty-minute drive from Maliana. Randy was one of the two Americans who were newly assigned to work in Bobonaro district. He was the unlucky one to get assigned with me. I could tell that he wasn't thrilled about working and living in the "Wild West."

I couldn't blame him, or anyone else, for that matter. Even Maliana now had reliable UN telephones, Internet connection, a couple of different restaurants, and electricity throughout the night hours. Bobonaro didn't have any of those things. Well, our Bobonaro Station had a UN telephone installed, but it only worked on rare occasions. I figured the UN put the telephone in the station to tease the UN civilian police who worked there.

Randy was in his early thirties about six feet tall, and muscular. He was in excellent physical condition. He had been a police officer in Mississippi until he got the opportunity to go on a United Nations mission. He was a SWAT team commander and instructor where he worked in Mississippi. I planned to use

Randy's skills to help me train a special team. I would use him on operations in the mountains if he showed me he could handle it. I knew Randy could handle the physical part of mountain operations but the toughest part of the mountains is the psychological part. Not too many people from western societies can handle the second part.

We turned onto the dirt road from the main mountain road that goes into Bobonaro Village. The dirt road was badly washed out in places. There were many deep ruts where civilian trucks and military trucks and APCs had gradually displaced the dirt of the road. A car could not have passed down this road. A car would be hard pressed to travel down the main mountain road. A kilometer later we drove past the Catholic church that is at the top of a hill on the edge of Bobonaro Village. The road then curves more than ninety degrees to the right and sharply drops down to the center of Bobonaro.

At the bottom of this steep hill I turned right onto the main street of the village. I drove to the end of the street then parked the truck beside a small single-storey building that I was told was the Bobonaro Station. We saw three Timorese men and one woman sitting on the two-foot-high cement ledge that ran the length of the veranda. All four of the Timorese were wearing the ETPS (East Timor Police) uniforms. Their light blue shirts and dark blue military style pants were immaculately cleaned and pressed. Their black boots were polished to the point of glowing.

The four police officers greeted Randy and me with big smiles and a handshake as we walked onto the ground level concrete veranda. We were then led into the building. The two offices on either side of the vestibule were the offices of the Bobonaro Zona (sub-district) Administrator and staff. I met the Zona Administrator, Mateus De Jesus, as we walked in the front door.

Mateus was a five-foot eight-inch, slim Timorese man. He didn't display a muscular image but I could feel his strength when we shook hands. I would later find out that Mateus was the commander of the infamous Falintil Clandestino group known as Colimau 2000. The group had disbanded in November of 1999 when there was no longer an enemy to fight.

We were next led to the rear office in this single-story building. The room was maybe ten-feet by twelve-feet. There was a desk top computer and printer on a folding table against the front wall. Next to that table was an identical folding table that was devoid of articles other than a telephone, which I would learn hardly ever worked. The left side wall had a five-foot high open face shelf cabinet that ran from the back wall to the large window. A long folding table was pushed up against the back wall. To the right of that table was one four drawer file cabinet. A large Indonesian military map hung on the right wall.

There were three men and one woman in my new office when Randy and I walked in. Two of the men were wearing Nepalese police uniforms. Both of these men introduced themselves as they shook our hands. The other two people in the room were Timorese wearing ETPS uniforms. Randy and I shook hands with the two Timorese police officers.

I could see the rank marked on the Timorese man's uniform epilates. This was the man that Jasper told me was my Timorese counter-part at Bobonaro Station. He was subordinate to my Command but he was the ETPS commander who would run Bobonaro Station when the ETPS took operational control from the United Nations in June of 2003. I quickly learned that none of my ETPS staff spoke English as I tried to talk with them. There was no interpreter assigned to the Bobonaro Station. Two Malaysian police officers had been running the station prior to my arrival. Both of those policemen spoke Indonesian so there was no need for an interpreter.

Later in the day Roshan and Rana, the two Nepalese, took Randy and me to a house on the other side of the market area of Bobonaro Village. The ETPS commander, Olavio, came along with us to help us negotiate a deal for renting the home. I had discovered that I could communicate with Olavio somewhat. Olavio spoke Portuguese and I could speak limited Spanish. The two languages were similar enough so that Olavio and I could talk.

We drove through the center of this small village on the rough concrete street. The center part of Bobonaro Village looked like a Mexican villa. Both sides of the street was lined with one-story concrete building. About fifty meters past the market area the street turned from concrete to a gravel surface. We soon crossed a small bridge that spanned a narrow ravine. Just past the bridge as we started up hill Roshan said, "Turn here." I looked to my right and saw a narrow driveway that plummeted to a concrete home that was built on a small flat surface twenty feet lower than the street.

I turned into this driveway and rode the brakes to keep the truck at a slow speed. The gravel driveway was so steep that I knew if the road surface was mud the truck would slip to the bottom, which was several meters past the concrete house. I pulled into the flat gravel area in front of the home. Several Timorese came to the front of the house to greet us. This was the family that owned the home.

They showed us around and through the home. I liked the house immediately. The concrete home had a nicely finished wide veranda in the front.

There was a small room that entered from the left side of the veranda. This was a storage room only. There was no doorway from this room that entered the home. The front door entered into the small living area that ran twenty-feet to the back wall. There were four equal size bedrooms, two that entered from the right side of the living area and two that entered from the left side.

Out the back door and fifteen-feet behind the home was the small bathhouse. Inside the bath house was a two-foot long by two-foot wide by two-foot high cement tank that held water for bathing. In front of this tank, cemented into the floor was the Indonesian style toilet, which we called a squatter. I could tell that Randy wasn't impressed with our new home but I was pleasantly surprised to find such a nice home in these mountains.

We made arrangements through Olavio to rent the house. We agreed to pay the family one hundred and fifty dollars a month, which would include the family cleaning the house and washing our clothes daily. Randy and I spent the last few hours of that day settling into our new home. We used the front left bedroom for storage and made the back left bedroom into our kitchen. I slept in the back right bedroom while Randy took the front right bedroom.

We spent the first few days getting familiar with our home, the village, the office and fellow police officers. I was surprised to see that the old TNI compound that had housed a Kiwi platoon during my first mission was now manned by a company of Australian soldiers. Australia's 4th Regiment Bravo Company was our neighbors. Bravo Company's compound was only twenty meters from our office.

We quickly became acquainted with our Australian neighbors. I told them how different their compound was from when the Kiwis occupied the same place. The compound now had a much larger perimeter that was well fortified with barbed wire fencing and concertina wire. There were sandbagged and roofed security positions around the perimeter. They had built two large buildings on the right side for barracks. There was a large roofed area between the barracks and the main building where a Gold's Gym-style weight room replaced the Kiwi caveman weight room that use to be there.

Two weeks after I arrived in Bobonaro I was ready to begin the secret side of what Jasper wanted me to do. The ETPS commander Olavio and I were communicating pretty good through our Portuguese and Spanish languages. Talking with him was still difficult because my Spanish was not very good but we got by. In addition to that I was gradually picking up Tetum words.

I took Olavio with me and drove to Maliana. As usual when I was doing something of a secret nature I looked for Domingos or Alfonso to translate for me. I had to be sure that there was no confusion about the conversation I was about to have with Olavio. I found Domingos at his home in Maliana. We sat on his front veranda where the three of us could talk alone.

Olavio was a man with a lot of experience. He was a low-level commander in the Indonesian police Force during the Indonesian occupation. secretly Olavio was a Falintil spy. Up front he performed his police duties for the Indonesians all the while he collected information to be passed on to Falintil commanders in the field. The Indonesian police force in Timor, known as Polri, was para-military trained, which meant Olavio was trained for military operations with military weapons.

Olavio was in his mid-forties and muscular. His black hair was combed back from his medium brown face. It was clear to see that he was well disciplined. He was devoted to the welfare of East Timor and the East Timorese people. This was the perfect man for my secret mission, or so it seemed anyway.

We went through the proper formalities as we sat on Domingos front veranda. Then while drinking coffee served to us by Domingos sister I told Olavio that I wanted to transform the ETPS assigned to Bobonaro Station into a special operations unit. All people that I have known that were once a member of an elite special operations team always have the itch to do it again. Olavio was no different. His eyes lit up when I told him what I wanted to do.

Then I told him what I planned to use the team for. We had to get out to remote villages to establish a network of informants. Eventually we would need to get investigators out to those remote villages to take statements, arrest suspects and capture documents. This raised the eyebrows of both Olavio and Domingos. I sat silently as I watched the reactions of Olavio.

Olavio didn't respond so I continued, "I have reason to believe that there is a group or groups of individuals that are conducting some kind of destabilization activities. We have been tasked to find out what is going on, identify the bad guys and then put a stop to their activities." I paused for a moment while I took a pack of cigarettes out of my pocket. I handed the pack to Olavio. He opened the top of the flip-top box and took a cigarette. Domingos didn't smoke so Olavio handed the box back to me.

After we lit our cigarettes I told the still-silent Olavio, "We will conduct our operations as though we are simply patrolling the villages. The eventual investigations and arrests will be conducted officially; however, during these same official operations, we will be collecting documents and other intelligence of the group's participation with those who intend to take control of East Timor. I need you now and eventually other ETPS who we can trust."

Olavio's face broke into a smile as I finished talking. Olavio responded solemnly, "It is like you said. The Indonesians will come back as soon as the United Nations leaves East Timor. They will regain control of East Timor through the Militia in West Timor and the supporters who they establish are living here. There is something going on out there but the people are afraid to talk to anyone." Olavio paused as he took a drag from his cigarette, "I was hoping someone like you would come here. East Timor needs you."

I instantly thought about the Jesuit priest who had said the same thing to me a month before I left East Timor, *East Timor needs me, huh? Maybe they do. I guess that priest's prayers worked. Here I am, back in East Timor, and God knows what I am getting into.* We finished our meeting and left.

Before driving back to Bobonaro I went to see La Faik. He wasn't home, but I talked with is wife. It was a struggle but I finally understood from Mrs. La Faik that her husband had gone to the jungle with some of his elements for a few days. I told her through Olavio that I would come back the next time I was in Maliana.

* * * *

With Olavio as my ally our secret operations came together quickly. We started training the six ETPS officers in special tactics. Randy assisted us with the building-clearing tactics" but when it came to the jungle tactics, Randy wasn't much good, or interested. There are not too many jungles in the cities of Mississippi. SWAT doesn't deal with jungles or mountains.

Olavio was a hard task master as he drove the six ETPS officer relentlessly. I was surprised at how fast those six young officers developed tactical skills. I had trained many American police officers special operations tactics. The tactics Olavio and I were teaching these young men and women were tougher tactics than what I taught in America but these kids caught on quicker than any group I had ever worked with.

There is something about training together as a tactical team that is a very bonding experience. The only thing that is more bonding then training together is when the team conducts actual operations. Everyone on this team already was very closely bonded from the training. We were like a family only after a few weeks of training.

I was quickly learning to speak many Tetum words as time went on. I was actually thankful that I never got an interpreter assigned to Bobonaro. I never would have labored to learn any of the Tetum language if I had an interpreter. As I learned Tetum, my teammates learned English. Olavio's Portuguese and my limited Spanish filled in the gaps. To effectively communicate our team had to mix and match four languages to accomplish one simple conversation. It was difficult at times but we were getting by just fine without an interpreter.

In between training exercises we were conducting patrols into many of the villages scattered throughout Bobonaro Zona. Many times we combined our patrols with the Bravo Company Civilian military Assistance team (CMA). It was their job to get out to as many villages as possible to promote the "winning of hearts and minds." They also were collecting any information available from village chiefs and other citizens about the villages and the people who live there. This four-man Bravo Company team was a great bunch of guys who did an outstanding job of both taking care of the people and collecting information.

The weakness of the information they collected was that it was what I call "surface information." You can't extract hard intelligence from "surface" contacts. To get the real juicy stuff you got to get into the bowels of a community. That was what the Bobonaro Special Operations team was doing. We developed secret informants who lived in many different villages. From them we learned everything there was to know about the people and groups of the informants' village and neighboring villages. As we discovered the existence of a group we would then seek to identify a member of the group that we could develop into an Informant. In some cases we were able to get our existing Informant involved with the group.

Once we had an informant who was an actual group member we collected a higher grade of intelligence about the group and what their intentions were. The ideal penetration was to develop an Informant who was a leader or administrator within the targeted group. The higher up the leadership chain of the group that we establish a secret Informant the higher the grade of information was that we could collect.

Within two months of my arrival in Bobonaro we had identified several groups throughout the Zona. We had managed to penetrate some of those groups with informants. Our network of informants was growing rapidly but so were the problems that go with maintaining an informant network. The hardest obstacle for us to deal with was communications.

Most places in this world take communications for granted. In this day and age of telephones, mobile phones, email, fax, and postal service the average person in this world has no concept of not being able to contact someone when they want to. In Bobonaro Zona there is no form of communication other than a face to face contact. The problem with a face-to-face contact is that most of the villages where our Informants lived had no roads.

The effort of walking to a village that was close by Bobonaro required walking down Bobonaro mountain, crossing a fast flowing river and then walking up the next mountain. If the village we had to go to was further out we would have to add another mountain and river to our walk. What would make this Patrol worse was the walk back to Bobonaro. Bobonaro mountain is the highest and hardest mountain to climb in all of Bobonaro Zona. Every time I climbed that mountain I swore I would never do that again. But of course I did do it again, many times.

By July of 2001 Jasper managed to get his hands on a Honda 400-cc Quad-Runner. He gave the Quad-Runner to us. The Quad gave us a much faster ability to contact our Informants. Before the Quad arrived we would have to spend at least one day just to make one contact. The Quad could be driven to several of the villages we had to get to. The Quad was a big help to us even when going to a village the Quad couldn't access. We used the Quad to get us to the bottom of Bobonaro mountain and walked the rest of the way from the river. That Quad saved us many hours of walking.

Our Quad had amazing power. There were times that I drove the Quad up such a steep incline that I had to stand up and lean well over the handle bars to keep the front end against the ground hard enough to steer. I swear that Quad could climb up the side of a concrete wall if you could figure a way to make it stick to the wall. The only weakness of the Quad was that only two teammates could go on the patrol. Jasper tried to get us another Quad but he had a hard enough time pirating the first one. Jasper's source of "acquiring" the first Quad didn't think he could successfully "acquire" a second Quad without getting caught.

By August our Bobonaro secret Special Operation / Intelligence Service team had collected enough information to give a fairly clear picture of what was going on in Bobonaro Zona. The CPD-RDTL was the most visible group operating in the Zona. Rosalino Cardoso conducted numerous flag raising ceremonies in many villages. This infuriated the Fretilin supporters and there were several times that they planned to attack the invading CPD-RDTL flag-raisers.

Captain Chris Thripp was the commander of Bravo Company's CMA team. Chris intervened on several occasions to convince the Fretilin members not to play into the hand of the CPD-RDTL who were deliberately provoking them. Chris was energetic, confident, and intelligent. He was about thirty years old and in excellent condition, which was typical of all the soldiers of Bravo Company. Bravo Company was a commando-trained outfit. Many of the command staff and team leaders were ex-SAS (Special Air Service). Chris genuinely liked the East Timorese people. Chris's respect for these people along with his charismatic charm prevented violence between the CPD-RDTL and the Fretilin Party on several occasions.

Daniel Mota was CPD-RDTL's commander of the CPD-RDTL Defense Force. I turned in intelligence reports to Jasper about Daniel Mota and this Defense Force along with many other reports of information we collected. I asked Jasper for permission to give a sanitized version of this information to my CMA friends. I knew that this commando outfit would follow up, in their own way, on the information. Jasper agreed to give them the information.

Daniel Mota was giving military drill training to a group of about thirty young men in Homesel Village. He was training a similar size group in a village just over the line into Kova Lima District. He had a third group he was training in a village on the other side of the mountain in Saburai Village, which is near the Indonesian border. Tapo Village, which is next to Saburai, was the planned Headquarter of this CPD-RDTL Defense Force.

The commandos confirmed the military training in Holmesel Village as they observed the training sessions from the recon teams hidden locations higher up the mountain that overlooks Holmesel Village. They also confirmed the Defense Force Headquarters in Tapo Village. There was even a sign that read, "CPD-RDTL Defense Force" posted in front of the once school now CPD-RDTL compound.

The next group we identified went by the name of *Bua Malus*, which is the Tetum word for "beetle nut." Beetle nut is a nut from a tree that many villagers chew. Those who chew beetle nut are easily identified by the bright red saliva and their red teeth. The first time I saw beetle nut chewers smile at me I thought they were bleeding from inside their mouth.

The Bua Malus commander was a respected Falintil commander during the war with Indonesia. He was now commanding a large group of ex-Falintil, ex-Clandestino and villagers in the Lepo area of Bobonaro Zona. The Bua Malus commander, Raimundo Karau Timor, had completely taken control of the Lepo area that is not near the main mountain road. The people of Lepo who were not Bua Malus members did not dare go into this Bua Malus controlled area. They had to walk around the area to get to their fields of crops. On two different occasions Raimundo and some of his members was seen target practicing with rifles.

We identified a group who at first caused a lot of confusion. This group went by the name of Colimau 2000. At first people thought this was the infamous Clandstinos who had wreaked havoc on the Indonesian Forces. Because of the reputation of the Colimau 2000 name many young East Timorese joined the group.

This group was well organized and controlled. The Colimau 2000 commander was a man named Gabriel Fernandes. The group Headquarters was in Maliana. We didn't try to penetrate this group. As I was becoming aware of this group La Faik had already penetrated the group with one of his Elements. It was better to penetrate the group from Maliana anyway. The Colimau 2000 Headquarters was in Maliana and most of their membership was in Maliana, Atabae, and Cailaco sub-districts.

Then one day an ex-Falintil commander from Dili came into Bobonaro. The commander was known by his code-name Labarik Maia. This commander had come to Bobonaro to recruit the many ex-Falintil who live in the area. Maia told everyone who would listen that an ex-combatant group was being formed to support the ex-Falintil and ex-Clandestino soldiers, much like America's Veteran Organizations. The ex-combatant group, known at that time as FBA, sounded like a good thing.

We were able to quickly penetrate this group. I actually had thought that we were wasting our time on this one but one never knows what a groups true intentions are unless you get into their head. Within two weeks of our initial penetration of the FBA we were getting a picture of what the FBA really was and it wasn't good.

The FBA was a Nationwide group who intended to unite all the ex-combatants into a security force. There was indications that this force would secure control of East Timor to establish what the FBA commanders felt was the proper Government and Constitution. Our informants who we had penetrated into the FBA gave us detailed information about the FBA structure and a secret headquarters that they were building at a very remote village in Manu Fahi district named Osanako.

The FBA struggled in the beginning. They originally planned to fill their ranks with true ex-warriors of the war with Indonesia. Many of the ex-warriors harbored strong devotion to the renowned Falintil Supreme commander, Xanana Gusmau. The Timorese people think of Xanana as a super hero who is like the father of East Timor. Probably much like George Washington was to the American people a couple of hundred years ago.

The Falintil who served under Xanana held the deepest respect for their commander. They responded to Labarik Maia's attempted recruitment with a question, "Does commander Xanana Gusmao support the FBA?"

Maia had to answer, "No."

The ex-Falintil then told the disappointed Maia, "Then we don't support the FBA, either."

After several months of trying to recruit the warriors of East Timor and failed the FBA hit upon another plan to fill their ranks. They opened the prospective membership to include any East Timorese who were a family member of an ex-Falintil or ex-Clandestino fighter. Virtually every East Timorese was a relative of an ex-warrior. The FBA organization then began to grow in numbers rapidly.

The more information we collected about these groups, the more confused I became about what all this meant. I was a field operator not an analyst; however, it was important for field operators to understand what was happening. A good understanding of the developing situation helps the field operator to better pick his targets. It also gives clues as to which strategies that can be used against the targets.

I had many discussions with Jasper about the information that we were collecting. There were many indications that these groups could one day become a threat to the stability of East Timor. Jasper told me that the United Nations wasn't looking at these individual groups as a serious threat. No one group had the strength to effectively destabilize East Timor; however, both Jasper and I felt there was much more to all these groups then what we knew at that time. The only way to find out was to burrow deeper into the groups.

On 30 August, 2001, the first free election in East Timor was held. The people were voting for their choice of who would hold the Parliament seats for the first Democratic Government of East Timor. The vote for the President would occur in April of 2002. I divided the Bobonaro Station staff to cover the multiple Polling sites throughout our Zona.

I was in the remote village of Sibuni for the event. After studying all the information that we had collected Jasper believed that the Sibuni Polling site was the "hot spot." We decided that I should physically be in Sibuni Village for the election proceedings. It turned out to be a good move.

I took one Australian civilian policeman who Jasper had assigned to my station and two of my Timorese teammates with me to Sibuni on 29 August. Bravo Company sent a section of soldiers to Sibuni to give us support and to provide radio communications capability. We spent the night before the election sleeping on the cement floor of the Sibuni school, which was also where the polling station had been established.

The following morning as the sky began to brighten from the approaching sun we could see many hundreds of Timorese who calmly sat in the schools athletic field waiting for the polls to open. Many of those people had walked through the night to arrive at their assigned polling station on time.

At 0700 hours the United Nations voting coordinators opened the polls. The many people filtered through the system to cast their votes. It was almost 0800 hours when three Timorese men singled me out to report a problem. One of the three men was from Anapol Village. My mind flashed back to my first ever walk through the mountains when the Kiwi section escorted us cops to Anapol Village to investigate the murder of four young men. The man from Anapol told me that he was sent by the Anapol Village chief to report that the people of Anapol will not be coming to vote today because they were scared to leave the village.

Last night unknown people came to Anapol Village and hid in the darkness near many homes. The unseen people in the darkness threw rocks at the many homes to cause terror. Any villager who tried to leave their home was hit with rocks. This act of terror continued throughout most of the night. I tried to get details of the incident from the man but I could see that he wasn't going to tell me any more than what he already had.

The Australian section with us in Sibuni radioed the information about the incident to his CP in Bobonaro. The Fiji military contingent was responsible for the security of lolotoe sub-district. Anapol was just over the sub-district line from Lolotoe into Bobonaro Zona; however, Anapol was more easily accessed from Lolotoe so Anapol Village was given to the Fiji company to secure.

A platoon of Fiji soldiers was immediately dispatched to Anapol Village. The platoon happened to be nearby the village so they arrived in Anapol within a short period of time. The people of Anapol felt safe with the Fiji platoon in the area so they left their homes and came to Sibuni to vote.

By mid-afternoon the athletic field was empty. Everyone had cast their votes and started their long walks home. The polling site would remain open until 1800 hours but I knew that there would be nobody else coming to vote. I told Bob, the Australian policeman, to handle the polling site while I took the Quad and one of the ETPS to Anapol Village.

Atanacio was a Timorese man who lived his entire life in Bobonaro Zona. He had gone through one of the earlier police academy courses, which made him a senior police officer among the Bobonaro staff. Atanacio had a stong Falintil background, which was common for people who lived in the mountains of East Timor. He was a good operator and a good friend.

Atanacio was in his late-twenties, lean but very muscular. He was very alert to everything around him including a natural feel for reading people or situations. I took Atanacio with me to Anapol not only because he was one of our better tactical operators but I needed his determined spirit to help drag out the truth of what was happening in Anapol.

We drove the Quad down to the river on the backside of Sibuni mountain. We couldn't take the Quad any further so we parked the Quad in Maui Village and walked the three Kilometers into Anapol Village. We were gratefully received by the Anapol Village chief, Helder, who served us coffee and told us about the events of the previous night. The big question was, "Who were these attackers and why did they terrorize this village the night before the elections?"

It was a good thing Atanacio was with me. Helder was holding back until Atanacio first badgered and then coaxed the truth out of Helder. It turned out that this terror had begun in April of 2000. There was a group of men who were commanded by a man who is known by the code-name of Tim Saka ("Tim" is pronounced "team"). This group was based out of a village named Pellet, which is where Tim Saka and many of his members live.

Starting in April of 2000 Tim Saka would lead thirty to forty of his members into Anapol Village armed with Katana's, sabers and bow and arrows. They claimed to be the Clandestino's for an elite group of Falintil soldiers who are still hiding in the mountains waiting for the right time to come and fight the enemies of East Timor. Tim Saka dropped the names of many well known Falintil hero's as being members of this elite Falintil Force. The interesting thing was that all these names were of "dead" Falintil hero's. Tim Saka claimed that they were still alive.

Tim Saka also told the people that the Izolados, which was the name Tim Saka called this hidden Falintil Force, sent him to collect contributions from the people to support the Izolado Force. Helder and his villagers didn't believe that the Izolado's existed so they refused to give anything to Tim Saka on his first visit in April of 2000. Tim Saka responded by ordering several of his men to severely beat Helder. The beating was followed by the coordinator of the Tim Saka group stepping up to the badly injured Helder who now lay helpless on the ground in front of his home. The Coordinator grabbed Helders hair and pulled him up to his knees. The Coordinator then held a Katana against Helders throat and orderd, "Tell your people to give us what we want or you die now." The name of this Coordinator was "Daniel Mota" from Holmesel Village.

Tim Saka and his group were then able to take over control of Anapol Village during their stay. The village women prepared a feast for the group at Tim Saka's direction. Tim Saka and his subordinate leaders helped themselves to any of the attractive young women of the village who they wanted through the night. The next day they collected money, cows, pigs, cigarettes, clothing, and lesser items from the people.

* * * *

Jasper and I discussed this information that Atanacio and I had brought back from Anapol Village. There was no prior knowledge about this unnamed group from Pellet Village. Pellet wasn't even marked on the military maps. There was only one name of the many names of the suspects that Atanacio and I collected from our Anapol trip that had been heard of before. The only known suspect named was the CPD-RDTL Defense Force Commander Daniel Mota. We had to question the legitimacy of Helder's story.

I believed the information was true. Unlike Jasper I was in Anapol Village to see the fear and sorrow in the eyes of Helder and many of the villagers. Jasper trusted my judgment. He wanted to begin building a criminal case against these unknown people who were from this seemingly non-existent village that isn't even on the map. I told Jasper that we were not ready for that yet.

We had the Special Operations team who could get investigators into these remote mountain villages. The problem was finding investigators who had the grit to make the trip with us. The other problem was that this investigation would become very dangerous very soon as we walked many miles through the mountains. This group in itself sounded like a Force capable of ambushing us. In addition there was a solid connection to the CPD-RDTL Defense Force under the command of Daniel Mota.

Jasper understood the problem. He told me that he would try and find me men who were good investigators and could handle long dangerous walks through the woods. In the mean time I was to continue our information collection projects.

* * * *

I took Olavio for a return visit to Anapol. I knew if we kept going back, Helder would open up more and more. He eventually gave us names of other villages who were being victimized by Tim Saka and his group. We intensified our patrols into the remote villages that Helder had named. One of those villages was a village called Atus. Helder had said that one of Tim Saka's leaders lived in that village along with four other Tim Saka members.

I took Atanacio with me to Atus Village. The truth is it was becoming dangerous for us in those mountains now, more dangerous then before. We had to assume that Tim Saka was getting information about our increasing inquiries about him and his group. The risk of getting ambushed by bow and arrow wielding Tim Saka or CPD-RDTL members grew by the day; however, by taking the Quad we could accomplish more in a shorter period of time. Besides that, I didn't want to climb Bobonaro mountain any more than I had to. The problem with driving the Quad was only two of us could go on the patrol. That wasn't enough to effectively defend ourselves should we walk into an ambush. Our survival depended on our ability not to walk into an ambush.

I drove the Quad with Atanacio sitting behind me. We worked the Quad down the mountain path slowly. The path was so steep and rough that to travel fast endangered us of tipping the Quad over. We parked the Quad at the side of the river when we reached the bottom of the mountain. It was only a one-klick walk down the river from where we parked the Quad. Atanacio was on point closely watching for danger to the sides and his front. I walked behind Atanacio and covered our rear and both sides of us.

We made our way through the rushing water of the river when the jungle became too difficult to pass through. Eventually we came to the path that led up to Atus Village to our left. I looked at the sharp incline of the path and knew this was going to be a hard one-hundred-meter climb to the top.

The climb was harder than I had thought by looking at the path from the riverbed. There were many times that I had to hang onto a piece of shale rock or brush to keep from falling from this narrow path that was on the side of this almost cliff. I hoped the weak shale rock wouldn't give way, which would have resulted in my very quick return to the riverbed below. Our ability to secure ourselves from attack during this climb was non-existent.

We entered the Atus Village and were graciously received by the village chief. While we sat on the veranda of the chief's home, Rafael came from the rear of the house and joined us. I was surprised to see Rafael there. He was the 2IC commander of the CPD-RDTL under Rosalino Cardoso. Rafael was a radical leader and prone to violence.

Rafael was a man in his late-thirties. He lived in and ruled the little village of Lactos, which was on the upper edge of Bobonaro Village. Rafael had family who lived in Atus Village, which is why he was there on that day that we visited. I actually had always got along good with both Rosalino and Rafael so I was not concerned for our safety by his presence. In fact Rafael was responsible for giving us more breaking news in our quickly building case of Extortion against the Tim Saka group.

Atanacio mentioned Tim Saka and his group from Pellet during our conversation with the village chief and Rafael. At first Rafael didn't say anything. Thirty-minutes later we were sitting quietly while we ate the Timor-grown roasted peanuts that we had been served. Out of the clear blue Rafael said, "I don't like Tim Saka."

Atanacio pushed his statement, "Why not?"

Rafael said, "Him and his men come here and demand money from the people."

I was a little surprised to hear Rafael tattle on Tim Saka. Because of Daniel Mota's involvement with the Tim Saka group I assumed that the CPD-RDTL was all involved as well. Now the second highest ranking CPD-RDTL leader was telling us about Tim Saka's atrocities. But then again Rafael's family living in Atus Village was being victimized along with everyone else.

We coaxed all the information that we could out of Rafael and the village chief. Rafael even pointed out to us the Tim Saka commander and four of his members that live in Atus Village. It was easy for Rafael to show the suspects to us because they were sitting at a home nearby watching us very closely.

As we were getting ready to leave Atus the Tim Saka commander, Alesu Sabrout, and his four men grabbed their Katana's and walked out of Atus Village in the direction of the path that Atanacio and I had climbed to get to Atus. Rafael watched the men closely as they disappeared in the jungle from the edge of the village. Rafael said, "Tim Saka and his men know that the police are investigating his activities. You cannot go back the same way you came. Those men will ambush you on the trail." I thought *I already had that figured out.*

Rafael and the village chief led Atanacio and I to the opposite corner of the village and showed us a path that is rarely used by the villagers. They told us to take this path back to the river, we should be safe. We shook hands and said thanks to our Atus Village hosts then started through the jungle toward the river.

Atanacio walked point as I followed, both of us completely alert for signs of an ambush. I was so focused on our back trail that most of the way through the jungle I was walking backward. Atanacio stopped at the edge of where the trail we were following dropped out of my sight.

Atanacio just stood there looking down. I finally moved up close to him so that we could talk. I asked, "*Saida?*" (What?)

Atanacio never moved or looked away from his fixed gaze, "*Perigozu makas?*" (very dangerous). I moved up along side of Atanacio and looked down. I could see why the villagers rarely used this path. We were about to descend a path that was so steep and rugged that we needed mountain climbing gear, which we didn't have. It wouldn't have mattered. I wouldn't know how to use the gear if we had it.

I told Atanacio in the best Tetum that I could, "We got to go so just go." I took a little comfort in the thought that if we fell we would at least deny Tim Saka the pleasure of killing us. It took us twenty-minutes to get to the riverbed below but we made it in one piece. We quickly but cautiously made our way up the river toward our waiting Quad.

Halfway back to the Quad we stopped on a little island in the middle of the river. This was a pleasant little place with a soft breeze blowing down the river. We could see any threat they may approach us on this little Island from any direction. We stopped to take a break and eat a little food that we had carried with us.

Atanacio and I lit a cigarette and enjoyed this little piece of paradise in the middle of nowhere. Atanacio said what I was thinking, "The work we are doing is very hard but at times like this I like it. I like working with you." The experience of being in those mountains cannot be described in words. I knew what Atanacio was saying and I felt the same love for him too. I smiled as I slapped him on the shoulder.

* * * *

By November we had everything we needed to begin operations against the Tim Saka group, everything except an investigation team. By now the two Nepalese had been transferred to Dili. The two Australians assigned to my mountain were about to end their mission and Randy was not an investigator. Jasper assured me that he would send me two good investigators from the new batch of Australian policemen that would replace the Australians soon leaving the mission.

I was very tired. I hadn't been on a CTO in nearly three months. I told Jasper that I needed a break. I made out the paper work right then for a CTO that would begin in about one week. Jasper signed the papers and told me to plan on leaving in one week. He would see to it that my CTO was approved.

A few days before my CTO started there was a serious incident that occurred at Maui Village. Rosalino Cardoso and Daniel Mota led a group of about sixty CPD-RDTL members to Maui Village for an unannounced flag raising ceremony. Maui Village was one of several villages that make up the Molop Desa. There was not even one CPD-RDTL member who lives in the Molop Desa.

The CPD-RDTL group walked to the middle of the wide gravel bottom riverbed and waited, they just stood there. The people from Maui Village, which is on the rivers edge, saw the group of invaders in the river. The Molop Desa Village of Omalai overlooked Maui and the river from the heights above. The people of Omalai Village also saw the large group of men standing defiantly in the river.

When the people of Maui Village and Omalai Village above could be seen gathering at the edge of the river Daniel Mota yelled as he held the CPD-RDTL flag, "This is the flag of East Timor. You must learn to respect the true government of East Timor."

Crowds of villagers soon collected in the riverbed to confront the invaders. The Maui Village chief and two of his sub-leaders took up positions in front of their people. They tried to convince the people to go back to their homes.

The village chief's efforts were overridden by the jeers and taunting of Daniel Mota and several of his men. By now the sixty-plus CPD-RDTL members had formed a skirmish line in front of the crowd of people from Molop Desa. The village chief approached Rosalino and asked him to take his men and leave before there is trouble. Rosalino yelled at the highly respected village chief, "You move your people out of our way now!"

A young man had moved up close to his village chief. When he heard Rosalino so completely disrespect the chief the young man stepped forward and struck Rosalino in the face with his fist. Rosalino crumpled to one knee on the ground. This was what Daniel Mota was waiting for. As Rosalino fell to one knee Daniel Mota shouted, "Attack!"

The men that formed the skirmish line of the CPD-RDTL all had rocks in their hands. They responded to their commander's order in unison as they threw the rocks they carried into the crowd of people. This proved to be a big mistake. It was clear that the CPD-RDTL had come to Maui Village to pick a fight with the people of Molop Desa. Their strategy was to lure many people close enough to be attacked. They believed the sixty-plus CPD-RDTL force could easily overwhelm the citizens by a fast and organized initial attack. It didn't work out that way.

The people of Molop was already angry because of the presence of this CPD-RDTL force along with their taunting's. Their anger grew when Rosalino disrespected their chief. Though many of the Molop Desa people were struck by the CPD-RDTL rocks the people didn't run away as Mota believed they would. The people picked up rocks and fought back with a vengeance.

The riverbed is covered with rocks that are the perfect size for throwing at another human being. The people of Molop outnumbered the CPD-RDTL force and they were standing in the middle of an ammunition rich riverbed. The CPD-RDTL skirmish line was crushed within moments. Daniel Mota and his men were forced to run for their lives. They run down river away from the angry crowd and then turned up the mountain, going back to Holmesel Village.

Rosalino didn't make it out with his Defense Force commander. A combination of the initial blow to his face that put him down followed by the many rocks that was bounced off his head and body left Rosalino in a crumpled heap in the riverbed. The village chief and other village leaders protected Rosalino from further injury. They took the injured Rosalino to the chief's home. The village chief's wife prepared food for Rosalino while the village medic treated his wounds.

Late in the afternoon of that day several battered CPD-RDTL members reported the incident at our station in Bobonaro. We took statements from the five CPD-RDTL members who had come to our station. The story above of what happened in the riverbed is what the five CPD-RDTL members wrote in their statements with the exception of they did not know what happened to Rosalino.

The following morning I led a patrol to Maui Village to find Rosalino and bring him back to Bobonaro. We found Rosalino sitting in the shade at the village chief's home being well taken care. We brought Rosalino back to Bobonaro. The following day we took a statement from Rosalino at our office. I was amazed at Rosalino's account of what happened.

Rosalino said that he was taking the CPD-RDTL group to a village in Kova Lima District. As they were crossing the river near Maui Village they were attacked by the villagers and forced to run away. Rosalino said that he had been captured, beaten and held against his will by the Maui Village chief and two other village leaders. Up until this moment I had always liked Rosalino. I didn't like his tactics of promoting the CPD-RDTL but he was doing what he believed in. He had never stepped over the line that separates right and wrong, although he frequently nudged the hell out of that line a few times.

Now Rosalino grossly stepped over that line. His blatant lies accusing the very men that saved him were amazing to me. I understood his strategy perfectly though. If Rosalino could accuse the innocent leaders of Maui and get them criminally charged this would infuriate the Fretilin members all through the Bobonaro Zona. This would cause the many people who believe in the existing democratic justice system to question their views and maybe change their support of the current Government establishment.

I spoke at length with Jasper about the Maui incident and warned him about what Rosalino was trying to do. Jasper assured me he would monitor the situation while I was on CTO. Two days later I did go to Darwin on my much-needed CTO.

CHAPTER FOURTEEN

The Team Saka Task Force

My CTO in Darwin was just what I needed. I had taken ten days of leave time and spent every day of that time in Darwin. I always stayed at the Mirambeena Hotel when I was in Darwin. The Mirambeena had two huge saltwater swimming pools, an outside bar and lounge area, big comfortable rooms, and everything that I wanted to do in Darwin was in easy walking distance.

As usual, on the day before my return to Timor, I went through the normal, "I don't want to go back" feelings. Darwin was so nice, clean, easy-living and safe. I hated to leave the comfortable Western style of living to return to a life of squatting to relieve myself, pouring cold water over myself to get clean, sleeping on the floor in a mosquito dome, and being isolated.

At least now I knew the natural cycle of my feelings. The first few CTOs I had taken in 2000 I was always depressed on my last day in Darwin. Now I knew that when I landed in East Timor I would be happy to be back. I wasn't depressed on this November 2001 day before my return. I just accepted the feeling of not wanting to go back.

* * * *

I stopped into the Maliana Station to meet with Jasper. I had just driven three hours from Dili. I needed a break from driving down the rough roads of East Timor anyway but that was a sideline benefit. There was a message from Jasper waiting for me when I got off the UN C-130 flight in Dili. The message was to meet with Jasper the moment I got to Maliana.

I walked into Jasper's office. A man I had never seen before was sitting at the front desk, which is the district operational commander's desk. The man was in his mid-thirties, five-foot-nine-inches tall and muscular. His short, dark hair and mannerism gave me the impression that he should be wearing an Australian Bravo Company uniform appose to the Australian police uniform he wore.

The man stood up from his desk and introduced himself to me as we shook hands, "Hello, I am Paul Blood, the new Bobonaro district operations commander." I shook Paul's hand as I remembered Jasper telling me that there was a new batch of Australian police coming. Paul was obviously one of them. I told Paul my name just as Jasper walked in the door.

Jasper's entry ended the small talk as Jasper said, "Jim, you're here. We must talk right away."

Jasper walked to his desk at the rear of the room and sat down. I sat in the chair beside his desk while Paul sat in the chair in front of the desk. Jasper took a cigarette out of the pack that was sitting on his desk. He then threw me the pack. I took a cigarette out, then offered the pack to Paul. I already knew that Paul was the type who didn't smoke but I could have been wrong. I wasn't; Paul politely said, "No thank you."

I was surprised that Jasper didn't shoo Paul away while we talked. Jasper got right to the point, "I have been waiting for you to return. I need you to conduct an operation immediately. The prosecutor's office in Dili has issued warrants for the arrest of the Maui Village chief and his two subordinate leaders. CPD-RDTL national-level commanders are putting a lot of pressure on the United Nations to bring these men to justice."

I was stunned. I told Jasper that we would be making a big mistake by arresting those men. I then calmly emphasized, "Those men are innocent. Everybody knows it except for the cowards who issued these warrants just to appease the CPD-RDTL." Jasper nodded his agreement with me but told me we have no choice. The warrants for the arrests are issued and the police commissioner wanted those men arrested two days ago.

I was closely studying Paul who I realized was closely studying me. He only sat and listened as Jasper and I talked. As our discussion continued, I eventually accepted the fact that we had no choice. The commanders in Dili are so out of touch with what was going on out here that there was no hope of knocking them into reality.

Once I realized the operation had to be done I started thinking of strategies to pull this thing off and somehow turn this around so that the CPD-RDTL didn't win in the end. Jasper knew me well enough by now that he calmly waited while I thought this thing through. The answer came to me in an instant. I knew what to do but I needed time to work it out. I could see that Jasper was under great pressure to get this thing done right now. I had to give him the ammunition to stall the police commissioner.

I stood up and walked over to the large military map on the wall. I spoke like a teacher in front of a class as I educated Jasper and Paul. I pointed at the location on the map where Maui was, "This is Maui Village. Maui Village is in the center of Molop Desa, surrounded by other Molop villages."

Paul was standing beside me by now. He looked hard at the map where I pointed, "There is no village there."

I looked at Paul, "The village is there. It's not marked on the map but it is there. Trust me on this."

I told the two commanders the hard facts, "We are going to have to walk from Bobonaro, which will take the better part of a day. When we get to the village we will grab these three guys and haul ass."

Paul interrupted me as he asked, "Why do you have to—haul ass?"

I looked at Paul, understanding that he was new to Timor and didn't know the people yet, "Because when we arrest these innocent men, there are going to be a few hundred angry villagers who are going to take our prisoners back from us, if they can catch us."

I told Jasper and Paul as I pointed out locations on the map, "We will make our escape going down this river toward Anapol. Anapol is the only Molop Desa Village that will not attack us when they see that we have the Maui chief in custody. We have built a strong relationship with them so we should be all right going through there. We will then go up the mountain on the other side of Anapol. At the top of that mountain is a road that goes to Suai. That same road also connects with the Bobonaro road in Laurba Village. We will have our truck waiting for us there. We will then drive back to Bobonaro with the three prisoners."

Jasper was well acquainted with the types of operations that I had conducted in the past. The operation plan I described was actually pretty normal, other than we would be in danger from the angry Molop Desa citizens. Jasper knew the plan I just outlined was an overview version. I would work out the details and write up an "operation plan" to turn in to him for his final review and approval. Jasper simply said, "That is good, Jim. Do it."

I could see that Paul was apprehensive as he fired questions at me, "What about back up? What about communications? What about—"

Jasper cut Paul off, "Jim, when your ops plan is complete turn it in to me through Paul." Jasper had always left the operations commander out of the loop before now. The operations commander had never even been aware of the operations that I ran. I knew the reason Jasper omitted the involvement of the operations commander was because he didn't trust him. Apparently he thought Paul was all right.

I told Jasper, "I will need a couple of days to get this worked out and prepare the team for the ops."

Jasper nodded his approval as Paul asked, "What team?" I didn't answer Paul. I figured if Jasper wanted Paul to know about a special team in Bobonaro he would tell him. I shook hands with the two commanders and left.

I drove up the mountain deep in thought. I had a lot of work to do and very little time to do it in. It was late in the afternoon when I arrived in Bobonaro. I went straight to the Bobonaro Station. I had to talk with Olavio and Atanacio immediately. My plan to deal with this situation in Maui had to be implemented now. There was no time to waste.

I was surprised to see three new UN police officers at the station. Two Australians introduced themselves to me as I walked in the door. The third man was wearing an American police uniform. He also introduced himself. I knew I was getting two new Australians but I didn't know about the new American. I asked the American as we shook hands, "Sooo you assigned to this station?"

Tom, the new American, answered, "Yes, I replaced the other American that was here."

I am sure the confusion showed on my face, "Randy's gone? Where did he go?"

The three new guys snickered as Tom replied, "Randy got transferred to Dili. I am his replacement."

Simon, one of the two new Australians, added, "You must not talk to the district commander much."

I smiled to myself at Simon's comment. If only they knew how much I talked to Jasper. I softly said, "Yeah, I guess it slipped his mind. Anyway, welcome to Bobonaro. You all are going to love it here. The restaurants, discos, and wild women here in Bobonaro will give you plenty of social life and the work is easy."

Simon and Tom looked at each other with a puzzled look on their face while Michael, the other Australian, said, "We have been here for three days. We haven't seen any of those things. Where do you hide them?"

I could tell already that I liked Michael. I answered, "I'll show you later." I told the three new guys to meet me at my house later in the evening. I then excused myself.

I met with Olavio and Atanacio in the interview room across the hall from our office. I described the ops plan for the Maui operation. Olavio and Atanacio was not happy about arresting the three men in Maui Village, either, but they were dedicated police officers and would do whatever the job called for. I brightened their spirits when I told them my real plan, "We will prepare to conduct this operation; however, I don't think we will have to implement it." My two teammates silently watched me while I continued, "We will write a letter to the Maui chief and tell him the situation. The letter will emphasize the treachery of the CPD-RDTL. We will ask for their help to put the CPD-RDTL in their place by the three men coming with us to Dili. We will go to the court and make sure the truth of this incident is known. This will reveal to everyone the true nature of the CPD-RDTL."

Olavio and Atanacio went to work drafting the letter. They were very pleased to hear the plan. They knew that the village chief and the other two village leaders would be obligated to comply with a formal request for their help to confront and expose the CPD-RDTL. All we had to do was stall the operation that we were planning. It would take a few days to find someone to deliver our letter and for the village chief to respond.

I got to the house just before dark. Tom had moved into the room that Randy had used. Michael and Simon had moved into a large tin shack that was next to Bravo Company's compound. The walls and roof of corrugated tin were fixed on top of a concrete platform. My three new policemen were sitting comfortably on the veranda when I drove in and parked the truck. I carried my CTO bag into my room, grabbed a beer from the kitchen, then went out onto the veranda to get acquainted with the new men.

Michael O'Grady was an old-time Australian police officer. He was about sixty years old and five-foot-eleven-inches tall. He was stocky of build with a bit of a gut. Michael had a keen but dry sense of humor. He was happy to see Australia's commando company next door to him. This was the same unit he served with during the Vietnam War. As I got to know Michael I knew he had the psychological grit to handle the rigors of mountain operations, but I was concerned about his physical ability.

Simon Mullins was in his thirties. He was five-foot-seven-inches tall, stocky but a little chunky. His eyes was the same shade of brown as his short-cut hair. Simon had spent a few years in the Australian Army before joining the

Australian Federal Police Force. Simon had an arrogant flair to him. I could see right away that he didn't like to be stifled by leadership. I knew we were going to clash until I earned his respect.

Tom McCarthy was from Texas. He had no military background. His police background was road patrol and investigations, no special operations stuff. He had a strong, determined spirit though. That along with his six-foot-two-inch slender-but-in-good-shape body was all that I would need. He didn't have to learn the tactics. All he needed was the physical ability to walk through these mountains. The team would handle the security part. What it really comes down to is if Tom had the heart to do the job or not.

I was pleased with what I saw. I just had to pull these guys into an Investigation team that could work with my East Timorese Special Operations team. I told these new guys about the operation that we would have to conduct. Tom and Simon were very apprehensive about the details of the plan. They didn't call me crazy but I knew that was what they were thinking. I could see that Michael was apprehensive about The team and my ability to lead such an adventure but that old Special Forces background in him was interested. This was a good sign.

The next two days was training and preparation days. I didn't include the new guys in the training exercises but I had them watch and assist me as trainers. This set the tone for there status of being mentors and trainers of the ETPS. It also gave them the proper respect for their many years of experience. They turned out to be good instructors. I could see their enthusiasm grow as they worked with a team of guys that really could do the job. Simon and Tom still didn't think that we could conduct the operation that I had outlined though.

They confronted me on this issue at the office on the second day. I finally told them, "Relax, I don't plan to actually conduct this operation anyway. If for some reason we have to actually go through with this thing you guys won't be going. It will be dangerous enough without having to get you guys through those mountains. You're not ready for this yet."

I told them my real plan. Olavio had sent the letter he drafted the morning after he wrote it. He found a person from Maui Village that was in Bobonaro. Olavio sent the letter with the Maui man. We will wait for a response. The two men were thrilled with my plan. I could see that I had just raised a couple notches on the "respect scale."

Later on this second day I drove the detailed operation plan down the mountain to Maliana. Jasper wasn't in the office so I handed the ops plan to

Paul. I sat at Paul's desk and waited while he read the plan. When he finished he said, "This is a good operation plan. But I have to refuse it."

I expected this response from Paul. No western nation police commander in his right mind would think that straight up police officers could conduct an operation of this nature. I responded, "That's fine with me. I don't want to go arrest those guys anyway, but Jasper is going to want this thing done."

What I was really happy about was the delay this rejection would cause. I had to stall this operation until I heard from Maui. I knew that if I had a written document that said the three suspects would come to Bobonaro and turn themselves into the police the police commissioner would have to be patient and wait.

Paul re-read the ops plan then commented, "This is a Special Forces-style operation. I wouldn't even approve a trained SWAT team to conduct this ops."

I smiled slightly, "This is pretty basic stuff in the mountains. We've done it before and we'll do it again—if you want. It doesn't matter to me but if you guys want those men arrested this is what its going to take to do the job."

Paul thought for a minute then asked, "Why didn't you plan for a helicopter insertion and extraction?"

I looked at Paul frowning, "I have requested helicopter support from the UN on numerous occasions. You want to know how many time I got any help from them?" I held up my hand with my fingers shaped in a "Zero." Paul lightened up a little as he nodded his head. He said, "Do an ops plan for a helicopter insertion and extraction. I will get you the helicopter."

I smiled again as I replied, "You got it. No offense, but I will believe we will get the airlift when I see it."

As I was driving back to Bobonaro, Paul contacted me on the radio. He said, "Your ops plan had been approved. Conduct the ops as soon as possible." I knew Jasper would approve the plan. Unlike Jasper, Paul did not yet know that we can actually do this stuff. I figured that Paul was probably smarting from being overridden on this decision. I would ease his suffering by doing the airlift ops plan that he requested anyway. Besides, just maybe he could get us helicopters.

When I got back to Bobonaro, Olavio gave me the good news that he had received a letter from the Maui Village chief. The letter said he and the other two men would be happy to turn themselves in to us and go to Dili to present the truth. The problem was that they couldn't walk to Bobonaro. They would have to walk through Sibuni Village and then Oalgomo Village. Holmesel Village was near the trail they would have to walk on as well. The Maui chief believed that the CPD-RDTL in those three villages would attack them. The chief asked us for an escort.

I knew the village chief was right. Sibuni was about thirty-percent CPD-RDTL. Oalgomo was fifty percent and Holmesel was one hundred percent and was also the home of Daniel Mota. We would have to escort the Maui men, which was fine. It was simple enough now. We would conduct the operation that we already planned for. The only difference was now we were avoiding the CPD-RDTL strong points by walking the men through Anapol. Now that we didn't have to worry about angry citizens this operation would just be a long walk.

Early the next morning, I wrote out the plan for a helicopter insertion and extraction. I took the new plan and the letter from the Maui Chief and drove to Maliana where I met with Jasper and Paul. Within three hours Paul had actually successfully arranged United Nations helicopter support for the operation. I was shocked. This operation just became a cakewalk.

The next morning Simon, Tom, Olavio, Atanacio and I were waiting at Bravo Company's helipad for the UN helicopter that would lift us into the target area. I was surprised when I saw Paul drive up to our station twenty meters away. He parked the car and walked over to where we stood. He was encouraging and supportive. I liked Paul so far. He was a good commander. Just the fact that he would drive up to see us off said a lot about this man.

Soon we saw a Russian-made MI-8 helicopter approaching. The big lumbering white helicopter with black UN letters stenciled on the sides settled onto the landing pad. We climbed aboard and we were off. The MI-8 flew over to the next mountain top and settled onto a grass-covered hilltop. I asked the pilot over the noise of the rushing rotors, "Why don't you take us to Maui?"

The hilltop where the pilot landed was in Sibuni Village. The pilot asked, "Where is Maui?"

I pointed down the backside of the mountain where we now sat. The pilot said, "There is no landing zone there."

I responded, "Yes, there is. You could park two MI-8s in there."

The pilot said, "Okay, show me the way."

I crouched behind the pilot as he lifted the big bird off the hilltop and flew in the direction that I had pointed. Within a minute, Maui Village could be seen from the air. I pointed at the village, "There is Maui. On the right side of the village is where you can park this thing." The pilot nodded as he flew toward Maui. A couple of minutes later, he was settling the MI-8 into the large flat area that was next to the Maui single-story school building.

Nobody in Maui knew that we were coming. There wasn't any time to send a message to the village before the operation. Olavio, Atanacio, and I walked across the village to the Maui Village chief's home. The chief greeted us warmly, surprised but happy that we had come to help him and his people. He sent for the other two leaders. When they arrived we walked together across the village to the waiting helicopter.

We all climbed aboard while the pilot fired up the engine. The big rotors quickly gathered momentum. The whole aircraft shuddered as it lifted off the ground. Within ten minutes we were landing on the helipad in Bobonaro. Simon and Tom stayed on the helicopter as the rest of us climbed out onto the helipad. I turned toward Simon and Tom before stepping out of the aircraft, "Take care of them." Tom nodded as Simon gave the thumbs up signal.

Simon understood the evil being done to these three men. He volunteered to go with the prisoners to Dili and make sure that the truth was known about what happened in Maui Village on that November day. Tom volunteered to accompany Simon and lend a hand. The five men would fly back to Dili with the MI-8. Paul had arranged for a car to meet them at the Dili helipad.

Paul was still at the Bobonaro helipad when we got back. We had only been gone an hour but I didn't expect that he would wait. Paul was very pleased with the results of the operation and complimented me for my work. I returned the compliment for his part, which to me was much more amazing then us taking a short ride in a helicopter, picking up three passengers and then flying back. Paul had done the impossible. He got us support.

I asked Paul to speak with me privately. We went to the nearby station and sat in the interview room alone. I methodically went through the developments of the Tim Saka case with Paul. I was careful not to reveal our secret information collection activities. I would never reveal that activity without Jaspers blessings.

I told Paul, "I think Simon and Michael can handle the psychological riggers of mountain operations, maybe Tom too. We can build a case against this Tim Saka group and arrest them if I can get some support. It looks like you can get the support we need. If those guys are willing I would like to form them into an investigation wing of our team and begin operations against Tim Saka."

Paul was interested. With his curiosity peaked he asked, "What team?"

I explained in detail the training Olavio and I had given this handful of East Timorese police officers. I gave him my evaluation of what their realistic capabilities were. Paul wasn't anywhere near convinced, but he was willing to take it one step at a time and see how it went. That was fair enough.

I wrote out the ops plan for the beginning Tim Saka operation. This was a fairly easy operation to plan and execute if we could get helicopter support from the UN. When I finished preparing the ops plan I drove to Maliana to present the plan to Jasper and Paul. Both commanders readily approved the plan. Once again Paul surprised me when late that day he announced that he had the helicopter support lined up for the operation that was now officially called Operation Double-Play.

The Operation Double-Play plan was to insert two teams, one in Anapol Village and the other in Atus Village. The Anapol team was designated team Alpha while the Atus team was designated team Bravo. The objective of both teams was to take official statements from the many victims and witnesses. This was not an easy objective. I knew the villagers were scared. Without the statements, we had no case. If we could get just one statement we could make an arrest or two, which would encourage the people and hopefully make them willing to give us more statements.

Team Bravo would have the toughest part of the operation. For one thing there were five suspects that actually lived in Atus Village. The second hurdle was that we had not made enough patrols into Atus Village to build a sense of confidence in us from the people. The last difficulty was when team Bravo was finished in Atus Village, Team Bravo would walk to Anapol Village and link up with team Alpha. team Bravo would assist team Alpha with statement taking if team Alpha needed the help.

The combined teams of Alpha and Bravo would be extracted by helicopter at 1700 hours. The helicopter would not be able to wait for us so at 1700 hours we had to be ready to climb on that helicopter or plan on a long walk home through "Indian Country." The possibility of getting ambushed as we walked to Bobonaro was a very real threat, which was why we started referring to CPD-RDTL and Tim Saka areas as Indian Country.

The only drawback to this plan was the comms (radio communications). Once on the ground Team Alpha and Team Bravo would be able to talk to each other but we would have no comms anywhere else. A relay Station in Bobonaro wasn't possible either. I knew from past experience that our radios could not reach Bobonaro.

I described the ops plan to Olavio, Michael, Simon and Tom as we sat on the veranda of my house. We were enjoying a warm Bintang beer while I used a map and went through the operation one step at a time. By now all of these men seemed to trust my leadership abilities, even Simon.

I made Simon the team leader (TL) of Team Alpha. His teammates were
Tom, Olavio, Paulina, and Mario. Paulina was a Timorese woman in her
twenties. She was from the Molop Village of Omalai, which was just up the
mountain from Anapol. Mario was in his late twenties. He was strong of both
body and will. He was from Sibuni Village, which was close enough to Anapol
that Mario's presence would give encouragement to the Anapol people.

I would be the TL for Team Bravo. Michael would be our investigator.
Atanacio and Ricardo would be on Team Bravo. Ricardo was only in his early
twenties but he was a fine special operator. He was five-foot-ten-inches tall and
stocky. Paul told me he would "flesh out" Team Bravo with a reliable tactical
man from Maliana. Paul knew team Bravo was going into Indian Country and
may need the support of another reliable "gun" (a man skilled in tactics).

I don't recall the name of this "top gun" that Paul sent to me, which I regret.
He really was a top gun. Mick, which is the name I am giving him, was from
Tasmania. He was six-foot two-inches, stocky like a NFL linebacker. His tactical
skills were superb. What made him even more perfect for our little team was that
he was a mountain climber.

Operation Double-Play began in the early morning. Teams Alpha and Bravo
waited at the Bravo Company helipad for the helicopter to arrive. I must say I
was a bit perplexed when a little French- made UN helicopter landed on the pad.
It could only carry three passengers at a time. All I could do was look at the teams
who stood behind me, shrug my shoulders, and say, "It's better than walking."

I was on the first lift into Atus Village. The Portuguese pilot lifted off the
Bobonaro pad and flew toward the northwest; Atus Village was southwest. I
asked the pilot, "Where you going?"

The pilot took a map and pointed at a spot on the map as he said, "Atus
Village." I looked at the map. He was taking us to Atus Village all right but it was
the wrong Atus Village. I told the pilot that he was going to the wrong Atus.

The pilot asked me for the grid reference for the right Atus Village. I said,
"I'll guide you. Turn left and follow that river." I pointed down to the river I
wanted him to follow.

The pilot made a sharp left turn and dropped down to the river. We raced
along at about two-hundred-feet above the river. Finally, Atus Village was in
sight. I pointed to the Village and told the pilot, "That's Atus Village." The pilot
swooped into the Village and dropped us off in a clearing that was in the center
of the Village. A few minutes later, he was back with the rest of Team Bravo.

We went to work on the people to try and get a statement. The Tim Saka
leader, Alesu Sabrout, and his four fellow members closely watched from a

distance. The situation wasn't good. These villagers would have been scared to give us a statement even if there was nobody in the Village at the time to intimidate them. We were about to give up the quest when a very elderly man walked over to the Village chief's veranda where we sat. The man said, "I'll give you a statement." And he did.

This man's statement was very detailed including dates, times and names of all the offenders that he knew. It took Michael several hours to get all the information down. Ricardo could speak a fair amount of English. He was acting as interpreter for Michael but the translation process was very time consuming. The statement was finished early in the afternoon.

Michael went through the statement with me step by step. We had all the elements of the crime of extortion to charge the offenders. Five of those offenders were sitting on the veranda of a home across the open area of the Village that we used for an LZ. I asked Michael, "We got enough to arrest Alesu Sabrout?"

Michael responded with a simple, "Yeah."

I pulled Team Bravo together so that we could talk. I announced to the team that we would arrest Alesu Sabrout and take him with us to Anapol Village. We couldn't arrest all five suspects. We simply did not have the manpower or resources to handle five prisoners. Next I explained to the Atus Village chief what we were going to do. I thought the chief may be a little upset but he wasn't. His face broke into a broad grin as he said, "Diak" (good).

We walked across the open space and approached Alesu Sabrout. The other four Tim Saka members moved away from the home as we approached. Alesu stood on his veranda giving us a defiant glare. I had spent many years as a police officer in Michigan. I always got special pleasure when the time came to arrest some bully that was stupid enough to think he could intimidate me. Those same feelings welled up inside me now as I looked at this man's face. He was about to find out he wasn't the powerful man he thought he was.

Olavio, Atanacio, and Ricardo did the honors and they did it well. There was no small talk or negotiations. Olavio told Alesu, "You're under arrest," as Ricardo and Atanacio each firmly grabbed an arm and put handcuffs on Alesu's wrists. Alesu's face changed from tough guy to a look of great concern. He thought we were coming to talk to him, which was why the other four men walked away.

We didn't waste time. Once Alesu was in custody we left Atus Village making our way to Anapol Village. It was possible that we could be ambushed by the other four Tim Saka members but doubtful. We took them by surprise so they had no plans in place. We had their leader, which left them without solidarity. On top of that we moved out of the Atus area quickly which didn't give them time to get prepared and then get in front of us. Besides all that, four men with bow and arrows were no match for six men, even though we were only armed with 9mm semi-automatic pistols.

Many people cheered and let out joyful whoops as we walked our prisoner into the center of Anapol Village. Simon told me that they were just finishing up the last of the statements. Out of all the hundreds of people who live in Anapol Village team Alpha could only get eight people to give statements. I was impressed team Alpha got that many. I was even more impressed that they were nearly finished taking the last of the statements.

At 1630 hours we moved the combined teams to the LZ at the river side of Anapol Village. We kept a four-man security screen around Alesu Sabrout at all times. We didn't think he would escape. The security screen was in place to protect him from the people of Anapol. I knew the Timorese people well enough to know that if they got a chance to effect revenge on a man who has greatly abused them they wouldn't hesitate.

I was relieved to see an MI-8 helicopter as it approached us on the LZ. An MI-8 could carry both teams and our prisoner in one lift. Soon the MI-8 was on the ground. The teams climbed aboard along with Alesu. I was the last one on the aircraft. Though we were not under any threat I always adhered to the principle that the team leader should always be the first person on the ground during an insertion and the last one on the aircraft during the extraction. I believe that leading by example marks the best team leaders.

Once again, Paul was at the Bobonaro helipad when we climbed out of the MI-8. Michael and I briefed Paul about the results of Operation Double-Play while Simon and Tom interviewed the suspect. Paul was deeply impressed by the operation we just pulled off. By the time we finished Paul looked at me and said, "Good job. Very good job. Let me know what you need next and I will do my best to get it for you."

I smiled and said, "Funny you should say that. I could use a little assistance in a project I am working on." Paul looked at me questioningly.

By now I was aware that Paul had a close relationship with his Australian commando counterparts. I told Paul that we would need a little military assistance for the next part of the "Tim Saka Campaign." I knew that the military couldn't get involved in law enforcement operations; however, if the military conducted an operation they could request a police presence and they would get it.

The plan was simple enough. We would feed information to the military through Paul. If Paul could expand on his gifted ability to get us real support just maybe he could convince the military to conduct an operation to capture a group of bad guys that was a potential threat to national security. Paul smiled a pleased smile, "I think that can be arranged. Give me the information when you're ready."

Simon didn't end the interview of Alesu until Alesu told Simon everything he wanted to know. Simon was the most amazing interviewer I had ever seen. He had the instincts to go into a man's mind and soul and get them to tell everything. He knew when to put the pressure on and when to give the interviewee an assuring pat on the shoulder or thigh. By the time Simon was through with Alesu we knew everything there was to know about Tim Saka and his gang of thugs.

Over the next few days Olavio and the team kept close tabs on the activities of all the identified groups. We still did not know how the team Saka group fit in with any or all of the other groups. We already knew that there was a relationship of some kind between Tim Saka and the CPD-RDTL. How close that relationship was, we didn't know yet.

As the days went by we collected bits and pieces of information from a variety of Informants that were in positions that up front had no connections with each other. The Tim Saka group turned out to be the central focal point as we put those bits and pieces together. It turned out that Tim Saka had a direct relationship with Raimundo Karau Timor and his Bua Malus group. Raimundo had even got involved with conducting his own extortion activities modeled on his buddy Tim Saka's tactics.

Then we came across another piece of the big picture puzzle that showed a strong relationship with CPD-RDTL. Operation Double-Play put a lot of pressure on Tim Saka. He and his members knew now that we were building a good criminal case against them. He expected that arrest warrants would be issued. He also knew that this Bobonaro team had the capability and will to make the arrests, even if it meant going into the mountains.

Tim Saka took many of his members and went to the Village of Tasqolo. There was a large group of his peers in Tasqolo who would support the evading Tim Saka and his group. Tim Saka's buddies in Tasqolo were a strong concentration of CPD-RDTL.

I gave this information to Paul. I told him the crop was ripe for picking. The Dili Courts had issued arrest warrants for twenty-seven named Tim Saka members. There were at least a dozen more that we did not have names for yet.

221

The information about Tim Saka being in Tasqolo Village was a sure thing. We had confirmed the information from several unconnected informants. We needed to conduct a large operation to attempt to capture the Tim Saka group while they were all together in Tasqolo Village.

Paul was into this thing we were doing. He now had confidents in my ability to lead this very unusual but capable team. He didn't know where we were getting the information but he had confidents in that too. I felt confidence in Paul as well. Paul had the capability to control and support our team. Paul and I had formed an unspoken bond.

When I had finished briefing Paul on all the information and the strategy for going after Tim Saka he said, "I'll see what I can do. Oh—by the way, your team has been given an official name. You guys are The Team Saka Task Force."

I corrected Paul's statement, "No, we are the Tim Saka Task Force. You are the commander; we are the sharp end of the sword." Paul smiled at my attempt to quote Japan's great WW II Admiral Yamamoto's statement to his emperor.

CHAPTER FIFTEEN

The Team Saka Campaign

On 28 December 2001, our Bobonaro team committed our first "over the fence" operation. By now every police officer who worked at the Bobonaro Station was a close knit family. This was the only Station in all of East Timor where the United Nations police and the ETPS were equal, both on the job and socially. On 27 December, the entire team trained for the coming operations that we now knew was going to happen. After the training session we all crowded on the veranda of the American House and drank warm Bintang beer.

As we unwound from the day of training we decided to have a team Christmas / New Year's Eve party two nights from then, Timorese style. Paulina and Raquel would organize the preparation of the food while the guys prepared the station building. The girls recruited the family Tom and I rented the house from to help cook. Raquel made out the shopping list of food for us guys to pick up.

Raquel was a pretty Timorese woman from Malilait Village. She was in her early twenties, five-foot two-inches tall, slender, and as was typical for Timorese women, very well-built with little to no fat. She had recently been married and was now pregnant, which was why she didn't go on Operation Double-Play.

As we guys went over the shopping list, I asked, "So where do we get all this stuff?"

Atanacio answered for the group, "We can get the vegetables and cooking supplies at the Maliana market. We can get the chickens there too. The pig and spices we should get from the Tunubibi illegal market."

Tom quickly pointed out, "That's West Timor."

I looked around at the faces of my teammates. All of the Timorese were looking at me like kids looking at their father, waiting and hoping the father says yes. Simon had that mischievous look of a child wanting to do something he knew was wrong. Michael had his normal indifference look. I asked, "Okay, who is going over the fence?"

Atanacio and Ricardo quickly volunteered as the eyes of everyone lit up. Tom's look was a look of concern mixed with unbelief, "You're not really going to go into West Timor, are you?"

I snickered slightly, "I'm not going over. They are. We will wait for them on our side of the river."

Tom responded, "We?"

I nodded, "Yeah, you and Simon haven't seen the border yet; it's time I show you guys around." The Timorese all laughed as Tom frowned doubtfully.

The next morning Tom, Simon, and I picked up Atanacio and Ricardo at Paulina's house. The three Timorese were dressed in civilian clothes as I had directed them the night before. Atanacio announced as he got into the truck, "Paulina is coming with us to make sure we get the right stuff. I thought, *Women are the same the world over.*

We drove to the market in Maliana. I parked the truck on the street while the three shoppers went through the market buying the shopping list items. An hour later they came back heavy laden with vegetables, bottles of cooking oil and chickens.

Ricardo carried five live chickens dangling from the strings that were tied around their feet. All the items were thrown in the back of the truck then the trio of shoppers returned to the market. A few minutes later they returned with more chickens and vegetables. Our three smiling from ear to ear teammates jumped into the truck as I started the engine.

I drove out to Tunubibi then turned onto the military made roadway that led to the river. This was the first time that I had been to the Tunubibi illegal market river crossing point since the Project Homecoming operations in 2000. The place had changed considerably. There was a larger group of Australian soldiers stationed there. In addition there was now a border patrol office that was manned by UN and ETPS police during the day.

As I parked the truck beside the border patrol office a UN police officer wearing a Shri Lankan uniform came out of the office and walked over to us. He was surprised by the many wing flapping chickens in the rear of our truck. We all piled out of the truck. Simon, Tom, and I greeted the Shri Lankan while our three civilian clad teammates skirted around the border patrol station and slipped across the border.

I told the Shri Lankan that I had brought Simon and Tom to see the border. The Shri Lankan was happy to show us around. As we stood on the rivers edge the Shri Lankan told us that we couldn't enter the river. The riverbed is now considered as "No Man's Land." Only designated police and military from both sides of the border are allowed to enter the riverbed.

As the Shri Lankan was explaining the new rules of the border, I could see Simon almost drooling as he looked at the many selling stalls that people had erected right in the riverbed. Soon Simon announced that he and Tom were going to walk down to the Australian position that was nearby. Within a few moments, I saw Tom's light blue UN cap as the two men wandered through the many shopping stalls and people in the riverbed. Soon the Shri Lankan saw them too. He became very excited as he said, "They can't be there. You must get them out of there right away."

I shook my head at my wrongdoing teammates, but I knew that Simon couldn't resist the lure of the markets. I was just about to call Simon and Tom back when Atanacio, Ricardo, and Paulina came walking across the river dragging a large goat behind them with the rope that was tied around the goat's neck. The trio wasn't bashful as they walked right past the Shri Lankan border patrol officer and me.

The Shri Lankan became even more excited as he saw this gross violation of the border. He pointed at the violators, saying, "That's an illegal crossing! They can't do that! They must—"

I interrupted the greatly upset Shri Lankan, "It's okay; they're police officers. Besides, they're already over here now."

The Shri Lankan sighed at the hopelessness of trying to control the activities of our outlaw Bobonaro team.

Soon the goat was secured in the back of our truck. Tom and Simon had returned from their walk through no man's land, so we said, "Thanks a lot for the tour," to the very perplexed Shri Lankan, and left.

As we drove away, I asked Atanacio, "I thought you went into West Timor to get a pig?"

Atanacio frowned as he said angrily, "They wanted too much money. Everybody over there with pigs wanted too much money, so we got this goat instead." I thought, *At least my boys are watching out for our hard-earned money.*

The 29th became a day off for all of us. The party wasn't until the evening, but there was a lot of work to do to get ready for the party. The men butchered the goat, gathered tables and chairs from various locations, and decorated our Station. Many of our team's friends and families came to help out through the day. The Timorese are not big on drinking alcohol, but we all sipped on beer and Tua Mutin throughout the day. (Tua Mutin is a homemade alcohol with a milky-white color.)

The women butchered the dozen or so chickens and started cooking in the afternoon. Everyone had been so busy preparing for the night to come and enjoying the gathering of so many friends that we forgot to check the fuel in the generator. At 1730 hours the generator stopped. We refueled the generator but couldn't get it to start. I sent Tom and Simon to the Bravo Company compound to get one of their engineers to help us with the generator. Tom and Simon both were dressed in Timorese sarongs, which wouldn't have been a big thing if they hadn't have run into the battalion commander who was visiting the company in Bobonaro.

The engineer had to clean the jets in the motor of the generator, which took some time. The party began on time at 1900 hours. The party guests ate by the light of oil lamps as we hoped that we would have electricity by the time we were ready to start the music. The engineer had to replace one of the jets. Bravo Company donated one of their own jets they had in storage. (I now give my deepest thanks to Bravo Company for your help.)

We started the music. There were many ETPS who had come up to Bobonaro from Maliana. Our Station was packed inside and outside. I took a break from dancing and watched the many Timorese and my three UN teammates as they enjoyed themselves together. We were like one big happy family. But I also thought about the problems I was going to have to deal with because of this party. There was no way that we could keep our many crimes secret.

The Shri Lankan from the border was surely going to report our illegal operation into West Timor. Many people witnessed our trucks passage through Maliana, heavy laden with chickens and a goat. Tom and Simon got busted by a high-ranking military commander wearing their sarongs and we took a day off from work that we were not supposed to take. Outside of all that, we did everything right, I think.

The party ended just before daybreak. The police officers from Maliana went to different homes of those who live in Bobonaro to get a few hours' sleep. The rest of us partygoers did the same. About noon, I picked up the Maliana police officers to drive them down the mountain. Several of them were supposed to be at work already. I thought to myself as I drove down the mountain with people spilling over the edges of the back of my truck, *I'll just add this to my list of many crimes that I have committed in East Timor.*

By the time I reached Maliana, I was told over the radio to report to the district commander's office. I responded to the radio call with a, "Clear on that," as I thought, *Man, bad news travels fast.* I dropped off my passengers then drove to the headquarters to face the music. I walked into Jasper's office. Both Jasper and Paul were there. I sat by Jasper's desk as directed. Paul sat beside me, looking at me with a frown.

Jasper began sternly, "It has been reported that you are responsible for ETPS crossing the border illegally. We also got a report from national headquarters that some of your international staff was out of uniform, dressed in sarongs. We have several reports about you transporting Timorese citizens and farm animals in a United Nations vehicle."

I interrupted Jasper, "Those were ETPS in civilian clothes, not citizens."

Jasper's response to my correction of the facts was a long silence. Paul still frowned at me from where he sat beside me. I hung my head slightly as a show of shame that I did not feel. I sat quietly and waited for the lecture to begin. Jasper broke the silence, "We just want to know one thing from you. Did you guys have a good party?" Jasper and Paul both broke out in laughter.

I snapped my head up from my shameful pose as I said, "Yeah, it was great. I would have invited you guys, but we thought we better keep it secret."

Paul laughed harder, "Secret! It's a good thing you don't run your operations the same way you ran that party. Everybody in this part of the world would know what you're doing."

Before I left the commanders office, Jasper told me to have my team ready to go. I asked, "Go where?"

Paul then jumped into the conversation as he gave me a wink of an eye, "Just be ready to go. We can't tell you any more than that for now." As I drove back to Bobonaro I thought about what was probably coming. The military had the information about Tim Saka and his members hiding with the CPD-RDTL in Tasqolo Village. It didn't take a rocket scientist to figure out the military was getting ready to take action.

About mid-morning on 3 January 2002, Paul came to the Bobonaro Station to talk to me. He told me that the military at the Bravo Company compound was going to invite the entire Bobonaro Tim Saka Task Force to come to the Bravo Company compound for dinner tonight. We would not be allowed to leave after arriving at the military compound. They would feed us dinner but the true purpose of this was to launch an operation into the Lour Desa (Area). The Target was Tasqolo Village.

The team Saka Task Force would take part in the pre-ops briefings and rehearsals. To maintain top secrecy of this operation we would be put into quarantine until the launch of the operation the following morning. Paul finished his pre-briefing briefing to me by saying, "This is top secret. You are the only one that is to know about this operation. Get your guys ready but don't tell them what they are about to do, not even Tom, Simon, and Michael."

After Paul left I announced to my teammates, "We will have a training session this afternoon starting at 1500 hours. Go home, get some rest, and be back here at 1500 hours with all of your equipment."

There was much speculation about the sudden training session. I told the guys that Paul wanted us to increase our training to be prepared for the upcoming operations that should start in a week or two. The guys bought my explanation and went home.

At 1500 hours everyone was back at the station. I held a meeting with the team. We went through every piece of intelligence that we had collected to this point. Next we went through the Tim Saka investigation. By the time we finished it was nearly 1630 hours. I told the team that we had been invited to attend dinner at the Bravo Company compound at 1700 hours. The CMA had visited me late in the morning and asked us to please come. I told my teammates to grab their kit and let's go. They looked at me questioningly as they picked up their gear. I led the team over to the compound. It felt strange when the gate closed behind us as we walked into the compound knowing that we couldn't leave.

We ate a nice dinner in the mess hall. Olavio and I were invited to sit with the company commander and the Battalion commander who "just happened to be visiting." Once dinner was finished the mess hall was cleared of any soldiers that was not needed to be present during the briefing that was about to start.

The briefing took about two hours as the details of Operation Katana was explained and discussed thoroughly. (Operation Katana is not the real name of this ops.) The basic operation plan was to "cordon and search." Australia's Charlie Company was making their way to their assigned cordon position at the time of this briefing. A company of Fiji soldiers and one platoon of Nepalese soldiers were also making their way to the target area to form an impenetrable cordon around the large Tasqolo Village.

United Nations civilian police along with one platoon of Australian military would be inserted by helicopter at first light. This combined Assault unit would sweep the Village for the Tim Saka members. The objective of this operation was to arrest as many of the Tim Saka members as possible.

The briefing then covered all the gathered intelligence about the Village, the people, the CPD-RDTL who were harboring the suspects and then the information on the Tim Saka group in Tasqolo. Olavio and I filled in some gaps of the intelligence briefing. The Battalion commander informed us that the Bobonaro team would focus on intelligence collection during the operation. The Investigation side of our team would be supported by UN investigators from Maliana who would arrive at this compound at 0400 hours.

We spent the next few hours after the main briefing with the "On the Ground" team Leaders. We went through the tactical stuff first with the use of a mud map. Then we walked through rehearsals of our expected tactics. We finally finished all briefings, rehearsals and preparations at 2300 hours. The company provided us floor space and gave us thin foam mats to sleep on for a few hours.

Nobody slept much that night. By 0330 hours the whole team was awake. At 0400 hours two car loads of ETPS and UN Investigators from Maliana arrived. I was glad to see that our one time teammate from Tasmania, Mick, was with them. By this time the whole Australian company was awake. The next hour went by fast as we all visited with the Maliana Investigators.

Shortly after 0500 hours two military Black Hawk helicopter landed on the landing pad in front of the compound. The pilots shut down the engines then entered the compound for a brief meeting with the operation commanders. At 0530 hours they returned to their waiting aircraft and fired up the engines. The rotors started to turn as our accompanying platoon climbed aboard. The platoon was the first chalk (lift) to fly into the LZ. They would secure the LZ for the police arrival. Both Black Hawks gracefully rose a few feet off the ground then nosed forward and shot down the side of the mountain that started its steep decent from the edge of the helipad. The helicopters were quickly out of sight as they dropped below the edge of the helipad.

Within a few minutes the birds were back. They swooped onto the landing pad like hawks snatching prey from the ground. As the skids touched the pad we moved to our assigned helicopter and jumped aboard. Within seconds the birds rose off the pad and we wear plummeting down the edge of Bobonaro mountain. The sensation was like riding down that first big hill of a large rollercoaster.

A few minutes later the Black Hawks were touching down on the grassy LZ on the east edge of Tasqolo Village. We quickly climbed out and joined the soldiers who held security positions, forming a circle around the LZ as they lay on the ground in firing positions.

Once on the ground we entered Tasqolo Village and went to work. We methodically cleared one home after another. This was a large village with many homes. By noon we still had a lot of homes left to clear. Our sweep operation had produced six prisoners so far. The military commanders were disappointed that we hadn't captured more suspects. The Bobonaro team was surprised we got that many. We knew that most or all of the suspects would escape out of the village when they heard the helicopters coming.

Falintil tactics for evasion during an attack of this nature was to scatter from the target area and go to preplanned defendable locations nearby. We just hoped the preplanned locations were on the other side of the cordon so that they would be captured by the soldiers that formed the cordon. Unfortunately that was not the case.

Our investigators spoke with witnesses and suspects to continue building the criminal case. The Bobonaro team interviewed people to discover the locations that the Tim Saka members had gone. We also conducted searches of homes that we believed may have documents of intelligence value.

By late afternoon the Black Hawks were back to airlift the six prisoners and the many captured documents that we did find. The second chalk of passengers was the remaining police, the military would stay in the field to conduct sweeps through the edges of Tasqolo Village. They hoped to capture a few more prisoners. I told the Charlie Company commander that I would like to keep three members of my team in the field with his soldiers. The commander readily agreed.

Olavio, Atanacio and I stayed behind. Mick, the Tasmanian, adamantly volunteered to stay with us so I kept him too. We watched the Black Hawks disappear in the distance knowing that was the last ride home tonight. The four of us grabbed our packs and moved into the Charlie Company perimeter that they had established next to the LZ. We picked out a place to sleep within the perimeter and dropped our packs. We then split into two teams of two. Mick and Atanacio would accompany First Platoon during their sweep along the south side of the village. Olavio and I would accompany Third Platoon with their sweep of the north side of the village. Second Platoon would secure the company position.

We worked hard during these sweeps walking through the very rough and heavy foliaged terrain that surrounds Tasqolo Village. We didn't get back to the company perimeter until 2200 hours. Our hard efforts produced nothing. The company commander was again disappointed. I would have been too but I was too tired. I was soaked from sweating all day. The air on top of this mountain was cool compared to the lowlands but the entire day and evening was pretty physical, which caused me to sweat heavily.

The sliver of the moon and surrounding stars did not give us a lot of light to find our intended sleeping positions within the perimeter. Flashlights were not permitted to be used inside the company position. Eventually we found our backpacks where we had left them. I pulled a small plastic tarp out of my pack and spread it out on the ground. We hadn't planned on spending the night in the bush so none of us brought our normal jungle excursion kit. The night breeze was still warm but I knew that would change in a few hours. I lay on my tarp and went right to sleep.

At 0230 hours I woke up shivering. The warm breeze had changed into a cold wind that swept across the little grassy mountain top where we slept. I sat up and looked down the mountain toward Suai. This was the last mountain before dropping down to the miles of flat land that stretched to Suai and the south sea. Lightening flashed repeatedly in the thick clouds over Suai. I still shivered as I hoped that the storm I was watching over Suai didn't come up here. I couldn't imagine getting wet on top of being so cold.

I curled up in my little tarp, which helped to keep some heat in my body. Soon I quit shivering but I was still too cold to go back to sleep. I looked over at my three teammates who seemed to be sleeping just fine. I don't know how they did it, but there they were. I puffed on a cigarette I had lit using the tarp to shield the lighter. I lay back against a dirt mound and looked up the mountain peak that started to climb near the edge of our company perimeter.

I thought about Lepo Village that was on the other side of that mountain. Then I thought about the Bua Malus group that controlled a large area of that mountain. I thought about the Bua Malus commander and his 2IC who lived up there. Our investigations into the Tim Saka Group revealed that Raimundo Karau Timor and his 2IC had participated in a couple of Tim Saka's extortion excursions. The Dili Courts had issued warrants for the arrest of Raimundo and his 2IC.

A plan formed in my head as I froze that night on that mountain top. At 0330 hours I woke my three teammates. I told them that I wanted to go up Lepo mountain to try and grab the two Bua Malus leaders. I planned to slip into the village at first light, grab the suspects and haul ass back to this company perimeter.

I told Mick that this could be dangerous and he didn't need to go if he didn't want to. Mick's response was, "You're not keeping me out of this. I'm in." Ten minutes later we were packed and ready to go. I informed the soldiers handling security near our perimeter exit point what we were doing. Once that was done we started up the mountainside with Atanacio on point. I walked the two-position Mick was in the three-position and Olavio walked the drag-position.

Atanacio stopped twice on the way up the mountain when he detected movement ahead. As Atanacio stopped and melted into the jungle at the side of the trail Olavio and I knew that people were coming. The first time Atanacio did this I dropped back to Mick and told him people were coming. I said, "When you see the man in front of you move off the trail and disappear then you do the same. After the threat has passed by us we will reform on the trail and continue the patrol." Mick started to ask a question but I cut him off, "The people who are coming are very close. We must move to hidden locations right now."

Mick and I no sooner got off the trail when two men carrying farming tools walked through our position. Once the men were past we reformed and started up the mountain again. Twenty minutes later Atanacio again disappeared to the side of the trail. The rest of us did likewise. We never saw the people on the trail this time but we heard them talking and walking as they turned from the trail we were walking and went down a smaller trail that led to fields of crops.

Atanacio stopped and moved into a defensive position about fifty-meters short of Lepo Village. Olavio did the same thing covering our rear. I moved back to Mick and explained that we would wait here until first light. If we entered the village now the dogs would start barking and the people would know someone had entered their village. Once it was light the dogs would not bark. Mick nodded and took a defensive position covering our left side. I moved to the right and covered our right side. Now we wait.

Soon we saw the first rays of light that turned the night sky from inky black to gray. As we looked down from our mountain perch to the east we could see the horizon start to glow pink. Without having to give any signals our little team reformed on the trail. Three of the four of us knew the time was right to cover the last fifty-meters. The sky would be light by the time we entered the village.

We moved quickly once we were in the village. Soon we were in team security positions at the side of commander Raimundo Karau Timor's home. We waited silently until the first occupant of the home opened the door. Within a few minutes the front door of this large multi-room concrete house opened. A young man in his late teens stepped out onto the veranda. That was our cue. We stepped up onto the veranda and swept past the startled young man. We swept through the house, clearing each room as we proceeded. By the time the surprised occupants realized what was going on, we were done, but we come up short-handed. Raimundo wasn't there.

We questioned the occupants who were reluctant but eventually told us that Raimundo and his 2IC had become aware that there were warrants issued for their arrest. The two men went to some place called Osanako Village to evade capture. Upon hearing the word Osanako I remembered a piece of our past information about Osanako Village. That was where the FBA was establishing some kind of Headquarters. I also wondered how the suspects knew there was arrest warrants issued for them.

Empty-handed, we made our return to the Charlie Company perimeter. There were now many people on the trail tending to their personal affairs. We took up positions to wait for the approaching unsuspecting travelers that we came across so that they wouldn't see us until they were close enough for us to take control of them. One group of men that came down that trail while we waited in hiding positions was from Pellet Village. Olavio recognized one of the men as the Pellet Village chief. We had a warrant for his arrest for his involvement with Tim Saka.

We stopped the group of men and arrested the Pellet Village chief. It turned out that a second man in the group of five men also was a Tim Saka member that we had a warrant to arrest. We took him into custody and sent the remaining three men on their way. We took our two prisoners back to the company perimeter and reported to the company commander.

The commander was ecstatic that our four-man team's special operation up the mountain had produced two more prisoners. I asked the commander if his men could secure our prisoners while we went to another close by village to attempt the arrest of a CPD-RDTL suspect named on the warrant list. The commander agreed but told me we had to be back by 1100 hours. The entire company would be extracted at 1200 hours. I gave the commander the thumbs up sign and led our four-man team out of Charlie Company's perimeter.

The suspect we had gone to try and arrest was not in the village. We did come across a ten-year-old girl who had a severe burn on her right leg. The burn area covered most of her shin. We took the injured girl and her mother with us back to the company perimeter. The company commander agreed to evacuate the girl and her mother with the extracting troops so that the girl could be taken to the hospital in Maliana.

At 1200 hours the first helicopter arrived to extract Charlie Company. The warrant officer organizing the extraction assigned our Bobonaro team and prisoners for the first chalk. We were glad to be getting back to Bobonaro soon. We were exhausted from lack of sleep and the physical excursion over the last two days. We were nearly out of water and the only food we had was the remainder of the military ration-packs that Charlie Company gave to each one of us the night before.

We waited kneeling at the edge of the LZ for the MI-8 to settle onto the ground. The military was using United Nations MI-8s because they could get the company back to Bobonaro much quicker then the multiple trips that two Black Hawks would have to make. As the MI-8 touched the ground we stood up and moved toward our ride home. As we neared the aircraft the helicopter crew chief waved us off. The flight pilot is God when it comes to his aircraft in the field. What he says goes. We didn't know why we got waved off but we turned around and went back to the edge of the LZ.

The warrant officer talked with the crew chief, then walked over to us. The warrant officer told us that the pilot will not transport anyone that is not wearing shoes or boots. Our two prisoners were wearing sandals. We had to find them shoes before they would be allowed in the aircraft. I looked into the warrant officer's eyes and could see that he was as upset as I was. I was sure that he had noticed that the injured girl and her mother were allowed onto that first chalk. The girl was barefoot and her mother wore flip-flops. I asked, "Where are we going to find shoes or boots out here?"

The warrant officer replied, "We are in contact by radio with the battalion commander in Bobonaro now."

A couple of minutes later the warrant officers radio man received a call from their commander in Bobonaro. The message was that they had successfully got two pair of boots onto the MI-8 that was now returning for the next chalk. The warrant officer told me, "We will get the boots off the helicopter and send the second-chalk. Get the boots on your prisoners quickly. I will send you guys on the third-chalk."

The boots came with the helicopter as the Battalion commander had said. We quickly got the boots onto our prisoners and moved up to the edge of the LZ to be ready to climb on the helicopter when it returned for the third-chalk.

Once again we moved toward the MI-8 after it settled onto the LZ. Once again we got waved off. The warrant officer was pissed. He climbed up into the aircraft to talk with the pilot. Soon I could see the warrant officer angrily waving his arm toward us and then toward Bobonaro. The pilot's actions also appeared to be movements of anger. Soon the warrant officer stepped from the aircraft and walked over to where we waited. The warrant officer told me, "The pilot is refusing to take your prisoners. The battalion commander is on the phone with the police commissioner at this time to get someone to order this dickhead to take these prisoners. Taking prisoners was the whole purpose of this operation in the first place."

A few minutes later the warrant officer got the bad news. When he had finished talking on the radio he walked over to me shaking his head. He told me, "You will have to leave your prisoners here. The pilot's commander in Dili has refused to override the decision of his pilot. You police will be on the next chalk."

I no longer felt tired or hungry or thirsty. All I felt was anger. I told the warrant officer, "I will not leave our prisoners."

He replied, "That pilot is not going to take these prisoners. There is no changing that now."

I said, "That's fine. We'll walk our prisoners out."

The warrant officer looked at me with a look of shock. He pointed to the distant mountain top where Bobonaro Village sat as he said, "Bobonaro is five kilometers away. It is nothing but jungle and rugged mountains between here and there. You guys haven't had a break in the action in two days. On top of that there are still a lot of Tim Saka bad guys here in the area. You really think you can run that gauntlet?"

I didn't hesitate to answer, "I will not leave my prisoners. We could use some water, though. You guys got any water to spare?"

The warrant officer shook my hand, "You guys got a lot of guts. You got my respect. We don't have much water, either, but we'll give you what we got."

The warrant officer walked over to the few soldiers still on the ground. The warrant officer said something to the soldiers. The soldiers then stood up and walked over to us as they pulled their canteens out of the holders. They lined up and poured what water they had left into our canteens.

By the time we took the last of the soldiers' water, our canteen still were not full, but it was enough. The MI-8 was on its way back for the fifth and last chalk. We gave a wave to the soldiers as we started off toward Bobonaro in formation. The warrant officer called out as we walked away, "I'll see you in camp tonight."

I stopped walking turned around and looked at the warrant officer. I yelled out, "Thanks for trying." The warrant officer gave me a smile along with a thumbs-up. I returned the thumbs-up turned around and marched with my team and two prisoners as we entered the jungle.

The jungle was so quiet. There was no breeze, but at least the shade from the tall trees that rose above us protected us from the sun. Atanacio was on point. The walking pace he set reflected the anger he felt for that unknown pilot who abandon us on the LZ. I didn't mind the fast pace; I was angry too. Strategically, it made sense to get out of Indian Country as soon as possible anyway. Tim Saka and his twenty or so men that were hiding in this mountain somewhere would think that we had extracted with the company. If we should happen to bump into them, they would be much more surprised than us.

We reached the bottom of Lour Mountain in about one hour of walking. We took a break when we reached the river. We took the handcuffs off our prisoners' wrists. We shared what little food we had left from our ration-packs with our prisoners. It was a strange thing. These two guys were acting like we were long lost buddies instead of the enemy. They seemed to have a lot of respect for us because we did not leave with the military. They knew that we could have left without them but we chose to stay with them.

We ate the food and drank the water that the soldiers had given us. Soon we waded across the river and started up Bobonaro mountain. We didn't put the handcuffs back on the prisoners. This side of Bobonaro mountain is so steep and rough that to climb the mountain, the climber needed to use his hands. I put Olavio on point. Atanacio was still pissed. I knew he would set into a Falintil pace up this mountain, which was a much faster pace than I wanted to keep.

Two hours later we walked into a little village that was a short distance from Bobonaro. Rui Barreto was an ETPS officer that was initially on our team but was transferred to Dili to train for the logistics officer's job. Rui was from this little village. We walked over to Rui's house to take a break before walking into Bobonaro. We were all exhausted by now. I wanted to walk into Bobonaro with a show of strength not as a haggard mob. If the people were going to trust us they had to see us as being invincible.

Rui was at his house when we got there. He had a couple of days off from work so he came to his home in Bobonaro. His wife served us coffee and biscuits while we rested and talked with Rui. Thirty minutes later we left. The short break along with the refreshments gave us the energy I was looking for. We marched into Bobonaro in formation. We made our way to the Bravo Company compound.

As we neared the front gate the soldiers manning the gate raised the crossbar. They had never opened the gate ahead of time before. We always had to stop at their guardhouse and wait for the soldiers to call into the command post and get permission for us to enter. We marched through the open gate. As I walked into the compound I saw Paul come out of the command post and walk toward us. The rest of our team came out of the mess hall. We could see the pride in the eyes of Paul and the rest of the team as they approached us.

Paul was the first to reach us. He shook my hand as he said, "Good job. Fine job." He then shook the hand of Olavio, Atanacio, and Mick, saying, "Very good job" to each man. The rest of our teammates shook hands with us. Once the welcome-home formalities were complete, Paul whisked me into the command post while the team took the two prisoners over to the Bobonaro Station. I could see that look in Simon's eyes. He was champing at the bit to start interviewing the new prisoners.

I had never been allowed into Bravo Companies Command Post before. I didn't realize how big the room was. There was several military commanders waiting in a large area of the CP when Paul and I walked in. All of these men were fresh and clean. My uniform was wet from river water and sweat. Mud covered my boots and pant legs. From the waist up I was covered in dried mud and dust.

We had got back to Bobonaro just in time for the official Operation Katana de-briefing meeting. I was warmly received by the many commanders in spite of my appearance. The de-briefing began right away. I was surprised when a soldier carried a plate of food and a can of Coca Cola into the briefing room and handed the items to me. I was starved but I tried to eat with some semblance of dignity.

During the meeting the Bobonaro team and I was repeatedly praised for our performance in the field. By the time the meeting was over I was feeling pretty special. I felt great pride for the team. When we left the compound Paul and I walked over to the Bobonaro Station. The whole team was still there. Simon was interviewing one of the two prisoners. I knew Simon well enough to know that these interviews could go on for hours to come. He wouldn't stop until he had everything he could get out of those guys.

Paul announced to the team, "I'm taking these guys home to get cleaned up and rest." He then turned to me, "These guys can handle everything. I'll take you home. You should rest tomorrow too."

I didn't argue. Olavio, Atanacio, Mick and I followed Paul to his Nissan truck and climbed in. Paul dropped Olavio and Atanacio off at Olavio's house. Atanacio lived in Laurba Village but he would spend the night at Olavio's house.

Paul then drove me to my house. I shook hands with my commander and Mick then got out of the truck and watched them drive away. That was the last time I ever saw Mick. A few weeks later he got a message that his father had died. He went home and never came back. He was a good teammate.

I didn't think that what we did was all that great, but everyone else did. The next day Michael told me that he was in Jasper's office with Paul and Jasper when the drama of the pilot refusing to take our prisoners was unfolding. Jasper and Paul had told Michael how pleased they were that two more suspects had been arrested. So was the police commissioner.

When the bad news came in that the pilot wouldn't take the prisoners, Jasper got on the phone to the commissioner to get that pilot ordered to take the prisoners. The commissioner called back a few minutes later saying that the pilot's decision was final. Jasper and Paul were furious that the two prisoners would have to be left behind and cursed the pilot.

Michael walked over to the holding cells to help book in the six Tim Saka prisoners taken out of Tasqolo the day before. Michael and two members of our team had driven the six prisoners to Maliana. Danielle, an Australian police officer who was the Maliana Station commander, suddenly poked her head into the booking room and told Michael, "They're walking them out. Those guys are going to walk those prisoners all the way back to Bobonaro."

Then Michael told me in his heavy Australian accent, "Everybody was shocked. Nobody expected you guys to do that. It never occurred to any of the commanders that walking those prisoners back to Bobonaro was even an option."

I could see that Michael was also thinking that we had performed some great feat. I responded to Michael, "Michael, it wasn't that big of a deal other than we were really pissed off. We had made that walk before. We knew what we were doing."

Michael just looked at me as he said with a feeling of deep respect, "What you did was legendary."

I took full advantage of our new-found "legendary" status. We were collecting information about the movements and locations of all the suspects left to arrest through our informant network. Olavio and I lined up one operation after another to go get the suspects. Each operation included search warrants for the homes we suspected may contain documents of intelligence value. Our new found reputation stretched all the way to Dili. We were getting virtually anything we asked for.

We started running operations back to back. Through our secret information network, we knew when a suspect became vulnerable to us. Since Operaton Katana, Tim Saka's group split up to evade capture. As soon as we saw an opportunity we took it. Paul offered to get us helicopter insertions but I refused them. We had to move into the target area during the night hours and pounce on the target at first light. The strategy was to hit the bad guys before they were awake and going to the fields, or the markets, or a friend's house and most importantly before he was awake and could see us coming.

We hit one target after another using this strategy. We never missed. Every operation yielded us the prisoners we expected to get along with many documents. We did our homework before every operation and paid attention to every little detail but the truth is our uncanny success was amazing. The only thing I could attribute this success rate to was that God was pissed at these guys and was helping us to knock the shit out of them. I mean that.

I wanted to hit Holmesel Village for a long time. The Holmesel Village chief was a named Tim Saka leader but we wanted to get Daniel Mota when we hit Holmesel. Mota had fled Holmesel back when the Tim Saka campaign began. He hadn't been back to Holmesel since. It was hard getting information out of Holmesel Village. There were only a handful of families that were not devoted CPD-RDTL members and allies to Tim Saka. Extreme measures had to be used to contact our informant that we had developed inside the village, which caused time delays in collecting the information. Hitting Holmesel Village required patients, a lot of patients.

Olavio and I were preparing plans for the future hit of Pellet Village as well. Pellet Village was a hard target for us. Pellet Village, which wasn't marked on the map, first had to be located. We eventually identified where the village was. Unfortunately for us Pellet Village was three hundred meters over the line into Kova Lima District. We made several attempts to penetrate Pellet Village by developing an informant. Our attempts failed.

Simon had collected a lot of detailed information about the village and people from the two Pellet prisoners that we had arrested during Operation Katana. It turned out that our efforts to walk those two men back to Bobonaro rather than abandon them on the LZ was going to provide us the best pre-operation intelligence that we were going to get. There were still too many "unknowns" to hit Pellet Village yet though. We would wait.

In the mean time, we stayed busy hitting other lesser targets. As our "first light" operations yielded us one or two prisoners at a time, our reputation grew to superhuman levels. The remaining suspects quickly figured out our strategy of first light assaults. They combated our strategy by sleeping in a different house every night so that if we should hit their village looking for them we would not find them in their own house.

That was a good counter-strategy to evade capture but it didn't work. Our informant network gave us information as to what houses a particular suspect was using to sleep the nights away. Armed with that information we simply searched each of the named homes and still got our man.

In addition to the arrests we were making we also recovered an amazing amount of documents. Some of those documents were evidence of the extortion cases we were investigating. Many of the Tim Saka, Bua Malus and CPD-RDTL leaders who were involved in this large extortion racket were recording the village they victimized, the date they victimized it, the names of who they took money or goods from, and what they took from those individuals.

There were also records of the membership lists of the different groups that we had identified in the Bobonaro area. Those lists gave us the names of the members, the rank of the member and the village they were from. We were discovering that these groups were much larger and better organized than anyone had realized, even us.

By the first of February, 2002, the only group that we had not recovered documents from was the Bua Malus Group in Lepo Village. The little suburb village of Lepo where Raimundo Karau Timor and his 2IC lived was as impenetrable as Pellet Village. We assumed that if Raimundo and his 2IC happened to be in the village when we hit it they would be sleeping in another home. We would never find them.

One day we got a fluke piece of information that the 2IC had returned to the village for a few days of visiting his family. Raimundo was not there but the 2IC was. We discussed the possibilities of hitting the Bua Malus stronghold. It was important to get the documents that we believed was in the home of the 2IC. The documents that we had taken out of Raimundo's home during Operation Katana was not the incriminating documents that we had hoped. I knew there were more.

The problem with launching the operation now was that we didn't have enough intelligence to know the homes the 2IC was using to sleep. We would be going in blind. Simon came up with a bold solution, "Why not go in and arrest the 2IC's family? We can hit the 2IC's home and pressure the family to reveal the 2IC's whereabouts. When they give us false information we can arrest them for harboring a fugitive."

That was a good plan. The Timorese have a strong sense of family. There was a good chance that once the 2IC realized that we were taking his family to jail he would give himself up to us to save his family. It was worth a try. The chances of getting any hard intelligence out of that village were slim to none anyway. We put the operation plans together over the next couple of days then hit it.

The "hit" was more successful than we had hoped for. As expected the 2IC was not sleeping in his home. The family did lie to us about where the 2IC was, so we arrested them. Once the target was secured we moved our truck near the 2IC's home from where we had hid the truck about one-kilometer away. We took the 2IC's wife and young brother to our truck in handcuffs. We stalled leaving with them right away to give the 2IC time to decide to do the right thing, which was to turn himself in to us. Simon's plan worked like a charm. The 2IC came walking up to us a few minutes after we had his family and introduced himself. We arrested him and let his family go free.

The biggest catch of that raid was the documents we took out of the 2IC's house. Not only was there evidence of the Bua Malus involvement with extortion but we got their membership list. Bua Malus had thousands of members throughout East Timor. In addition to that we had numerous documents that clearly identified a direct link with the CPD-RDTL national commanders.

As we basked in our rising glory over the extreme success of all these little operations we started making plans for the two big operations left to be done. We decided on the first of the two targets, "Target Holmesel."

* * * *

We gave Target Holmesel the code-name of Operation Home Plate. This was going to be a tough operation. Holmesel Village sat on the far side of Indian Country. We knew that the chances of catching Daniel Mota in that village was slim to none but the Holmesel Village chief and the documents that we were sure was there was a worthwhile prize to go after.

Operation Home Plate would require a lot of support. First we needed a sizable Force to seal off the village while we searched the two homes of Daniel Mota and the home of the village chief. Next we could use a helicopter extraction. We would have to walk all night to get on the edge of Holmesel Village by first light. When we left Homesel Village after the raid we hoped to have the influential village chief in our custody. It would be better to take the chief out by helicopter rather than walking him through several kilometers of Indian Country.

I worked the operation plan out through Paul. We couldn't use military resources so Paul lined up assistance from the Portuguese special police unit (SPU) based in Dili. The SPU was two platoons of specially trained police officers who were paramilitary trained. Most of the police officers in the SPU were prior Special Forces of Portugal. The SPU roll in East Timor was primarily for crowd control and riots. We were about to give one platoon of these elite warriors a break from the boredom of Dili.

The final operation plans were ironed out to this. The SPU would drive out to Bobonaro from Dili on the day of the operation. Upon their arrival I would conduct a briefing of all involved members. This would be followed by operation rehearsals and preparations. The combined teams would then be free to rest until 2300 hours, which would be the time we "staged" (gathered) at the Bobonaro Station. The team leaders would conduct equipment and weapons checks at that time. The combined teams would begin the long dark walk to Holmesel Village at 2330 hours.

Michael, Paulina, and Raquel would stay at the Bobonaro Station and maintain radio relay communication between the teams and Paul who would be based in Maliana. I designated four rally points (RPs) to better mark the teams progress and to provide a point of gathering should the team run into trouble or become separated during the operation. The Bobonaro Relay Station (BRS) and Paul could keep track of the teams general location as we reported from the specific RP.

The teams would move through the mountain without the aid of flashlights, which would give our movement away to the CPD-RDTL trail watchers in Oalgomo Village, Sibuni Village and Holmesel Village. The teams would check in with the BRS at RP#1, which was half way down Bobonaro mountain where we turn left onto the trail that goes to Sibuni mountain. We would check in again at RP#2, which was at the cemetery just before entering Oalgomo Village. We would check in when we arrived at RP#3, which was at the river that flows between Bobonaro Mountain and Sibuni Mountain. We would take a break at RP#3.

The combined teams would then climb Sibuni mountain toward Holmesel Village. RP#4 was one-hundred-meters before reaching Holmesel Village. When we got to RP#4 we would check in, set up a hidden security perimeter and wait for first light. At first light the teams would enter Holmesel Village. The SPU would secure the village while the Bobonaro team secured the three Target homes within the village.

The objective of Operation Home Plate was to arrest the village chief and collect documents. Once those objectives were completed the combined teams would move to the top of Sibuni Mountain where there is an LZ on a grassy hilltop. The teams would be extracted from the hilltop by helicopter at 1000 hours.

* * * *

The afternoon of the planned launch date of Operation Home Plate the Portuguese SPU Commandos arrived in Bobonaro. This twenty-four man platoon looked like commandos. Every one of them was tall with bulging muscles that was easily seen through their dark blue uniform t-shirts they wore. I met with the platoon commander and went through the operation with him step by step. This was followed by a briefing meeting with all the members of both teams involved.

We conducted some walk through rehearsals, which completed our pre-mission activities. There was four hours before we would "stage" at the Bobonaro Station so everyone went to get a little rest. The SPU set up camp in our station. At 2300 hours we staged and did the equipment/weapons checks. As we went outside to prepare for our departure I noticed the SPU were still wearing their t-shirts and only carrying small backpacks. I asked the SPU commander if his men had raincoats. The commander said, "We don't need them."

We always took raincoats with us. Raincoats were the best thing to wear in the mountains at night. Besides keeping you dry when it rains the coats do a good job of keeping you warm. I told the commander, "This is the wet season—it is going to rain on us later. The mountains gets cold at night even if it is not raining."

The commander replied, "Its okay, we don't use them." I thought *These guys really are tough.*

We made our way out of Bobonaro Village going toward RP#1. I had Mario on point followed by me. Olavio was in the three-position and Atanacio in the four-position. The SPU filed in behind Atanacio. The remainder of the Bobonaro team brought up the rear. The Bobonaro team was accustom to walking through the mountains without the aid of flashlights, the SPU was not. I heard men slipping and sometimes falling behind me from time to time as we walked down the dark trail.

We checked in with the BRS when we arrived at RP#1. We continued down the left trail that led to Oalgomo and Sibuni Mountain. We reached RP#2 and again checked in. So far we were maintaining the timings that we figured it would take us to get to the different RPs. We were a little late getting to RP#3. Mario had neglected to tell me that the CPD-RDTL had recently established an additional Observation Post (OP) at the lower edge of Oalgomo. This was not good, especially to learn about it just before we entered Oalgomo Village.

The OP was located at a spot that we could not skirt around. Oalgomo Village to the left of the OP was inaccessible to us because the dogs would bark and announce our presence. The steep mountain side to the right of the OP could not be accessed. We had to neutralize the OP. I moved back and briefed the SPU commander. We decided to send a small detachment to secure the OP. If the OP was manned we would capture the occupants and take them with us to Holmesel. The CPD-RDTL has radio equipment. It was imperative that we prevented the OP in Oalgomo from warning Holmesel Village that we were coming.

I sent Olavio and Mario with four SPU members who had night vision goggles. The rest of us waited on the upper edge of Oalgomo Village. Thirty minutes later the team who went to neutralize the OP reported that they are in the OP site and nobody was there. I moved the waiting combined teams up to the OP site. The combined teams then pushed on toward RP#3. After crossing the river at RP#3 I checked in with the BRS.

We were late getting to RP#3 but we still had time for a thirty-minute break, which was well needed by everybody by this time. During this break the wet season rains came, soaking everyone. At least it wasn't cold by the river but that would soon change as we climbed to the colder heights of Sibuni mountain.

The trail going up to Holmesel Village was a tough thing to negotiate when it was dry. Now it was very wet and very dark because of the thick clouds overhead. Even us mountain-seasoned Bobonaro guys were slipping from time to time. The inexperienced SPU had a hard time of it but they kept going and never complained. We got to RP#4 on time, which gave us one-hour to wait for daybreak. It was still raining as a cold wind howled through our perimeter at RP#4 while we waited. The SPU team suffered from the cold but held their security positions and never complained.

At first light I moved the teams into Holmesel Village. The SPU had the outer village secured instantly. The Bobonaro team swept into the three Target homes and soon had all three locations secured. Once again we enjoyed complete success. The Holmesel Village chief was found and arrested. We recovered multiple documents out of the chief's home and also one of the two homes of Daniel Mota.

With the captured treasures in hand we started up the mountain toward the LZ. Mario was still on point. The climb from Holmesel to the LZ wasn't that far but it was a tough part of Sibuni Mountain to climb. Mario stopped about halfway up to give everyone a break. I told him to keep moving. I wanted to see what these Portuguese were really made of. We went all the way to the LZ in one push, which meant we didn't take a break the entire way.

As the exhausted teams lay down in the grass to wait for the extraction helicopter I talked with the SPU commander. I told him how impressed I was with him and his men. This SPU team was one of the finest outfits I had the privilege of working with. Their tactical ability was superb. Their politeness and professionalism could never be out done. And they were one tough bunch of guys. They made Portugal proud.

Soon we saw an MI-8 approaching. It would take two chalks to lift our teams back to Bobonaro. I sent most of the SPU on the first chalk. The SPU commander told me to take my team out first. He was trying to be polite. I told the commander that we had to be the last ones out. I had to be the last one on the aircraft. The SPU commander smiled his understanding as he reached out and shook my hand saying, "I knew you were Special Forces."

I replied, "No I'm not."

The commander slapped me on the shoulder, smiled and walked away to tell his men they were the first chalk.

There was a bond forged between these two teams during Operation Home Plate. After the de-briefing meeting at the Bobonaro Station the SPU grabbed their kit and prepared to make the four-hour drive back to Dili. The SPU and the Bobonaro team exchanged handshakes, slaps on the backs and even some hugs. The SPU commander told me, "It was an honor to work with your team. I hope we have the opportunity to do it again."

I smiled at the commander as I said, "We will, in two to three weeks."

The commander smiled back saying, "You let us know when your ready. Don't leave us out." We shook hands. The commander jumped into the waiting truck and they were gone.

Three weeks later we did Operation Out of Bounds, which was the long-awaited raid on Pellet Village. Pellet was out of bounds for us, about three-hundred-meters out of bounds. To make matters worse I decided that we could not assault Pellet Village from the Bobonaro Zona boundary line. By now the CPD-RDTL, Bua Malus and Tim Saka groups were very much aware of the Bobonaro teams tactics of moving through the mountains. They had tightened their security tactics of detecting our teams movements all through Indian Country. There was a lot of Indian Country between Bobonaro and Pellet Village.

We still had not been able to penetrate Pellet Village with an Informant. Pellet Village was one-hundred-percent Tim Saka. Because of the extreme pressure we exacted against Tim Saka the village of Pellet was not allowing anyone who wasn't part of their group into the Pellet area. This left us with some huge intelligence gaps for planning this operation.

One of those big gaps was not knowing who was actually in Pellet Village. We had identified the homes of Tim Saka himself and his 2IC's home. We identified the homes with the use of aerial photos of Pellet Village. The two men that we captured during Operation Katana and walked back to Bobonaro provided us most of our intelligence for Operation Out of Bounds, including identifying our points of interest of Pellet Village from the aerial photos. We confirmed much of the information from the two prisoners through other informants who were familiar with Pellet Village.

We knew the target locations of the two homes we would search for documents. We were reasonably sure that Tim Saka and his 2IC were not in Pellet Village. They were believed to be in Osanako with Raimundo Karau Timor, the Bua Malus commander; however, with Pellet Village being one-hundred-percent Tim Saka Group the village was a target rich environment. The chances of finding suspects on our warrant list were very good.

We had to use a different strategy for this operation. Up to this point we knew exactly who we were going after and where they were at. This time we didn't know who was there and we certainly didn't know where they were at. We come up with a plan to overcome this seemingly impossible hurdle. The key role to capture the bad guys went to the SPU.

This time when we hit the village we would telegraph our assault as we entered the village. This would give anyone with a guilty conscience the opportunity to try and slip out of the village in the opposite direction of the Assault team. Assuming the SPU is able to get into cordon positions in time to intercept the conscientious evaders they will capture the possible suspects. Our teammate Mario can identify the suspects whose names are left on our list. Any of those suspects caught in the SPU screen will be arrested as Mario identifies them. While the SPU and part of our Bobonaro team attempt to scoop up bad guys the rest of the Bobonaro team will search Tim Saka's home and the 2IC's home for documents.

The other big gap of ignorance we had to overcome involved the combined teams' target approach route. Normally we would approach from the mountainous jungles on foot; however, all of our targets before now were areas that we knew and we had prior intelligence of any local security measures in place before the operation was executed. None of us had ever been to Pellet Village before. We had no informant in Pellet so we had no intelligence about the village's security other than what the two Pellet prisoners had told us two months ago. Two-month-old information could not be considered reliable.

We solved this problem by planning an "up the gut" target approach. We would drive our teams to the far side of Pellet Village on the Suai road. We would hide our transport trucks about one-kilometer from a little dirt drive that goes to Pellet Village from the Suai road. There is a house at the Suai road that is beside the dirt drive. That house is occupied by a family of Tim Saka members who sells TNI uniform shirts, pants, etc. to members of Tim Saka, Bua Malus and CPD-RDTL. The Bobonaro team would raid this house while the SPU team started to work their way to Pellet down the dirt drive.

The almost one-kilometer to Pellet Village on this dirt path had to be cleared as we went on the outside chance that there was a village security OP somewhere along the length of the drive. Once the drive was cleared the SPU and four Bobonaro team members working with them would set up a team security perimeter near Pellet Village.

The Bobonaro team elements who secured the house near the Suai road would search the house. The mobile radio relay team, which would be Tom, Raquel, and Paulina, would move their truck from the hidden location on the Suai road to the now secured house. They would handle the control of the Tim Saka family from the house while the Bobonaro team that assaulted the house moves up to the perimeter position on the edge of Pellet.

Just before first light Mario and Atanacio would lead the SPU to the intended cordon position. After first light when we see that villagers are awake and moving around outside their homes the Bobonaro team will enter Pellet Village as a highly visible sweeping line to make sure anyone trying to evade had to go out the backside of the village. The Bobonaro team would stop their sweep of the village when they reach the two target homes, which are both at the rear of the village.

This operation plan looked good on paper. We were trying out new strategies so the effectiveness of this plan remained to be seen. Jasper and Paul felt confident in the abilities of both the SPU and the Bobonaro team. What they had to work out was the feathers that were going to be ruffled because we pulled off a major operation in Kova Lima district.

Jasper and Paul decided not to inform the Kova Lima district commander about this operation. They knew this man well enough to know that he would demand to have control of the operation. The man was not capable of handling a special operation of this nature. Our teams were going up against enough hard obstacles already. We didn't need the added frustration of falling into the grasp of a commander who knows nothing about these mountain operations. Jasper told me, "You do the operation. We will handle the Kova Lima commander." That was good enough for me.

In the afternoon of the Operation Out of Bounds launch date the SPU arrived in Bobonaro Village. Warm greetings were exchanged as these two teams were reunited to conduct yet another daring operation. We went through the plans, conducted briefings, did our rehearsals, made our preparations then rested.

At mid-night we staged, did our equipment/weapons checks and climbed into our trucks. We drove almost two hours to get to the first RP (Rally Point) where we would leave our trucks. The combined teams quickly covered the distance to the Target-number-one (T#1), which was the house near the Suai road. The seven men from the Bobonaro team designated to secure T#1 raided the house as the rest of the teams began clearing the dirt drive to Pellet Village.

The teams stopped fifty meters short of Pellet Village, which was RP#2. Shortly before first light the seven man Bobonaro team who had cleared, secured and searched T#1 joined the perimeter at RP#2. Pellet Village was not as high in the mountains as many of our past targets had been. The breeze was cool but not bone-chilling cold. We were fortunate that there was no rain that night. The cloudless skies allowed the starlight to give us limited visibility of our surroundings.

Atanacio and Mario led the SPU out of our perimeter as the sky began to turn gray. Twenty minutes later Olavio led the Bobonaro team to the edge of the village. We could see a few people moving inside the village. There was smoke coming from cooking fires behind several of the homes. Young women were sweeping the ground around their homes. Now was the time to make our move.

Olavio took half our team to the left side of the village. We waited for Olavio to get into position. From the aerial photos we could see that there was one trail that left the village on the left side of the village. It was imperative that we secure that trail during our initial sweep. This would force anyone evading our assault to go out the rear of the village. The rest of the area around the village was inaccessible because of sheer mountain walls that dropped from the edge of the village.

We began the sweep by calling out loudly between the two sweeping halves of the Bobonaro team. As we swept slowly into the village the activity of the village increased dramatically. It was kind of like disturbing an anthill. Olavio's sweep was stalled near the center of the village when he ran into a large group of villagers who had gathered to protest our assault. I moved my group over to

Olavio to back them up. We recognized this as a probable tactic to give suspects time to flee. Whether this was the case or not we will never know.

We were in no hurry so Olavio negotiated with the acting village chief about our actions (We had arrested the Pellet Village Chief during Operaton Katana). Fifteen minutes later we were on the move again. The people of Pellet were not happy with us but Olavio had settled them down enough to prevent any violence. By the time we reached the two Target homes at the rear of the village the SPU had caught three men trying to slip out the back of the village. All three men were Tim Saka members that we had warrants for. They were arrested. Mario picked out two other men who were hovering in the background while crowds of people moved close to our areas of activity to see what we were doing. Those two men Mario saw were also on our warrant list. They were arrested too.

All five prisoners were walked out to the established Radio Relay Site at T#1 to prevent any provocation of the crowds by seeing their fellow villagers in handcuffs for a long period of time. We searched the homes and recovered documents out of both homes. We also recovered a TNI uniform and military web gear out of both homes. Olavio gave the proper respect to the people of Pellet Village by meeting with the acting village chief before we left Pellet Village. Olavio explained in detail about the atrocities done to neighboring villages at the hand of the active Tim Saka members.

While Olavio talked with the chief I saw one New Zealand soldier walk into the rear of Pellet Village with a Timorese man. I talked with this soldier who was wearing the rank of a lieutenant (Lt.). It turned out that the Lt. was a military intelligence Officer from Sector West Command Center located in Suai. The Timorese man with him was his interpreter.

The Lt. was obviously happy about seeing us in Pellet Village. After the formalities of introducing and identifying each other the Lt asked, "You guys are a little out of your area aren't you?"

I raised an eye brow at the Lt.'s smiling comment knowing he was enjoying seeing our unapproved assault of a village that was not in our area of responsibility. I said to the Lt., "I noticed you walked into the village from that rear trail. It appears that you may have been in our Bobonaro Zona, which happens to be out of your area."

The Lieutenant laughed, "Oooh, You saw me walk in here, huh? We just took a little walk up through Anapol, Sibuni, Holmesel, and then here."

I laughed as I told the Lt., "We are three-hundred-meters into Kova Lima, you were over three-kilometers into Bobonaro Zona."

The Lt. also laughed as he replied, "Yeah, but I didn't tear up any villages like you guys just did to Pellet."

I shrugged my shoulders and confessed, "You got me there. What can I say? Sorry about that."

This ended the playful bantering so we got down to business. We exchanged information about the Lt.'s little foray into Bobonaro and our little village tearing up excursion into Pellet. The Lt. was excited to hear about the TNI uniforms that we had found at the two homes. We had also taken several uniforms out of T#1. I allowed the Lt.'s interpreter to look through the documents we captured while we talked. The documents proved to be more evidence against the Tim Saka extortion operations as well as the normal membership lists.

We left Pellet and made the long drive back to Bobonaro. Once again we said goodbye to our SPU brothers. The prisoners were subjected to Simon's methodical techniques of extracting information. By the time he had finished we knew we were done conducting operations in the wild mountains of Bobonaro for the time being. The only suspects left to arrest were the top leaders and they were long gone. They had fled the mountains in Bobonaro for safe havens in remote areas in other parts of East Timor. We would have to wait until they surfaced.

I was long overdue for a CTO. I took this opportunity for a much needed break. I spent ten glorious days in Darwin Australia. Once again I went through the normal "I don't want to go back" feeling and as usual when the C-130 touched down on the tarmac in Dili I was glad to be back.

Simon and Atanacio were waiting for me in the Dili airport terminal when I got through customs. They announced that they were in Dili because they had arrested Daniel Mota a couple of days ago and had driven him to Dili to go before the Court. Simon and Atanacio were beaming. Not only had they arrested the CPD-RDTL commander of the CPD-RDTL Defense Force but Simon's subsequent interview revealed that the last of our suspects to arrest were right here in Dili right now.

Our raid on Pellet Village had resounding effects on all the organized groups throughout East Timor. Everyone believed that the Bobonaro team could only operate in Bobonaro Zona. Our raid on Pellet scared them because now they believed that the Bobonaro team could go anywhere in East Timor. Raimundo Karau Timor, Tim Saka, Tim Saka's 2IC and two other lesser leaders had been taking refuge at this unknown headquarters location in Osanako Village. Now they were afraid that the Bobonaro Tim Saka Task Force would assault Osanako. The five leaders fled Osanako and came to Dili.

I called Jasper and asked for permission to keep Simon and Atanacio with me in Dili while we hunted down the last of the fugitives. Jasper gave us his blessings. The next several days were filled with finding these suspects. We eventually discovered where friends and families of the five men lived. Then we found people who we could trust that lived in those same areas thus creating an impromptu information network. Within a few days we were getting information about the suspect's whereabouts.

The suspects were paranoid enough that they didn't sleep in the same house two nights in a row. Eventually we had enough information to make an aggressive move to capture the Bua Malus' Commander Raimundo. It wasn't a sure proof plan but Simon backed up the plan with the strategy we had used in Lepo Village.

The two homes that we had targeted to capture Raimundo were lived in by people that were close to the Bua Malus commander. One home was a family of his life long friends and the other was where his sister and aunt lived with their families. If we missed Raimundo we would arrest his friends and families when they lied to us.

We raided the two homes with the assistance of Dili police units. Raimundo was not at the friend's home. As we had figured they would do the family at the home told us some outrageous lies. We arrested two men out of that home. The home of Raimundo's sister and aunt was the same outcome. Raimundo was not their. Simon pushed the sister and aunt until we caught them in lies to protect Raimundo.

Raimundos young sister was standing with us on the veranda of her home nursing a baby as she talked to us. He aunt sat in a chair on the veranda also nursing a baby. Finally Simon grew impatient with the sister's lies and arrested her. The sister immediately began to cry. As Atanacio and a Dili police Officer grabbed onto the sister to take her to the police car the sister said as she pointed her finger at her aunt, "If you arrest me you got to arrest her too. She lied too."

Simon listened to the translation of what the sister had said. Simon nodded his head as he said, "Okay, she is under arrest too."

Both arrested women were driven to the prosecutor's office in custody and both of them still nursing their babies. I thought the Timorese prosecutor would be upset with us for bringing the babies into his office with the women. When the prosecutor heard our account of the women's lies to protect Raimundo the prosecutor told us to take the women to jail. He would take care of the paper work to hold the women in custody. Simon asked, "What do we do with the babies?"

The prosecutor said, "Take them with their mothers," So much for the Prosecutor being upset with us.

We were just driving out onto the street from the prosecutor's office with the women and their babies when we saw Raimundo Karau Timor step out of a Taxi and walk toward us. He turned himself in to us. We talked to the prosecutor after arresting Raimundo about letting the women go free. The prosecutor was reluctant but eventually agreed to let the women and their babies go free.

The next day Tim Saka called us through the Dili police Station. He wanted to turn himself in. We drove to a house where Tim Saka said he was staying. Tim Saka, his 2IC and the other two Tim Saka leaders were sitting on the front veranda as we walked up. They offered us a chair to sit down, which we did. We were served coffee and crackers by the family who lived at the house.

For thirty-minutes we drank coffee, ate crackers and talked about our Tim Saka campaign as if we were friends playing some type of "cops and robbers" game. When we finished we took the four men into custody and drove them to the jail.

This was the end of the Tim Saka campaign. There was nobody left to go after, we had caught them all. We had arrested thirty-four Tim Saka members, including Tim Saka himself and his 2IC. We completely "crushed" the Tim Saka Group. In addition we arrested the Bua Malus commander and 2IC. We also deeply gouged the CPD-RDTL by arresting the commander of their defense force, Daniel Mota. All these men would be in prison for a long time to come.

The intelligence we collected during the Tim Saka campaign was worth its weight in gold. We now had a clear picture of the individual groups. We knew their numbers, the names of their members, their command and administration structure. We established clear connections between the different groups. We also had some solid clues about who was at the hub of the spokes of this group wheel.

We had developed all that we could from Bobonaro. The rest would have to be done from Dili on a national level. That was not my concern. I was in Bobonaro without the ability to follow up on all the information we had submitted to the national level intelligence division known as Strategic Information Division (SID). I only had one month left in this United Nations mission to East Timor, anyway. I planned to take it easy for my last month in the mission. There wasn't anything left to do, anyway.

CHAPTER SIXTEEN

City Life

After the destruction of Tim Saka's goup I suddenly found myself with nothing to do. We still had a police department to build, though. I had built a special operations unit out of the men and women that were suppose to learn how to become everyday police officers. The team learned how to patrol, run the office, handle normal investigations and other little tasks that go with the everyday work of a police officer but they were as bored as I was. Jasper and Paul had talked me into requesting an extension of mission for an additional six-months of service, which I did. Now I was thinking I may have made a mistake. With no real bad guys to go catch the mountain living was petty boring.

I went to Maliana one day in the middle of April. There was a message waiting for me when I got to the Maliana Station. The message was from Ron Redfield, who was the Dili district commander. Ron was a fellow American civilian police officer; however, I didn't know him too well. I saw on the message note that Ron had actually called two days ago. As usual he couldn't get through to us in Bobonaro because of our phone that rarely worked.

I called Ron from Jasper's office. Ron first complained about how hard it is to get a hold of me. I knew Ron had never served outside of Dili so he had no real understanding of the difficulties that exist outside of Dili. Soon Ron got down to business. He asked me to transfer from Bobonaro to Dili district and work for him. I was surprised that he was requesting me personally like that. Ron didn't know me any more than I knew him.

I asked Ron, "What will I be doing in Dili district?"

Ron's voice became more serious, "I need an intelligence unit. I want you to build me one."

I was immediately interested but I was also very apprehensive. Doing this stuff in the mountains where there is nobody to see what we are doing is one thing. Working in Dili is very visible. Every top United Nations commander, both police and administrative, is right there in Dili. The United Nations functions by the old saying "out of sight, out of mind." In Bobonaro I was out of sight, way out of sight.

I hesitated to answer either way for a few seconds as many questions rushed through my head. Finally Ron said, "Look, come into Dili and meet with me. I can tell you everything when we meet. I can't say much over the phone." I agreed to meet Ron at his office the following morning.

I got to Ron's office about 1000 hours. He received me gratefully for my sudden notice drive to Dili. As we sat in his office trying to have a conversation we were continually interrupted by his phone ringing and people coming to his door. It was obvious to me that Ron was a very busy man. After about twenty-minutes of constant interruptions Ron said as he stood up, "Fuck it, let's go get some coffee."

Ron was a big guy with a firm voice that backed up his strong personality. He was a decisive person whose mannerism naturally demanded others to submit to his will. In this case submitting was a pleasure. A cup of coffee sounded good after my four hour drive from Bobonaro. I followed Ron to his Nissan pick-up truck parked outside his office. I jumped in the passenger side of the truck as Ron brought the engine to life.

Ron drove his truck with that same indomitable attitude that he displayed in the office. He wasn't reckless or inconsiderate of others but at the same time he owned the road. He didn't move for other people on the road they moved for him. I liked what I saw so far. My biggest fear of coming to Dili to work was knowing that when the going got tough I would need a commander that was strong enough to deal with any blowback that may come my way. Ron appeared to have that strength.

Ron took me to a restaurant called the Metro, which was on a street he called restaurant row. I spent very little time in Dili up till now. When I was in Dili I was either at National Police Headquarters or the Timor Lodge for one night before leaving on CTO. I didn't know Dili at all. I didn't know that there were several Western-style restaurants that ran the length of a street for two blocks.

Ron led the way into the restaurant and sat at a table near the front picture windows that covered the front wall on both sides of the front door. Ron sat at the table and motioned me to sit in the chair across from him.

Ron was six feet tall and about two hundred forty pounds. He may have had a little fat around the gut, but this was one stocky man that dwarfed the chair he sat on. He ran his fingers through his short, almost black hair as a young Timorese girl walked up to our table. Ron looked at this pretty young woman. His brown eyes actually softened a little as he ordered us two cappuccinos. I looked at Ron and couldn't help but say, "Oh my God."

Ron looked back at me asking, "You don't want a cappuccino?"

I gave Ron a severe frown, "The cappuccino is fine. I just can't believe I am sitting in a nice restaurant in Dili and I am about to drink a cappuccino." I had heard so many UN civilian police complain about how tough it is to live in Dili. I continued my comment, "I better never hear another Dili boy complain about how tough they got it." Dili boys are what us guys from the outer districts call those who have never left Dili.

Ron laughed as he said, "I am a Dili boy, too, but at least I know how good I have had it through this mission. I get pissed off, too, when I hear some of those guys complaining all the time."

I nodded my approval of Ron's comment, then asked, "So, what's on your mind?"

Ron held nothing back as he told me the situation, "The police commissioner and the SRSG (Senior UN Representative) are very concerned about the upcoming Independence Day celebrations this coming May 20th. They have heard about possible problems developing from these groups that have formed throughout East Timor. We need to know what is going on—what is really going on."

I gave Ron a little frown, "We?"

Ron smiled, "I want to know."

I asked, "Those guys got the SID to collect information Nation wide. What do you want me for?"

Ron responded with a hint of frustration, "Those guys aren't collecting anything worth a shit. The Commissioner and the SRSG know it but they can't do anything about it." Ron stopped talking as the cute little Timorese girl brought us our Cappuccinos.

This girl was different from the Timorese women I knew in Bobonaro. Several of the younger women in Bobonaro dressed in Western-style blue jeans, blouses, and shoes, but this woman dressed very Western. Her blue jeans were decorated with sequins and were intentionally faded down the front of the thighs. The jeans fit snug against her firm body, revealing every curve of her buttocks and legs. The pants legs flared into bell bottoms that covered most of the high heel shoes that she wore. Her white pull over blouse also fit snug against her body. The short length of the blouse exposed her dark brown skin of her lower back and belly. Like most other Timorese, there was no fat on this woman.

The woman gracefully sat one cappuccino in front of Ron. She then slowly sat the other cappuccino on the table in front me. Her dark brown eyes were fixed on my eyes as she put a napkin and spoon next to my cup. Her black hair outlined the chiseled features of her face as it hung loose running down to the middle of her back.

At first I thought this woman was giving me that "come on" look that was common when a woman from a Western country wants a man. As I looked into this young woman's eyes, I could see that she was interested, but there was something different about her. She was dressed to kill, but there was a proper modesty about her as well. I watched her walk away, not only because she was beautiful, but out of confusion.

Ron broke my trance, "You remember that Timorese women are off limits to international staff?"

I answered as I turned my attention back to Ron who was smiling at me, "Yeah, I remember. I thought I knew her from someplace."

Ron rolled his eyes at my comment, "Can we get back to business now?"

I took a slow deep breath, "Yeah, but let me get my breathing back to normal first." I took one more slow, deep breath, and exhaled, "Okay, I think I'm ready now."

Ron's brown eyes steadily were on my eyes as he sighed, "I can see working with you is going to be a challenge."

Ron told me that I would be the officer in charge (OIC) of the Dili district information unit (DDIU). That unit has been in existence for a few months but has produced very little. The purpose of the DDIU was to collect information that is pertinent to Dili District to support policing needs. Ron said, "I want you to run the DDIU so that straight up it looks like you guys are simply doing that, collecting policing information. Covertly, I want you to build an intelligence unit that is capable of getting all information that is important to East Timor."

This was all sounding pretty familiar. I asked, "What are my limitations?"

Ron laughed, "Don't kill anyone, unless you have to." Then he got serious, "If anyone gets in your way from the UN let me know and I will take care of it. You got more support than you realize."

I told Ron, "I will need to have the flexibility to go out of Dili district. I need to establish strong relationships with East Timorese people. Foreigners don't know any more than you or I do. I need a four-wheel drive vehicle that can get me into the mountains, preferably a Nissan truck. I need the po—"

Ron cut me off, "I will get you whatever you need. You just do what you got to do to get this secret side of your unit up and running as soon as possible."

I had a lot to think about during my drive back to Maliana. Ron told me to get my gear packed and get moved to Dili. My transfer to Dili had already been approved. My six-month extension in this UN mission has been approved. Ron further had told me, "The Commissioner will call Jasper and tell him about your immediate transfer. I am sure that call will be made before you get back to Maliana. We need you here, now."

Jasper was upset that I was leaving Bobonaro. I sat in Jasper's office after my long drive from Dili. As Ron had said Jasper had received a phone call from the Commissioner. Jasper understood that I was needed in Dili but he didn't want to see me go. We said our farewells and good lucks. It was hard to leave this man whom I had developed so much trust and respect for. Saying goodbye to Paul wasn't much easier. During the short time I had worked under Pauls command I had grown to respect him very much.

I met with La Faik next. I hadn't worked directly with La Faik during the year I spent in Bobonaro; however, we continually stayed in contact to exchange information. La Faik had kept me up to date reference the activities of the Colimau 2000 group that dominated the four sub-districts north of Bobonaro sub-district. As we were crushing the groups in Bobonaro the Colimau 2000 was getting stronger. There was now an alliance between the Colimau 2000 and the FBA. In fact, the 2IC of the Colimau 2000 was now working daily at the office that the FBA had established in Maliana as an administrative organizer.

I new this man that was now actively involved with both of these groups, he had been an interpreter during my first mission in the year 2000. Ozorio Leke was educated, intelligent and hungered for further education. He had never struck me as a person to become involved with radical groups. Now here he was holding a high position within two groups at the same time.

I made plans for organizing continuing coordination between La Faik and me as I change my base of operations to Dili. This was actually going to be a good move to enhance our information collection activities. I will be able to support La Faik's operations, which will in turn give me the information that La Faik collects.

I stopped and talked with Ozorio on my way through Maliana after talking with La Faik. Ozorio received me as he always had in the past. Ozorio lived alone in a bamboo home on the outskirts of Ritabou Village. After the traditional protocol of my arrival at Ozorio's home I got right down to it. I asked Ozorio about his involvement with the Colimau 2000 and the FBA. Ozorio and I always had a good relationship before now. I was pleased to see that had not changed.

Ozorio said, "I know that you are intelligence. I know that you are friends of Senior Alfredo but I will tell you anyway because we are friends."

Senior Alfredo was a highly influential Fretilin leader. Ozorio also knew that Senior Alfredo was a Segrada Familia commander. Ozorio knew this because Senior Alfredo was Ozorio's uncle.

Ozorio told me that he was the secretary commander under Gabriel Fernandes who was the commander of the Colimau 2000. Ozorio had recently started doing all the administrative work for the Bobonaro District area FBA because of his computer skills. I asked Ozorio, "What interest does the Colimau 2000 have with the FBA?"

Ozorio gazed into my eyes with a serious look in his eyes, "All of the groups are together. The FBA groups all through East Timor, Bua Malus, Tim Saka, CPD-RDTL, the Militia groups in West Timor and Colimau 2000. For now the groups will appear to be separate but they are one. What the UN is doing here is not the right way for East Timor. When the time is right we will establish the proper Government for the Timorese people."

I took a breath as I wondered if what Ozorio said was true. Then I wondered why Ozorio would tell me this plan to change an existing Government. This was a very serious matter if true. I responded to Ozorio's statements, "That's some pretty serious plans that would take a lot of organizational skills. The groups would need a lot of support too."

Ozorio was a young man in his mid-twenties. He was five-foot nine-inches tall with a lean but muscular build. His brown eyes continually gazed into my eyes closely studying my reactions. Ozorio calmly said, "We have the organization and we have the support from Indonesia." Ozorio smiled a very slight smile while he continued to calmly look into my eyes. He said to me very seriously, "You should come with me and meet Gabriel. Your skills are very well known to us. You could be a big help to the East Timorese people."

I felt myself becoming very confused. I must say I was a little overwhelmed by what Ozorio was telling me. As we continued to talk about the current and future politics of East Timor I became more confused about whom the good guys and bad guys were. The one thing that was clear to me was that somebody had a solid plan for taking control of East Timor at some future point and time. Developing a plan and implementing the plan was two different things but if what Ozorio was telling me was true there could be some big problems coming to East Timor.

I knew I was getting played by Ozorio as he politely pushed me to go with him to visit Gabriel. Ozorio was good at selling the "movement," as he called it, for the betterment of East Timor. By the time he finished I was even more confused.

There was no threat of my being sucked into these groups though. I may have felt confusion about who the good guys and bad guys were but I knew what side I was on. That was not going to change. I would always do what I could for "my side." The rights and wrongs would have to be ironed out at a higher level than I had access to.

My mind was swimming in thoughts as I drove up the mountain to Bobonaro for the last time. Ozorio had told me about a place called Osanako where there was a large headquarters compound being built. This headquarters would be the central control of all the groups during the upcoming struggle for control of East Timor. All of the groups were involved with the building of the complex and also the security. Small contingencies of members from all the groups rotate into the headquarters complex to do their share of the building and security duties.

I left Bobonaro Village on such short notice there was barely enough time for me to pack my gear and say goodbye to my many friends. Saying good bye to the family that we had rented the house from was hard. They had become like my own family. There were many hugs and tears. I threw my gear in the back of the truck then turned around to say a personal goodbye to each family member. I drove to the Bobonaro Station to grab a few of my remaining personal items and to say goodbye to my team.

This was a hard thing to do. Every member of that team was so tightly bonded together we were like one body. Now a part of the body was leaving. The only relieving thought was that I would stay in contact with them as much as I could to collect information from the informant network that was still in place.

The emotional stress of leaving my many friends and family in Bobonaro faded away as I drove to Dili. Thinking about my conversation with Ozorio made me realize why I was wanted so badly in Dili although I doubted any of the United Nations top leaders realized just how serious of a situation these groups could be. I tried to work out the degree of truth of what Ozorio had told me.

There was no way to know at this point. That wasn't my job, anyway. Some trained analyst would have to work that out. My job was to get the analyst the information so that the analyst could properly do his job. This thought led me to the next perplexing thought. If the only analysts are at the SID then just how well is my information going to help?

Ron had said that the SID wasn't doing much. Actually what Ron had said was, "Those guys aren't collecting anything worth a shit." Does that mean that they don't know how to collect high grade information but their analyst side is good or is both sides of their intelligence game bad? There was so much that I had to figure out. I took a deep breath as I decided to slow down and take things one step at a time.

I got to Dili and rented a room at the Timor Lodge. There were several hotels in Dili but I knew the Timor Lodge. Several Americans lived at the Timor Lodge. The other benefit of the Timor Lodge was that the company I worked for had created a weight room at the rear of the Timor Lodge. I had never been a weight lifter but I thought I might try it out.

The Timor Lodge was nothing more than several rows of mobile home type structures that had individual rooms built inside. Each room was accessed by one exterior door. There was one small window on the back wall, an air-conditioner mounted high on the back wall, one twin size bed, a small closet cabinet and a small shelf built onto the side wall and chair to use that shelf as a desk. This was all crammed into a six-foot by twelve-foot room.

The shower and toilet facilities for the many guests was in a mobile home structure that had six small shower stalls on one end and eight toilets, a long urinal and a line of sinks along the opposite wall of the toilets. There was a separate structure for the women guests.

At the rear of the rows of would be hotel rooms was the bar and restaurant area. The bar was inside a concrete building that sat behind a large grass roof structure that had open walls from the roof's edge to the four-foot high bamboo walls that lined the exterior of this restaurant area. A TV was on a high shelf in the right front corner of the restaurant. The Timor Lodge was my new home for the time being anyway.

The next morning an Australian police officer named Rod came to the Timor Lodge and picked me up for work. He was driving a beat up Tata that had all the police markings. Rod was wearing his full uniform and United Nations cap. I had to ask myself, "*What kind of intelligence unit is this? Why don't we just get a megaphone and drive up and down the streets announcing who we are?*" I would change this in short order but I wanted to spend the first few days observing how things have been done up until now. I went and changed into my uniform before leaving with Rod to go to work.

Rod briefed me on several police type situations of concern in the Dili area as he drove that piece of shit Tata down the crowded narrow streets of Dili. He told me about the several martial arts groups that occasionally warred against each other. He told me about the many crimes of theft that victimized Internationals that live in the Dili area. He also told me about the possible gathering of ex-Falintil fighters in four different areas of Dili. The ex-Falintil was gathering in Dili to celebrate the coming Independence Day celebrations.

I liked Rod. He was a good, dedicated police officer. He was a man in his late fifties five-foot ten-inches tall and slim build. He had short gray hair, which was the only thing that gave away his age. Rod was very courteous as he showed me around Dili. We arrived at Dili district police Headquarters about 0830 hours. Rod told me that Dili Station and Dili district share the same heaquarters. Dili Station is under the command of Dili district. Dili Station is the Largest of all the Dili stations and also handles the jail behind the Dili Station.

I followed Rod into the DDIU office, which was a large one room office area built inside a mobile home type structure. I thought as we walked in *Wow—this is just like my home, only a much bigger room with bigger windows and a cheap sliding glass door.* The DDIU staff was all in the office, all of them wearing uniforms. They all stood up to shake my hand and welcome me as their new OIC.

Alan was a Bosnian police officer and the only other United Nations worker in our unit. He was in his late-twenties and small build compared to all the other Bosnian police officers I had met over the past two-years of mission work. He was five-foot eight- inches tall and slim. His light brown hair was just long enough to touch the top of his ears. Alan always had a smile and enjoyed day to day life. He was a good kid, but had little interest in work.

Jose Nunes was an ETPS officer. He was the longest serving member of the DDIU. He started in DDIU when the unit was created a few months before. Jose was in his mid-twenties about five-foot seven-inches tall. His body was lean but muscular. Jose could speak limited English that was good enough to avoid the use of an interpreter.

Arnoldo Soares was an ETPS officer who hadn't been assigned to the DDIU very long. He was five-foot ten-inches tall, slim but muscular. His short black hair didn't cover an area on the left side of his head in front of his ear where there was visible burn scares. Arnaldo was in his late-twenties. He had no knowledge of intelligence work. His personality wasn't really good for intelligence work but he had a lot of heart and dedication to his country and his team. Arnaldo would do anything that was asked of him he simply didn't know what to do.

There were two other young Timorese police officers who were in the process of transferring to other divisions. I am sure they were good kids, but I was glad to see that we would be getting a couple of new guys. This would give me the opportunity to have a say in who gets assigned to my new unit.

The DDIU office was equipped with one computer and printer that sat on a large wooden folding table. There was one four-drawer filing cabinet, one telephone and one wooden folding table that had several padded steel chairs pushed under the table's front and sides. There were three two-ring notebooks neatly stacked on the wall edge of the table.

I looked in all four drawers of the file cabinet. There was nothing there, just empty drawers. Rod told me their reports were in the notebooks. I looked through those notebooks and saw copies of reports from the community policing unit, the UN military observers and even some SID reports. There was nothing that had been generated from the DDIU other than cover reports that described the reports from other units and divisions.

I asked, "What contacts and informants do you guys have established?"

Rod told me that he was going to take me to meet all their contacts later in the afternoon. I thought *We can meet all your contacts in one afternoon?* I could see that I would be building an intelligence unit from scratch.

I turned to my new Timorese staff and asked, "*Imi iha ema bele foti informaci segredo?*" (Translated: Do you guys have people who give you secret information?)

The four Timorese police officers looked at me with their mouths open. Roberto said, "*Ita kolia Tetum.*" (Translated: You speak tetum.)

I answered, "*Ituan diet.*" (Translated: only a little.) My status as a new commander just shot to the top of their grading scale. There were UN workers who could speak Indonesian and some that could speak Portuguese, but never had any of these young men heard a foreigner speak their island language of Tetum.

After we worked through their initial shock of my speaking Tetum—the answer to my question was "no." They did not have anyone that can give them secret information. I told them in Tetum, "I am going to change that."

In the afternoon Rod took me to meet the UNMO's (UN military Observer's), the military intelligence Analysts and we finished our tour at the SID office. These were all excellent contacts for exchanging information and head shedding but there was no value for actually collecting information. Although the UNMO's did enlighten me on one issue that I found important.

I had asked them if they had ever heard of someplace called Osanako. They knew the place right away. They even showed me some aerial photos of a large building being built in Osanako. The UNMOs told me that they had gone to Osanako once to inquire about the building. They took a helicopter because Osanako could not be accessed by vehicle. The UNMO commander said, "You have to drive two hours from the village of SAME down very rough mountain roads to get to Turiskain. From Turiskain you have to walk two to three-hours through the mountains to get to Osanako."

I asked the UNMO commander, "So who is building this building and why?"

The UNMO commander answered, "Marcos Da Costa is the Osanako Village chief. He is an ex-Falintil commander and a current CPD-RDTL leader. He told us that they were constructing the building for a wedding reception. He later told a Portuguese military patrol who went through that area that the building was going to be used for the upcoming May 20th Independence Day celebrations. I don't think there is much to this building they are constructing."

I told the UNMO commander as politely as I could, "There is an organization constructing a building that is four times bigger and more elaborate than any school outside of Dili—in a village that is two to three hours' walk from the nearest roadway and you don't think there is much to it?" I paused briefly before continuing, "I have information that Osanako is the planned site of a major headquarters location for several of these groups that have formed in East Timor."

The UNMO commander raised an eyebrow as my statement caused him to remember something. He leafed through the Osanako file in front of him then read a page of a report. The UNMO commander said, "Yes, here it is. The Portuguese unit that went through Osanako reported having seen and recognized several Colimau 2000 members who were helping to construct the building."

I thought, *Well, that's a big yes. Marcos Da Costa is a known CPD-RDTL leader and Colimau 2000 members are helping to build the place.*

While Rod and I visited the SID office, I brought up the subject of Osanako. The SID knew nothing about it. They told me they have regular meetings with the CPD-RDTL national leaders and also Eli Seti who is a powerful ex-Falintil commander who now Commands a well organized ex-Falintil group in Baucau District. The SID officers told me that if there was some kind of headquarters being planned they would know about it. They believed that Eli Seti would know if the CPD-RDTL was building a headquarters and Eli Seti would tell them.

I looked at the SID analyst shocked by what he had said, "Why would Eli Seti tell you anything about the secrets of CPD-RDTL. Eli Seti is CPD-RDTL."

The analyst laughed at me, "You don't know much about Eli Seti, I guess. I talk to him all the time. Eli Seti has no involvement with the CPD-RDTL. Eli Seti is devoted to Xanana Gusmao and the new Government of East Timor."

I looked at this analyst more amazed at what he was saying. Xanana Gusmao was the newly elected President of East Timor. He was the hero of the war with Indonesia and completely respected by most of his Falintil Troops. Eli Seti was not one of those who completely respected Xanana Gusmao's authority. I told the analyst, "In the year 2000, Eli Seti was a CPD-RDTL leader. He sent two of his clandestine members into Atambua to smuggle two assault rifles and four hand grenades from West Timor back to Baucau. He was dealing with the commander of the infamous Tim Saka Militia organization originally from Baucau. Does this sound like a loyal patriot of East Timor?"

The analyst laughed again as he asked me, "Where do you get your information? You've got it all wrong." I knew then I was wasting my time talking to those guys.

I now understood why the commissioner and SRSG were frustrated with the SID. There whole source of collecting information was going up to the bad guys and asking them what they were doing. That would be like a narcotics investigator going up to a drug dealer and asking him for information about his drug business. Of course the drug dealer is going to say, "Oh, I don't do that any more. I am now a loyal citizen of my community."

The military intelligence analysts we visited appeared to be a well-run outfit. The problem with those guys was I knew from past experience that they would only share information that they felt we needed to know. Besides that I had worked in the field with their intelligence collection teams. They did a good job but they didn't conduct Targeted penetration operations.

I went back to the Timor Lodge that night more than ready for a few cold beers. It was so hot in Dili that I sweat all day long, even when I was in the DDIU air-conditioned office. The air-conditioner mounted in the back wall of our office was too small and too old to have much effect on the heat. I took a shower, dressed comfortably, then walked over to the restaurant. The half-dozen or so Americans who lived at the Timor Lodge were all sitting at one long table near the TV and eating as I walked in.

I grabbed a plate that was near the beginning of the cafeteria-style food line. I walked down the short line of entries for the night. Soon my plate was heaping over with food. I ordered a beer as I paid for my dinner. The Timorese lady working the cash register took my money and gave me my change along with the cold can of Australian Victoria Bitter beer that she took from the cooler behind her.

I sat among my fellow Americans and ate what I thought was a pretty good meal. I listened to a couple of the guys complain about the food, the living conditions at the Timor Lodge, and the heat. I noticed that the men who were complaining were men who had never worked and lived outside of Dili.

The rest of us sitting at that table had no complaints. We had a bed to sleep in, air-conditioning, hot and cold running water that didn't have to be boiled before drinking, a restaurant that served good food that didn't come out of a can, and cold beer. The only issue I could agree with the two Dili boys on was the heat. Dili was the hottest place I had been yet and I didn't like it.

For the next two weeks I maintained what the DDIU had been doing before I arrived as I studied the men in the unit. We drove around to the four different locations around Dili where the FBA had prepared camping areas for their members. The ex-combatant members would be gathering in Dili for the upcoming Independence Day. We took head counts of the members at the four locations everyday. Their numbers were increasing daily.

I started to make contacts during the evening hours on a few nights. Through La Faik, I was aware of another active intelligence organization operating in East Timor. The newly established East Timor military known as the "Federal Defense Force of East Timor" (FDTL) had a military intelligence unit that was commanded by an ex-Falintil commander known as "Mau Nana." All intelligence operators knew about commander Mau Nana and the FDTL military intelligence unit. This is a common necessity of any military anywhere in the world.

What the rest of the International intelligence community in East Timor did not know was that the FDTL intelligence was a much bigger operation than what the United Nations plans had called for. I was close friends with one of the FDTL secret operators since the year 2000. I made initial contact with my friend and started the plans for future joint information gathering operations.

After two weeks of driving around in a fully marked police car and wearing uniforms I had seen all I needed to start putting a team together. By this time I had built a good relationship with the Timorese Dili District commander, Babo Ismael. A man in his early thirties, Babo was very intelligent, educated and had a charismatic personality. He was a strong leader of his people. I talked with Babo about the kind of person that I would like to have assigned to the DDIU.

Babo was very supportive of the DDIU as anyone who fought in a war realized the importants of good intelligence.

I told Ron that it was time to get the DDIU out of uniforms and into a reliable vehicle that did not have "police" written on both sides, front and rear. The next day Ron gave me a Nissan pick-up truck that was marked with big UN letters only. That was perfect. There were many UN trucks just like this Nissan that were driven by UN staff from many departments with no connection with the police.

I told the DDIU team members to come into work dressed in civilian clothes, everyday type clothes nothing fancy. I wanted our members to look like everyday nobodies. It was important to keep the lowest profile possible. I began working directly with my Timorese staff all day everyday. I was giving them lessons in establishing secret informants. I taught them by walking them through an actual target, choosing a target and then develop that target.

Jose was a natural for this type of intelligence work. He knew many people and he had the personality to convince people to work for him. The first Target I chose was the CPD-RDTL. I asked Jose and Arnaldo, "Who do you know that is a CPD-RDTL member?"

They both personally knew members. My next question was, "What positions do they hold within that organization? The most important information is going to come from commanders and administrators." Jose knew one mid-level commander.

I continued the lesson, "Can you befriend this commander?" Jose didn't think he could.

I asked, "Do you know any of his friends or family?"

Jose said, "I know the commander's uncle."

I moved on to the next step, "Can you talk to this uncle?"

Jose answered, "Yes."

I smiled at Jose and said, "There you go. There is a possible beginning of developing an informant into the CPD-RDTL."

Jose said with a big smile, "That's easy."

I corrected Jose's statement, "It's not that easy and it's dangerous." I explained that before making contact with the uncle he must first try and establish what side the uncle is on, whether the uncle is prone to work both sides to the middle or worse yet may be devoted to the target but convinces Jose that he will be loyal to the DDIU.

I made the following point very clear, "You pick the wrong person to develop into an informant, you endanger yourself and your team to exposure by enemy assets."

I then explained specific strategies to develop a possible informant that allow the operator to "feel out" the potential informant and suck him into the operator's control at the same time. The most important principle for the operator who is developing an informant is patience. Whether the process takes one day or one year is not near as important as developing the right informant without exposing the operator or the team.

Jose picked up on intelligence tactics very quickly. I could see that Arnaldo did not have the aptitude for this type of work without becoming dangerous to us. I started working with Arnaldo on the other side of the intelligence coin, Counter-Intelligence.

The DDIU was so vulnerable to exposure. There was no doubt that our secret operations would be exposed at some point. We had to prolong that exposure for as long as possible. A counter- intelligence program helps to protect our DDIU from being penetrated by enemy assets and also may give us forewarning of when we are "hot" (exposed).

At the same time I was beginning to develop the DDIU, I got a message from my sister. She was concerned that I may not know about a serious situation that involved my wife and our other sister. My wife had gone to our other sister and convinced her to co-sign for a car that my wife wanted to buy. My sister believed my wife's sob story about our current car needing to be replaced. She co-signed for the car. A few months later, creditors were calling my sister about two cars that she had co-signed for which had been repossessed.

I knew immediately what my wife had done. She conned a signature for one car and forged my sister's name on the other one. I was furious, and that was the end of my marriage. Communications from Timor were difficult and many times just not possible. Email was the only constant means of communication. I emailed a friend of mine who was an attorney and asked him to handle my divorce, which he agreed to do.

At the end of April, 2002, I was building a straight-up police intelligence unit, a secret intelligence operation, adjusting to living in Dili, and now going through an Internet divorce. I was a little stressed. I spent my free evenings sitting outside with some of my fellow Americans who lived at the Timor Lodge. It was nice being around some Americans again. We were all old-timer cops from back home, which provided us with many war stories to exchange, as well as current event topics.

Being an active field intelligence collector was a twenty-four-hour a day activity. I quickly learned that one of the best resources for getting information from other districts throughout Timor was the Timor Lodge. Many people from the districts who were going on CTOs would stay at the Timor Lodge the night before their flight to Darwin, Australia, or Bali, Indonesia. I started spending part of my evenings in the restaurant area that became the TV room after everyone had eaten. I struck up conversations with likely candidates who I thought may know something of interest to me. This proved to be a very effective tactic.

As the reality of being a "free man" settled into my head, I began thinking about a social life. I went out on a couple of nights to the two discos in town. There were lots of people who went out to these Western-style dances. Most of the customers were foreigners. United Nations soldiers and other United Nations workers were a large percentage of the foreigners; however, there were several businesses from other countries in Dili that catered to the United Nations too.

The huge UN staff and soldiers who all had lots of money to spend was a target-rich environment for hookers. There were plenty of prostitutes available at the discos as well. There were women from Indonesia, Thailand, Philippines, and a rare few from East Timor. Getting laid in Dili was an easy thing for any man who was looking to do so.

In addition to the prostitutes, there were several East Timorese women who went to the discos. Some had learned to be whores who spread their legs easily for men who bought them drinks to cloud the Timorese culture of not being sexually involved with a man before marriage. Others came to the disco to dance and hopefully find their true love. Most of the women in this category had been married once and had one or more kids. There were many young women in Dili who had been abandoned by their Militia member husbands in 1999. By Timorese standards, these women were "tainted goods." Timorese men for the most part didn't want a marriage with a woman in this situation.

Most Timorese women were pretty naïve when it came to the Western way of thinking at a dance. Timorese dances were real social events that went on all night long. The difference was that the Timorese drank very little throughout the dance. There was no groping of the dance partner, even subtly. The results of such an offense at a Timorese dance would be a stout beating of the violator by family members and friends of the molested woman.

If a woman met a man she was interested in, they may sneak into the shadows and exchange kisses, hugs, and I am sure some groping; however, this was not a meaningless thing. There would be the intentions of both parties to be boyfriend and girlfriend with the possibility of marriage if everything went well during their building relationship.

Timorese women coming to these Western-style discos found out the hard way that to sneak off with a foreign man resulted in many promises of commitment before and during the sex the woman would be compelled to give only to find out that commitment was for one or two nights only. After a few experiences of these types of relationships, the woman was known to be an easy lay by the regular patrons of the discos, and in fact she had become an easy lay as her sense of morality became deadened by repeated meaningless relationships. The once-modest Timorese mountain girl had become a whore.

I liked the music at the discos but I didn't like the atmosphere. I should have wanted to jump right into this type of action but I didn't. I wasn't interested in a meaningless relationship that could cause me big problems. I wasn't interested in having any relationships.

I did meet a couple of different East Timorese women with whom I considered having a relationship. It was easy for me to meet Timorese women because I could speak Tetum and I was well grounded into the Timorese way of life. The first woman I met was an interpreter that I had known when I worked in Maliana in 2000. I hadn't seen her since then. She had moved to Dili in early 2001. Our by chance run in with each other turned into getting reacquainted over dinner followed by lunch together. Our relationship was quickly becoming more than friends. I became paranoid about the repercussions of a love relationship with this woman so I broke it off.

The other woman I started to become involved with worked at the Timor Lodge. She was an attractive Timorese woman with a real proper Timorese way about her. She was a little closer to my age too. Her children were all in their teens. Her Militia husband had abandoned her and the kids in 1999.

There was little danger of serious problems resulting from a relationship with her, but I saw her as a good person I would have to leave someday. It was better not to get involved in a deep relationship that would ultimately hurt this woman more than she had already suffered. I was better off alone, anyway.

I focused one hundred percent on work. Soon Babo assigned a couple more ETPS to the DDIU. One of those men turned out to have the qualities necessary to be a good intelligence officer.

Cesaltino was in his early twenties with only a few months of police experience but he knew a lot of people. He also knew how to influence people.

Like Jose, he took to the tactics of establishing and controlling Informants like a fish in water.

In a short amount of time we had penetrations of varying degrees into the CPD-RDTL, two ex-Falintil groups that were part of the FBA and several of the Martial Arts groups. We were writing intelligence reports daily that could be attributed to the DDIU police side of our operations. I was also daily writing reports that were turned into Ron directly. Our DDIU file cabinet was filling up.

Working and living in the city was a hard adjustment for me to make but it was now paying off and it was getting interesting. The city life was difficult by American standards but after being in the mountains for so long I found life in the city very comfortable, other than the extreme heat of Dili. It was going to get much hotter for the DDIU.

CHAPTER SEVENTEEN

Levels of Terrorism

September 11 of 2001 brought the existence of terrorist organizations to the front of everyone's minds world wide. East Timor was no different. I thought about that early morning when I first learned about the attack on the World Trade Center as the man sitting in front of me brought the incident up in our conversation.

Randy, my fellow American and house mate, and I were sleeping in our individual rooms at the house we rented in Bobonaro Village. At about 0500 hours we heard the engine of an Australian military jeep up on the roadway. The sound of a military vehicle on the roadway usually meant that someone from the Bravo Company compound was coming to see us. Both of us always woke up at the sound of a jeep, no matter how hard we were sleeping.

We listened to the engine, hoping that it would drive past our house. Soon we heard the pitch of the engine change as the large four-wheel-drive vehicle came down our steep driveway and to the front of our house. I heard Randy say what I was thinking as we both unzipped our mosquito domes and rolled out onto the floor, "Now what happened?" Every time the military came to see us in the middle of the night there was always work for us to do.

Randy went and opened the front door and stepped out onto the veranda. I walked up behind Randy and stood in the doorway. As we greeted the Bravo Company CMA team we could tell even in the dark that something was terribly wrong. Captain Thripp told us about the horrible attack on the World Trade Center and on the Pentagon. He invited us to come down to the Bravo Company compound and watch the news on their recently acquired TV system.

The reality of what Chris, Capt. Thripp, had told us didn't sink in until we saw the news footage of the jet slamming into a World Trade Center tower. It was hard being so far away from home realizing that our country was under attack. The Australian soldiers of Bravo Company felt deep sorrow for what had happened in America too. Everyone watched the news in silence too deeply shocked at what they were seeing to speak. It was a bad day.

* * * *

The man in front of me continued, "We have reason to believe that there is a terrorist cell operating here in Dili." The man produced a file from his desk and handed it to me. I opened the file and scanned through its contents. There were several photos of a building that I recognized as a local restaurant in Dili. There were also photos of five men who were involved with the restaurant. The names that went with the photos were all Arabic names. The faces of the men also looked Arabic.

The man sitting at the desk told me to read the file later then continued, "It is important to collect as much information as possible about these men and what their activities are—their true activities."

The man sitting in front of me was not a United Nations worker. He had no involvement with the United Nations. I had known this man during my first mission in East Timor. I told the man, "I'll see what I can do."

As I drove down the crowded streets of Dili I thought about this new revelation of a possible terrorist cell operating in East Timor. I would add this new terrorist investigation to the one I received through Ron. The Muslim mosque in Dili was suspected of having Terrorists living in the mosque. I was given the names of two suspects that were the possible terrorists in the mosque.

These were both real possibilities of terrorist activities; however, I was equally concerned about possible Terror activities against the people of East Timor. Our rapidly growing informant network was reporting the plans of the Colimau 2000 and the CPD-RDTL to develop "Ninja units." The purpose of these black clad shadow warriors was to begin their activities with acts of theft. Stealing from homes and also organizing roadblocks along lonely mountain roads to stop passing vehicles and taking things of value from the vehicle occupants. These Ninja units could handle any covert operation needed up to and including murder.

Rod had left the DDIU in May 2002, when he rotated home. Ron replaced him with a new Australian who was one of many Australian police replacing the Australians who just left the mission.

Mick was a very welcome addition to the DDIU. He was about forty years old and five-foot-nine-inches tall, with a medium build. He had silver hair and a short silver beard to match. Mick had a lot of experience with the Australian Federal police intelligence unit. He knew what he was doing and he adjusted to the working environment in East Timor very well.

Mick knew all the information that was coming through our office but I had to keep some of our collection operations secret from him. Some of the intelligence trails we were following were leading back "over the fence." It was better that Mick didn't know about any espionage activities much less become involved with them.

Mick spearheaded some of our counter-intelligence investigations that up front looked like nothing more than Militia and East Timorese TNI who had returned to East Timor to live. He was responsible for putting great pressure on a cell of operators in the Hera Village area.

There was a Koppassus commander and several Militia members who had moved back into the Hera area. Hera was a small village about ten-kilometers east of Dili along the north coast road. Our Informant Network gave us the initial information that the group of Koppassus and Militia had returned to Hera. They were holding secret meetings to help organize a large black market smuggling operation that was smuggling a huge amount of goods from West Timor into East Timor. The smuggling was being conducted by the Aitarak Militia who use to dominate the entire Dili area including Hera. The other purpose of their secret meetings was to organize a Ninja unit.

Mick took away their ability to operate as he worked up a murder case against every one of the Militia currently in Hera including their Koppassus commander who was living in Hera. Mick had dug into this group of Militia until he discovered a murder that happened in September of 1999 in Hera. The witnesses named the group of murderers. The list of murder suspects included all of these men we wanted to neutralize. This was the case we would use to accomplish our purpose.

* * * *

Mick took initial statements from witnesses and identified the names of other witnesses. He then turned the case over to the Serious Crimes Investigation unit (SCIU) as we were directed to do by Ron. We were an intelligence unit. Ron didn't want us being tied down with completing investigations that would draw us into Court. The SCIU quickly put the finishing touches into this case then arrested the Hera Militia members and the Koppassus commander.

We were identifying several returned Militia and TNI that were in East Timor. Some of them we knew were conducting espionage activities. Many of them we could never get beyond the suspicious stage. We did identify an SGI controlled operator who had managed to penetrate the SCIU. The operator was a member of UNTAS, which is an SGI group creation of East Timorese who were spies.

We thoroughly investigated the UNTAS spy in the hopes of criminally charging the man with espionage. All we were able to actually prove was that the man was an UNTAS Agent who had been sent from Bali, Indonesia. We couldn't criminally charge the man but at least he was immediately dismissed from the SCIU.

* * * *

Our information network was getting better and stronger as time went on. Soon we knew almost every move and intention of the CPD-RDTL and to a lesser degree the FBA. We were getting information about CPD-RDTL, FBA and Colimau 2000 members who had become ETPS police officers. Several of these ETPS was actively collecting information for their group leaders. The ETPS ranks had become generously "salted" with spies.

The Colimau 2000 was increasing the pressure out in Bobonaro District. They were conducting open terror campaigns to gain control of many remote areas during the day. At night their Ninja units terrorized the population. In July, 2002, the Colimau 2000 were trying to dominate the now very large markets in Maliana. The people were resisting the Colimau 2000 terror tactics. This caused the two Colimau 2000 top commanders to make a big mistake.

One day in July 2002, a group of Colimau 2000 members entered the Maliana market. Gabriel Fernandes and Ozorio Leke had sent them to attack a man who ran a selling stall inside the market. The Colimau 2000 commanders believed this man's strong will was influencing the other people to stand up against the Colimau 2000. The man was savagely attacked and beaten severely. The injured man had to be flown to the hospital in Dili. He was in a coma and near dead.

La Faik and his Segrada Familia had been closely monitoring the Colimau 2000. La Faik tried several times to feed information to the ETPS in Maliana so that they could deal with the Colimau 2000. La Faik did not understand why the police were not getting aggressive against this rising threat to the citizens of the entire Bobonaro District. The terrorized citizens could not understand that in situations like this western style Law and Order fall short of the needs of the public.

La Faik would no longer exercise restraint after hearing of the attack on the man in the Maliana market. He summoned Senior Alfredo to lead an assault against the Colimau 2000. He included the FBA organization as a Target for this assault too. The two groups were basically together and shared the same 2IC, Ozorio Leke. Segrada Familia attacked Gabriel Fernandes's home and the Colimau 2000 office next door. After a short hand to hand battle the many defeated Colimau 2000 members were forced to run for their lives while Segrada Familia burned the office building and Gabriel's home.

The Segrada Familia then turned their wrath against the FBA Headquarters near the downtown of Maliana. The FBA also fled as smoke bellowed in the sky above their Headquarters building. The Colimau 2000 fled to the remote areas of Ermera District to evade the rampaging Segrada Familia. The FBA membership was largely ex-Falintil soldiers. They eventually negotiated a truce with their once Brothers in Arms Segrada Familia.

The police were now able to take their shots at the Colimau 2000. The police investigation of the attempted murder at the Maliana market gave them solid evidence against the men that actually conducted the beating of the victim but also solid evidence of the conspiracy to beat that man. United Nations and ETPS Investigators arrested several Colimau 2000 members including the two top commanders, Gabriel Fernandes and Ozorio Leke. The Investigators had arrest warrants for many more Colimau 2000 members but the suspects were all hiding in Ermera district.

A few days after this incident in Maliana I was summoned to the chief of operations office at National Headquarters. I was told to be prepared to give a full report of everything I knew about the Colimau 2000 group. The UN police and military liaison (PML) officer was requested to attend the meeting between the chief of operations and me. I was surprised to see my old teammate, Tom McCarthy, sitting with the chief of operations when I walked into the office. Tom was the new PML.

I briefed the chief of operations about the Colimau 2000 and provided him with the numerous reports that I had written including my discussion with Ozorio Leke before leaving Bobonaro three months ago. The chief of operations was stunned at all the detailed information that I provided him. He asked me accusingly, "Why haven't I heard about this before now?"

I calmly replied, "I don't know. I turn copies of my reports into the SID, I would have thought they would keep you informed."

The chief of operations nodded his realization of the problem. He then said, "I suspected that was the case but, Jesus Christ, this is a lot of good information that I should have known about a long time ago."

The chief of operations then calmed himself, "Well, that's why your sitting here with me now and not them. I have another reason for your being here too." The chief of operations motioned toward Tom, "Tom here tells me you have a trained team that can perform special operations in the mountains. We need a special operation conducted immediately."

The chief of operations told me that there were several existing warrants for the arrest of Colimau 2000 members and there were more warrants that would soon be issued. This was an opportunity to greatly weaken the Colimau 2000 group by putting many of their members and leaders in prison. The problem was that the entire remaining group was hiding somewhere in the remote mountains. The chief of operations looked at me silently for a moment, then said, "Your mission is to find these bastards and bring them in. I realize it could be dangerous out in those mountains, so I am not ordering you to conduct this mission. It's up to you if you want to volunteer to conduct this mission."

I told the Chief of Operations that I would be happy to go after the Colimau 2000 but I would need a lot of support when the time came to start the campaign to arrest them. I knew that the Portuguese SPU was no longer on the Island. I asked about the possibility of getting military support for the campaign.

The chief of operations replied, "That's why Tom is here with us. You tell him what you need and he will work with the military to get your support." The chief of operations paused, then said almost apologetically, "You have seven days to complete this mission."

I think my mouth dropped open, "Seven days? It took us three months and nine tough operations to crush the Tim Saka group. The Colimau 2000 is a much bigger group and they are better organized."

The chief of operations flatly said, "There is nothing I can do about the time limit. It's out of my hands. I know the odds are against you but I would appreciate anything you can do to help out in this matter."

I left National Headquarter and prepared for the Colimau 2000 mission into Bobonaro district. I had been training with Jose and Arnaldo since May. They knew the special tactics side of this game, so I told them to be prepared to leave for Bobonaro in the morning. I left Mick in charge of the DDIU.

Jose, Arnaldo, and I drove to Maliana early the next morning. We linked up with La Faik as soon as we could get to him. He was thrilled that we had come to lend a hand. We made plans for several reconnaissance operations to locate the Colimau 2000 members. The recon operations would be run by the Segrada Familia.

Once the plans were in place, Jose, Arnaldo, and I went to Bobonaro Village. The house that I had rented for one year was occupied by an American police officer who had replaced Tom a few weeks before my transfer to Dili. Marion was a good cop. He had become heavily involved with the Bobonaro team training exercises. Jose, Arnaldo and I moved into my old house with Marion.

The next morning I met with Atanacio who was now the ETPS commander of the Bobonaro Zona. Olavio had transferred to Dili in June. I briefed Atanacio about the situation and my mission. Atanacio agreed to bring the old Bobonaro team under my command for an operation against the Colimau 2000. Marion, Atanacio and I made plans to conduct team training exercises over the next two days. This would sharpen everybody's skills and also get Jose and Arnaldo meshed into the Bobonaro team.

The three of us DDIU drove down to Maliana later in the morning to meet with La Faik. The rest of that day was spent delivering three separate Segrada Familia recon teams to their operation insertion points. Late that afternoon I met with the Bobonaro district commander. Jasper had ended his mission and gone home in June. Paul had also returned home. The current commander was Danielle from the Australian Federal Police Force. I had known Danielle when I was working in Bobonaro. She was a very good choice to take command of the Bobonaro district.

I kept Danielle informed of our activities so that we could coordinate a joint effort against the Colimau 2000. Danielle had an aggressive investigation team that was hungry to go get the bad guys. They were anxiously awaiting our information as to where the Colimau 2000 had gone. I hoped that we would be able to throw these investigation dogs the piece of raw meat they craved.

The next two days we were in Bobonaro training. It felt good to be back home. It was like I had never left. We trained hard as we always had. Our training sessions, as always, were based out of my house. We trained in that part of the village part of the day then went down the mountain from the house for the remainder of our training. The people of Bobonaro Village had become accustomed to our training sessions. The people were visibly pleased to see us training again.

The day following our training sessions Jose, Arnaldo, and I moved our kit to Maliana where we would be staying for the remainder of our mission. We needed to be closer to the Segrada Familia to do our intelligence thing. By the time we met with La Faik that afternoon two of the three recon teams (RT) were back. The RT that we had sent over the line into Ermera District had located a contingent of the Colimau 2000 at a small village in Hatulia sub-district. The members were sleeping in different homes in the village.

La Faik had guessed that the Colimau 2000 had splintered into two or more groups to evade capture. The Ermera RT confirmed this theory. The other two RT"s were covering areas in Cailaco Sub-District that at one time the Falintil used to base attacks against Indonesian Forces. The second returned RT reported that there was no sign of the Colimau 2000. La Faik decided to send a recon team into Atabae Sub-District. There was one possibility of a location in Atabae where the Colimau 2000 could take refuge. It was unlikely that they would go there but like La Faik said, "If I were them I would go there just because the enemy wouldn't think that I would."

I reported the location of the Colimau 2000 group that we had found in Hatulia, Ermera district to Danielle when we returned to Maliana that night. The following night the Maliana hungry dog Investigation team went to Hatulia and pounced on the Colimau 2000 members hiding there. They came back to Maliana heavy laden with prisoners. It felt good to see our information acted upon. The effectiveness of the operation was completely the results of the Investigation teams abilities but we took pleasure at having pointed them in the right direction.

The third RT got back late the following day. They had found where the Colimau 2000 had been but they had moved. The third RT tracked the Colimau 2000 to a point just over the river into Atabae Sub-District. The third RT determined that the group had gone into the Ouipua area, which was the mountain that Augustinho Bili Tai had used to stage for the assault on the Australian platoon in Aidabasalala back in the year 2000.

La Faik's hunch had paid off. I went to Maliana to begin planning the operation to assault Ouipua while we waited for the Atabae RT to return with updated information. On the sixth day of our mission, the Atabae RT was back with the information as to where the Colimau 2000 was in Ouipua Mountain. I completed the operation plan and had the Bobonaro team briefed and ready to launch the following morning.

That's when I got a call from the chief of operations with the bad news that we would not be getting any military support. I told the chief of operations,

"Without the military we cannot assault Ouipua Mountain. We need the military to set up the cordon positions around the Colimau 2000 otherwise they will simply escape as we approach."

The chief of operations sighed his frustration, "This is politics at its worse. We cannot use the military. I am very sorry."

I discussed this unfortunate development with Danielle and the Maliana chief of investigations. We focused on possible actions that we could take rather than complain about something we couldn't change. We decided to attempt a two prong probe into the fringes of the Ouipua area.

The Investigation team would drive the roadway from Aidabasalala to Ouipua to attempt to locate any Colimau 2000 members that may be moving through the area. I would lead the Bobonaro team supported by Segrada Familia into Ouipua from the wild area north of Ouipua. This operation wasn't much more than a fishing trip but we reasoned that at the very least we would put pressure on the Colimau 2000 in Ouipua.

We launched the operation before daylight the following morning. The Bobonaro team/Segrada Familia managed to capture two suspects and collected a surprising amount of intelligence throughout a long hard day of walking. We even identified a group of bamboo huts where the Colimau 2000 was beginning to build a whole new village. The Maliana Investigation team had the biggest success of the operation. They captured nine Colimau 2000 suspects.

Early that evening, I made it back to Maliana. The Maliana chief of investigations, Danielle, and I de-briefed the operation outcome. When we finished, I took Jose and Arnaldo and drove to Dili. We had to be back in Dili on that day. I got back to the Timor Lodge for a much-needed shower and cold beer about 2300 hours.

The next day was business as usual. Other than a call from the chief of operations thanking and congratulating me on a job well done, everything was as if we had never left Dili for a week. Because of the many arrests made during the seven day Colimau 2000 operation the commanders at National Headquarters felt our activities were a success. I felt that we were just partially successful. We could have accomplished four times as much if we could have got the military support.

About one week after the Colimau 2000 mission I went to a restaurant and bar that was located on the beach. I liked the restaurants that were on the beach because of the serene atmosphere and the sea breeze that helped to relieve the heat. I ate dinner at the Purple Cow restaurant as that sea breeze turned a little cooler with the night. Tonight was a Friday night so the bar and restaurant would turn into a disco at 2200 hours. I didn't plan to stay for the music. I had been working day and night for the past four days and I was very tired.

I paid my bill at the bar and started to walk out to my car when I saw Gherdy walking toward the entrance. Gherdy was the company representative who was assigned to East Timor to take care of all us American police. Gherdy was alone. He had stopped into the Purple Cow for a drink before going home. I walked back into the bar with Gherdy and joined him for a drink. The beer was cold and going down good as we sat and talked. One beer led to another as many people started arriving for the dance. Soon the music began to play.

Gherdy and I were not paying to much attention to the growing crowd and loud music as we sat at a table away from all the action. I was getting pretty buzzed when a Timorese man I knew as Antoni came up to me. Antoni talked to me for a short while then asked me if there was anything I wanted. I knew Antoni was a hustler, but I couldn't help but like the man. I was just drunk enough to be playful as I told Antoni in Tetum, "I want a whore, a very pretty whore, not one of these regular prostitutes." I then laughed as I continued, "You can bring one of the regulars for my friend here."

As Antoni scurried off Gherdy asked me, "What was that all about?" Antoni and I had been speaking Tetum. I told Gherdy about Antoni and what I asked him for. Gherdy rolled his eyes, "There you go again. I just know you are about to get into trouble with these games you play." Gherdy no sooner finished talking when Antoni came back to our table with an East Timorese hooker behind him.

Gherdy looked the woman over as Antoni presented her to him. Gherdy played the game too, "How much?"

The woman boldly responded, "Fifty dollars." Gherdy toyed with Antoni and the woman for a while, then sent them on their way. Gherdy and I then exchanged old war stories of our police career days that involved prostitutes. We finished our cans of beer, then ordered two more.

I had forgotten about Antoni as Gherdy and I continued our discussions and drank. Antoni came back to our table and said with a smile, "Here she is," As he motioned to the other side of me.

I turned and looked in the direction Antoni had motioned as a Timorese woman was sitting down in the chair beside me. I looked into this woman's dark brown eyes and thought, *I told Antoni I wanted a pretty whore, and that's what he brought me. This woman is very beautiful.*

The woman had long dark brown hair that hung loose to her sleek butt. Her body was petite. She was under five feet tall and probably didn't weigh ninety pounds, but she was well-shaped. Her tight-fitting jeans and pull-over blouse revealed every important curve on her body. Her dark brown face had the chiseled features of high cheek bones, tiny nose, and nicely thick lips that glowed crimson from the lipstick she wore. I was impressed.

The woman sat properly erect in the chair next to me as she looked at me with that normal East Timorese look of indifference. I asked the girl in Tetum, "What's your name?"

She was surprised to hear me speak to her in Tetum. She answered, "Nina."

I asked her questions like, "Where are you from, How long have you lived in Dili?" and so on. She responded like a normal Timorese woman would, not like a whore or prostitute.

I grew tired of feeling this woman out, so I asked her, "How much for one night?" The woman didn't respond, but I knew the Timorese well enough by now that I could see that ever-so-subtle change in her eyes that told me she was offended by my question. I thought, *I have managed to piss off the most beautiful woman in this establishment, but at least I know she isn't a prostitute.*

Antoni was standing behind this beautiful young woman while I talked to her. He told me, "She wants to dance; go dance with her."

I continued to look into this woman's eyes as Antoni spoke. This woman, Nina, would not look back into my eyes. I now knew this woman was not a prostitute, and I had my doubts if she was a whore, either. She was acting very Timorese. I continued to look into this woman's eyes as I answered Antoni, "Maybe later. I have to discuss some things with my friend right now." I then turned away from the woman and Antoni as I resumed talking with Gherdy. The woman stood up and walked away.

I was interested in this woman, not only because she was beautiful, but because I had noticed something very special about her. On her left shoulder were five raised bumps of her skin in the shape of a square with one bump in the center. I recognized this as the mark of the Cinco-Cinco (5-5) Clandestine group who performed secret activities against the Indonesians during the occupation of East Timor. This beautiful woman could have value to me whether she was a whore or not.

I observed this woman as she danced with a group of other Timorese women. The men who normally aggressively pursued the known whores at the discos around town showed no interest in her. I had to question again whether this woman was a whore. So far it didn't look like it.

About one o'clock in the morning, Gherdy went home. I walked up close to the dance floor. I saw Nina dancing with two other Timorese women who I recognized as waitresses from the restaurant next door. I walked out onto the dance floor and stood in front of Nina looking into her eyes. Nina stopped dancing and looked back into my eyes questioningly. I raised my head ever so slightly, which is a Timorese thing from the mountains. With that slight raise of my head, I had asked Nina to dance. Nina nodded back at me and started dancing with me.

We danced together for one hour. At two o'clock in the morning, Nina suddenly announced she had to go. She just quit dancing and walked toward the front door with three of her girlfriends. As I watched her walk away, Antoni reappeared, telling me to go with her. I told Antoni that I wasn't invited.

Antoni said, "She will go with you, but you must go now." It was obvious to me, even in my semi-drunken condition, that Antoni was playing both Nina and me. I told Antoni that I wasn't interested and walked away.

As I walked outside, I saw Antoni yelling to a group of women who were walking toward the next-door restaurant. I could hear part of what Antoni was saying. Nina was apparently one of the women. Antoni was trying to convince her to go with the foreigner she had been dancing with. The women were trying to ignore Antoni.

Antoni saw me as I was unlocking my car door, which was parked near where Antoni stood in the middle of the street. Antoni came right over to me and began nagging me about taking Nina home with me. By this time all I wanted to do was go home and go to sleep. Nina wasn't interested, anyway.

I scolded Antoni for nagging me. I also informed him that selling women for sex was against the law, especially when the woman doesn't want to be involved. When I finished, Antoni hung his head in shame, then asked, "Can I get twenty dollars from you?"

I looked at Antoni in disbelief for a moment, then laughed at him, slapped him on the shoulder and got into my car to leave.

Two weeks later I went back to the Purple Cow to have a few drinks and listen to the music. I hadn't thought about my encounter with Nina until I walked into the bar. I walked up to the bar and ordered a VB (Victoria Bitter beer). The music from the large speakers that sat on the otherwise empty bandstand was spewing out "Who Let the Dogs Out" as I waited at the very crowded bar for my beer.

It was after eleven o'clock at night when I finished meeting with a couple of FDTL secret operators. I was very tired, but I was a little wound up, so I decided to come unwind at the Purple Cow for a little while. This was the first time I had come back to the Purple Cow since my little drinking binge with Gherdy two weeks ago.

The man behind the bar put the can of VB on the bar in front of me. I handed him a five-dollar-bill and waited for my change. The man hurriedly got my change and placed it on the counter in front of me as he took the drink order from the man standing next to me. I stuffed the change in my front jeans pocket as I walked away from the bar.

The dance floor was crowded. It didn't look like there were any tables open on the other side of the dance floor so I started working my way through the crowd trying to get up the stairs where there was an area that overlooked the dance floor. I was halfway up the stairs when I ran face to face into Nina who was coming down the stairs. We exchanged *bo noites* (Portuguese for "good evening") and a handshake. We looked into each others eyes for a few moments. I asked Nina, "*Danca* ?" (Dance) Nina smiled slightly and nodded.

We danced together non-stop, except for twice when we went to the bar for a drink. I bought Nina two whisky and Cokes, which the Timorese call "whisky-Cola." I found out Nina's true name when a girlfriend of hers approached us on the dance floor and called her Ely. After the girlfriend walked away, I asked Nina about her name. She confessed that her name was actually Ely. I nodded my head as I stopped dancing and properly shook Ely's hand and said in Tetum, "Hello, Ely, my name is Jim. Would you like to dance with me?" Ely smiled at me and resumed dancing.

Ely didn't seem to be interested in the many men who couldn't help but watch this brown beauty dancing with me. She had acted the same way two weeks ago when I secretly watched her dancing with her friends. At exactly two o'clock in the morning she announced that she had to go.

I stopped her as I asked in Tetum, "You want to go get something to drink and eat?" Ely stopped and looked into my eyes for a few moments. I could tell she was trying to read my mind. She finally answered, "*Bele.*" (Translated: I can.)

She turned and walked out to the street. I followed close behind her. I walked to my car which was parked across the street from the front entrance to the Purple Cow. I opened the passenger door for Ely to sit in the truck. Ely looked inside the truck and then looked at me, studying me closely. I could see that she was concerned about what I had on my mind. I could also see that she was very interested in me.

A Timorese man came out of the bar and stood at the side of the street talking to a couple of friends. I recognized this man as an ETPS who was assigned to the special police unit (SPU). This was the police unit that the

Portuguese SPU had trained. Ely walked across the street and talked to this SPU Officer. I could tell I was the topic of their conversation as they both kept glancing over at me as I stood beside my truck.

About five minutes had passed when finally the SPU officer walked Ely across the street to where I stood waiting. I was concerned that I may have a problem with this very husky police officer. The Timorese were not fond of Timorese women getting involved with foreign men. They had good reason to feel this way. Foreign men often have smooth-talked Timorese women until they get the woman alone, which always results in the foreign man having sex with the woman, either through false promises, pleading aided by aggressive foreplay, and sometimes out and out force. Even seemingly sincere relationships end in the abandonment of the Timorese woman.

I was a little surprised when the husky SPU officer told me, in English no less, that it was okay for Ely to go with me. He continued, "I know you are a good man, not like the other *malais.*" (Foreigners.) I really didn't know this SPU officer. I only knew that he was an SPU officer because I had seen him a few times with his unit. He seemed to know me though or know of me anyway.

I thanked him as I shook his hand. He held the passenger door open for Ely to get into my truck while I walked around and got into the drivers side of the truck. The SPU officer then stopped traffic in the street and directed me as I backed up. We waved at each other as I drove off toward the main part of town. I drove down the street known as Restaurant Row. I planned to buy Ely something to eat but the restaurants were all closed.

I drove across town toward the Timor Lodge. I tried to have a normal conversation with Ely but I discovered that I couldn't speak Tetum. I had never had conversations with Timorese women about things that men and women would talk about. I could carry on lengthy conversations about training, operations, intelligence activities, etc. but when it came to a simple conversation with a woman, I found myself without the vocabulary.

I pulled into the Timor Lodge and parked near my room. Ely became very nervous as I shut the engine off. She asked, "Where are we going?"

The outside Area lights of the Timor Lodge were not sufficient to light up the entire area. There were deep shadows where I normally park. I calmly looked into Ely's shadowed face as I told her, "You don't have to do anything you don't want to do. If you want, I will take you home right now."

Ely sat silently for a few moments. I knew that she was interested in me. There was a price to pay for a Timorese woman to get to know a *malai* (foreigner). It looked like she had been on the hard end of this process before.

After about two minutes, Ely opened her door and stepped out of the truck. I got out of the truck and led Ely to my room. I opened the door and turned on the light. Ely again hesitated before stepping into my room.

By now I had upgraded my room at the Timor Lodge. The bedroom area was the same as before, including the one twin size bed. My new upgraded room also had a shower, toilet, and sink in a small-side room. There was a doorway but no door to separate the bedroom from the bathroom.

Ely sat on the only chair while I sat on the bed. I could see that Ely was becoming very nervous again. I offered her a Coke or a beer, which I had a few cans of both shoved under my bed. Ely took a can of beer that I had opened before handing it to her. She started drinking the beer in short bursts of gulping as I could almost see her blood pressure rise. I would like to have thought that her extreme anxiety was from overwhelming desire for my body but that wasn't the case.

Actually, I felt sorry for Ely as I watched the fear grow inside of her. I could only imagine the bad experience or experiences that had caused her to be so afraid. But then again, I had to wonder why she would come to my room with me if she was so afraid.

I reached out and lightly rubbed her forearm as I said softly, "I will not hurt you. We can sit and talk, go to sleep, I'll take you home, or whatever you want to do."

I could see Ely's blood pressure dropping as I talked. I then added with a big smile, "Or we can have wild sex." Ely actually giggled a little. That was the biggest display of emotion that I had seen in her yet.

We sat and talked for a long time. Conversing with her was a struggle. Many times she would say something I didn't understand. Ely would look at me as she realized I didn't understand. She would patiently say, "For example," and then explain what she had said using other words that she hoped I might understand.

Eventually she told me that she was scared to go home during the late night hours. She lived with her younger sister and aunt in an area of Dili called Bebonok. Ely was scared of the Ninjas who prowled the dark neighborhoods throughout the night. She wouldn't go home until daylight.

We ended up sitting on my little bed together. I held her and kissed her repeatedly. Eventually we were lying on the bed wrapped in each other's arms exchanging soft kisses. I did my man thing of trying to get her clothes off while she did her lady thing of trying to keep her clothes on. I could have badgered her to get what I wanted, but that would have changed our growing relationship. I didn't push the issue.

We eventually fell asleep in each other's arms. By daybreak, she was awake and waking me up, which wasn't easy. We had only slept two or three hours at the most. I wasn't even sober enough to have a hangover yet.

As we left my room, Ely was very nervous about any Timorese seeing her with me. I asked her where she wanted to go. She told me that she wanted to go near the bus stop. She had to go to Liquisa today. Liquisa is a town that is about a forty-minute drive west from Dili along the north coast road. I told Ely that I would drive her to Liquisa if she wanted me too. She was surprised that I would do that. She agreed to my offer.

I was being polite to her but my motives to drive her were a little more sinister. To satisfy my personal interest in this woman, I wanted to know if she was telling me the truth about going to Liquisa, and if so, I wanted to know where she was going. I still hadn't forgotten the Cinco-Cinco Clandestino mark on Ely's left shoulder. This woman could possibly be of value to the DDIU growing intelligence network.

When I worked in a narcotics unit back in America, it was unthinkable to mix passion with work through an informant. But this wasn't America. I hadn't been playing by any rules up to this point in my mission anyway, so why start now? I had every intention in the world to abuse this poor lady professionally, and maybe physically, too, if things worked out.

However, there was a reason for not mixing pleasure with work in narcotics units back home, other than when it was time to go to court. That volatile mix became a very unstable emotional explosive that must be handled carefully to avoid dangerous results.

I drove Ely to a house in Liquisa and dropped her off. I asked her to meet me later that evening. She agreed to meet me at six o'clock at the Purple Cow restaurant. I handed her ten dollars, telling her it was for her bus fare back to Dili and for a taxi to take her to the Purple Cow. She thanked me then walked toward the house as I drove off.

That night I arrived at the Purple Cow Restaurant a little before six o'clock. I drank a beer while I sat near the sea and waited to see if Ely would show up. I wouldn't have been surprised either way. About six-thirty a taxi stopped in front of the Purple Cow. I watched Ely step out of the Taxi, then walk toward me. We sat at a table that was close to the sea and talked while she drank a Fanta and I drank beer.

Later we ordered dinner and ate together. About ten-o'clock, I asked Ely if she wanted to go back to my room with me. Ely thought for a minute then asked, "The same as last night?"

I told her, "The same, I won't do anything you don't want." She agreed to go. I paid the bill and we left. Before going to the Timor Lodge, I drove around Dili as we listened to music.

That night we started out talking as we sat in my room but quickly escalated to hugging and kissing. I naturally wanted this beautiful woman; however, I found myself deeply attracted to Ely's personality. I hadn't realized just how lonely I had become until now. I could feel my spirit meshing tightly with Ely's spirit. Our passion grew naturally. There was no wild, lustful groping or tearing off of clothes, just passion that slowly grew in intensity.

Ely said to me almost pleading, "I want to be loved. I want a man who cares about me. If we make love it should be the same as husband and wife." My tough-guy, unfeeling front that I tried to fool other people with had only fooled me. That all melted away now. What Ely had said to me should have scared me to death and sent me running away from her, but it drew me closer.

I made love to Ely, the kind of love that left us both hungry to remain in each other's arms after the pleasure. We slept entangled for a few hours. I woke up with Ely's hair in my mouth. My arm under her sleek body was so numb I couldn't move it. I struggled to slide my arm out from underneath her. Ely woke up while I was laboring to save my arm. She laughed at me as I rubbed my now-salvaged arm to get the blood flowing again.

I lay down next to Ely again and wrapped my arms around her as she snuggled tightly against my body within my grasp. Soon we were making love again, at first slowly and passionately but gradually increasing in intensity as we kissed an unending kiss. The first of the new day's gray light began to penetrate our room from around the closed window curtain as we reached our climatic pleasure together, still closely intertwined and our lips gently pressed together in that unending kiss that had begun nearly an hour earlier.

We knew we should get up and get ready to go, but neither of us moved. I don't know about Ely, but I couldn't find the strength to move. I didn't want to move either. I rationalized, "This is Sunday morning. I work day and night most of the time anyway, so if I'm not into work at 0800 hours this morning, its okay." We fell asleep again, still embracing.

Actually, we had to embrace. There wasn't enough room on that twin-size bed to sleep separate. An hour later, we were awake and making love one last time before we got ready to go. After another hour of loving passion, we showered and left. Ely was so paranoid about someone seeing her with me. She directed me to a secluded area in the Manleuana area of Dili. I stopped the car and let her out only after she was sure nobody was around. We made arrangements to meet at the restaurant in the evening.

As I drove away I thought deeply about what I was doing. I was already too emotionally attached to Ely. I knew the attachment would grow as time went on. I wasn't necessarily opposed to falling in love with the right woman, but this wasn't the right woman. She was twenty-five; I was fifty. She was Timorese; I was American. She could be hanging out with me because she truly was looking for love, but she could be a hustler looking for dumb, lonely, and horny foreigners to get access to their money, but I didn't think so. She was too Timorese. Time would tell.

The DDIU continued to grow in intensity too. We focused our straight-up cop operations to support the DDIU secret operations. Operation "Hot Stuff" was a straight up continuing operation to identify the black market smuggling from West Timor into East Timor. Our secret investigation into the possible foreign Terrorist Cells was going well and it didn't look good for the security of the many embassies and United Nations installations in East Timor.

We looked into the resources available in East Timor that could be used to build large destructive bombs. There didn't appear to be the possibility to build a bomb from existing resources. Should an attack be planned the terrorists would have to smuggle the needed ingredients and equipment into East Timor. Our investigation into the suspected Arab cell revealed to us that three of the five men who owned and managed the Taj Mahal restaurant had married East Timorese women. The three suspects used their marriages to attempt to acquire East Timorese ID cards and East Timorese passports.

One of these three men had married the daughter of the highest-ranking commander of the notorious Los Palos Militia group known as "Tim Alfa" ("Tim" is pronounced "team"). We also established that there was a continual flow of communication between the Tim Alfa commander in Indonesia and his daughter in Dili, East Timor. This gave the suspected terrorist cell the very real possibility of access to the Militia controlled smuggling operation into East Timor. This was why we focused so hard on Operation "Hot Stuff."

The United Nations commanders wondered why we were so interested in the black market smuggling. The smuggling was against the law; however, those laws were not in place within the developing East Timor system yet. Therefore smugglers could not be criminally charged. Any smugglers caught would simply be returned to West Timor.

By mid-September our informant networks and our active separate entity contacts were producing an enormous amount of information. Most of that information was low-grade but we continued to tighten our networks onto their targets like a python tightening around its victim. A lot of our information had to be reported through the normal chain of UN information flow. We had to refer to an information source so we established a code system for our sources.

I gave our information networks color codes. For example, Team Green was the code-name for any of our informants reporting information about the CPD-RDTL. Specific informants were given a number so we referred to an informant as G-1 or G-3 or whatever the informants number was. We had to protect these informants as best as we could. This code system could easily be figured out by an analyst so we included a code rotation system.

Team Green was our penetration into CPD-RDTL, Team Blue was our penetration into the Militia and Koppassus in West Timor. Team Red was into the ex-Falintil groups, Team Yellow was into the Colimau 2000 and Team White was into the newly elected and established East Timor government. We rotated the color designator for a team regularly so that anyone not knowing my system would be mis-directed should they somehow get access to my reports. To get clues about who our informants were you had to know how the rotation system worked in correlation with the date of the report.

The reports had to be written in a manor that appeared there was no rotation system. Every report I wrote was a time consuming ordeal to give our commanders the information they needed but still protected our Informants and the code.

Information from our separate intelligence entities was also given codes. La Faik's Segrada Familia was team Luckys Star, The FDTL intelligence was team Friendly Fire. Short term operations into Indonesia were referred to as team Cold Turkey no matter what designated team was conducting the over the fence operation.

In mid-September I added a new team to our list of operators. As Ely's and my love affair grew I also worked the angle of using her for information collection purposes. It turned out that Ely was an intelligence gold mine. Her entire family was devoted supporters of the current government. Most of them were either ex-Falintil soldiers or ex-Clandestino operators. Ely's father was a Falintil Battalion commander during the first years of the war. Ely had also been a secret operator for the Cinco-Cinco Clandestino organization. In 1999 she had the opportunity to perform a special service to her country.

In April of 1999, Ely was living with her Aunt in Liquisa while she went to the Liquisa High School. Like the rest of her family, Ely's Aunt had strong Falintil convictions. She was married to a man who by day was a respected leader of the Indonesian community and by night was a Falintil commander. When a Falintil unit was operating near Liquisa Ely and her Aunt would assist the unit by cooking them food.

The SGI collected information that made them suspect the two women. The Besi Merah Putih Militia began a covert surveillance of the two women. Soon they confirmed the women's involvement supporting the Falintil guerillas. The Besi Merah Putih arrested the two women at the first opportunity and took them to the Militia headquarters in Liquisa.

The interrogation began with the normal question and answer sessions. The interrogation was about to escalate to torture and rape when a Koppassus soldier arrived. The soldier had heard about Ely's capture and came to the Militia headquarters to take Ely away from the Besi Merah Putih. The Militia was quick to comply with this renowned Koppassus soldier who was assigned to oversee Militia activities in the neighboring Ermera district.

As the Koppassus soldier took Ely out of the headquarters, the Besi Merah Putih began their physical abuse of Ely's Aunt. Ely had been saved, but her Aunt would endure days of torture and rape. Ely could hear the screams of her Aunt as she got onto the back of a motorcycle behind the man who rescued her.

The Koppassus soldier took Ely as his own. He was Timorese so he made the proper arrangements through Ely's family and married her in the Timorese tradition. He moved Ely into a TNI military provided home at the TNI compound in the city of Gleno, Ermera District. Ely and this man developed a true love relationship over the next few months; however, Ely never lost sight of her family and the war against Indonesia. She now had access to a lot of intelligence. She provided that information along with ammunition that she slipped out of her husband's large cache, for her Cinco-Cinco organization.

In September, 1999, Ely's husband took Ely and fled to West Timor. Ely came back to East Timor to live after her husband abandoned her in Atambua. He had moved into a home with an Indonesian woman that he had met. The now-pregnant Ely was left alone in a strange country. She came back to her family in East Timor at her first opportunity.

* * * *

One night Ely and I were catching our breath after a long session of love. I told her that she had beautiful brown skin. She then thought she would attempt speaking a little English as she smiled widely and announced, "I am chocolate."

I smiled back at her as I said, "Yes, you are chocolate." Her statement about her color stuck in my head. Thus became the code-name I gave Ely and the network I was already building around her.

By September I had not been on a CTO in six months. I was getting pressure to take a CTO but I didn't want to go to some other country and spend several days alone. I didn't want to be alone any more. I decided to take Ely with me. I helped her get her passport and made plans for us to go to Bali Indonesia for ten days. Ely had never been anywhere other than Timor before.

We spent ten beautiful days in Bali. Because Ely could speak Indonesian, we met people who lived in Bali who were from both Bali and Jawa Indonesia. These people showed us around the Island giving us the experience of the true Bali, not what most tourists who come to Bali experience. Although we did spend some time at the tourist markets, ate at tourist type restaurants and so on.

Our last night in Bali we went to the disco at a place called the Padi Club. This was a two-story building that had a dance floor and bar on both floors. Ely and I danced the night away in this very crowded disco. Most of the people were tourists from several countries. Australia is close to Bali so a large percentage of the customers were Australians.

There were also several local Balinese that were there enjoying the music, drink and dancing. I was impressed with one attractive Balinese woman who was dancing while she balanced her glass of beer on her head. She brought the glass down from her head from time to time, took a drink, then put the glass back on her head never missing a beat. I guess using her head for a counter was better than holding the drink while dancing.

It was easy to pick out the Indonesians who were regulars here at the Padi Club. They were not the whores and roughnecks I would have expected them to be. They were just local citizens who enjoyed a night out at a nice place.

The next morning, Ely and I flew back to East Timor. We had to be careful who we told about our wonderful experiences in Bali. Ely's family could not know that she was heavily involved with a *malai*. The UN could not find out that I was heavily involved with an East Timorese woman. It was so ironic. Many of the United Nations staff, including some of the top leaders, were violating their local staff and interpreters through lies and false promises. I could brag about having wild sex with some poor East Timorese woman who I conned into "putting out" and nobody would think a thing of it. But to have a meaningful relationship with a Timorese woman would bring me big trouble. It didn't make any sense to me, but this was what would prevent me from ever being able to have a life-long relationship with Ely, and I knew it.

We did have a handful of friends that we could show our pictures and tell about our Bali vacation. I sent my attorney and friend an email telling him about Bali and suggested that he spend some of the money I was paying him and go to Bali. A few days later, my attorney sent me a message back saying, "Thanks for the bad advice. I'll go to the Bahamas instead." This response was because of the news of a terrorist bomb attack that happened four days after Ely and I left Bali.

Everyone working in East Timor was stunned by the news of the terrorist bomb that was detonated at Kuta Beach in Bali Indonesia. Most of the international workers in East Timor, if not all International workers, had spent CTO time off in Kuta Beach. A Jawa-based terrorist group known as JI (Jemaah Islamiah) had mastermind the attack. The JI cell that conducted the attack was led by a man from Jawa known as Ambrose.

The terrorists had done their homework. They prepared a large bomb inside the closed paneled vehicle they used for the bomb delivery system. They drove the "bomb on wheels" down the crowded narrow street that ran in between the two most popular discos that was frequented by the many tourists in Bali, especially Australian tourists.

The Sari Club was on one side of the street and the Padi Club was across the street from the Sari Club. Ambrose's cell operator stopped the bomb-laden vehicle in the middle of the street exactly in between the two bars. The driver shut off the engine, got out of the vehicle, locked the doors, then walked away. The vehicle caused an immediate traffic jam. The street was always packed with cars at that time of night. The street was so narrow that there was no possibility to drive around the obstruction.

An Australian football team was at the Padi club that night enjoying the night in beautiful downtown Kuta Beach. Some of their members went out into the street to help the Indonesian citizens by pushing the vehicle that was obstructing traffic out of the roadway. That was the last anyone would ever see those men.

Ambrose detonated the bomb as the Australian men started to push the truck. You can't get any closer to "ground zero" than that. Hundreds of people died in an instant as the shock wave of the bomb destroyed everything in its path. Many survivors of the initial blast soon died from the terrible burns that covered their broken bodies. Some of the victims survived both the blast and their terrible burns.

The shock wave of the news of this bomb now tore through the international population in East Timor. There was many United Nations international staff that was on CTO in Bali at the time. Nobody knew who the victims were, not even the Indonesian investigators who would spend hours and days trying to identify the hundreds of victims. Communications with Bali at that time was near impossible. There was not one International staff member in East Timor that didn't have at least one friend that was in Bali on CTO that could have been a victim.

Another part of the aftermath shock wave in East Timor was the realization that East Timor could be a very real terrorist target as well. During the following weeks and months the many embassies and the United Nations prepared huge sandbag and concrete barriers to protect against vehicle bombs.

In addition to the many added security measures being installed to protect an installation there was the need for intelligence, hard intelligence that could prevent a terrorist cell from ever being able to carry out an attack in East Timor. The DDIU had three ongoing operations underway that just got pushed up to the top of the priority scale.

CHAPTER EIGHTEEN

Under Attack

The DDIU was a busy unit. When I took command of the DDIU in April of 2002, The DDIU struggled daily just to find things to occupy their time through the normal working hours of the day. Seven months later we had more work to do then there was hours in a day. We had to prioritize what projects we could actively pursue. Many of the projects flipped flopped back and forth from the front burner to the back burner as circumstances changed our priorities.

I was thrilled when a special team of investigators arrived at my office one day asking for any information we had about any suspected terrorist cells that may exist in East Timor. These men were professional Terrorist Investigators from Australia who had been requested by the UN to lend a hand. I handed them our Operation Peachtree files and our Operation Flower Land files. Operation Peachtree was a file five-inches thick on the suspected Arab group who run the Taj Mahal restaurant. Operation Flower Land was an assortment of suspected Terrorists that were linked to a faction at the Mosque in Dili.

This temporary special investigation team was very interested in both files. They asked for our assistance. I offered to turn the investigation over to them if they would like. They took me up on my offer without hesitation. This was a good thing for the DDIU. We had pretty much exhausted all that we could do covertly against these targets. I knew that this Australian special investigation team would take our information and do an "up the gut" run with it. That was exactly what was needed on both operations. The DDIU was organized for covert stuff. The aggressive "go and talk" to the suspects was not our cup of tea.

While the special Investigators did their thing on these two operations we were free to work on other important matters at hand. Our "Cold Turkey" operations into West Timor were reporting renewed training of the Militia at the TNI Jungle Training facility near Atambua. This was not a good thing. If the Militia were again going through training programs that meant there was going to be some Militia infiltrations of East Timor again. This was an important development that needed to be pursued aggressively.

Our Cold Turkey operations (operations into Indonesia) to this point had been nothing more than occasional "fishing trips" that required little effort or risk. That was about to change. For operation purposes and our security we assigned a code-name to our DDIU team. The team code-name was Makikit (Eagle). All of our staff involved with secret operations picked a code-name. After our team was named and the secret Makikit operators were named my teammates looked at me saying, "You got to have a code-name too."

I told them, "I have a code-name. La Faik gave it to me back in 2000."

We had conducted this meeting in the DDIU office. We sat comfortably scattered around the large folding wood table. The Makikit team consisted of Jose, Arnaldo, Cesaltino, and me. Mick was ending his mission in East Timor and going through the check-out procedures so he was no longer coming into the office. Our other two DDIU East Timorese members who were not involved with the Makikit activities were running an errand that I had given them.

Arnaldo, Jose and Cesaltino watched me anxiously waiting to hear what my code-name was. I teased them by changing the subject to another project that we needed to work on. Arnaldo could no longer take the suspense. He asked pleadingly, "Come on, Commandante, what is your code-name?"

I looked into the anxious waiting faces of my teammates one by one then smiled, "My code-name is Karau Timor Mutin." (White Buffalo.) The boys smiled and nodded their approval of the name.

We then got down to the business of espionage. I made it very clear to the Makikit team that what we were about to do was espionage. The act of espionage is not a big thing unless you get caught. We could get caught by the UN, ETPS or East Timor government authorities which could cause whoever got caught some serious personal repercussions; however, the real danger was to become exposed to Indonesian Authorities. That would be a very dangerous situation for the members caught and possibly the whole Makikit team.

Now that I had the attention of the Makikit team, I laid out the game plan. We would coordinate our activities with team Friendly Fire (The FDTL intelligence) and team Lucky Star (La Faik and his Segrada Familia). What we were about to do was very dangerous but also very necessary for the survival of East Timor.

Over the next few weeks our coordinated operations identified the training location in West Timor, which had moved from the location used in the year 2000. We established that there were Koppassus units in Atambua, actually staying at the home of Joao Travaris who was the infamous top leader of all the East Timorese Militia in West Timor. The Indonesian military had claimed that there were no Koppassus in West Timor. We now knew that, in fact, there was.

We also established that Tome Diago was in Atambua. Tome was the SGI creator of the Militia units during the Indonesian occupation of East Timor. Our information was that Tome was organizing some plan of infiltration into East Timor. The information also included Tome's secret penetration of a spy cell currently in East Timor. Something was about to happen in East Timor, very soon.

I turned in reports about the growing threat in West Timor. I couldn't report everything I knew because that would alert people to the espionage activities I was now heavily involved with; however, I got enough information up the line to properly warn those who needed to know. The results of our information were all pretty negative. Nobody wanted to believe that Militia was getting ready to enter East Timor. It was like the year 2000 all over again. Nobody would believe until East Timor soil again was soaked in blood.

Some of the SID staff openly scoffed at my reports and made jokes about the DDIU. Military intelligence was riding the fence about the information, whether to believe or not believe. The analyst I was talking to one day focused on the one piece of information that was happening right now. I could tell that he would judge the future plans of the Militia, if any, by being able to prove one piece of our information.

The analyst was deep in thought and almost asking himself as he asked, "How do you know the Koppassus is at Joao Travares's house? How do you know they are training?"

I responded sympathetically to this man who was looking for some kind of proof that he could present with our information, "Known Koppassus soldiers and commanders have been seen at the house. The training has been limitedly monitored by informants."

The analyst continued his internal struggle as he pushed me for proof, "Can't we get photos of the Koppassus at the house? How about photos from the training site? Maybe the Informant can bring back some shell casings from the training site after the militia's alleged shooting practice?"

I couldn't help but smile at the analyst as I said, "Listen to yourself. You are trying to find evidence to give to your commander whom you know will not believe this information. If I bring you photos of soldiers at the Travares home or the training site the response will be that the photos could have been taken anywhere and the people in the photos will not be known to any of us. If I bring you a bag full of spent cartridges the response will be that the cartridges could have come from anywhere, also how do we know that the Militia was doing the shooting even if the cartridges did come from some secret training site."

The analyst nodded as he said, "You're right."

I liked this analyst. I could see that he was concerned about this information. I told the analyst as a friend, "You take this information and do with it what you think is best. As a friend I want you to remember all this information I am giving you. When the Militia from West Timor becomes highly visible here in East Timor I want you to remember that I told you so, there coming and their coming soon."

I was frustrated and very tired by this time. I decided that it was time for another CTO. I made plans to take Ely with me to Darwin, Australia, and left the following week. We had another wonderful ten days together staying at the Mirambeena Hotel, eating at the many restaurants, swimming in the Mirambeena pools, and dancing at the discos. Ely saw a "his and hers" gold wedding band set in one of the downtown stores. We had talked about a possible future marriage.

I was actually very receptive of the idea, but I doubted that it would ever happen. I knew that a day would come when I would have to leave East Timor. The possibility of successfully going through the immigration process under our circumstances was slim to none. But by the end of our ten days in Darwin, I was deeply in love with Ely. I bought the rings.

We got back to Dili in late November. The Makikit team was waiting for us at the airport when we arrived. They had come to welcome us home but they also wanted me to know the developments while I was gone. The Cold Turkey operations were providing good information and a lot of it. A Militia infiltration was eminent.

The Militia would enter East Timor some time in December. In addition to the Militia the CPD-RDTL was getting more aggressive. They planned to hold a demonstration in front of the government building the first of December. What a coincidence that was. The Militia is going to start operations in East Timor the same month that the CPD-RDTL is starting to flex some muscle.

The days off in Darwin were fantastic but I almost regretted taking the time off. Things were escalating rapidly in East Timor. I should have been there to help take care of our covert business. But then again I guess it really didn't matter what information we collected. Nobody would believe the information anyway much less take action on it. This complacent unbelieving attitude of the rest of the International intelligence community in East Timor was about to see the truth and get there eyes opened in a violent way.

On 3 December, 2002, the Dili investigation unit received an arrest warrant for a man who was a student at a high school near downtown Dili. The Dili investigation unit went to the high school and arrested the young man. This would be an acceptable action of the police in many countries around the world; however, in East Timor this showed complete disrespect to the school, the teachers of the school and the students. The arrest of this student sparked an immediate riot of the schools student body.

Special police units (SPU) was sent to bring the rioters under control. By the time the mini riot was over two ETPS motorcycles were burning in the street, many police cars had broken windows and dents and several police officers had minor injuries from thrown rocks. Everybody thought it was over.

The Makikit team wasn't so sure so a couple of our guys went into the bowels of the student community to see what may be brewing. They came back an hour later with the news that there were many university students who were angry about what the police had done at the high school. There was a plan to conduct an organized and violent demonstration against the Untied Nations and ETPS police the following morning at 0900 hours. The student assault would be against the National Headquartes, which is across the street from the rear of the University.

I immediately turned in a report to the Dili district commander and sent a copy to the SID office so that they could inform the police Commissioner. By this time the Dili district commander who had brought me into Dili had rotated home. The new Dili district commander was a Portuguese man named Antonio Da Silva. Antonio was a good commander that I had already developed a lot of respect for.

On the evening of 3 December, the Makikit team prepared for the battle we knew was coming in the morning. We established an informant who could be close to the coordinating student leaders of the planned assault of the National Headquarters. We would communicate with the Informant by use of mobile phones.

By 0800 hours the following morning our informant was in place on the university grounds. There were already many students gathered for the assault. Our Makikit team was in position for the believed coming battle at 0900 hours too. We were monitoring the rear of the university, the front of the University and we had one member monitoring the still ongoing peaceful demonstration by the CPD-RDTL at the front of the government building, which is across the street from the front of the University.

So far the CPD-RDTL had not become a problem but we were suspicious of this group of two-hundred ex-Falintil fighters. Actually who we were suspicious of was the commander of this group of CPD-RDTL demonstrators. Gil Fernandes was a radical CPD-RDTL commander that was always involved in the "seedy" side of CPD-RDTL activities. Any time CPD-RDTL got caught involved with activities that were against the law Gil Fernandes or Americo Menesis, another CPD-RDTL commander, was the scapegoats.

Both Gil Fernandes and Americo Menesis were arrested in early 2001 and did time in prison for smuggling hand grenades into the University Gymnasium where Xanana Gusmao was going to give a speech. In addition to this Gil Fernandes was a student at the University where this assault on National Headquarters was about to be launched from. Gil was a student activist and probably had a hand in the planning of the assault on National Headquarters. If Gil wasn't directly involved with the students we knew that he at least knew about the plans to assault the National Headquarters.

The street in front of National Headquarters was empty by 0830 hours on the morning of 4 December, 2002. This is normally a busy street but there was no heavy traffic flow on this morning. It was like someone had put a sign up on both ends of the street before entering the block where the National Headquarters was located that said, "War Zone, enter at your own risk."

I was driving around the three block area that encompassed the front of the government building (GPA), the university that was behind the GPA and the National Headquarters that was across the street from the rear of the university. At 0855 my informant that we had planted inside the University called me saying that about one-hundred-fifty students would attack the National Headquarters soon. They planned to storm the front gate. They had gathered many rocks that they would throw at the police.

I drove up to the front gate of the GPA to make sure the ETPS were ready. I could only see about one squad of SPU in the background and a half-dozen regular ETPS police at the front gate. There was no UN police. I told the ETPS at the front gate that the students were getting ready to come.

I then drove down the street to take up a position where I could watch the other end of the rear of the university campus. I figured that if the students were serious about actually taking control of the National Headquarters they would launch a second attack against the opposite end of the headquarters long front face. If they did that they would have to move through this area at the rear of the university.

I no sooner got into position than the assault began against the main gate located at the front left end of the headquarter building. There was no movement where I was. The street near the front gate filled with people instantly. This was an organized coordinated assault by the students as they formed in layers and in depth. First came the verbal assault followed by a barrage of rocks. There was not enough police defending the front gate to do anything more than form a skirmish line to prevent the students from entering the headquarters.

The ETPS skirmish line became sitting targets for the rock assault. Without the numbers to counter assault the rock throwing mob the students stood at a distance and continually threw their projectiles. Soon through a little fear and lot of frustration the police opened fire on the students. The first volley of shots fired was in the air to disperse the students. The students didn't flinch as the rocks continued to batter the ETPS. The next volley of shots fired by the ETPS was into the mob of students.

The students soon disengaged fleeing into the rear of the university campus. Two of their numbers had been shot. A few minutes later I was called by our Informant on the inside. He told me that one student was dead and another student he felt would soon be dead from the bullets the police and fired. The students became even angrier. They carried the dead body out the front side of the university and then around to the front of the GPA where the two-hundred-plus CPD-RDTL were passively demonstrating.

Upon seeing the dead student and hearing the angry student's account of what had happened, the ex-Falintils joined the students cause. Gil Fernandes took over command and control of the now combined groups. As Gil organized for the next assault against National Headquarters the beleaguered ETPS police was reinforced with other ETPS and a platoon of SPU. United Nations police were also being gathered to defend the National Headquarters.

With Gil Fernandes in command of the combined groups the nature of the assault changed. First there was a probing frontal assault to see what strength the police now had in place. The probe assault was pushed until the police again started to fire warning shots. The attackers retreated back into the university campus. Our informant on the inside called me frantically warning that we must leave the headquarters. Gil was preparing a strong attack against the police. The informant did not believe that the police had the strength to stop the assault.

I finally got the informant over his panic and got from him the tactics that Gil was planning. They planned to lore the SPU away from the main gate with a contingency of members who would attack the police at the front gate from the street, left of the front gate. The attackers in this group would be few in numbers and mount their attack weakly and unorganized. When the SPU formed a skirmish line and moved toward this group of attackers the assaulting group would slowly move away from the approaching police skirmish line to draw the SPU further away from the front gate. When the SPU were far enough away from the gate the combined groups of students and ex-Falintil would assault the front gate and the rear of the SPU skirmish line in strength.

I passed this information on to the Dili district commander who was the commander in charge of the police units defending the headquarters. I had to make contact with the Dili district commander, Antonio, by mobile phone. The assault began as I was giving Antonio the assault plan. Before Antonio could understand the assault plans and coordinate his many units it was too late. The SPU began their crowd control tactics going after the rioters down the street to the left of headquarters.

I watched helplessly as the SPU marched into Gil's ambush. Within two minutes the main assault began. This proved to be a vicious assault against the now split power of the police. The SPU was trapped in the street. Within a few minutes the remaining police who held control of the front gate collapsed in disarray. The many gunshots the ETPS fired in the air and into the crowd had failed to stop this assault. The headquarters was open to the attacking combined groups but the groups didn't enter the headquarter compound. After the SPU fought their way back to the headquarter grounds the combined groups broke off from their attack and went back into the university compound.

By now I was getting frustrated with trying to give information to Antonio. Antonio had his hands full just trying to coordinate his resources. I moved to the upstairs of the headquarters main building where the chief of operations was based. As I made contact with the chief of operations our informant called me. He told me that Gil had a plan to draw the police out into the open where they would be attacked. The informant said, "The police must not leave the headquarters." By now it was obvious that the focus of Gil was not to take control of the National Headquarters. He wanted to attack the police officers, the ETPS police officers.

A moment later the Informant said, "They're attacking Hello Mister. I think they are going to set the building on fire."

Hello Mister was a Western-style small grocery store that was one block to the left of the front of the university. I told the chief of operations that Hello Mister was under attack. His response was to send the SPU to the Hello Mister store. Before he could give the order I advised him not to do it, it was an ambush.

The chief of operations looked at the phone I held in my hand and asked, "Who is that?"

I answered, "It's an informant who is standing near Gil Fernandes who is the commander of the ex-Falintil who is orchestrating all of this."

The chief of operations looked at me surprised, "The ex-Falintil?"

By now we could see huge clouds of black smoke that was billowing above the Hello Mister store one block away from us. I slowly said, "Don't send the SPU."

Shortly after Hello Mister was burning, a platoon of UN Brazilian military police arrived in full riot gear. A platoon of Portuguese military arrived behind them to back them up. Gil made a couple of attempts to divide the United Nations growing forces by moving small harassing elements to the Dili Stadium one block south of the headquarters. Gil reasoned that the police and now military would attempt to save the Stadium from being burned. We didn't fall into their trap. For whatever reason, the ex-Falintil did not set fire to the Stadium, probably because there was very little of the large concrete building that would burn.

President Xanana Gusmao arrived and spoke to the crowd of rioters. Blood dripped from the side of the president's head where he had been struck by a rock while his motorcade entered the embattled area. When Xanana finished speaking the rioters calmly turned and left the area. It looked like it was over as we watched the hundreds of people disperse. It was a false perception.

Sticking to old Falintil doctrine Gil was not going to continue operations against a strong force. He would evade the enemy's strength and attack our weakness, which he did with a vengeance. Gil reorganized his force of ex-Falintil and students and launched an attack down the Comoro road toward the airport on the west edge of Dili. They burned Indonesian owned businesses and assaulted any UN vehicles and personnel that they came across.

Gil's assault force went into Bebonok and burned the home of Mari Alcatiri, East Timor's Prime Minister, and the home of Alcatiri's brother who also lived in Bebonok. This delayed the assault on the airport, which was Gil's primary target. This delay gave the UN forces the time needed to secure the airport. Gil's forces made a push toward the airport but broke off the assault when they encountered heavy resistance.

Gil then reorganized his forces for an assault on the Becora prison, which was on the opposite side of town. Our Informant heard the plans being made for the assault on the prison. I passed this information to the chief of operations. A platoon of Portuguese soldiers soon arrived at the Becora prison to aid in the defense. This was enough to deter Gil's planned assault.

On the morning of 5 December 2002, the ex-Falintil and the students gave Dili back to us as they dispersed their organized groups. The aftermath of the 4th of December would continue for months as investigators worked to build criminal cases against the many crimes that were committed during the day long battle. Investigations was also being conducted reference the many shootings by ETPS police.

The police commissioner's staff at National Headquarter was conducting an investigation into the shortcomings of intelligence collection that maybe could have prevented the disaster of 4 December. This brought both the DDIU and the National Headquarters SID under the microscope. I didn't have time to worry about this investigation. I knew we didn't to anything wrong anyway.

The Militia threat from West Timor was a serious matter. We focused all of our efforts to find out what was coming at us so that we could get the information up through the chain of the information flow. On 20 December we got information from a Cold Turkey operation that the Militia was now in East Timor. Five small Militia units had crossed the border into East Timor on 18 December 2002. The Cold Turkey team knew that two areas of planned Militia operations were Loes, Liquisa District and Atsabe, Ermera District.

As usual our information about this Militia incursion was discreetly scoffed at by the rest of the intelligence community. That changed a little when a Militia member of the Militia unit assigned to the Loes area was captured by a group of ex-Falintil who lived in a village in Loes. It was still questionable whether there were actually armed Militia units actively operating in East Timor, after all there was only "one" Militia man caught. Nobody will believe anything they can't see for themselves, except for one man this time.

Dennis McDermet was the deputy police commissioner and at this time he was the acting commissioner while the actual police Commissioner was off the Island on CTO. commander McDermet was an Austalian Federal police force commander. I was summoned to attend a meeting at commander McDermet's office on Christmas Day, 2002. I didn't know what the meeting was about. We had so many operations going on right then it could have been about many different things.

Commander McDermet held the meeting in his office. There was only he, the director of the SID, and me. Commander McDermet was not the type of man to beat around the bush. He got right to the point as he asked me what, if any, information the DDIU had on Militia activities in East Timor. The SID director opened his briefcase and rummaged through files as he told commander McDermet some information. He never mentioned the information that I had reported on for the past six weeks.

When the SID director finished commander McDermet asked me, "Did you know about this?" I raised an eyebrow in surprise as I looked across the table at the SID director. I was waiting for him to tell about the rest of the information, my information. The SID director sat calmly looking at me with a little smirk on his face. I figured I was getting set up for something.

I told Commander McDermet, "Yes of course I knew about this but there is a lot more."

Commander McDermet looked at me sternly, "I want to know everything you know about these Militias. I will not ask you how you got the information."

I told the commander everything, starting from the first report we got about the Militia training. When I finished, Commander McDermet looked at the SID director and asked, "Did you know about all this?"

The director shook his head, "No."

McDermet then asked me, "Did you report your information?"

Before I could answer the director admitted to receiving reports about the Militia from me; however, there was nothing in the reports that could be verified. The director continued, "There is nothing now to verify his information."

Commander McDermet turned his attention back to me, "What is your evaluation of your information?"

I hesitated before answering. I was feeling a little uncomfortable talking about this situation. I suspected that I was about to step into a giant bear trap that this director of the SID had hidden. I finally answered, "I'm not an analyst, sir. I know how to get the information, but the value of that information and predicting the future from that information is above my qualifications."

Commander McDermet looked at me with that same calm but stern look, "I would like to know what you think about this."

I took a breath and figured I might just as well walk into the bear trap like a man, so I held nothing back, "The Militia are here. I don't know what their intentions are, but I find it interesting that they supposedly went to the two areas of East Timor that are controlled by the remnants of the Colimau 2000. We have a lot of information that the Colimau 2000 members are largely either low level Militia members who have returned to East Timor to live or they are relatives of Militia who are still in West Timor. A second name the Colimau 2000 goes by is the 'Sons of the Militia.' During our operations against the Colimau 2000 last July we established beyond any doubt that one entire group of Colimau 2000 from the Bili Mau area are one hundred percent Guntar Militia members."

Commander McDermet asked the SID Director, "Did you know about this?"

The director shook his head, "No."

I had one more issue of concern that I thought the commander should know so I just came out with it, "One more thing, sir, the CPD-RDTL headquarter complex in Osanako has had a recent increase of activity over the past few weeks. There could be a connection between that complex and the Militia now operating in East Timor."

The SID director rolled his eyes as commander McDermet asked, "What headquarter complex?"

I happened to have the file on the complex with me. I produced the file and showed the commander the aerial photos of the large building as I told him everything I knew about the complex. Commander McDermet asked the director, "Did you know about this?"

The director answered, "Yes but there is nothing to indica—"

The commander interrupted the director, "Why didn't you inform me of this complex? Don't you think that a place like this in a remote area could become a big concern?"

The director did not respond.

After a few moments of silence, the commander dismissed the SID director. I thought as the Director walked out the door, *Yeah, see ya.*

Commander McDermet then told me that he had independent information that was similar to most of my information but not as detailed. We discussed the need to collect as much information as possible about the development of these issues. He was pleased to learn that the DDIU was already doing just that.

Commander McDermet was very concerned about the Osanako complex. He said, "We must find a way to get information about what is going on there."

I told him, "I am sending a team into that area in a few days. The launch date is 28 December." The commander smiled at me as he realized that the DDIU was on top of the Osanako situation too.

Team Chocolate left Dili in route to Osanako on the evening of 28 December. My girlfriend Ely and one other Team Chocolate operator were conducting this covert operation to find out what was going on in Osanako. I had used Ely on other information collection excursions but nothing as potentially dangerous as this one. I didn't want to use her but she was the only one that had the connections to infiltrate the area.

Team Chocolate returned to Dili late at night on 30 December. Team Chocolate's information was a little unsettling. There were two to three-hundred men dressed in TNI military uniforms and conducting military training at all times. The "soldiers" would rotate through the training program from other areas of East Timor every few weeks. There was a hidden underground facility located underneath the large building. There are assault rifles and grenades stored in this underground facility.

A second smaller building has been built. There is one large generator inside the smaller building that supplies electricity to the complex and also to the village of Osanako. A second generator will be added to the first generator soon. Team Chocolate even had the make and model number of the generator. A third large building was under construction at the time of Team Chocolate's operation.

There were many members of this Osanako group that were moving their families to Osanako. The entire area around Osanako is aggressively patrolled by uniformed units of Osanako members. There were also static security positions where people had to identify themselves to access Osanako.

The information from team Chocolate raised some eyebrows to say the least. Finally it was realized that the activities at Osanako just might be a matter of concern to the United Nations and the future of East Timor. The UN military sent a patrol into Osanako to verify team Chocolate's information. They confirmed everything except for the hidden underground facility. Nobody would believe that existed until July of 2003 when the Osanako group invited Xanana Gusmao to the facility and gave him a guided tour. Part of the president's tour was into a large underground facility that was under the first large building.

On 5 January, 2003, Militia units from West Timor attacked a small village near Atsabe, Ermera District. There were many shots fired that left four East Timorese dead in the wake of this Militia attack. A village leader was kidnapped from the village. His dead body was found near a river the following day.

A few days after the attack in Atsabe the ex-Falintil villagers near Loes, Liquisa District captured a nine-man Militia team that was operating in the area of their village. The investigative interviews of the captured Militia revealed that there were five Militia teams operating in East Timor. Two more teams would be launched at the end of January. A man named Tome Diago was the commander and strategist for these Militia incursions. The captured Militia also gave the investigators the names of each Militia member of the two combined Militia teams who attacked the Atsabe area village.

Now there was no doubt in anyone's mind about the value of the DDIU information. Virtually everything that we had been reporting for months was now verified. We suddenly got support that we had been begging for. Simple things like office equipment and transportation. We were suddenly on top of the world so to speak.

However, on top of the world for a covert intelligence unit is not a safe place to be. It is much safer to be unknown and unseen. The DDIU's raised status only meant that we had a long way down to fall. We basked in our hard earned glory but prepared for the assault against us that we knew would start soon.

CHAPTER NINETEEN

Hunting the Eagle

It was decided to give the newly trained East Timorese Defense Force (FDTL) the opportunity to gain some operational experience and at the same time encourage the people of East Timor by seeing their military securing East Timor. The FDTL went after the marauding Militia units in Ermera District. This was their land, their mountains and it was their people who were murdered on 5 January, 2003.

The FDTL showed what they could do. Many of the FDTL soldiers had not fought with the Falintil against the Indonesians but these young men were well trained and Commanded by ex-Falintil commanders who had fought the Indonesians. These FDTL soldiers had grown up in mountainous jungles just like the mountains in Atsabe.

The small Militia teams knew they were out matched. It was time to haul ass back to West Timor and get out of the way of the East Timorese war machine. The Militia had a place to escape but the Colimau 2000 did not. They had been safe in their mountain hideaways until now. The Timorese commanders and their troops were not handicapped with the need for proof of what they already knew. The FDTL did not differentiate between Militia who came from West Timor and the Colimau 2000 who lived in East Timor, they were all Militia.

Over the next few weeks the Colimau 2000 did everything they could to evade the FDTL but to no avail. A combination of FDTL intelligence and the professional aggressive tactics of the FDTL captured one group of Colimau 2000 members after another. The FDTL broke the back of the Colimau 2000, an injury that group would never recover from.

While the FDTL were methodically crushing the Colimau 2000 the Makikit team got a piece of information that put us to work day and night again. Tome

Diago was the SGI / Koppassus commander of the invading Militia but he was also the mastermind of active intelligence operations in East Timor. The Makikit team had identified some of Diago's intelligence operators, including his niece who was an ETPS police officer. One day in late January, 2003, we received information that Tome Diago was in Dili.

Information from one source is always questionable. We eventually confirmed the information beyond any doubt through two other informants, Tome Diago was in Dili. Capturing Tome Diago would be a tremendous intelligence victory. In addition to that the Serious Crimes Investigation unit had multiple arrest warrants for murders orchestrated by Tome Diago throughout the year of 1999.

Going after Diago was not a simple matter. The type of operations to capture this highly trained individual would require continued coordination and control of informants supported by surveillance. We needed a lot more reliable manpower. We turned to the SID for help.

The former SID Director had been removed from his position. The man who replaced him was an American police officer from New York, Jeff Craig. The DDIU relationship with the SID changed over night. It was now an easy matter for one or the other intelligence units to get support from the other. The next seventy-two hours was a busy time for both units. We came very close to capturing our prey but the elusive Tome managed to escape our traps. A few days later a Cold Turkey operation confirmed that Tome was back in West Timor.

All was not lost though. During that difficult seventy-two-hours SID / DDIU operators identified several of Tome Diagos contacts in Dili and Liquisa. We also collected enough information to begin a criminal investigation into Tome's niece's involvement with her uncle's espionage activities. The niece was eventually arrested and jailed.

In February, the Fiji military in the Atabe sub-district of Bobonaro district struck a blow against Tome Diago. Diago had sent a small Militia unit to Loes from Atambua, West Timor. The team he sent was a bottom of the barrel group. They entered East Timor and wandered through the Atabe sub-district area trying to figure out how to get to Loes. One day they ambushed a local bus on the main north coast road just three-kilometers from Atabaleten, which was where a Fiji company military compound was established.

The Militia attack of the Timorese local bus known as "Bulldozer" resulted in one man shot and killed. The Militia stole food and money from the survivors. The Militia then kidnapped a local man. They wanted the man to show them the remote mountain trails through Atabae sub-district to Loes. For two days the kidnaped man led the Militia unit through the jungles. On the second day the kidnaped man escaped, leaving the Militia on their own in an area that they did not know.

The Fiji company in Atabaleten hunted the Militia unit day and night ever since the attack on the bus. The Fijis finally found the Militia they so aggressively sought. The Militia unit had found their way to the Loes River that divided Atabae and Loes. All the Militia had to do was get on the other side of the river and they were in Loes. They never made it.

A Fiji platoon ambushed the Militia as they entered the River. The Militia fought back as they fled back into the jungles of Atabae leaving behind two of their dead teammates. The next day the wounded and exhausted Militia could not move fast enough to evade the pursuing Fiji's. The Fiji's again engaged the Militia killing half their numbers and capturing the rest.

This put an end to Tome Diago's Militia incursions. The FDTL destroyed the resources that the Militia needed to operate in East Timor. The SID and DDIU had his intelligence operatives on the run in both Dili and Liquisa. The Militia team captured in Loes had given a lot of incriminating statements against Tome Diago. Now the survivors of the Militia group the Fiji's neutralized was giving more statements about Tome Diago's involvement with the Militia incursions. The TNI High Command had no choice but to assign Tome Diago to another Indonesian island to get him out of the spotlight.

Somehow, in the middle of all this intrigue, I still found time for Ely. We were still meeting almost every night. It was getting very hard keeping our relationship secret from her family. It was time to do the right thing by her or end the relationship. Ending our relationship was unthinkable to both of us by this time, so we made the arrangements for a traditional Timorese engagement ceremony called a "Prenda."

The ceremony was held on the night of 18 February, 2003. Ely spent two days before the ceremony at her father and mother's home in Railaco, which was about a forty-minute drive up the mountain from Dili. I had made arrangements with my close friends and former interpreters from Maliana, Alfonso, and Domingos, to go with me as my family. Alfonso and his wife would be my family spokespersons. The Makikit team members also represented me as my family.

I had never met Ely's mother or father before this night. It was not appropriate that I meet them until after the initial ceremony was complete. I drove Alfonso and his family, Domingos, and some other close friends of Ely's and mine up the mountain to Ely's parents' home. It was completely dark and a light rain was falling when we arrived.

A twenty-five-foot by thirty-five-foot tent made of bamboo framing and covered with plastic tarps was erected in front of Ely's parent's home. A small generator hammered away to provide lights inside the home and the tent. There were many people waiting in the tent when we arrived. Alfonso and his wife met with Ely's parents to discuss why Ely and I should plan to be married.

When this ritual meeting was completed, Ely's Uncle Jose and his wife came to where I sat and led me out of the tent and into the home. Two women waited in front of a closed door. As I was led toward these two ladies, one of the ladies held a small wooden box up to me and opened the top of the box. I put the customary ten dollars into the box. The lady closed the box as the second lady handed me the key to the door that was behind the ladies.

I took the key and opened the door. Ely was waiting for me on the other side of the door, sitting on a sleeping platform that at one time was hers. I walked into the room and stood in front of her. I extended my hand toward her. Ely reached up and took my hand. I gently pulled her up to her feet and led her through the house and into the tent.

Ely was beautiful. She wore a pinkish-colored gown-type dress that clung tightly to her sleek body. Her long dark hair hung loose down to her butt. Even in the dull light, her hair shone. The makeup she wore accented her already distinct facial features, especially here luscious lips that were lightly coated with a glossy red lipstick.

Once inside the tent Ely's Uncle Jose and his wife led us to the nicely decorated place of honor at one end of the tent. We stood there looking into each others eyes as Jose handed me a necklace. I gently put the necklace around Ely's neck as she held her long hair up and out of the way. When the necklace was fastened and I pulled my hands away from Ely everyone stood and clapped long and loud. This completed the engagement ceremony. As far as the Timorese were concerned, Ely was mine. When we left after the party, I would take Ely and all her belongings with me to live together.

The women brought dishes of food into the tent and set them on a large table. There were so many dishes of food that they had to use a second smaller table that was brought into the tent from the house. Ely and I did the customary walking up to everyone present and inviting them to come and eat. Once this ritual was done, Ely and I filled our plates from the many platters and bowls on the tables. Then everyone was free to collect the food they wanted to eat.

Following the dinner, the women cleared the tables while the men rearranged the chairs and removed the tables. The music started to play and everyone danced and danced and danced. This went on for hours. I finally asked Ely, "When does the dance stop?"

Ely answered, "When it is daylight." I thought she was kidding. She wasn't. The music stopped when the early morning sky turned gray.

There was one more event to complete this engagement ceremony. Ely's parents, Alfonso and his wife, and Ely and I ate breakfast together in Ely's parents' home. After breakfast, we got ready to go. Ely had already packed everything she owned, which wasn't much. She went and got her three-year-old son, Rikki, and carried the still-sleeping boy to my truck. I followed her to the truck carrying her small bag of belongings.

Ely and I were married by traditional Timorese standards; however, I needed a marriage certificate and I needed it soon. I was due to end my mission in April, 2003. I would have to return to the states. There was no way that I could get immigration visas for Rikki and Ely without being legally married. I couldn't get legally married because the divorce I started almost a year ago was still dragging on in court.

I discussed this dilemma with a close friend who was a Timorese government official. This man had the normal Timorese outlook about everything, which was, all problems could either be solved or lived with. His answer to my problem was simple: Take Ely to Indonesia where we could get married in a church. When the ceremony was over the church would issue us a marriage certificate. He told me not to register the marriage certificate in Indonesia; bring it back with us to Timor.

With that marriage certificate in hand, I could live in East Timor indefinitely. When my UN mission was over, I could stay in East Timor until the divorce was legally completed. Then I could register the marriage certificate in East Timor. My legal date of marriage would be the day we registered the certificate. It was the only solution for Ely and me to stay together.

By the end of February, East Timor was settling down, so now was the time to take a CTO and get that marriage certificate that Ely and I needed so desperately. We went to Bali, Indonesia for a much-needed CTO and to get married. I figured we would just do a simple ceremony, just to get the certificate, but Ely had to have a full-blown wedding.

Our Indonesian friends were all excited about the wedding. They jumped right into the preparations for the event with all their energy. Our wedding was on a very rainy Thursday night on 13 March, 2003. Ely had spent the entire day of the wedding with three Indonesian women who did her hair, did her makeup, and got her into her very beautiful wedding dress.

After the ceremony, the wedding party returned to our hotel and spent the evening enjoying food and drinks in the hotel's lavish garden at the rear of our room. We then had a couple of days to relax in Bali before we flew back to East Timor. This was a very special moment in my life. I am thankful that I will always have this special memory of Ely's and my relationship together.

The Makikit team was waiting for us again at the airport when we arrived in Dili. This time it was to welcome home the newlyweds only. The situation in East Timor was pretty stable now. I had time to spend with my new family in the evenings over the next couple of weeks. My mission would be over on 8 April, 2003, so my days were filled getting prepared to leave the mission. I wouldn't be leaving East Timor, but I still had to get everything in place at the DDIU. I was supposed to begin my check-out procedures to end my mission when I received a call from my contingent commander. In the last possible second I had received another extension of mission.

Now that I knew I would be around a while longer I got back to work with the DDIU. There was plenty of work to do but there was no big threats to deal with, no big operations. We maintained all of our networks and stayed in contact with our brother intelligence organizations but everyone was reporting there were no activities of big concern. It was like the calm before the storm. The big question was, "When does the storm begin and what was the next storm going to be?"

I knew that the Makikit team was being hunted by enemy intelligence operators. For several months there were ETPS police officers that we knew was giving information to the outside groups that they were members of. At first they made normal curious inquiries of what the DDIU was working on. By April, 2003, those inquiries were about things that they shouldn't have known about. That wasn't a good sign.

We started paying closer attention to the counter-intelligence side of the coin. We had been so busy collecting information we hadn't had time to spend on counter-intelligence for our teams defense. One area of weakness that came to mind was our collection activities that were outside of Dili district. By UN Rules and Regulations anytime we went outside of Dili district we had to turn in a "movement of personnel" (MOP) form. If someone was able to get their hands on the MOP forms they would know the date we left, where we were going, who was going and the general purpose of the trip.

There was one suspicious ETPS officer who worked in the logistics office where the MOP forms were filed. That officer always made small talk inquiries to one of our DDIU members who was not part of the Makikit team. It was time to find out if this man was getting access to the UN files.

I made out an MOP form for a trip to Manatutu, which was about a one and a half-hour drive east of Dili. We didn't go to Manatutu on the date the MOP said we were going. I took the Makikit team and spent the day in Railaco where I knew we wouldn't be seen by any spies.

Sure enough, the ETPS officer who worked in the Logistics Office was trying to find out our purpose for going to Manatutu. The officer subtly opened the conversation with his DDIU friend about our believed excursion to Manatutu with, "I was in Metinaro yesterday and saw your commander, Jose, Arnaldo, and Cesaltino drive through Metinaro coming from Manatutu. What were those guys doing in Manatutu?"

I informed my district commander, Antonio, of this monitoring of our MOP forms and the threat it posed against our operations. The solution was simple enough. We would no longer fill out MOP forms. The chances of having a problem with the UN over not having an MOP form filed were slim, and even if we were to have a problem, Antonio would take care of it.

This was only the beginning of the threats against the "Eagle." Up until the end of January, 2003, the CPD-RDTL was an open book to us. We knew every move they made and every move they intended to make. In late March, we started getting an increase of information of CPD-RDTL activities. As we looked into the activities and at times prepared to offset the expected activities we discovered that the information was false. That was not a good sign either.

The incident that told us that the Makikit team was in serious trouble was in June of 2003. I had managed to acquire three top of the line two-way-radios/scanners. We re-opened the Sig Int (Signal intelligence) project that was so effective against the Militia in the year 2000. team Lucky Star, La Faik, was running the Sig Int Project.

Team Lucky Star had identified two frequencies that were being used by Militia from West Timor and their Colimau 2000 little brothers in East Timor. In June there was an instant change in the radio communications on those two frequencies. Team Lucky Star was now listening to some man carrying on with some lady about illicit affairs. The Sig Int project had been discovered, but how?

The only people who knew about the project were team Lucky Star and the Makikit team. Two weeks before the change in radio conversations I had turned in a report to the SID about the two identified frequencies being used by the

Militia. The report did not mention who was running the Sig Int project but whoever read that report would know that the DDIU was overseeing the project. There was no doubt in my mind that the enemy discovered the Sig Int project from my report through an Asset they had planted inside of the SID. The SID had been penetrated.

The penetration of the SID meant that the enemy knew that the DDIU was responsible for a lot of the information that helped to defeat the latest Militia incursions, the disruption of the various group's activities and the dismantling of intelligence Cells operating in East Timor. They knew everything that we had done, that we had reported to SID anyway. The Makikit team was being hunted.

We had received information from a Cold Turkey operation about the enemy intelligence operators in West Timor organizing Indonesian prostitutes from Kupang and Atambua to go to Dili to ply their trade and collect information. The many horny and money-laden internationals working in East Timor created a target-rich environment for these attractive Indonesian whores.

In July, 2003, a fellow American police officer who was in the command staff at Dili district approached me with some sizzling information. My brother American had received the information from a pretty Indonesian woman who he had been seeing on a regular basis for several weeks. I was instantly suspicious. Eventually I agreed to meet with this woman. The results of my interview of this woman were that she was being fed this information from an Indonesian man who wanted to meet me. I refused to meet the man.

The next thing I knew, this Indonesian lady was trying to befriend my wife. One day she brought the man she had wanted me to meet to my home. Ely told me that while the Indonesian woman talked with her the man closely examining everything in our house, especially family photos on the walls and tables.

This nearly ended my mission in East Timor immediately. There was a man that had become a sort of control agent for me. When I met this man I was told that I could tell this man everything without fear of any repercussions. I began to enlighten the man about several projects I had going on at the time. When I told the man about my "over the fence" activities, I commented, "I have to be very careful about these operations. If the UN found out about them, they may construe the activity to be espionage."

The man looked at me seriously as he said, "That is espionage."

I rolled my eyes along with a slight frown as I said, "See, you have known me less than five minutes and you're already accusing me of espionage."

As I discussed the situation about this Indonesian woman with this man, he told me, "You're burned. It is now very dangerous for you here. We have to get you off this island."

I was a breath away from a sudden exit from East Timor. That would have happened, but I convinced the man that I was not in any immediate danger and I could still operate to a limited degree even now that the enemy knew who I was. The final issue of my being allowed to stay and work was Ely. With my marriage certificate in hand, I would be back in Timor on my own in less than a week. Since I would be in Timor anyway, I might just as well be working. I was allowed to stay to see how things developed.

The Makikit team continued to collect information from our Informant Networks but now it was very difficult to sort through all the collected information and figure out what was misinformation and what was true. The enemy could not shut down our Networks but they were doing a good job clouding the water with a strategic propaganda campaign.

Makikit members were under surveillance by unknown persons at least part of the time too. All of the Makikit members reported to me from time to time that they believed they were being followed. There was two different nights that Ely and I were clearly being followed. One of those times I believed that we were going to be "hit" (ambushed).

Ely and I were eating dinner late at night at Diana's Restaurant, which is on the beach. I was suspicious of a dark-colored four-wheel-drive Hilux with tinted windows that made a couple of slow passes by the restaurant where we sat on the beach side of the road. The Hilux then made a third pass by the restaurant going away from Dili toward Hera. Ely and I waited and watched for over an hour to see if the Hilux would come back. It never did. I paid the bill and we left.

I drove away from Diana's Restaurant going toward Hera. I wanted to see if that Hilux was still around. Sure enough, it was sitting down the street on the side of the road as if in a surveillance position to watch who comes and goes from Diana's. We could see that there were two people sitting in the front seat of the Hilux, but because of the tinted windows, we couldn't tell if anyone else was in the backseat.

I didn't want to drive past the Hilux again, so I planned to drive the ten kilometers to Hera and then come back to Dili on the mountain road that enters Dili through Becora. It was about eleven-o'clock at night, which meant that the long trip through the desolate areas of Dili District was not all that safe. The Ninja teams had been setting up roadblock operations periodically throughout East Timor. The roadblock operations were conducted usually between 2200 hours and 0300 hours. There had been two incidents of Ninja roadblocks and thefts from the people unknowingly driving into the Ninja trap right on the roadway we would be taking to Hera.

Ely knew what to do should we ever run into one of these Ninja roadblocks. She knew that I would not stop for any reason unless it was just not possible to get over or around whatever obstacle the Ninjas used to block the roadway. For example, rocks and jagged glass scattered across the roadway would be a "no stop" barricade; a tree across the road would be a "stop" barricade. If I had to stop the truck for any reason, Ely knew to exit the truck, go into the jungle, and keep going. She was a mountain girl and would know how to take care of herself. While she escaped, I would neutralize the roadblock. Assuming I survived my one-man assault against the Ninjas we had a code that I would use to call Ely back to the truck. If Ely didn't hear the code she was to make her own way back home, which she was more than capable of doing.

* * * *

The road to Hera from Dili goes up and over a low mountain. On the other side of the low mountain the roadway runs along the sea line for several kilometers. There are no villages or even single homes along this stretch of road. As Ely and I neared the crest of this low mountain two vehicles, one right behind the other, suddenly appeared in my rear view mirror from out of no where. For me not to see them approaching behind us they had to have been driving with their lights off.

The front vehicle moved up close behind me and flashed his lights, which was asking me to let him pass me. I could see by the moonlight that the second vehicle back was a Hilux. I couldn't tell if it was the same Hilux or not but I had to assume that it was.

We were vulnerable on that mountain road. If this was an ambush and I let that first truck in front of me Ely and I were screwed. The front truck could easily block the narrow roadway leaving us no way around the vehicle in front of us. The mountain along this roadway was a solid rock face on our right side and a cliff on our left side. Ely would not be able to escape. There was no way I was going to let that first truck pass me.

As we continued down the other side of the mountain the truck behind me was becoming more aggressive about making me move over for him. He was riding my bumper, flashing his lights, and honking his horn. I had increased my speed to appease anyone who was legitimately driving down this road. The man behind me still wanted to pass. I knew now that we were under attack.

As we neared the bottom of the mountain I knew that the front vehicle would get past me. The roadway becomes wider and runs straight as an arrow across the flat low ground. I would have two options when the attack comes. I could evade the attack by turning off the roadway onto the flat terrain that is on both sides of the road and go back the way we had come. That was a good option and probably would be a successful one but by now I was getting a little pissed off so I decided on the second option.

I would allow the first vehicle to drive past me. As soon as the first vehicle was in front of me I would slam on my brakes and block the roadway with my truck. This would catch the enemy by surprise and trap the Hilux close behind me while the truck now in front of me sped away from us until he figured out what was happening. I will have successfully divided my enemies force. I could easily neutralize the occupants of the Hilux before the truck in front of us could turn around and engage me.

I told Ely what my plan was. She was a little scared but having grown up in a combat orientated environment she appreciated winning strategies. She had been around enough of my special operations training to have faith in my ability to knock the shit out of these guys using this strategy. She didn't even want to run into the jungle. She wanted to watch.

We reached the bottom of the mountain and continued down the now flat and straight roadway. The two trucks behind us slowed down creating more distance between us and them I slowed down too trying to suck them in. They slowed down even more and then stopped. I stopped too. We sat motionless on the roadway watching each other from about a half kilometer apart. Less then two minutes later the two trucks spun around going back toward Dili at a high speed. Ely and I sat on the roadway and watched them climbing back up the mountain until they were out of sight. Ely and I took a nice drive along the beach road and then over the mountain that enters Dili from the backside.

In December, 2003, Dili district handed over complete control of police functions to the ETPS. The only UN police that would remain at Dili district would be a handful of advisors. I was reassigned to the SID unit at National Headquarters. The SID director at that time was an Australian Federal police commander who had only been in East Timor only a few weeks. The director was a man well trained and experienced in the arts of intelligence.

Two months before my transfer from DDIU to SID I had pretty much shut down most of the Makikit covert operations. We were under too much pressure from enemy intelligence operations to continue effectively. The last super-secret operation we tried to run in October, 2003, got burned right out of the chute. I stood in front of Cesaltino, who was the bearer of the bad news, in the DDIU office rubbing my hand across my face in frustration as I said, "Damn, those guys are a pain in the ass." I knew it was time to follow the advice I got from my unofficial control agent. I would just do the straight up work and ride out my time to the end of my mission.

It was a hard adjustment when I transferred to the SID unit. Working out of National Headquarters puts a man in plain sight of the UN police hierarchy. I was so use to breaking every rule in the United Nations book that I kind of forgot some of the rules even existed. None of the commanders who had wanted my kind of work were around any more. Even Antonio had recently ended his mission and went home.

The SID commander, Cedric Netto, was a patient man who took care of his troops. He helped me over the rough spots as I learned to walk the straight and narrow path of the United Nations. I am sure he saw me as being rough around the edges and uncouth but he recognized the skills that I possessed and knew how best to use my skills. Soon he had me blended into the SID team, which really was a good team. Besides Ced and myself there was Matt and Julian from Australia, Chan from Malaysia and Patricia from Africa. Each one of my teammates that I would serve with for the last six months of my mission in East Timor was "top shelf" all the way.

This was the first time since coming to East Timor that I worked with a team of international police. I could tell that Ced was more than capable of managing the deep covert stuff that the Makikit team had been doing. I would have loved to do some of our normal type of intelligence operations with commander Netto at the helm but we would never get that opportunity.

We were very busy in spite of being restricted to performing police intelligence only though. We continued to collect information on the various groups throughout East Timor that were now "outlawed" by the East Timorese government. The situations involving these groups were heating up as the government directed the ETPS to stamp out these groups.

Our biggest claim to fame would be a "human trafficking" case we stumbled into. The initial information that we received pointed us in the direction of the many massage parlors that were operating in Dili. Everyone knew that there was prostitution going on at the massage parlors; however, there were no laws against being a prostitute. There were laws against those who provided prostitution services. When it was discovered that many of the prostitutes were victims of human trafficking we went after the organizers of the human trafficking with a vengeance.

Ced put me on undercover status to penetrate the traffickers. Ced and I had discussed my undercover assignment at length. There was no question about targeting the traffickers, who was the criminals. The women were the victims so there was no purpose to pose as a client to build a case against them for an act that we couldn't even charge them with.

The brothels used women from other countries only. The women came from Thailand, Philippines, Indonesia, and China. The traffickers had "talent scouts" in those countries who would pick out pretty young women who were vulnerable. The scout would smooth-talk the pretty young woman into a money-making opportunity that she couldn't refuse. The young woman believed that she could work for this "company" in East Timor in a legitimate capacity for six months, then return home with lots of money.

When a group of recruited women arrived in Dili they were met at the airport by brothel managers, which was to be expected. What wasn't expected was that the brothel managers took the women's passports from them right at the airport. The women were taken to the hotel where they would be working and then told the details of their job duties. This was when they learned that they were now prostitutes.

Several of the women victimized had good moral backgrounds with no desire to be fucked several times a day by any man who had the money. All the crying and begging to go home didn't save them. The brothel managers had the women's passports. They were in a strange country. They didn't speak the language of East Timor. The women had no choice but to become prostitutes.

As I worked my way into the managers of the massage parlor brothels it turned out that many of the brothels were interconnected. I started getting information about when new girls would arrive in Dili. Ced decided on a plan to have SID agents at the Dili airport to intercept the arriving women. The women would be refused entry into East Timor and sent back to where they had come from.

This put the brothel managers in a bad way. They were out the money for the airfare for the women's tickets. They were also out the money that they would have made from those women's services. The brothels that were once well stocked with prostitutes suddenly didn't have enough women to handle their established clientele.

As I burrowed deeper and deeper into these traffickers and got more information, Ced coordinated with the national investigations division and launched into a campaign of raiding some of the brothels. We always got feedback about the effects of the airport operations and brothel raid operations when I revisited my newfound friends who managed the brothels. They labored real hard to figure out strategies to outmaneuver the police operations against them. Many times I was able to find out what their new plan was. This enabled us to always be one step ahead of the traffickers.

* * * *

In February, 2004, I was getting a lot of pressure to take a CTO. I hadn't been on a CTO in five months. I decided to take Ely and go to Bangkok. I didn't want to go to Darwin. I would like to have gone to Bali and spent time with Ely's and my Indonesian friends who had become like family to us, but I couldn't do that. In January of 2004, my secret friend had told me not to take any more CTOs in Bali, Indonesia. He never said why not, but I could assume that it was no longer safe for me in Indonesia. Since we had to go to another country, I thought we would try Thailand.

We flew out of Dili in late February, excited to get twelve days of being alone together away from Timor where there was no escape from all the work that rolled in daily. We flew into Bali where we would connect with a flight to Bangkok. Within an hour, we were on the next flight to Bangkok. As we approached from the air, we were both amazed at how huge the city of Bangkok was.

We spent ten beautiful days in Bangkok, taking in many sights and enjoying the lavish hotels. Ely and I were both martial artists so we had to go see the infamous Muy Tai kickboxing on one of our nights in Bangkok. The arena was just like the arena scenes on the movies. Ely started taking pictures at first from where we sat just behind the rows of chairs at ringside that was reserved for the professional gamblers. The next thing I knew Ely was standing in front of the rows of gamblers right at the ring itself. I saw her standing there snapping pictures and thought, *That's my Timorese wife. The next thing she will do is climb into the ring and ask the combatants to pose for her."*

She didn't get the chance to do that, however. Security guards quickly responded to the complaining gamblers and escorted Ely out of the restricted area. After the Muy Tai fights, Ely and I walked through the sprawling open air market that was next door. We bought nice clothes at a cheap price for us and several of our family members in East Timor. Our time in Bangkok was very nice.

Ten days later we flew out of Bangkok on our way back to East Timor. We had to change planes again in Bali. The flight into East Timor would not leave until the following morning. Since we had to spend the night in Bali anyway we had made our flight arrangements so that we had two days in Bali.

Ely wanted to buy some things at the Mata Hari square in Kuta Beach. More importantly, we knew that this would be the last time we were in Bali before the end of my UN mission. We wanted to meet with our friends and properly say goodbye. I remembered what my secret friend had told me about taking a CTO in Bali but we would only be there two days and we were entering the country from Thailand not East Timor. I figured our entry into Indonesia was safe enough. It wasn't.

Ely and I stepped off the Thailand plane and walked up the tunnel ramp along with the many other passengers on our flight. As we approached the top of the ramp I saw three Indonesian men standing together closely watching the many arriving passengers walk past them. One of the three men held a large white cardboard sign for all the passengers to see as they walked past the men. When I first saw the three men and the sign I thought *These guys must be here to pick up some VIP to be allowed to come and find the person they are responsible to meet before the arriving person is even processed through customs.*

As Ely and I walked closer I saw the names written on that white sign. My heart suddenly pounded in my chest as adrenaline shot through my entire being. "Amaral E." and "Martin J." were the only two names on the sign the one man held in front of his chest (Ely was still going by her maiden name, Amaral). My first thought was to turn around and get back on the plane. My next thought was to walk past the men as if we didn't notice our names on the sign. Both options were losers, though. We would be picked up going through customs. Going back into the plane wouldn't save us either. We had no choice but to present ourselves to these men.

I confidently approached the man holding the card with Ely's hand in mine. I asked, "What do you want?"

The three men were all burly guys compared to most Indonesians. They looked professional in there slacks, shirts and ties. They wore ID cards on the front of their shirts that identified them as immigration agents. All three men studied Ely and me closely. I could feel Ely's hand trembling as the fear of falling into the clutches of Indonesian intelligence surged through her. She harbored very bad memories of what these men were capable of doing.

I discreetly rubbed my finger back and forth across the top of Ely's hand, which I held, to try and calm her down. She didn't show the fear she felt, other than the trembling, which only I could feel. The man in front of me lowered the card he held to his side. They had found who they were looking for so the card had no further use. The man stood silent for several moments but finally answered my question, "We wanted to meet with you before going through customs. We want to make sure you have no problems entering into Indonesia."

I thought, *There are over two hundred people on this flight into Bali, and they are only concerned about two of those passengers.* That was not a good sign.

It was a good sign that we had not been arrested yet. We had room to maneuver. I asked the man, "What do you need us to do?"

The man just looked into my eyes without saying a word. After several seconds of silence I asked, "Do you need to see our passports and visas?"

The man continued to study me but then finally nodded his head. I handed the man Ely's and my passports. The man studied the passports closely. He seemed to be more interested in Ely's passport than mine.

The man then started questioning me about when we would be leaving Bali, where we would be staying, what we would be doing, who we would be visiting, what work did I do for the UN and on and on and on. When the question and answer session was over the man stood silent still looking deeply into my eyes. Finally he handed the passports back to me and told us we could go.

We were in great danger and we both knew it. These men were looking for a reason to arrest us. I knew that we would be watched very closely during our stay in Bali. Any move we made that raised the suspicions of the Indonesian intelligence would result in our arrest. It was also possible that they intended to arrest us after they identified who we contacted in Bali, which would result in the arrest of all those we contacted.

If I was not a United Nations employee there was no doubt that we would not make it out of Bali. Being a United Nations employee created a problem for those intelligence agents. They would have to respond to UN inquiries as to why a United Nations worker was arrested while on CTO in Bali. Bali was a designated location for United Nations workers to take their CTOs.

That left the third and most dangerous possibility available to the Indonesian intelligence. Ely and I could be snatched off the streets by an Indonesian intelligence Asset group, much like the Militia groups from East Timor. In fact, our kidnapers would probably be a team of Militia from East Timor. Ely and I both knew that if we were kidnaped we would both be killed eventually.

We made it through customs. I exchanged some money then we got a taxi to take us to a hotel. We went to a different hotel than what I had told the man with the card. I knew this would make Indonesian intelligence agents suspicious but I had decided that we were too vulnerable of being kidnaped from the hotel where we originally planned to stay.

As soon as I could I got to an internet service and sent my secret friend a message telling him the situation. I included the name of the hotel we currently were at and the name of the hotel we would stay the following night. This would give my friend a starting point to start looking for us should we disappear.

Ely and I spent a couple of tense days in Bali. We couldn't contact our friends who live in Bali because that would endanger them. We would never have the opportunity to see or talk to them again, not ever. Two days after our arrival in Bali Ely and I took a Taxi to the airport. Ely was scared to death. She believed that Indonesian intelligence would never let us out of Indonesia. She could be right.

We got to the airport and checked in our bags. As expected we were detained when the immigrations officer punched our names into his computer. I knew our names had to be "flagged." The immigrations officer studied our passports closely, especially Ely's passport. He looked up from the passports and told us to wait.

We watched him walk over to the main Immigrations office nearby. There was a large picture window that allowed us to see the interior of the Immigrations office. Ely was trembling again as we waited several long minutes. We closely watched the Immigrations Officer along with the man who was sitting in the Immigrations office work on the computer, make phone calls and occasionally looked at us through the big window.

My mind was working furiously to figure out what these guys were planning to do. As I figured out all the possibilities I also thought about possible counter measures. The more I thought about it the more I realized there were no "save the day" solutions. This wasn't like spy novels or spy movies where James Bond would pull off some heroic audacious escape to freedom. We were at the mercy of Indonesian authorities.

I kept wondering why the first men we encountered when we arrived in Bali were more interested in Ely than me. Now the immigrations officer did the same thing. He was clearly more interested in Ely. Ely was a beautiful woman but that was not their interest. Suddenly it occurred to me what these guys were thinking. They would have a problem arresting me but they could arrest Ely with no repercussions from the United Nations.

I knew that, intelligence-wise, arresting Ely would be a good move on their part. The torture and rape of Ely would give them everything she knew about my activities. I looked into Ely's fear-filled eyes and squeezed her hand. I was about to lose this woman who I had come to love so deeply. I was going to lose her to a horrible fate that was my fault. I cursed myself for being so stupid to have put us in this no-win situation.

The immigrations officer finally came back to where we stood waiting followed by the man who had been sitting in the immigration office. I sighed a long slow breath as I waited for the boom to be lowered upon Ely and possibly me too. The immigrations officer stepped into his little booth followed by the other man. The immigrations officer stamped Ely's and my passports and handed them to us.

I couldn't believe that they had allowed us to leave. But then again we were just on the departure side of the immigrations counter. There was a lot of airport terminal between us and our airplane ride to freedom. We walked to our departure gate which was to the far left of the terminal. The security screening station that enters our gates departure lounge was not open yet so we went to the coffee shop that was near our gate. We drank coffee and I ate a couple of small sausages wrapped in pastry.

While we ate and drank there were two men, dressed in shirts and ties, who were watching us closely. Both of these men were huge for Indonesians. They were both taller than me and built like big-time wrestlers. We weren't out of danger yet. When we finished our morning coffee we walked down to the departure gate. The security screening station before entering that gates departure lounge still wasn't opened so we sat down in the chairs in front of the gate.

The two big burly guys we had seen watching us while we were in the coffee shop followed us then stood on either side of where we sat. They stood with their hands properly folded in front of them and stared at us. Anyone seeing them would have thought they were our professional bodyguard service. Anyone who looked into the eyes of those two men would see that these were hard men who had no friendly intentions toward Ely and me whatsoever.

It seemed like hours, but ten minutes later, the security gate was opened and the passengers going to East Timor lined up to be screened for entry. The two men stood on either side of Ely and me while we waited for our turn to be screened through the gate. I could now read the ID card that was on the front of these men's shirts. The ID tags identified both men as "Indonesian intelligence." We were allowed to enter our flights waiting area. A few minutes later it was announced to board the bus that would take us to the jet flying to Dili.

Ely hadn't quit trembling since our initial encounter with the immigrations officer. Now as we walked to the waiting bus, being intimidated by our two burly bodyguards, Ely's legs hardly had the strength to walk. I helped her onto the bus and got her sat down in an empty seat. I looked out the bus window and saw our two bodyguards still standing formally watching us through the bus window. I was a little upset that those two men didn't at least wave goodbye to us as the bus drove away from the terminal.

The bus came to a stop next to the jet. Ely slowly made her way up the stairs to enter the waiting jet, her legs still lacking the strength from the fear she felt. We found our seats, fastened our seat belts, and waited for the jet to take off. There was no sign of anyone watching us since we left the terminal in the bus that brought us to the jet. I tried to sooth Ely's fears by talking to her, but she wouldn't respond—she just sat quietly.

After what seemed to be an eternity, the jet took off. As soon as the wheels left the runway, Ely started to cry. She buried her face into my shoulder and cried. I held her close and let her tears soak my shirt. We had made it out. We had both made it out together. Ely didn't stop crying for ten minutes. Then she took a few minutes break before she started crying again. We would have kissed the tarmac in Dili after we landed, but the hot asphalt would have burned out lips.

My special friend was waiting for us before we even got to customs. He had another man with him that I had never seen before. My friend slapped me on the shoulder with a big smile on his face saying, "Hey, you made it out."

I smiled back at him, "Yeah, we were lucky."

He told me to go through customs, get our bags, and meet him in the parking lot. He would give us a ride home.

As we rode in my friend's car, the man with him sat quietly on the passenger's side while Ely and I sat together in the back seat. I asked, "Can we talk?"

My friend said, "Yeah no problem."

I then blurted, "Man, are we hot in Indonesia."

My friend was real sympathetic as he said, "I told you not to go to Bali."

I explained, "We came into Bali from Bangkok. I figured nobody would notice."

My friend laughed, "Well, now you know. You aren't going up against the little intelligence outfits any more; this is the big league. Indonesian intelligence isn't anyone to take lightly."

Ely and I told my friend every detail about what happened. My friend responded to our description of what happened over the past two days, "You were lucky they let you both leave. The two men watching you before you left was a message to you that said, 'Don't ever come back.'"

My friend was silent for moment, then added, "It's time to get you off this island—both of you."

The next few weeks that I had left in the United Nations mission were a busy time. We still had to go through the immigration visa request process for Rikki and Ely. We received a lot of help from the United States Embassy staff in Dili. We never would have got the visas without their help. I was still working up until the day I began the UN checkout procedures.

It was hard leaving our Timorese family and many friends. I had become very close to all of Ely's family. They were my family now, too. We had a series of going away dinners. The last one was at Ely's and my house in Dili two nights before we left Dili. Close friends and family attended the dinner and the dance that followed the dinner. This was a very special time.

I had the opportunity to spend some time with many of the Timorese that I had worked with secretly over the past four years. My family and I were leaving East Timor. We were going to America where there were no Ninjas, no outlaw groups threatening to forcefully take control of the government, no guerilla forces that may show up in our home town and kill whoever they want.

My friends would remain in harm's way and carry on. They had no place to run so they had to remain and fight no matter how long it took. I felt guilty because I was running away. My friends were sorry to see me leave but they understood.

On the morning of 21 May, 2004, we woke up at daybreak to prepare to leave. Our house was full of people from the mountains who had spent the night so that they could see us off. The pastor of Ely's Assembly of God church came and prayed with us in our living room just before we left for the airport. Many of the people who had stayed at our house the night before came to the airport with us to say one final goodbye.

The Makikit team met us at the airport. Any Timorese will tell you that when the United Nations leave East Timor the Militia will come over the border from West Timor and join forces with those who want to change the government that the United Nations has helped to establish through free elections. Whether this is true or not remains to be seen but it is what the Timorese believe.

The Makikit team believes this too. Naturally they are afraid but they never let that fear stand in their way to do the best that they could for their country.

I gave Jose, Arnaldo, and Cesaltino one last piece of advice, "Stay true to the cause. Remember what side you're on. East Timor is a free country now. Many Timorese died for this freedom you now have. If the current government is no good, the people can change that the right way when they vote. Anyone who wants to forcefully take control of this country by killing and terrorizing East Timorese does not have good intentions for the people."

I looked into the tearful eyes of each of these brave young men as I shook their hand one last time. I called each one of them my son and wished them and their families well. There was nothing more that needed to be said.

My American contingent commander along with other American police officers was at the airport to say farewell to us. I was honored that they would take the time from their truly busy day to pay my family and me this respect. We all stood outside waiting until the last minute for Ely, Rikki, and I to enter through the secured area of the airport. There were many hugs, kisses and tears and then it was time. Ely, Rikki, and I walked away hand in hand: a family born from the turmoils of a struggling people.

[1] The "company" does not refer to the "CIA." I am choosing not to reveal the name of the legitimate company that recruited me. This company has no known affiliations with the CIA or any other intelligence agency.

CRISPY WINTERS & UNBROKEN SHELLS

by Amanda Kroll

My name is Amanda. *Crispy Winters & Unbroken Shells* is the heartwarming story of my childhood experiences with epilepsy, divorce, the death of a friend, first love, and lasting friendships.

From my first memory—playing with roly-polies on the sidewalk—to the unbearably hot day I received my college degree, this creative memoir is filled with colorful memories covering the span of twenty years.

Crispy Winters
&
Unbroken Shells

Amanda Kroll

Paperback, 108 pages
5.5" x 8.5"
ISBN 1-4241-9861-5

About the author:

These experiences, along with the wonderful relationships that have developed between myself, my mother, my twin sister, and my baby brother Ram, have molded me into the quirky individual I am today.

Don't Praise Me, Praise God

by Shirley Edwards

It's time to put God's will first in our lives and live for the Lord. Some pastors are focused on members, money and the luxurious lifestyle. "If you have the members, you have the money; if you have the money, you have the luxurious lifestyle." How can someone lead you when he or she is doing wrong? Also, we need to search God for ourselves and ask Him to give us understanding. Many things have changed in life, but I know that God has not changed His word. Man has made things suitable for his own purposes. Also, many pastors are preaching for the wrong reasons. Their luxurious lifestyles have taken their mind off the important things of what the real meaning of serving God is. God knows our hearts and He knows a true leader. Having a fancy car, fancy clothes, and a fancy home— what good are they when your soul is not right with the Lord? When you step out of God's boundaries, there is no hope without repentance.

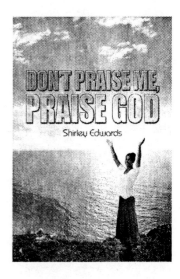

Paperback, 90 pages
6"x 9"
ISBN 1-60563-181-7

People need to take control of their lives and let "God use them."

About the author:

As you read this book I hope that you will be encouraged. I do believe that *Don't Praise Me, Praise God* will be one of the most talked-about books that has ever been written. May God bless you all.

also available from publishamerica

COPS, DONUTS, AND MURDER
by George Galjan

A police pursuit turns ugly and the suspect is shot to death. The community is up in arms. The coroner and the police forensics team conclude that it was an accidental shooting. However, the FBI believes otherwise. The officer involved turns up dead. Is it murder or suicide? Crew members from the tugboat *Bufford*, which included the son of Cleveland's mafioso, turn up dead in various parts of the city. All this awaits newly promoted Lieutenant Pavlick and his partner Sergeant Fu Chu Lai. When Sergeant Fu Chu Lai was shot, by of all people, the FBI, a newspaper columnist blamed the incident on donuts, and published an article, "Why Cops Crave Donuts." The following day the police were overwhelmed with donuts, and...

Paperback, 283 pages
6"x 9"
ISBN 1-4241-4284-9

About the author:

George Galjan was born in 1942 in Berlin, Germany. In 1956 he immigrated to the United States with his family. After high school, he enlisted in the Navy. He served two tours in Vietnam and later transferred to the Navy Reserves. He retired from the Reserves with the rank of senior chief. In 1969 Galjan joined the Cleveland police department. He retired in 1998, holding the rank of lieutenant. He currently resides with his wife, Margaret, in Avon Lake.

available to all bookstores nationwide.
www.publishamerica.com

also available from publishamerica

SON SHINE

A DIVORCED FATHER ESTABLISHES PRINCIPLES FOR THE FULFILLMENT AND GROWTH OF HIS SONS

by Paul Marascia

Son Shine is not an exposé on the problems of growing up in a divorced household. However, it does challenge all parents, divorced or not, to answer for themselves, did we do our part? Are we raising our children to be fulfilled, proud, and happy adults, or are we giving improper examples and providing little direction or focus? The resulting discussion provides a set of principles that are building blocks to help all children develop their personal creed: knowing who they are, what they aspire to be, and how they plan to live their truth.

Paperback, 107 pages
6" x 9"
ISBN 1-60563-426-3

About the author:

Paul Marascia grew up in Brooklyn, New York, as the son of first-generation Italian immigrants. He attended West Point, Brooklyn College, and New York University, where he received an MBA in 1992. Paul's professional career includes founding two software companies, serving as an adjunct professor of mathematics, school board president, baseball coach, and commissioner for youth sports programs. Currently, Paul is a vice president of investments for one of the nation's largest financial services firms.

available to all bookstores nationwide.
www.publishamerica.com

WHEN MOMMY WAS A SOLDIER

by Fran E. Orr

Maggie is very proud of her mother. She and her Nana sit together looking through a photo album of photographs of her mother's life. Maggie asks Nana to tell her again why her mother joined the Army. She learns about the values and strengths that make her mom a winner.

Paperback, 26 pages
8.5" x 8.5"
ISBN 1-4241-9576-4

About the author:

Fran E. Orr is married to a retired naval aviator. Their youngest daughter served almost four years in the Army. You will enjoy this story of a young woman's choice to serve her country as seen through her daughter's eyes.

INNOCENCE DECEIVED
by V. K. Ezzo

Dating back to 1914 and spanning over three generations, lovers and husbands have always deceived the women in Sara Marino's family. Left with broken hearts and broken trust, each learned to face the hard, cold facts of life, alone and scared, gaining inner strength from each hardship thrown before them. From a tarnished love affair to murder, rejection and abuse, the women rise above the strife and learn to cope and go on. Sara and her children fight for their very existence against one of the most insidious acts ever committed against another person. The inner strength of this family will give hope to those who have had to face the disillusionments of life. Amid all the turmoil, Sara meets a man whose determination to overcome her aloofness and distrust of men leads them into a romance that she neither wants nor is ready for. Sara is faced with the decision to begin living again or continue hiding in the world of hate and disenchantment.

Paperback, 138 pages
5.5" x 8.5"
ISBN 1-4137-3966-0

About the author:

Victoria Ezzo is a single grandmother who has raised three children and is now raising her autistic nine-year-old grandson. She began writing novels in 1986 after a family gathering revealed an earth-shattering secret that changed everyone's life forever. *Innocence Deceived* was inspired by that fateful revelation. This suspenseful tale explores generations of secrets and the series of dysfunctional consequences that resulted from a lifetime wrought with turmoil. Ms. Ezzo has written eight novels, a satiric play and numerous children's stories, all in an attempt to survive the past, the present and, hopefully, the future. When she is not creating literature, she enjoys painting and spending time with her six grandchildren in the lovely mountains of her hometown, Vernon, New Jersey.

Also available from PublishAmerica

VERTICAL BLINDS
by Stefanie L Plaud

Poetry is pain, identifiable, raw and unpolished. *Vertical Blinds* is like a heart sliced into four chambers: anger, jealousy, resignation, and hope. Each section is a tomb, a dedication to stages of life that are in a constant card game, shuffling for position. These poems are a calling to those that feel the darkness coming, and don't have the words to expose it. The cult of beauty is outdated, and these words—gritty, exposing, sometimes brutal—are a window into a trapped mind, reaching out to those who feel the same. They are not alone.

Paperback, 63 pages
6" x 9"
ISBN 1-60672-899-7

About the author:

Stefanie L Plaud is a 2006 graduate of Roger Williams University's Marine Biology program. She currently works at the University of Maine's Center for Cooperative Aquaculture Research. *Vertical Blinds* is her second book. *Rib Tunes*, Plaud's first volume, was released in 2005.

Available to all bookstores nationwide.
www.publishamerica.com

DESTINY OF A WAR VETERAN
by Sal Atlantis Phoenix

Destiny of a War Veteran depicts the life of a conscientious veteran. The subject matter of the story is serious and tends towards the realistic side of the aftermath of war. The story is about the analysis of the human soul lost in fantasy and in reality, about submission and rebellion, and about philosophy and tyranny. The story is vivid with images, and complex and rich in characters. It is an intriguing tale that defines the socio-political scenarios.

Vietnam War veteran Joe is tempted to participate in Middle Eastern and international politics, compelled with insinuated illusion of establishing freedom and democracy. The subsequent effects of the human tragedies engulfed from the political scenarios devastate him, and he seeks refuge beyond the realm of humanity.

Paperback, 188 pages
5.5" x 8.5"
ISBN 1-4241-8005-8

About the author:

Sal Atlantis Phoenix, a veteran of life and a conscientious citizen, is a playwright and fiction writer. His lifelong experience convinced him that "…with all its sham, drudgery and broken dreams, it is still a beautiful world. Be careful. Strive to be happy."